FALSE IDOLS

Karla Marie Sweet

Thank you a chance. Enjoy!

MLP

First published in 2025 by Mountain Leopard Press
An imprint of Headline Publishing Group Limited

1

Cataloguing in Publication Data is available from the British Library

Hardback ISBN 978 1 0354 2206 7
Trade Paperback ISBN 978 1 0354 2207 4

Typeset in Dante MT by CC Book Production
Printed and bound in Great Britain by Clays Ltd, Elcograf S.p.A.

MIX
Paper | Supporting
responsible forestry
FSC® C104740

Headline's policy is to use papers that are natural, renewable and
recyclable products and made from wood grown in well-managed forests
and other controlled sources. The logging and manufacturing processes are
expected to conform to the environmental regulations of the country of origin.

HEADLINE PUBLISHING GROUP
An Hachette UK Company
Carmelite House
50 Victoria Embankment
London EC4Y 0DZ

The authorised representative in the EEA is Hachette Ireland,
8 Castlecourt Centre, Dublin 15, D15 XTP3, Ireland
(email: info@hbgi.ie)

www.headline.co.uk
www.hachette.co.uk

For my family

PART ONE
LIMERENCE

ONE

It's the sound that usually wakes me. The loud crunch on impact. The shattering of glass. That harrowing scream that makes my blood run cold. And there's the jolt forward, of course. That feeling of falling coupled with my own desperate attempt to catch myself. Slow the momentum. Even though, by then, I know it's too late.

It happens again the morning we move out of our house, ready to leave Georgia for good. I wake in a cold sweat, just like all the times before, and hurry to the bathroom so as not to disturb Derek. He's been sleeping soundly next to me, completely unaware of my violent dream.

In the bathroom, I collapse beside the toilet bowl, the bones of my backside bumping against the black-and-white tiled floor. My stomach heaves, my heart clenches into a bloody fist and then the tears come. Once I am sure I won't vomit, I clasp my hand over my mouth so that Derek won't hear my loud, shuddering sobs – it's also a reminder to myself, not to let out a wail.

Then, I reach for it – the only thing I know will make it all stop. It is taped under the cabinet we keep by the bathtub, the cabinet that is typically stuffed with numerous 'self-care' items.

On top there is a burnt-out candle, a novel I haven't read and a bath bomb, all ready to be packed into a moving box. I slide my nail under the tape and peel it off.

The inside of our new Los Angeles home is bare but beautiful. Wooden parquet flooring, spotless marble countertops, ample space and a sprawling, lush green garden complete with a giant rose bush and a small pool. The pool is empty, the rose bush not yet in bloom, but still I can see the potential of our pristine new home. Our furniture hasn't arrived yet, thanks to some screw-up with the removals company, so, until it does, we'll have to make do.

'It'll be romantic,' Derek croons, cupping my face in his hands. 'Like it was in college when we were poor.'

I force a smile, knowing how important it is to him, to us, that I make an effort.

'In fairness, I did like the mattress on the floor. And the exposed brick. It all felt very artsy.'

'Well, that was entirely the point,' Derek replies. 'I wanted to help feed your creative energy.'

He winks, I scoff and push him away playfully.

'You know you're never going to see me now I have a studio in the house, right?'

'Maybe that's the point?' He says, with a smirk.

I roll my eyes and groan melodramatically before heading down the steps into the garage. Natural light streams through the windows and the entire space is painted white. The decision to park our cars in the driveway so I could use the garage as studio space was a large part of our agreement when we'd first had the conversation about moving to LA. While Derek schmoozes the rich and famous, furthering his directing career one handshake at a time, it will be important for me to have something of my own.

'You gonna try and get some work exhibited here in LA?' Derek asks, stepping into the studio behind me.

I hesitate.

'I dunno . . .'

I'd painted for years back in Savannah, but had never had a single piece of work shown. Mainly because I'd never tried.

Derek had, of course, given me endless speeches about my fear of success.

'Sadie, come on,' he'd say. 'What's the worst that can happen?'

I'd smile, embarrassed, and tell him I didn't know.

But I did. I knew exactly what I was afraid of. Exactly where success could lead. I couldn't risk it in Georgia. Could here be different?

He steps towards me and catches me in an unexpected embrace. I breathe in the familiar smell of Italian lemonade, vanilla pods and leather car seats: an aftershave he's been wearing for years.

'You can be whatever you want to be here, honey,' he whispers into my ear. 'That's the beauty of this place.'

I nod into his shoulder. He pulls back and looks me in the eye.

'*And* it's a great city for networking. You could speak to galleries. See about—'

I cut him off. 'I'm not doing an exhibition, Derek. We've talked about this. I'm not in the right place.'

'Are you kidding? You're in exactly the right place!'

I pull away from him. 'You know what I mean. It's not the right time.'

He sighs. 'Just think about it, okay? Give yourself a chance.'

I nod and it seems enough to placate him. His face creases into a grin.

Of course, he has no idea how dangerous sticking my head above the parapet could be for me.

'How about we get Chinese takeout? We can sit on some cardboard and eat it right out of the boxes, you know? With those splintery chopsticks that always come with the delivery?'

His warmth is infectious and I can't help but smile.

'Sounds perfect,' I say.

An hour later, we're living out Derek's vision and I'm forced to admit it *does* feel romantic, if slightly uncomfortable. As I chow down on teriyaki tofu chunks and stir-fried broccoli stems, Derek tries not to slurp his noodles as he waxes lyrical about his LA dreams.

'Man, I can't *wait* to sign up for gym around here. The standard of fitness in LA is *crazy*. I seriously need to up my game. Venice Beach, honey. One day . . . I'll be there.'

'Why not now?' I ask.

'When I go to Venice Beach, I want feel like I can hold my own. When I wrap this movie, I'm gonna be like . . . two workouts a day. Low sugar, low salt, high-protein diet. Arms. Abs. Legs. Derek 2.0.'

I smile, proudly. 'You'll be swinging from those hoops and doing backflips and shit in no time.'

'It'll be incredible, honey,' Derek says. 'We'll have a whole new life here.'

I pause, despite the fact that nothing in the world has ever felt more appealing to me than the prospect of being able to trade my life for a new one.

'Look, I'm in this with you,' I say. 'One hundred per cent. And I'm so proud of you for pursuing your dreams like this. It just might take a little time for me to adjust. Back in Savannah, there was this whole community of artists . . . *friends* . . . that I knew understood me. That had my back. Sure, I'm excited to have a space of my own to paint, but . . .'

'You'll miss Raheem. Of course you will. You guys practically grew up together. And there's the girls too,' Derek says, understandingly. 'I get it. I do. But they can visit any time. And we'll be back in town every once in a while too.'

'I know. But it's not the same. The shared studio wasn't just a place to work. It was home.'

I blush a little as guilt begins to edge in on me; I know what a privilege it is to be here. Jenna and Ashley, even Raheem, chatty as he is, would kill to have the space I have now. The opportunity to make art without a closing time or having to clean up for other people. Without the drive to get there or having to think about what you might wear. Just rolling out of bed and getting to paint without limit is a luxury most can't afford.

'I just worry I might get a little . . . lonely,' I muse out loud.

Derek puts down his noodles, wipes his mouth on a paper napkin and scoops me up with one arm, pulling me close.

'Anybody would feel like this, moving to a new city. But

you'll find your place here, baby. I promise. LA is like the creative capital of the whole country. There's bound to be an incredible community just *waiting* to take someone like you in. Until then . . . you've got me, right?'

I chuckle and wriggle free, telling him I don't want my food to get cold. But the truth is that I already feel like a spare part. An afterthought in the great success story of Derek Perkins.

Later, we blow up the bed we bought at the local Walmart and rummage through our suitcases before laying out our skincare products below the mirror in the en suite. His: shaving balm, aftershave, a foaming cleanser and a moisturizing SPF. Mine: six different serums, a retinol cream, two SPFs, some under-eye masks, four different cleansers, two different clay masks, a pumpkin enzyme jelly mask, a 'make-up melting' balm and a bottle of the perfume I'll probably wear for the rest of my life. Derek jokes that it's *my* bathroom. I tut and try not to laugh, knowing that, once we've fully unpacked, I'll likely commandeer the larger bathroom down the hall.

Once Derek has left me alone, I'm able to begin my night-time routine. It all starts with me playing wave music from my phone while I go through at least five of my skincare products. I'd usually light a candle, but, due to the moving situation, I don't have one to hand. I cover my hair in my trusty golden bonnet in a bid to avoid nappiness forming at the nape of my neck in the night and, once in bed, I spray lavender spray all over my pillow. It seems a little redundant, given we're sleeping on a squeaky, ready-to-deflate blow-up, but, when it comes to sleep, I'm not shy of putting in the work to facilitate the best night's rest possible. After all, I know what happens when I don't. I journal for a few minutes, then read for a few minutes, then put on my 'Sleep Sounds' playlist before turning out the light. Derek pulls me close.

'You always take so *long*,' he murmurs, already half asleep.

'Worth the wait, though, right?' I joke, snuggling into his side.

I think about my last nightmare, the one I had almost a week ago, on the day we moved. It's a brief flash of trauma lasting barely a split second, but it's enough to make me panic that the extensive routine that came before it may not be enough.

As Derek drops off, I fumble for my phone in the dark. Moments later, I'm scrolling through Astrid Michaelson's social media feed. There's a photo of her at her recent high-school graduation and I read through every single comment underneath. I've lost count of the number of times I've done this recently, but each time is like picking a scab: satisfying and only mildly contemptible. In the picture, she is smiling and, even though we've never met, I believe wholeheartedly that she is happy. That her grin isn't the mask mine so often is. It takes at least forty minutes, but, eventually, I drift off to sleep, on a wave of hope: the possibility that I didn't wreck her life beyond repair.

TWO

I put a fresh canvas on my easel and mix Cadmium Yellow with Prussian Green. The objects carefully laid out before me blur for a moment as I narrow my eyes to adjust my perspective. This time, I won't draw out the shapes, marking their territory on the canvas, giving my brush a roadmap. Instead, I simply make a few marks where the negative space should be. Then, I put logic aside, choosing to paint freely in the hope of finding my flow in this strange new space.

Before I know it, it's seven thirty and I hear Derek clatter through the front door. I clean off my brushes in the adjoining bathroom, wash my hands, slip out of my overalls and head back into the main house to greet him. He is the first person I've spoken to all day and I instantly overwhelm him with questions.

'Honey,' he says, all empathy. 'Why don't you go out tomorrow? Maybe to the grocery store or . . . there's a place doing pottery classes nearby. You could enrol. Meet some new people?'

We order takeout again – this time, Italian – and he tells me about his exciting day of meetings, the brilliant new script he's read from a first-time writer 'you'd never guess' was a debutant, and how much he's looking forward to 'hanging out' with his new producer tomorrow. He talks fast and energetically, as if his work isn't really work. But I know it is. I've seen the hoops he has jumped through to get here, lain beside him during the sleepless nights, witnessed the endless hours he's put in. And I know the pressure he is under now he's being heralded as 'the next Barry Jenkins'.

'You know they only say that because I'm Black, right? It has nothing to do with talent or even the type of movies we make.'

'I know, sweetie,' I reassure him. 'But it doesn't mean you *aren't* hugely talented. It just means that critics struggle to recognise it outside of a certain context. That's their failing, not yours.'

The next day, I do what he suggests and head to Gelson's. On the way, I pull up at the side of the road and peer into the pottery studio window. I'm disappointed to see that the attendees of this afternoon's workshop are all ancient and the work that is scattered around looks overly simplistic. I get back in the car, deciding I might circle back in a few days, if I still haven't found my community by then.

I call Momma on the way to the store, filling her in on the latest developments with Derek's film and how we're settling into our new home.

'Are you driving?' Momma asks, nervously. 'You know I don't love you calling when you're driving, baby.'

'Mom!' I groan, like a teenager. She knows I only call her that when she's getting under my skin, but part of me knows she's right. I know only too well what can happen if the focus slips away from the road. Even if only for a split second.

Momma tells me she has a pot on the stove and rushes off to rescue it. I'm not sure if the pot is even real but I've run out of things to say anyway, my life in LA suddenly feeling so small.

The Silver Lake branch of Gelson's is a real feast for the eyes. There's a level of variety that almost feels overwhelming and everything seems at least a dollar more expensive than it may have cost at our local Kroger back in Savannah. A reminder that being able to shop at Gelson's is like being allowed into an exclusive club. A club that offers environmentally conscious wellbeing, a precious commodity in times of global warming and mental-health warfare.

Despite having written a list of exactly what we need, I decide to take my time, zig-zagging in and out of each aisle, gazing at every shelf so as not to miss exciting ingredients for meals I may never actually cook. Shiny fruit and vegetables, wet beneath the sprinklers, freshly baked bread, a perfectly presented deli counter and the smell of the hot food buffet all serve to inspire my inner chef. I decide to create something magical for me and Derek with the limited kitchenware we've managed to accrue over the last few days. Sure, we'll be sitting on the floor, but that doesn't mean we can't indulge in whatever Greek feast or South Asian supper I'll manage to conjure up from the ingredients currently in my cart. I envision presenting Derek with a stunning fruit platter tomorrow morning and drop in a couple of large magenta dragon fruits, a pack of passion fruit and some apricots. He'll raise an eyebrow, tell me he's happy just eating eggs and waffles for brunch, and then eat at least two thirds of the platter anyway, just to make me feel validated. He'll know, as well as I do, that this is about keeping my mind occupied. It's the boredom that kills you, of course.

'I wouldn't if I were you,' a voice says. I'm standing in the cereal aisle, weighing up the pros and cons of buying a bumper pack of Chocolate Pillows. Pros: they will, undoubtedly, make Derek smile, transporting him back to those halcyon college days he mentioned only the other night, triggering a nostalgia for late nights back from partying, foraging for snacks in our kitchenette or lazy Sundays curled up on the battered old couch, watching old movies on his projector screen. Cons: Chocolate Pillows are, absolutely, terrible for your health.

'They're full of preservatives,' the voice pipes up again, as if able to hear my thoughts. I turn forty-five degrees to address the woman next to me, small talk at the ready, but my charm quickly dissolves when I see who I am talking to.

The woman is about six feet tall, golden hair down to her waist, dressed entirely in white linen, long loops of gold chains draped down her chest, each ear adorned with multiple little hoops and studs. There are rings on each of her slender fingers, and she has perfectly manicured nails – turquoise – detailed with tiny gold moons and stars that glitter beneath the harsh strip lighting of the store. Her eyelashes seem to go on for ever and I feel as if I am looking into the darkest depths of a rainforest when I catch sight of her astonishingly green eyes. She wears virtually no make-up but is still, somehow, utterly pristine.

'Sorry,' she says. 'It's completely none of my business. I didn't mean to startle you.'

She smiles, warmly, and looks down at her sandalled feet, as if slightly embarrassed.

'Not at all,' I say, her blushes further endearing her to me. 'It's just . . . you're literally the first person I've spoken to all day, so . . . my communication skills are a little rusty.'

'New to LA?' she asks.

'Very. Everything feels so . . . big.'

'Well, you're not alone. You might feel like you are, but this city is a revolving door. A conveyor belt. New arrivals every day. You just need to find your tribe.'

'That's what my husband keeps saying,' I reply.

Only he hadn't used the word 'tribe', of course.

The woman smiles again and I feel a sudden responsibility to fill the silence and a desperate urge to impress her. I don't want her walking away thinking that I'm a bad conversation-alist, even if I am, currently, going through a social drought.

'I thought about joining a pottery class,' I tell her. 'I'm an artist, you see. Had a really great community back in Georgia. But part of me feels like, now I'm here in a LA, I should have some hobbies outside of my vocation. Like-minded people are great, but it's also good not to be in an echo chamber, right?'

I'm babbling now, realising that the only reason I suddenly care about seeking out people who are so different to me is because I think she might be one of them, and I am eager for her to be my friend. Even if only for a few more minutes.

'You think too much,' she tells me, before handing me a gold-embossed business card. It's only then I realise I'm still clutching the box of Chocolate Pillows in the other hand.

'If you ever want to get into your body and out of your head, I run a movement and wellbeing class you might find . . .

enlightening. Women only. It's a very safe space. And the community we have is incredible.'

The cards shimmers as the store's lighting bounces off the shiny lettering: 'Deep Flow' it reads on one side and, on the other, 'Lilith Winters'. There's a West Hollywood address, a website and nothing else.

'Is it yoga?' I ask. 'Zumba?'

Lilith laughs, seemingly at my stupidity, and I regret having asked.

'The class is a blend of several disciplines and rituals. Ancient and modern. Predominately Eastern. Certainly divine.'

'And you teach every class?'

That laugh again, only this time shorter, quieter.

'I'm less of a teacher and more of a guide. A facilitator. A conduit. I'm just here to help you tap into the divine feminine energy that already exists within you. The class is about enabling *you* to harness *your* creative life force and see the universe from a new perspective. Of course, not everybody is ready to go on that journey, but, if you feel you are, come along.'

'I'll give it some thought,' I tell her, and she smiles in return.

'You have a beautiful energy,' she says. 'And *gorgeous* hair.'

She reaches out and I clench my teeth, bracing myself. But, instead of sticking her hand in my curls, she takes the box of cereal I'm still clutching, puts it back on the shelf and winks at me, as if I am in on the joke.

And, with that, she is gone, her business card the only real proof she wasn't a mere figment of my imagination.

THREE

Derek appears in the doorway just as I place a giant bowl of salad on the table. The novelty of finally having furniture still hasn't worn off and every meal feels like a huge event. Tonight, it's crab linguine made with fresh pasta, chili and crab meat that I bought from a fishmonger by the beach. Fresh ingredients only from now on, I tell myself. Even if I *do* have to drive a whole hour to get to Sal's Seafood. No more additives. If I want the ethereal glow Lilith Winters possesses, there will have to be sacrifices.

'You should write a cookbook, baby,' Derek says, polishing off his second portion. 'I'd buy it.'

'You wouldn't have to,' I laugh. 'You're married to the chef.'

'I'd still buy it,' he says. 'Gotta show my support!'

That night, we finally have sex in an actual bed – the first time in our new home. We both finish quickly and then shower together, lathering lavender and bergamot onto one another's skin. Just as I anticipated, Derek doesn't bat an eyelid at the thin lateral scab about an inch away from the back of my knee. He probably assumes I cut myself shaving. That is, if he noticed it at all.

After drying off and pulling on my pyjamas, I stumble into

the kitchen, peckish, but unable to commit to much. I slide open the cutlery drawer and find a few fortune cookies left over from the multiple Chinese takeouts we had when we first moved in. I crack one open and allow the buttery sweetness of the first half to melt a little in my mouth before I crunch down on it and then unfurl the message it has left behind. 'Yesterday's disasters often come dressed in tomorrow's clothes,' it reads.

I roll my eyes and toss the strip of paper into the trash.

Returning to bed, I lie awake, staring at the ceiling and listening to Derek's muffled snores as the clock speeds towards the early hours of the morning. Lilith dances through my thoughts and I picture her business card burning a hole in my jacket pocket. I start to consider the idea that she is just what I need to find my place here. But then fear comes creeping in the night, into my bed and then into my mind. I can't shake it. The thought of being in a class again makes the thin, downy layer on my arms stand to attention.

The next morning, I decide to remind my body what movement feels like. Could I really be fit enough to take Lilith's class without all the other members laughing at me the moment my back is turned? I'm full of doubt, but, nonetheless, I find myself scrolling through YouTube in search of the perfect yoga video. 'Intermediate' seems ideal for where I'm at these days but, twenty minutes in, I'm sweating and it feels as if I may have pulled a muscle. As I fumble through the final few poses, I start to feel silly. How could I have believed this was a good idea? I'm nowhere near fit enough for my gangly, awkward frame to be seen moving around in public places.

In my teens, I'd been a dancer, but what may have been a

promising career fizzled into nothing before I even reached adulthood. In my twenties, I'd found other ways to stay fit. Derek and I would go on a long bike ride almost every Sunday morning. During the week, I'd do a hatha yoga class with Ashley on a Tuesday morning and Pilates each Thursday lunchtime, often dragging Raheem along with me. But then, one day, I missed my footing coming down the rickety staircase in our old Savannah home and, in an instant, it was all over. A torn cruciate ligament took me out for months and I never quite got back into the flow of things after that.

I remember driving to the gym one rainy morning in a bid to sign up for a membership. Instead, I stood outside for fifteen minutes, my hair frizzing in the drizzle, wet leggings sticking to my thighs. I didn't want to watch myself in those floor-to-ceiling mirrors as I surreptitiously compared myself to the reflections of the glistening, tanned, muscle-bound regulars around me. I missed the endorphins I knew a decent workout would undoubtedly give me, but my sense of shame quickly overrode all that. Instead, I went to the Publix on the other side of the parking lot, bought some Pillsbury cookie dough and ate it straight out of the package while I watched a storm brew through my car window.

Throwing myself into Lilith's class when I barely understand what it entails could lead to the same feelings of inadequacy I felt back then. I take her card out of my jacket pocket and allow it to follow my fortune-cookie message into the trash.

Two nights later, however, I'm wide awake, my eyes chasing the shadows on the ceiling. When I finally begin to drift off, my body lurches and I'm in the car again, slamming on the brakes a moment too late, the windscreen shattering in front of me. I wake up in a cold sweat and run to the bathroom. When my feet touch the cool tiles, though, I snap out of it, and the rattling of my breath and shaking of my shoulders ceases for long enough for me to drop into reality: I need to be careful. I can't risk Derek growing suspicious.

I creep back towards our bed and take my cell phone from the nightstand.

Once I'm in the hallway, I switch on the flashlight function and use it to guide me into the kitchen and towards the trash can. Digging through the dregs of last night's dinner, Derek's protein-shake bottles that should almost certainly be in the recycling, and reams of balled-up cellophane and aluminium foil, I eventually find what I'm looking for: Lilith's card. It's stained with soda, red wine and God knows what else, but I can still easily read the golden lettering.

After washing my hands, I take care not to scrape the chair along the tiled floor as I pull it out, sit down and open up my laptop, my face illuminated by the blue screen light.

The Deep Flow website is stylish, laden with celebrity endorsements and images of perfect bodies, skin slick with sweat. There are pictures of candles and a graphic of a wave rolls across the screen in sync with the movement of my cursor. The classes are described as a 'transcendental internal cleanse', but, beyond that, the site is so minimalist it's hard to get a real understanding of what participants actually *do* during the sessions.

Maybe it doesn't matter. These women look happy. Confident. Glowing. And I could use a dose of that. I click the link and sign up for the four-week free trial.

*　　*　　*

Sunlight illuminates the studio as Lilith walks towards the front of the class, reaching out to touch various members of the gathering as she goes: a hand on a shoulder, a stroke of someone's back, a moment where she holds hands with someone else. She looks like a golden angel, sent from the beyond to guide us all towards peace, and I find myself yearning for the same sort of attention she has given those select few.

The studio itself is sparse. Sprung wooden floorboards, changing rooms tucked away at the back of the class, floor-to-ceiling windows at the front. I'd expected to have to check in with a receptionist before class began but this place is far too economical for that. Instead, I stepped straight off the sidewalk and into the studio, abandoning my shoes on the way.

'There's cubbies here,' another member of the class informed me, demonstrating where I should put my stuff by putting her own things in the cubby closest to me.

The room smells of Palo Santo, there are candles lit in each corner and the windows are hung with soft drapes in muted pinks and purples. The sound of low drums and a simple stringed instrument plays through the speakers, just loud enough to be heard over the murmurs of my fellow classmates.

I am the only person of Black heritage in the class and, save for two young, giggly Latinas at the back of the studio, I am the only person of colour, period. What's worse is that everyone in the class is dressed in white or cream: tight sports bras and matching leggings or shorts. In my bright red onesie, I realise I couldn't stand out more if I'd tried.

But, just as anxiety begins to take hold, there's that soft

smile again, that patient pause that says, 'I am here, join me when you're ready.'

I feel the nervous energy of the class begin to settle and soon we are all breathing as one, a singular organism led by Lilith's own breath as she guides us, gently: 'Inhale . . . exhale. Inhale . . . exhale.'

Before long, my pounding heart slows to a steady beat as Lilith instructs us to hold our breath between inhalations and exhalations. It's nothing I haven't done before, but, today, it feels somehow magical.

And then the music creeps in. At first, a complicated but calming piano solo, then a voice laden with vibrato, singing lyrics about the limerence of first love. My chest swells and I find myself, suddenly, on the brink of tears. I'm back where it all started for Derek and me, eyes catching across a cluttered bookstore: him, holding Toni Morrison's *Song for Solomon* in his big, strong hands; me, full of mystery – or so he says when he tells people how we met. Our story would play out like one of those romantic comedies we used to watch together on rainy Sundays in New York – that is, if it weren't for my chequered past.

When I met Derek, I didn't want to let anyone access the little box of secrets hidden inside me. Love felt dangerous back then. Sometimes, it still does.

'Now, we sway,' says Lilith.

I open one eye and watch the tree-like limbs of the other attendees caught in an invisible breeze. I attempt to move in tandem with them and close my eyes again.

Soon we are moving at a faster pace and now allowed to

'observe' our fellow fitness fans. Only this isn't fitness, Lilith reminds us: 'This is wellbeing. This is harmony. This is *love*.' And, on the word love, the entire class shouts 'LOVE!' in unison. The music changes pace and we follow Lilith as she orders us to 'fling open the doors' to our hearts, throwing her arms back theatrically as she does. We all copy her and then send our heads down to the floor between our legs before rolling our spines slowly upwards until our heads reach towards the ceiling again. Then we're flowing, side to side, arms waving as if attempting to move through water. The music changes again, this time to a tribal beat. Lilith says, 'You know what to do,' and I momentarily panic because I don't. Before I have time to truly consider this, however, she tips her head back and lets out a war cry that makes me almost jump outside of my skin. Is she serious right now? I wonder. Is everyone really going to be down with this?

My questions are quickly answered as a cannon of whooping and hollering from those around me begins. Surely, I can't be expected to—

'Sadie!' Lilith shouts. 'Show us who you are, Sadie! Lift your voice to the sky!'

I grimace.

This *isn't* who I am.

Admittedly, I want to be a part of something, want to feel less alone in this sprawling metropolis, but I am like wall-paper – happiest when allowed to sit in the background, present but without demands, observant but unquestionable.

'Come on!' Lilith cajoles. 'You are safe here! You are loved! We honour your spirit, Sadie!'

I can't help but think that, if I were *genuinely* loved, hon-oured and safe, Lilith would leave me the fuck alone. Instead, she does the opposite.

'Keep moving, class,' she tells the others, and then steps towards me, holding out her hand as if she wants me to shake it. I accept her approach and she takes my hand between both of hers and looks into my eyes. It's awkward as hell.

'You're not ready,' she says. 'But you will be.'

My hand feels sweaty between hers and I feel more self-conscious than ever. I fight the urge to pull away and, then, the urge to cry.

'Let it go,' Lilith tells me.

Then she says it again, this time addressing the whole class. And the arm flinging begins again. She tells us to feel the universe entering our body, filling us up with energy, filling our lungs with air and our hearts with love. As soon as the word 'love' leaves her lips, I hear the chorus around me again.

'Love!'

Lilith tells us to let go of our lives before this moment. Our relationships. Our work.

'Release!' she cries. 'Release it all! This moment is for you and you only. In this moment you are free!'

It's time to 'ground' ourselves and I have no idea what that means, but my classmates soon begin to squat in time to the music, fingers spread wide, pointing down to the laminate floor and then clenching their fists as if pulling something up from the earth below. Lilith tells us to uproot the weeds that surround us and plant our own roots anew. She says something about chakras too, but I don't catch it. I'm too busy trying not to think about the agony building in my leg muscles.

Right when I think I can't take it any more, Lilith orders us to 'sink into the earth' and begins drumming on the floor between her legs. All standing in a grande plié, the women in the class follow suit, and soon there is a chorus of battle cries around me. They seem euphoric, but I am just uncomfortable, and that discomfort goes way beyond the physical.

Lilith reaches above and tells us to pull the light of the sun into our bodies and push it into our emotional centre. Then she lifts each hip to meet her hands, twisting the corresponding knee in as she goes, her well-toned backside swaying from side to side as she does. This, like everything else she's done today, feels borrowed, only, this time, it's from somewhere much closer to home. I am reminded of childhood cookouts and dancing with my aunties in the front yard, of Aunt Sheila and Aunt Lenora moving their powerful hips in time to the music while I copy their every move, of Cousin Niecy bringing out a fresh tray of cornbread before dumping it down so she can join in with us.

And here I am now, joining in again, against my better judgement. This feels familiar and that feels good. I'm not floundering like I feared I would. Instead, I'm thriving, enjoying the nostalgia of doing something I already know so well. More than anything, I feel myself leaning in, trusting my body more than I have in years. It is a body that has, before, failed me when I've needed it most. Failed to defend itself under attack. Failed to have quicker reflexes in the most dangerous of moments. Failed to carry love to term. But now my limbs are embracing movement and I feel such unity with the women around me as we all move in perfect sync to the music. Lilith catches my eye and smiles before beginning to spin on the spot, like the whirling dervishes I remember seeing in a black-and-white documentary when I was a teenager.

Soon, I am twirling too, fighting dizziness and, at first, the urge to laugh. But before long the others are giggling too and I give in. Lilith shouts that we should 'submit to joy' and, in this moment, joy comes easily. I feel it envelope me. Consume me. I laugh and laugh and spin and spin until I am too dizzy to stand up any more. I collapse onto the floor, panting and smiling, my fallen classmates surrounding me. Lilith joins us on her back and tells us to close our eyes and dream of stars. She recites something she has memorised, about moonlight and the water in our bodies, about women and our blood cycles, about balance and peace. The music fades away in the background and, suddenly, I can hear everything: birds singing outside, one mimicking another, then two new birds with entirely different mating calls. I can hear the quiet drone of the air conditioning. The soft snores of one of my classmates. The rev of engines as cars speed by. Someone next to me breathing, heavily, and then . . . a bell. No. Not quite. An instrument of some other kind. Perhaps.

I open one eye and see Lilith tapping the side of a brass bowl with a short stick covered in leather. She is squatting, the bowl between her thighs as she smiles that same smile I saw at the beginning of the class. She lights a candle in front of her, then some incense, and I quickly close my eyes again before she spots me spying.

Eventually, she starts to speak.

'Acceptance,' she says. 'What is acceptance? Accepting difference. Accepting others. Accepting our partners, our friends, our family members, warts and all. What does it mean to accept our environments? Our past mistakes? Our current life situation? Can we truly learn to accept ourselves? And if so, how? It's easy to love ourselves when we are achieving. Easy to love the parts of ourselves that others regard as beautiful and brilliant. But true self-love is accepting ourselves when we fail. On the days we feel ugly. Or the days when we don't receive a single compliment despite how long we spent doing our make-up or choosing *that* outfit. True acceptance is choosing to be ourselves even in the times we feel stupid or awkward. And every time we make a mistake.'

Her words melt into my ears like honey and I can hear at least two of my classmates quietly weeping as she talks.

'What we're talking about here is so important. But, instead of doing the work required to achieve self-acceptance, we desperately seek external validation. We people-please in a bid to control what others think of us. We forget our boundaries. We give away our bodies and our minds to people who don't have the capacity to embrace them in the way they deserve.'

I think of the time Derek and I broke up for six months back in college and my subsequent online dating crash course. I remember meeting men, expecting a date, only to quickly discover they expected sex. Not that they *hoped* for it. But that they felt *entitled* to it. And, thanks to the patriarchy brainwashing me, I'd felt obligated to give it to them. Even when I didn't really want to.

The sound of the brass bowl vibrates through my memories, bringing me back to the present moment. We all take a deep breath and, in unison, breathe out hard through our mouths, expelling self-rejection and any residual negative energy.

'I forgive all those who have hurt me, including myself.'

We all speak Lilith's words back to her, aloud. Or, at least, the others do. I open and close my mouth like a fish, murmuring inaudibly, unable to lie out loud.

'I let in light and love. I am whole and complete,' she says, and a tear unexpectedly slips out of my right eye and dribbles down the side of my face and into my hair. A shuddering sob fills my chest and becomes desperate to release itself. I refuse it, unsure of where this sudden wave of emotion has come from. *I was only ever here to go through the motions*, I remind myself. *The point of this class is to fill my time. Give me a sense of routine. Maybe make new friends. That's it.*

After class, I'm putting on my shoes when Lilith approaches me from behind. I smell her first, a waft a white lilies and lavender overwhelming me.

'Did you enjoy the class?' she asks.

'I did. You . . . kind of remind me of a therapist I had back in Georgia. Not the way you look or anything. But the way you talk. It's very . . . soothing.'

Lilith smiles and is silent for long enough to make me nervous. Eventually, she asks if I'll come again. I hesitate.

'There's no pressure, of course,' she says. 'But if you'd like to, you can invest in some Deep Flow apparel of your own.'

She gestures to the white bodies now scattered around the

studio, some chatting, most gathering their things, a few still lying on their mats.

'It's nice to feel a sense of unity, isn't it?'

I nod and her voice suddenly grows louder as she addresses the whole class.

'Flow family!' she says. 'I almost forgot! I have *some*, albeit limited, availability for one-on-one Spiritual Cleansing sessions, if any of you would like to . . .'

I don't hear the rest of her announcement due to a sudden swarm of Deep Flow students surrounding Lilith. Eventually, there's a wall around her, shutting me out, and there is nothing left for me to do except quietly head out to the parking lot.

FOUR

'You sound like you've joined a cult.' Mumtaz laughs and, not for the first time in her presence, I feel the joy drain out of me as a tidal wave of shame crashes down.

Mumtaz is the 'straight-talking' British wife of one of Derek's closest friends, Mehdi Nasir. I say 'straight-talking' rather than just straight-talking because that is how Derek fondly describes her, whereas I just think she's a straight-up judgemental bitch.

I put up with her, though, as I have done for years, while the Nasirs have passed in and out of our lives. First, during college, when Derek and Mehdi became close, even though Mehdi was pre-med and it seemed unlikely they'd have anything in common. Then, when Mehdi finished medical school and slept on our couch in Brooklyn during the beginnings of his rotation at a local hospital – 'Just 'til he finds his feet,' Derek said at the time. It lasted four months.

We moved to Savannah and, after a year there, Mehdi came for Thanksgiving, with Mumtaz in tow. At first, we'd gotten along, bonding over how problematic we found the principles of a holiday that celebrated the massacre and colonisation of indigenous peoples.

'Why on earth would Black and Brown people want to celebrate *that*?' Mumtaz had asked, rhetorically, as we chowed down on turkey, collard greens, candied yams and mac 'n' cheese.

Washing dishes with Derek later on, I'd smiled and told him Mumtaz was 'my kind of person' and, soon, I wanted to be around her all the time. There were afternoons spent at the mall, cocktails downtown, dinner dates and a trip to the nail salon that ended with us accidentally leaving a sushi bar without paying, on account of us getting very drunk on the way there. When their ten-day stay was over and Mehdi and Mumtaz headed back to New York, it felt like a real wrench. Before long, I had plans to visit during a period when Mehdi was due to be out of town at a medical conference. It was the ideal opportunity for us to have our own space and go out as much as we wanted – after all, Mumtaz could only ever get smashed in secret.

'He's a lot more practising than I am,' she told me over drinks in Soho one day. 'I mean, he definitely does coke and smokes weed with his colleagues sometimes, but he never drinks alcohol. So, I have to keep it on the down-low, you know?'

I understood. If Derek knew how much I drank when I was with Mumtaz, he'd be shocked too, especially given the fact I'd been virtually tee-total for years.

'Come *on*,' Mumtaz had cajoled, the first time we'd gone out together in Savannah. 'Life is way too short to be drinking Virgin Pina Coladas.'

I'd told her I wasn't good with a drink in me. That I'd barely drunk at all since I was legally able to. That I didn't trust myself inebriated. But she'd told me one or two cocktails wouldn't get me *that* drunk and had called the waiter over to order me a Long Island Iced Tea. Two hours later, we were singing the world's worst version of 'Islands in the Stream' at a downtown karaoke bar and, half an hour after that, I was on my ass in the street, heels off and unable to get up without assistance.

In New York, Mumtaz took things to a new level. We went out for tapas on what Mumtaz had described as 'a low-key weeknight', but, before I knew it, I was in a toilet cubicle with her and she was offering me some white powder on a key.

'Don't be boring,' she said, sighing irritably when I refused. 'In London, everyone does this *all* the time. It's like . . . *totally* accepted. You're only in New York for a few days. Have some new experiences, Sadie. Make it count.'

Walking back into the restaurant, everything felt brighter, louder, heightened. We went to a club with flashing blue, purple and red lights, music pounding, writhing bodies and us in the centre of it all. I felt more confident than ever. Mumtaz kept hugging me, pecking me on the cheeks and lips, telling me I was special. I loved it. Loved her. It had been a long time since I'd had a close girlfriend.

We danced and danced. Harder, faster, our bodies colliding over and over. There was another club after that one, then another and another. More drinks. More bumps. More dancing. High as the light flickering across the ceiling. Seeing ever so slightly double whenever I tried to focus.

But then, like a jump cut in a film I was watching, I saw myself vomiting into a gutter. Mumtaz, holding back my hair while she checked around for onlookers.

Looking back, it's clear that her reputation mattered more to her than my wellbeing. But it wasn't until weeks later that I figured that out.

In the car on the way back to hers, I started crying, trails of mascara running down my face. I hadn't liked the way those guys we'd been talking to in the bar had touched me. One had leaned in a little too close, all garlicky breath and bad aftershave. The other had grabbed me just a little too hard as I'd moved away to head back to the dance floor. A hand on my neck. Another on my thigh. It had all brought back memories I'd been pushing down for years.

I tried to talk to Mumtaz about it afterwards, but she'd only rolled her eyes.

'You're just fucked, Sadie. We've had a good night. Don't ruin it now.'

The next day we went to a rooftop bar and drank Bloody Marys before getting facials. I felt embarrassed. Ashamed. Why couldn't I handle 'fun' with the level of aplomb Mumtaz clearly could? She was capable of getting totally wrecked and partying into the early hours while still working an important job, making it to beauty appointments on time and keeping it all a secret from her husband. How had she learned to do all this?

'London,' she said, popping the olive from her newly arrived martini into her mouth. Her lips were flawlessly rouged, her skin so immaculate I doubted she even needed the facial we were due to have. 'London was like a trial run for New York. And practice makes perfect.'

The next day I was on a plane back to Georgia. I still felt phenomenally rough, regretting being weak enough to give in to Mumtaz's peer pressure and mildly humiliated when I thought of my reaction to those guys in the bar. Flashes of the night were still coming back to me and too many of them made me cringe.

In the months that followed, I'd heard less and less from Mumtaz. It was as if she was freezing me out and I couldn't make sense of it. Against my better judgement, I'd done everything she'd wanted in New York. Surely I'd earned her friendship in return?

Eventually, after I'd mentioned to Derek more than once how Mumtaz's ghosting was making me feel, he told me he'd talked to Mehdi about it.

I was aghast.

'Why would you do that? I don't want him thinking . . . I dunno. That I'm some kind of beg-friend. And he can't know that Mumtaz drinks.'

Derek gave me a look somewhere close to pity and then told me what Mumtaz had told Mehdi. That she liked me, but felt I was a bad influence. That I was 'too chaotic'. That if she and Mehdi were going to keep trying for a baby she had to start thinking like a mother. 'Is Sadie someone we'd really want in our lives if we had children to think of?' she had, apparently, wondered out loud.

I remember feeling like I'd been kicked in the face. None of this made sense. It had been Mumtaz that had insisted on the drinking. Her, who had dragged me into that toilet cubicle and given me cocaine that she had bought with her own money. How was I the chaotic one?

Then I thought of myself throwing up into the gutter, crying in the cab and how worse for wear I'd felt the next day. Maybe that was it. Maybe she didn't want to hang out with people who showed weakness.

The humiliation and rejection I felt then has never really gone away. I feel it every time I think of Mumtaz and certainly every time I'm forced to sit through a dinner like this one. The Nasirs moved to LA years before we started thinking about it, and I know having 'friends' here was a major incentive behind Derek's decision. But, for me, they don't feel like friends. Mumtaz feels like an ex who broke my heart and Mehdi is someone I feel ashamed to have conspired against. Every day, he falls for Mumtaz's lies and, despite the fact he has only ever shown me kindness, I can't help but see him as an idiot.

'Well, it might sound like a cult to you, Mumtaz,' I finally say. 'But it's working for me. Seriously, it hasn't even been a month yet and already I feel amazing. If nothing else, it's clearing my head so I can be more creative.'

'I can vouch for that,' Derek affirms. 'You were in the studio yesterday for what? Twelve hours?'

I blush slightly. 'Something like that.'

'I barely see her these days,' Derek smiles.

'Sudden obsession, disappearing for days, lack of communication with loved ones . . . it *is* a cult!' Mumtaz laughs again and the men join in. It feels like it's all at my expense and I'm thankful when their baby cries from the next room and Mumtaz jumps up to attend to her. Within that relief, however, I find myself questioning how the worst people so often seem to get exactly what they want. Life isn't fair, I tell myself. As if I need a reminder.

Later, on the drive home, I'm silent. Derek prods me, hoping to provoke me into talking. But I won't bite.

'Come on. She just has a very British sense of humour. I know you're not Mumtaz's biggest fan, but she means well. She does.'

'Why do you always say that?' I finally snap. He'd said something similar when I'd told him that Mumtaz's story about me being 'chaotic' was far from the whole truth, that she'd instigated it all.

'Honey, I'm sure she's just concerned,' he'd said. 'Mehdi's always talking about what a golden heart she has.'

Years later, I still haven't forgiven him for trying so hard to see the best in her and, as he fumbles for a similar justification for Mumtaz's behaviour this time around, I decide I don't want to hear it.

'Forget it,' I say, leaning my head against the car window. 'You never have my back.'

'That is *not* true,' he retorts. 'You're being dramatic.'

It is on those words that I see red. We pull into the driveway, gravel crunching beneath the wheels, and I leap out of the car, slamming the door behind me. *I'll show him dramatic*, I think.

In the bedroom, Derek pleads with me as he slips between the sheets and into the bed beside me.

'So, we're really not gonna talk?'

My back towards him, I blink into the dark.

'I'm tired, Derek,' I say.

He sighs, loudly, and I feel him roll over, his back now facing mine. From his side of the bed I hear him mumble: 'I just don't understand you sometimes, Sadie.'

And I know that he is right. He doesn't.

But maybe that's okay now. Maybe there is someone here who does.

'You're Sadie, right?'

I turn round to find a flame-haired, blue-eyed Deep Flow devotee stood before me, grinning ear to ear.

'I've noticed you keep coming back.'

'It's my eighth session,' I smile. Then I lean in. 'You're actually the first person who's spoken to me other than Lilith.'

'Well, people are probably intimidated. I mean . . . look at you!' She waves her hand up and down my body, as if I'm supposed to know what she means. I decide to take it as a compliment, however, and extend my hand.

'I'm Natalia,' she says, taking it. 'Welcome to the community!'

We pick up our things and say goodbye to Lilith. Then, we grab smoothies from a nearby stall and sit outside on tinny metal chairs under a parasol stuck in the middle of a tinny metal table.

'I've been part of the Deep Flow family for, like, three years now, and it's really been a game changer for me. It got me out of a relationship that wasn't right, helped me release myself from some toxic family members and friends, and work is going better than ever.'

I ask Natalia if she misses the relationships she's ended. If she ever gets lonely. She looks at me seriously and says: 'The only relationship that really matters is the one you have with yourself. Deep Flow has helped me see that. It's peeled back the layers of my reality.'

Cold, pureed strawberries slip through my lips and onto my waiting tongue as I contemplate these ideas. I wonder what 'layers' I need to peel back. It's a strange metaphor, but Natalia seems genuinely happy. Who am I to question that?

When it's time to say goodbye, she catches me in a slightly unexpected embrace.

'Thank you,' I say. 'This has been lovely.'

'No worries,' Natalia smiles. 'Us women of colour gotta stick together!'

Confused, I refer back to her red hair, her blue eyes, the smattering of freckles across her nose.

'Oh. You're . . . sorry . . . I didn't realise you were . . . What's your . . . heritage?'

Natalia doesn't miss a beat.

'I'm an eighth Kazakhstani. On my mom's side.'

'Oh. Wow,' is all I can manage, and we agree to see each other again soon. Then, I walk away, dumbfounded, and feeling lonelier than ever.

'You left so early this morning,' Derek says, on my return home. He's tenderizing lamb on the kitchen countertop and I'm sure his choice of what to prepare for dinner and how to prepare it has *absolutely nothing* to do with his current mood. 'It's my day off. We could have done something together.'

'Why are you making dinner so early? It's barely even lunchtime,' I say, ignoring his diatribe.

'I'm experimenting with a new recipe,' he tells me, growing snappier by the second. 'The longer it marinates, the better it'll taste.'

He slams the fridge door. I shrug my shoulders and head

for a shower. Behind me, I hear him make a little sound of frustration. 'What's going on with us, Sadie? This isn't how we do things.'

I stop in my tracks. 'I don't know what you want from me. I told you how I felt last night.'

Derek sighs. 'I can't understand why you would think I don't have your back. I love you. I'm on your side. Always.'

'It didn't feel like that. You're so busy protecting your friendship with Mehdi that it feels like you don't believe me when I talk about how Mumtaz makes me feel. She's a bitch. And I don't say that about other women lightly. You know that.'

Derek nods. Admits Mumtaz is not perfect. Says her behaviour in the past has been reprehensible. He washes his hands and takes me in his arms, breathing into my hair. I accept it, all of it, trusting that this hug, these statements, are acts of contrition. That is, until he says the one thing I cannot believe he doesn't realise will twist the knife like nothing else: 'She's a mother now though. I'm sure it'll be the making of her.'

I pull away. He realises his mistake. But it's too late and I can hear him calling after me, full of apologies, all the way to the bathroom. This time, I don't turn back.

FIVE

'Where's your head at, Sadie?' Lilith asks after another perfect morning of Deep Flow.

I tell her I feel amazing, that it's taken a while to get into these classes but I've finally found my stride. I think about how I'm truly back in my body for the first time since my short-lived teenage ballet career and it feels like coming home. This class has been a reminder that there is magic in movement, something I've been afraid to fully lean into since my dream of being a dancer died. Sure, I'm not crazy about the rampant cultural appropriation and I don't yet feel like the other members of the Deep Flow community are 'my kind of people', but I am prepared to give them a chance. After all, my experience with Mumtaz taught me that friendships that start with an exciting spark of connection can often burn out quickly.

Since starting Deep Flow, my head has been clearer and my creativity and productivity in the studio has soared. It's hard not to feel like a walking, talking advertisement for the programme when I feel on such a high as a result of doing it.

'I wanted to know what your plans are now your four-week trial is up,' Lilith says, and I realise, with a jolt, that I'll no longer be able to attend classes without some financial commitment.

'How much is a full membership?' I ask. 'It doesn't actually say on your website.'

'You can join at the Basic level, if you wish, but that's really for more . . .'

She trails off and Natalia, who has been listening in nearby, interjects. '*Basic* people,' she says, laughing and subtly gesturing towards Debbie, a red-faced mom of four who often stumbles in late and never quite seems to have her shit together. I wonder if I would do any better, should motherhood ever find me, but quickly decide one way to avoid doing it poorly would be to start investing in myself before I even get there.

'Now, now,' Lilith says, softly chastising Natalia but unable to hide a faint smile. 'The next level is the Amber Membership. As well as unlimited classes, that would give you access to a weekly one-on-one Spiritual Cleansing session, invites to our socials, life-coaching newsletters and priority booking on my retreats.'

'That sounds great,' I say. 'How much is that membership?'

'So that would be a quarterly investment of just $2,500,' Lilith smiles, and I find myself straining my chin muscles so my jaw doesn't hit the floor.

'How much?' I ask again, checking I haven't misheard. Lilith repeats the figure again and I swallow hard, thinking about how Derek will absolutely kill me if he ever finds out how much I'm spending on all this.

'It's *totally* worth it!' a voice chimes in from behind me. I look over my shoulder and see a petite, tanned brunette grinning at us both. I later find out she is Ruby Sutherland, celebrity stylist and heir to the Sutherland Continental Cookies empire. She is, no doubt, one of Lilith's richest clients, but, in this moment, I imagine she is just like me, that this quarterly investment is a stretch she too will have to make sacrifices for. But it's 'totally worth it', so I nod and hear myself say yes.

Lilith hugs me. 'Get ready for your life to change,' she says, and I've never been more sure that it will.

A week later, I'm at a day spa in Pasadena with Ruby, Natalia and another Deep Flow attendee I've seen at every class. Emily Le Page has bleached blonde hair, a wiry physique and a well-defined set of abs she isn't afraid of showing off. Her most notable feature, however, is her eyes: one blue, one green. Outside of Deep Flow, she's into roller skating and surfing, both of which give her a sense of community, she says, but 'nothing like Deep Flow'. Like Natalia, she is a 'Carnelian' member, paying twice as much as I do for many more perks. Ruby, on the other hand, is the proud owner of an 'Obsidian' membership. I don't even ask what she's paying.

As we lie out on our lounge chairs by the pool, Emily flips onto her side so she can talk to me.

'The thing about Deep Flow is the spiritual interactions we get to have. Like, it's not just fitness or fun. It's all this internal work as well. It's transformative for so many people. The Spiritual Cleansing sessions are just . . .' She mimes a chef's kiss and shakes her head as if she can't quite believe she gets to be a part of something so wonderous. 'Have you booked your first one-to-one with Lilith yet?'

The truth is I haven't even thought about it yet. I've been so busy moving cash around our accounts and hoping Derek won't notice the money I've spent, I've hardly been able to enjoy what

I've spent it on. If Ruby hadn't insisted on treating us all to today's day spa trip, I wouldn't be here. Which seems a silly thought the moment I think it – if Derek doesn't notice $2,500 missing, it's unlikely he'd notice another $550. If anything, he'd be pleased to know I'm finally settling in here. Finally finding some friends. Even if they do seem like surprising choices. But I don't want to push it, and who knows precisely how much would have to go missing before he would start picking up on things. All I need to do is hang in there until I get paid the advance for my next freelance job. Contracts for the tech company logo design I've been booked for are already being drawn up. It won't be long before I have some cash of my own.

'After my first three one-to-ones, I left my marriage,' Ruby says, just as a tray of mimosas is delivered to us by an exceptionally good-looking waiter.

'You're kidding.'

'Nope.' She takes a sip. 'The crazy thing is, I didn't even realise I wasn't happy. It took some seriously deep work to understand that I hadn't been for a long time. That I'd fallen into a rut, you know? I married my high-school sweetheart and I didn't know any different.'

'And now?'

'I'm single. And I'm good with that. I finally have a chance to get to know myself.'

'*Girl*, that is so important,' Natalia says, clicking the fingers of her right hand above her head as she does. I quietly cringe before the voice in my head chastises me for it: *These people have been good to you*, it says. *Stop judging them.*

'Have any of you done therapy before?' I ask, thinking of

44

my former therapist back in Georgia and what a wrench it was to leave someone I had built such a strong level of trust and rapport with.

'Lilith *is* my therapist,' Emily says.

'Yaaaas, sis, same!' Natalia squeals, and the voice inside pipes up again: *Stop it, Sadie. Remember where you are. You're here to make friends and keep them.*

'I mean, she's not technically a therapist. More of a life coach. But the impact is the same,' Emily clarifies.

I confess I'm not sure what a life coach does that is different from a therapist. Surely both guide you through life, presenting you with tools to navigate it better?

Ruby's smile is only a tiny bit patronising.

'Therapists are more about dealing with the past. Not that Lilith won't talk to you about that. She totally does. It's just that life coaches are more about the future. Which I think is, like, way more useful. Traditional therapists get so caught up in childhood trauma that it can almost make you feel like you're stuck back there, unable to progress.'

Despite her delivery, Ruby makes a good point. I'd spent so many years working hard to bury the past that I'd barely even thought about the future. And yet, despite getting along with Ruby, Emily and Natalia better than I thought I would, I still feel sure they are not my people.

I decide to call my girlfriends back home on the journey back from the spa. When Ashley doesn't pick up, I call Jenna: straight to voicemail. I picture them both in the studio together, too busy to even notice my calls and, when I pull up outside the house, I quickly search for Ashley on social media. Sure enough, a post in which she is announcing her latest exhibition pops up. There are samples of her work included in it: a bold November sky, a reclining woman deep in thought, a child playing amongst daisies. Each painting shows Ashley's ability to convey breath-taking realism and there are dozens of compliments in the comments beneath. It's hard to admit to myself that it is only jealousy that stops me leaving one too.

I switch to Jenna's profile and what I find there is even harder to swallow.

'Congrats, beautiful!' one comment reads. 'So happy for you and Jamie!'

I stare for what feels like hours at the pregnancy scan she's posted. How could I be the last to know about this? I message her and ask just that: 'Why didn't you tell me?! You'll be a wonderful mother. Such incredible news.'

Then I go through all 168 of her previous posts, studying her face, her body, the way her and her husband Jamie hold hands and kiss. *What is it she has that I don't?* I ask myself. *How has she managed to sustain a pregnancy longer than I could? Is it genetics? Luck? A love stronger than what Derek and I have?*

She was always the one who got the most attention on nights out. Always had a slew of boys running around after her. Now, it's hard not to feel as if the universe simply selected her to have a life more perfect than my own. I consider the idea that perhaps there are the anointed ones and perhaps there are the rest of us. Never quite good enough. Lives littered with failure.

The phone suddenly starts buzzing in my hand. It's Jenna, returning my call.

'Hey, sweetie,' I say, attempting to give no clue as to my current mental state.

'Darlin'!' Jenna exclaims, in her familiar Southern drawl. 'I just saw your missed call. And your message. Look, honey, I'm so sorry I didn't tell you I was pregnant. I was trying to be . . . sensitive . . . you know?'

So you posted the news all over social media instead? I want to spit back at her. Instead, I thank her for trying. Tell her she was sweet to consider me and that I'm oh-so-happy about her amazing news. Then I lie about a friend arriving to meet me for coffee and hang up the phone.

I tear through the house and lock myself in the studio, returning to the painting I started weeks ago, when I first began attending Deep Flow classes. I strip down to my underwear in an attempt to mitigate the warmth of the garage space and, once comfortable, I paint and paint and paint, getting lost in burnt umber, chrome green and cobalt blue. I paint with passionate rage, tears bubbling beneath the surface, a spectrum of emotions pouring out of me and onto the canvas. When Derek finds me hours later, I am wired, half naked and covered in paint.

'Wow, there really is a fine line between genius and insanity, huh?' he says.

'What do you think?' I ask, gesturing at my creation. It's far from finished but it's starting to become clear what I'm attempting to achieve. Derek steps towards the piece and is silent for a moment. He frowns, strokes his chin and then nods.

'It's good, Sadie. Very, very good.'

'Yeah?'

'Yeah.'

We laugh as he scoops me up, ignoring my filthy state, forgetting the minor arguments and simmering tension we've endured over the last couple of weeks. In this moment, Derek sees only a creative success, and that is something he values and understands beyond anything else.

Over his shoulder, I can see the photo I've pinned to the corner of my easel, the image that has inspired my art: A ballerina, poised with arms outstretched, reaching into the void.

SIX

Six weeks into my Deep Flow journey and I'm feeling more connected with myself and aligned with what I want than I have for a very long time. Since that day in my car, descending into my Jenna / Ashley social-media black hole of despair, I've muted their profiles and made no further attempts to reach out to them. I'd expected the decision to feel like a huge loss, but the truth is that we don't have much in common any more, and continually comparing myself to them was both time-consuming and painful.

The only drawback of the wholesome new life Deep Flow has gifted me is that it seems to be at the expense of my connection with Derek. My Spiritual Cleansing sessions with Lilith however, have made me realise that, for years now, I've been making myself smaller to accommodate him: his talent, his dreams, his friends. After all, that's why we're in LA in the first place. Now that I'm here, though, Lilith has encouraged me to make the most of it, and being part of the Deep Flow community is one way to do that. The expense seems minimal, in retrospect, given how much I'm getting out of it. It's an investment in my wellness, my creativity and, above all else, my soul.

In today's session, we sit opposite one another as usual and Lilith holds both my hands in hers. I think about my first Deep Flow class and how reluctant I'd been to let her touch me. It seems so silly now and I confess it to Lilith out loud, apologising for being so guarded.

'It's important to realise not everyone is a threat,' Lilith says, a dream-like quality to her voice. 'But, of course, if people who should have taken care of you have made you feel unsafe in the past, it's easy to see why you may be suspicious of people.'

She's right. I've been operating in fight-or-flight mode for years. It's exhausting.

'Is there anyone in your life right now who is making you feel unsafe? Or maybe even just let down?' Lilith wants to know.

I plumb the depths of my mind and Jenna and Ashley float to the surface, their insensitivity still stinging. Lilith tells me I'm right to take a step back from them both.

'Protecting your energy is important,' she reminds me. 'What happens if you pour the love you used to give them back into yourself instead?'

After I leave our session, I feel radiant and worthy. Knowing I was right to shut Jenna and Ashley out of my life gives me a little spring in my step. *I'm doing the right thing for me*, a voice in my head says. And I'm delighted to consider the idea that removing them from my life will ultimately make room for something better.

The impact on my art has already been incredible. It's as if something has opened up within me and my work rate is through the roof. I'm just finishing up my second ballerina painting in what I hope will be a series of five or six. For the first time in as long as I can remember, I'm considering getting my work exhibited and have been googling local galleries that might accept the series. There's no one here who knows the person I was in Georgia, so if I keep it small and local, maybe I've got nothing to worry about, maybe I could even work under a pseudonym.

When I'm not googling that, I'm googling Lilith, obsessively poring over her social media and reading think pieces and articles about her. There's a four-page spread in *Harper's Bazaar*, detailing her morning routine, her journey into the wellness world and what to expect from her retreats. The feature is mostly made up of pictures of her staring beguilingly into the camera surrounded by giant plants or supposedly candid shots of her cutting up fruit or tending to her garden. There's also one of her meditating and I contemplate just how mindful you can truly be when you know you have a camera pointed at you.

I stumble across a profile on her in the *New Yorker* that reveals Lilith has multiple studios across the country, all manned by 'exceptional lightworkers' she knows personally, who she has trained herself and who she would trust with her life. In the piece, she talks a lot about 'the democratisation of wellness' and I wonder if, three years since it was written, Lilith feels her current pricing structure really reflects that goal. I've spent the last few weeks drifting between the stinging sensation that naturally comes with spending so much money on something that might not change my life after all and the feeling that it absolutely will. *It'll be worth it,* I tell myself. *My classmates are the perfect proof.* I just have to hope being an Amber member will be enough.

In every article I read, Lilith is described as 'magical'. One piece says she is 'beautiful inside and out, and generous to a fault with both her time and energy'. Another calls her 'iridescent' (a word I've never heard used to describe a human being) and 'magnetic', explaining what an 'immense privilege it is to be invited into her world'. The journalist who wrote the *New Yorker* profile says his 'soul feels washed clean' after a single session with her, and I realise that's exactly how I feel after spending time with Lilith too.

I find myself deconstructing every newsletter she sends, looking for hidden meanings, staring at photos of her from her personal Instagram, trying to figure out how I can have a life like hers. In one photo, she's picnicking with her husband in a gorgeous field of wildflowers somewhere out of state. In another, the two of them are caught mid-laugh as they dance together at a salsa night they're attending. They gaze into one another's eyes in each of the pictures and something like envy stews in my stomach.

Jeremy is what many would describe as a 'silver fox': grey hair coiffed to perfection, steely blue eyes, a dabble of stubble over his strong, square jaw. But he's more than just a trophy husband. Apparently, he was a millionaire long before he met Lilith.

He also has a child from a previous marriage, a twenty-year-old daughter named Izzy, and two sons from two other relationships. I reckon he's about twelve years older than Lilith, but, given he writes a lot of Instagram captions about working out, health supplements and skincare, it's fair to say he could be an even older man doing well for his age. He also talks a lot about steak, which, he claims, he eats at least once a day and would swear on a stack of bibles that the rest of us should be doing the same. He doesn't, however, discuss how he expects us all to afford to do so.

In one video, he shows us how he cooks his steak: 'Grass-fed butter. Salt and pepper. It's not complicated,' he claims, and I marvel at how, with all that money and all those resources, he is still not capable of seasoning his food in a way that would truly bring joy to his plate.

I *am* surprised Lilith isn't vegan, given how often she talks about 'Mother Nature'. But it seems both Lilith and her husband are part of a growing number of people who have shunned veganism and vegetarianism and, instead, preach the virtues of eating carnivorously but organically. After scrolling through several posts extolling this particular diet, I'm left wondering if these people tried veganism once upon a time and found it too hard, but still wanted to stand for something. This alternative appears to be the perfect way to have your meat and eat it.

I find myself googling 'grass-fed butter'. *What is this mysterious product Jeremy claims will revolutionise my life?* When the results of my search load, I'm disappointed to discover that it's essentially just ghee – a rich oil substitute Mehdi introduced me to when I was in college and something I've used to grease frying pans for years since. My life will not be transformed today. Nor will the lives of millions of Brown and Black people who have been using 'grass-fed butter' under another name for centuries.

When he's not talking about diet, Jeremy likes to talk about virility. A lot. So much so it actually makes me uncomfortable. One of his many business ventures, next to his superfood company and podcast, is his 'Guys-Only' Love Guru coaching company. I'd read about it in magazines before, but didn't realise that Lilith was married to the man behind it until now. I guess being in a successful relationship with someone as amazing as Lilith has given him the necessary authority to be able to advise other men on how to achieve the same. But knowing this doesn't make me cringe any less.

The more I read about Jeremy and watch his videos, the more I realise that I kind of hate him, and I wish I knew if that's because I disagree with his opinions and find his captions ridiculous or because he has Lilith in a way I never will. That's not to say I'm attracted to her. At least, not in the traditional sense. But I *am* drawn to her magic and I can't help but wish I could have her full attention sometimes. Go on adventures with her the way Jeremy does. Have the intimate conversations he gets to have with her and the commitment she has shown to him by deciding to become his wife.

As I scroll through Jeremy's profile, there's everything from anti-vaxxer propaganda to conspiracy theories and motivational quotes. Only most of the quotes don't come from religious leaders or philosophical thinkers, even though many of them feel close to stuff I've read or heard before. Instead, they are written by him and placed on red or black backgrounds. Some of them sound intellectual but don't quite make sense. Others proclaim 'what women want' and I wonder which women he has spoken to about this.

He talks a lot about wanting to be 'honoured as a man'

and the importance of men being allowed to 'be monsters'. I don't know what either of these things mean, but there are lots of men liking his posts and responding with things like, 'Fuck, yeah!' and 'Embrace the beast within!'

On YouTube, there are multiple videos of him on stage at various conferences. I click on the first clip. A short, curly-haired compere with one of those annoying headset microphones stands before an audience of about two-hundred or so people.

The whole room is chanting in unison: 'El-eh-ments! El-eh-ments!'

'Now, I want you to put your hands in the air and shout, "I am ready for change!"' the curly-haired man roars. The crowd mimic him, but he's far from satisfied.

'Is that all you got?' he yells. The crowd scream back at him a further three times. Some of the men in the audience jump up on tables in a desperate bid to prove how energetic they can be. Eventually, the compere is happy enough to reward them with an appearance from 'the man, the myth, the legend . . . Jeremy Winters!'

The audience totally lose their minds as Jeremy (also wearing a headset microphone) jogs onto the stage as a cringeworthily euphoric U2 track plays. When the music and applause dies down, Jeremy asks, 'Are you ready to take the red pill?' and the crowd shout 'Yes!' in unison. Jeremy grins.

'That's good. Because you know what we are? All of us in this room? We are gamechangers, changemakers, *chainbreakers*. So, I sincerely hope you're all ready to take the rules of this world we live in and throw 'em right outta the window.'

His fans go wild all over again. Then, I listen to him talking about the importance of breath, pausing for effect after each piece of information, as if he's dropping huge truth bombs, rather than just stating simple facts about how the human body works. He talks a lot about the amount of money Elements affiliates can make, the opportunities for travel and how much their lives will change. But at no point does he mention what they're actually selling.

After doing some digging in a Reddit forum dedicated to Elements, I discover their high ticket offer is an eye-wateringly expensive air purification system. In order to become an affiliate and sell the system, you have to buy (sorry, 'invest in') a system for yourself.

There's another video from the same conference that looks like it was recorded via a drone. It's a montage of event highlights soundtracked by Coldplay and featuring members of the crowd dancing, laughing, meditating together and more. There's a weird mix of people in 'corporate casual' attire and hippies that look like they live out of vans. About twenty per cent of people are inexplicably barefoot.

In the depths of my Jeremy-shaped rabbit hole, I find another video of a woman called Becki, talking about how she 'manifested' her place in Elements and how the business has changed her life. A former addict and teen mom, she tells a harrowing story about surviving domestic abuse and homelessness before discovering spirituality.

'The income from Elements feeds my higher purpose,' she says and it's hard not to find her journey compelling and inspiring, despite my misgivings about 'affiliate marketing'.

Jeremy has over 158,000 followers and, as I scroll through

them, they are almost entirely made up of white men. This doesn't surprise me. What does surprise me is just how many women there are. And that there are a fair few Black men and a lot of Arab and South Asian men too. I do a quick search to see if Mehdi is one of them and, the moment I type the first few letters of his name, a profile picture of him grinning in a grey suit pops up.

I wonder if he follows Jeremy for his Love Guru tips and if that's how he charmed Mumtaz. Or maybe he uses Jeremy's advice to cheat on her. It could be that he's more interested in Winters's world of nootropics or perhaps he's considering giving up medicine to become an Elements affiliate. I sigh and imagine him doing coke with Jeremy at a post-conference party. No wonder it's so easy for Mumtaz to lie to her husband if he's fallen so easily for this guy.

But, then again, so has Lilith. Only she has fallen so hard she's actually married him. For a moment, I question if this blind spot of hers is a fatal flaw, something I just can't look past. What other poor choices has she made if this is who she has chosen for a husband? Then I think about the litany of exceptional women I'm aware of who have chosen awful men. I think about how I've done it myself, in the past, with catastrophic consequences. And so I forgive Lilith for Jeremy, only wishing I could forgive myself quite so easily.

Today's cyberstalking comes to an end when Derek comes home and asks if I want to do date night at the movies. He's exhausted and confesses he 'might not be the best conversation tonight'.

'The movies it is then!' I say, suddenly struck by how lucky

I am to have ended up with a man who, unlike Jeremy, isn't completely dripping in pretence.

I kiss Derek on the cheek as I head off to get changed.

'You mind driving?' he calls after me.

'Happy to!' I yell back.

Half an hour later, we pull into the movie theatre parking lot and Derek gives me such a broad grin I have to ask him why.

'Nothing!' he chuckles. 'Just proud of how far you've come, you know? A couple of years back, you'd be *so* nervous about driving round a new city. Now look at you! All the hours we put in really paid off.'

I smile back, wishing I didn't have to continue the sad charade that comes with choosing to hide my darkest secret from the person I love most. If only I could tell him the reason I couldn't legally drive until two years ago wasn't because I didn't know how.

If only I could tell him the truth.

Eighteen Years Earlier

Elijah grabs the steering wheel and yells into my ear. 'Fuck, Sadie. If we're gonna do this, you gotta keep your eyes on the road!'

He instructs me to pull into a nearby cul-de-sac and park up next to a battered metal mailbox outside a weather-beaten wooden house. A giant American flag covers almost half the porch and I spy a confederate banner on the licence plate of the beat-up burgundy pick-up truck parked in the driveway.

Our state flag officially changing three years ago hasn't seemed to stop a great many people proudly toting the old version. It's hard to tell who is actually a white supremacist and who simply hasn't caught up with the new legislation yet. It's safest to guess the former in most cases, however.

Elijah spots it too.

'Okay, well, obviously not here.'

He points to a spot further down and guides the wheel as I tentatively tap the accelerator.

'I *was* looking at the road,' I protest. 'I swear.'

'You're too young for this. I knew it,' my brother sighs.

'You learned when *you* were fourteen,' I spit back.

'Thirteen, matter of fact.' He smiles a toothy grin and I look out of my window to avoid giving him the satisfaction of reacting to his smug, told-you-so face.

'You're going away again soon,' I whine. 'This could be my last chance for, like . . . *a year.*'

A year feels like for ever and childhood promises of driving lessons with my parents quickly faded into dust the moment Daddy's cancer got worse. He's too sick for me to bother him with it now and, when she isn't working two jobs to cover medical bills, Momma only seems to have time to take care of him.

I have visions of Elijah dying in Afghanistan, an IED exploding in his face, of Daddy's cancer finally crushing him in its deadly grasp and Momma and I becoming a family of four reduced to two, forced to fend for ourselves. I *needed* to drive.

'I was thinking I could get a job at the restaurant next summer,' I tell Elijah.

'And give Aunt Sheila another member of staff to worry

about paying?' he snorts. 'Nah, man. That's just another head-ache. How would you even get there?'

Counting the math out on my hands, I explain how I plan to get my driver's licence as soon as legally possible. 'It's twenty months 'til I turn sixteen,' I tell him. 'I'll take my test on my sixteenth birthday. Then, say I start the job at the restaurant next summer, that's like . . . nine, ten months before I might be able to drive there alone.'

'And in the meantime?'

'It's a thirty minute walk to Aunt Sheila's. She could drive me when she goes into work.'

Elijah laughs. 'I know you ain't walking thirty minutes in this damn heat. There ain't even a sidewalk half the way.'

I feel my lips grow smaller as I clench the front of my jaw. Why does he always have to make me feel so stupid?

Eventually, he stops laughing and puts a hand on the back my neck, now burning with embarrassment.

'You wanna help out Momma and Daddy that bad, huh?'

I nod.

'I be sending money back, you know,' he says. 'Help out all I can. One day, you may be able to help out too, but, right now, you too young.'

He pauses, long enough to take a sip out of the cup of Mountain Dew he bought at the drive-thru twenty minutes ago. It's the last of it and I hear what's left of the ice rattle as he puts the cup back in the holder.

'There is another way you can help, though.'

'Oh yeah?'

'Yeah!' he says, enthusiastically. 'Just keep doing what you doing, kid. Get good grades in school, keep up with your dancing and don't give them nothing to worry about.'

I manage a smile, thinking about how my 'dancing' will be done with if I don't manage to get another scholarship for the next year of classes.

'You smart,' Elijah tells me. 'Smarter than me, anyways. You *articulate* and all that. You can be anything you wanna be.'

He gives me a playful punch on the shoulder.

'Okay then?'

I nod, reluctantly. 'Okay.'

We switch places and my brother starts the engine, firing up the car radio as he does. Fat Joe's 'Lean Back' blasts out of his speakers and we immediately start to sing along, pushing our shoulders into the leather seats as we yell out the chorus. We only make it about a hundred yards up the road before the blare of an approaching freight train begins to drown out the lyrics.

'Shit!' Elijah shouts, before jamming his foot down on the gas in a bid to beat the train and make it over the tracks. I genuinely believe he'll do it until a rusty old Lincoln pulls out in front of us. Elijah slams on the brakes and I lean towards the windscreen of his pride and joy and spot the curly white hair of the other car's geriatric driver in her rear-view mirror. The freight train horn blares again and we watch the red-and-white barriers float down on either side of the tracks. Defeated, we collapse onto our headrests in unison. Who knows how long we'll be stuck here now.

'Do you know what my name means?' my ballet teacher asks, keeping a watchful eye over us all as we gently plié and relevé at the barre. 'It means ruler of the army. And you, my students, are my little army.'

Gaultier pauses to bring one of my fellow dancers into correct alignment.

'What do you think is most important for an army to be successful?' he enquires, placing a hand on another dancer's back to remind her about her posture.

Eventually, I speak up.

'Discipline?'

'Correct!' Gaultier smiles. 'Discipline, discipline, discipline. Be intentional with your movement. Create a sense of integrity with each bend, glide, lift. Your body is your instrument. Use it well.'

The music changes, commencing our port de bras section, Erik Satie's 'Gnossienne No. 1' drifting into my ears as I attempt to move my arms from first to fifth position as smoothly as possible. I sense Gaultier behind me and find myself torn between wanting to impress him with perfection and my desire to have him close. He moves his hand slowly down my arm, encouraging me to soften it into a rounder, more elegant shape. My eyelids flutter closed for a moment as I breathe him in.

'Almost,' he whispers, his French accent sending a slight shiver down my spine.

After class, Kirby and Marianne accost me in the corridor.

'He's so fricking hot!' Marianne announces, now well out of our teacher's earshot.

I bite down on my lip and try to picture what the expressions on their faces would be if I let my secret pour out.

'He's super strict, though,' Kirby sighs. 'I dunno if I'm gonna make it through this semester, you guys. I've been dancing on this injury for too long now.'

We look down at the scar on her knee, peeking out below the aquamarine-coloured skirt she put on in the locker room before we left.

'How many Black dancers actually make it anyways?' she asks. 'In ballet, I mean.'

'You could join Ailey,' I say. 'Focus on contemporary.'

'Girl, you know I ain't good enough for Ailey.' She pauses, thoughtfully. 'You are, though.'

I smile and attempt to be modest.

'Maybe a smaller company,' I say. 'Closer to home.'

'Things still bad with your dad?' Marianne asks, and I nod in response. It's clear I don't want to talk about it, though, and Kirby quickly brings the conversation back to dance.

'Maybe you'll be one of the first Black ballet dancers to make it. You light-skinned anyway. Mixed race, mixed race,' she says, referring to the dual heritage of both my parents. I wonder how much what we consider 'light-skinned' depends on context and if even I, within the sprawling white landscape of the ballet world, would be considered as such. I had a considerable advantage over Kirby, yes, but the likes of petite, pale-skinned Marianne would almost certainly pip me to the post.

'Mom's made it clear I have to get an academic degree before I can think about dance,' Marianne says, as if she can hear my thoughts. 'She has her heart set on law. Which is stupid, because everyone knows you need to start a dance career as early as possible. By the time I sit the bar, I'll be too old to be a dancer.'

'Maybe that's your momma's plan,' Kirby giggles.

We exit the building and squint into the sunlight, the blistering heat immediately beginning to scorch our bare arms and legs. As cars roll up to collect my friends, I hover near the entrance in the hope of catching a glimpse of Gaultier.

Last time, Gaultier had stopped to talk to me before getting into his car and I was mid-conversation with him when Momma showed up to take me home. Allowing myself to be ripped away from him is not a mistake I intend on making twice, so I've told Momma to pick me up a whole twenty minutes after class, just in case.

Sure enough, I spot Gaultier leaving the building, about to head through the parking lot.

'Thanks for class today, Mr Fontaine,' I call after him.

He turns round, all million-dollar smile and jet-black hair.

'I've told you, you can call me Gaultier.'

I blush as he comes closer. 'Did you have a nice time in the pool last weekend?' he says, lowering his voice conspiratorially.

'It was lovely,' I nod.

'We'll do it again sometime,' he says, satisfied. 'It's important to keep up with your physiotherapy.'

Then, unexpectedly, he runs his index finger under my jaw, softly lifting my gaze towards his steel-grey eyes. My heart catches in my throat as I suddenly become conscious of how public this is, how exposed we are. He lifts my arms up, one at a time, and steps back to look at me.

'Beautiful,' he says. Then, louder, 'Perfect posture is important. Remember that for your next lesson, okay?'

Any suspicious eyes turn away. He is a teacher helping his

student become the best she can be and that's all there is to it. I smile, taking care not to show my teeth, or, rather, my braces.

'Thanks, Gaultier.'

He walks away and I allow my arms to float down but my heart does not stop thudding inside my chest. Was that another invite to his house?

The previous weekend, I'd planned to go to Marianne's with a few of the other girls for a slumber party. It had been marked in the diary for weeks and I'd been really looking forward to it until, one day in class, I tweaked my hamstring. Gaultier and I had gotten talking while I waited for Momma to collect me and he had casually mentioned that some 'young people' from the neighbourhood often came over to swim in his pool.

'Swimming is the very best thing for injury recovery,' he'd said. 'In fact, a few people might come round next Saturday, after I'm finished here. Could be the perfect time.'

My heart sank. How could this amazing opportunity to see inside Gaultier's home clash with one of the most important events in my social calendar? Then it occurred to me that not only would Marianne's party provide the perfect cover story, but there was also a possibility I could do both.

'Would you be able to give me a ride after?' I asked Gaultier, already fantasising about sitting in the passenger seat of his silver Lexus, feet up on the dashboard as we laughed about whatever men like him laugh about.

When the day came, I told Marianne I needed to go home for a few hours after class and that I'd try to come over later on. She assumed it was something to do with Daddy's chemo and I didn't correct her. The lie felt bitter on my tongue, but I knew its fruit would taste sweet.

After class, Gaultier took great care to be discreet. 'I don't want my friends to be mad at me,' I explained, and he told me he understood. That it was 'a mark of good character' that I was so considerate.

He had, as I'd suspected, a beautiful home – like something out of a magazine. I remembered reading about Art Deco while flipping through the pages of *Home & Garden* during one visit to Kroger. I'd been so lost in its aspirational dreamscape that I'd barely noticed when the store clerk barked at me, 'Are you gonna buy that, miss?' I giggled and put it back on the rack, but the images stayed with me. Seeing Gaultier's house for the first time was as if they had all come to life.

His pool is large and miraculously blue, as if someone is employed full time to keep it clean. When we arrived, we both slipped off our shoes and he made a couple of calls that lead to the appearance of three local kids – a boy of eleven and two girls, one sixteen and one around ten. The sixteen-year-old, April, flirted with Gaultier the whole time she was there and I felt my jealousy bubbling under the pool as I swam quiet lengths, barely taking my eyes off her, like an alligator stalking its prey. It's clear she knows him better than I do and this enrages me. When Gaultier offers us all popsicles, she shrieks, 'I'll get 'em!', and dashes inside. *How dare she know where his freezer is*, I found myself thinking.

While we waited for her return, I got out of the water and plopped myself down at the side of the pool, feet still dangling, making tiny ripples as I swung them back and forth. My two-piece swimsuit sticking to my body, offering some cooling respite from the heat as I dried off in the sun. Gaultier's sun lounger was a mere two or three yards from where I sat and I planted my hands behind me, arching my spine back and lifting my face towards the sky. I wanted him to look at me, to tell the other kids to leave and give me his undivided attention. I've earned it in a way they never could. I am his student. Maybe, even, his protégée.

Forty-five minutes later, I got my wish after their mothers called them all home for dinner. By then I was mosquito-bitten and bored, having taken up a sun lounger of my own, not nearly close enough to Gaultier.

'Would you like to eat something?' he asked.

He invited me inside and soon there was a pot bubbling away on the stovetop.

'That looks like a nasty bite,' he said, nodding towards my ankle as I stood in his kitchen, still dressed in my swimsuit.

'Come here,' he said, abandoning the food for a moment. 'I have witch hazel.'

I followed him into the living area and, through his floor-to-ceiling windows, I noticed the last traces of the sun, now a deep red orange, sinking low in the sky. He instructed me to sit on his couch while he rummaged in a drawer.

'Et voilà!'

Gaultier brought the little tube over, talking as he did.

'You know, you're so much more mature than my other students. Even more than April, who you met today, and she is older than you. Perhaps it is because of your . . . situation . . . at home. You've had to grow up very fast.'

He sat down further along the couch and then tapped the

space next to him – a signal for me to turn my body to face him, lifting my legs up as I do. He started to apply the ointment to my bite and then to a few others dotted elsewhere on my legs. His hands were big and strong, but he applied the witch hazel so gently. I could feel my heart beating in my ears, making me barely able to concentrate on what he was saying. I'd gotten my first period five months ago and, as I felt fire in my blood and a rush of energy to certain parts of my body, I wondered if this is what it is to be a woman. These feelings. This sense of desire.

'Sadie, I want you to know I'm always here if you would like to talk about things. Anything at all. I like to think that I am not just your teacher. I'm also . . . a friend?'

I nodded. His warm hands were still on my legs. I felt full of both terror and excitement, my tongue stuck to the roof of my mouth, a knot twisting in my belly.

'How's your hamstring feeling?' he asked.

He started to move his hands further up my right leg, massaging the muscle as he went. I looked ahead at my bare feet, pressed against his thigh. They looked so tiny. So far away.

'Does this feel good?' he asked. 'Is it helping the pain?'

I tried to say something, but there was a hurricane happening inside me and I could only nod again. His shirt had been off while we sat beside the pool and he removed it again. I stare at his perfect body, lean muscle rippling as he moves.

'It's warm in here, don't you think?' he said. 'And this work I'm doing, this physiotherapy, it requires a lot of effort.'

He moved down on the floor beside me, crouching on one knee, as he rubbed from the top of my thigh downwards and back up again.

'Thank you,' I said gratefully, unsure of what else to say.

'My two favourite words,' he smiled, and I was glad to have pleased him.

'I can never hear them too much,' he continued.

And so I said thank you again. Over and over.

As his car pulled up outside Marianne's house, Gaultier reached for my hand.

'I hope our time together has been helpful. It was very nice having you.'

The knot in my stomach felt larger than ever but I managed a smile.

'Thanks for the ride.'

'That's okay,' he replied. 'I'm sorry you have to keep secrets from your friends. But you're right. It might upset them and we wouldn't want them thinking there's any . . . favouritism.'

'No,' I said, swallowing hard. I felt like I might vomit and, in my head, I silently prayed to God I wouldn't spew up all over his leather upholstery. Is this what it means to be lovesick?

'I'll see you in class.'

My legs were like jelly as I tumbled out of the car and made my way towards Marianne's porch. Gaultier sped off and I was left half wondering if the evening had all been a dream.

Inside, the girls were watching a scary movie and jumped out of their skins when I suddenly came through the door. Popcorn flew everywhere and there were cries of 'Oh my gosh!' and 'What the hell?!' But Marianne was quickly on her feet, dashing towards me and locking me in an embrace.

'We missed you,' she said into my hair. 'Is your dad okay?'

'Uh huh,' I managed, attempting to make the lie feel as small as possible.

When I returned home the following morning, I ran into my room as if it was an emergency and dug my diary out from under my bed. Its cover was made up of dark purple sequins and there was a tiny lock on the side. I reached for the key, taped under my nightstand. Then, suddenly, a lightning bolt of fear that my mother – or worse, my brother – might discover the key's location at some point in the future made me hesitate about detailing the previous night's encounter in a journal entry.

I wanted to shout my feelings for Gaultier from the roof-tops. Especially now I finally had proof he felt the same way. That all the times he'd put a gentle hand on my shoulder or stroked the curve of my spine in class meant more than a reminder to keep good posture. That months of stolen glances and parking-lot conversations had not been misinterpreted.

In a situation where no one could truly understand what we share, Gaultier had already risked so much for us. Keeping our secret would be hard but perhaps it is the least I can do. It would all be worth it, one day, years from now, when we were reminiscing about the start of our story and how we went against everything and everyone around us to be together. Star-crossed soulmates, just like in all the books and plays and movies.

I opened my diary on a blank page and wrote the word 'love' in as many fonts as I could muster until there was no space left and my hand started to hurt, the pen bleeding red ink onto my fingers.

SEVEN

Crowning Glory Hair Salon has had a recent refurbishment, my stylist, Trina, tells me.

'We'd been chasing that modern look for too long,' she says. 'In the end, we decided we wanted something different. Because *we* are different. So, we went for this retro vibe instead and, I don't know about you, but I think it's real cute.'

I make some enthusiastic sounds of agreement and continue to admire the 1950s-style interior – cotton-candy-coloured leather upholstery, highly polished silver equipment and back-stage dressing-room-style lighting. It feels like stepping into the kind of hair salon the Pink Ladies might've visited in *Grease* – that is, if the Pink Ladies were all Black and biracial.

Having had some terrible experiences in hair salons as a kid, sitting with my back to a stylist can often feel as scary as sitting in a dentist's chair, softly trembling in the knowledge that one snip could so easily ruin my social life for months. But there's something about these surroundings and Trina's soothing voice that helps me trust that I am in capable hands.

The smell of rose, vanilla and something else I can't quite place fills my nostrils as I sit back and catch a whiff of the cream the stylist next to us is rubbing into my neighbour's scalp.

'Lily of the valley!' the woman in the chair announces.

'How do you know that?' her stylist asks, unable to hide her surprise.

'I run a perfumery business,' she replies.

'But I thought you were a—'

'It's a side hustle. For now. But . . . I have big dreams.'

'Wow,' says Trina, getting in on their conversation. 'Do you make original stuff? Or designer dupes?'

The woman tilts her head towards us, her eyes briefly meeting mine. 'A bit of both. It's early days, so, you know, I'm still trying to find my voice.'

I sigh and mutter, 'I know that feeling.'

I hadn't really intended anyone to hear, but the woman immediately pounces.

'Oh yeah?'

'I . . . I'm new here. In LA,' I respond. 'Still trying to figure things out.'

'What's the dream?' the woman asks.

'Art,' I say, eventually. 'I paint. Landscapes. People. Still life.'

She snorts. 'I always found that phrase a funny one. Still life. What can that possibly mean? Nothing about life is still. It's chaos.'

Trina laughs.

'You getting *real* philosophical this morning, Veronica!'

'She's always like this,' her stylist retorts. 'Crowning Glory's answer to Socrates!'

The three women dissolve into giggles and I chuckle along, outside their little circle, looking in. Veronica's laugh sounds like a feather duster cleaning a chandelier, a hundred tiny pieces of glass tinkling together, light beaming through each finely cut shard.

'What's your name then, sweetie?' she eventually asks.

'Sadie Perkins,' I reply, before openly cringing at my over-share. She didn't need my full government name.

'And have you made many new friends since you've been here, Sadie Perkins?' she replies, as if my first and last name are glued together.

'Um . . . well . . . maybe not "friends". I *have* joined a class, though. It's kind of a community, really. The people there are . . . nice. Interesting.'

'You don't sound so convinced.'

'Oh, it's just early days. The class itself is great, though. Kind of lifechanging, actually.'

Veronica grins. 'Well, sign me up!'

I know she's not serious, but I find myself imagining the two of us side by side at Deep Flow nonetheless, an invisible thread of camaraderie hanging between us.

Later, she asks for my Instagram handle on her way out of the door. It's a private account that's really just for my artwork. Despite knowing I'm merely throwing it into the void, it can sometimes feel good to put my art out there. As if it exists all the more for being present in the world.

As I crawl into bed that evening, my phone pings – a direct message from veronicaharper058: 'Forgot to say – your hair looks damn good, girl!'

I smile to myself, send her my number, and ask her if she might like to go for a drink sometime.

* * *

Sometimes, when I'm not dreaming of crunching metal and broken glass, of an empty crib or hands inappropriately drifting where they shouldn't while I am pressed against a wall, I dream of dancing.

In one dream, I begin as a butterfly, morphing into different shapes as I flutter across the open-plan living space of a house I do not recognise as my own. At first, I am yellowy orange, with long wide wings, exploring kitchen countertops and a refrigerator covered in magnets and postcards of places in Europe.

Then, I am small and blue, lighting up as if electric, before disappearing altogether. I feel myself grow into human form, my powers of invisibility and flight choosing to remain with me. The pain of growth is agony, but I remind myself that even butterflies must suffer as they bloom into their truest selves.

Once my metamorphosis is complete, I glide across a studio floor opposite a mirror that reflects nothing back. *Perhaps I am a vampire now*, I think. *A monster moving in silence.* I twist and turn and pirouette. Then, as I leap through the air, I am caught in flight, suddenly aware of being pursued by men who wish to kill me. I'm a freak, they tell me in whispers. An abomination.

The scene around me changes as I flit over empty fields and drift through snow. Time passes at great speed. Days. Months. Years, perhaps.

I find myself in a new town. Home, at least for a while. Change my name, my clothes, maybe even my face. My powers don't seem to work here, it seems, but I have found new ways to become invisible. I take a job in a bar. Exposed brick walls, high ceilings and a boss who pays me in cash.

But none of this is enough. One morning, I wake to one of my persecutors tying a blindfold made of white cotton around my eyes and gagging me so I cannot scream.

Somewhere, a butterfly beats its wings against the inside of a bell jar.

Then, I wake again. This time in the real world. My hands flying to my face to tear at the cloth. There is nothing there, yet still I am gasping for breath.

'Honey?' Derek says, as he gently stirs beside me. 'Did you have a nightmare?'

'I was dancing,' I murmur, my dream quickly dissipating.

'Oh,' he replies, softly, before slipping back into his slumber. 'That's nice.'

My hands drift towards my belly, where, for a brief time, I had once felt the fullness of a different dream gently kicking against the wall of my womb. She had been so wanted, so loved, but, in the end, none of it had been enough.

I never had the chance to bury all the tiny parts of her in a box in the ground. To build a shrine to what I'd lost and say a real goodbye. Instead, I buried a wooden rattle I'd already bought, engraved with the name we'd decided on far too soon. Patted the earth down until it was flat and wrote a note in the dirt: 'I love you. I miss you. Be happy. Be free.'

And I'd meant every word. But how can you truly love someone who was never fully realised? Only ever on the brink of being? It seems to defy logic and yet I am so sure of it and so grateful she found a home in me. If only for a short while.

On nights like this, I often find myself cradling the place where she used to be, wondering if her absence is my penance as I try not to think about metal crunching against metal. The smell of exhaust fumes. Leather smashing into spine as the airbag sends me ricocheting back against my seat. The sound of glass cracking as the windshield collapses in on itself. Just as I, for such a long time, collapsed in on myself.

My dark dreams feel like angry tree roots that wrap themselves round my ankles, attempting to drag me into a peat-filled bog. All I can do is fight against them. Make the most of my waking life, this fresh start I have now. In LA, no one knows my past, my failings, my crimes. Here, I have the chance to be who I was always meant to be.

In our fifth one-to-one, Lilith reminds me of that. Perhaps she senses the bulky awkwardness of all I have to hide. An emotional fatberg, floating through the waters of my soul. She takes my hand and presses it against one side of her chest and, as she leaves it there for a moment, I feel her heart beating against the top of her rib cage. She closes her eyes and I follow her lead, before feeling her own hand press against me.

'You hold my heart in your hands,' Lilith says. 'And I hold yours in mine. A sacred bond of trust. I give myself to you endlessly. And all I ask in return is that you are open to receive whatever the Universe chooses to send your way.'

I'm two and a half months into my Deep Flow journey, so, by now, I know the drill.

'I am open,' I respond. 'I am open. I am open. I am open.'

For a split second, I am transported back to a former therapist's office and I realise that I have been building towards the inner work I'm now doing for years. That my journey with Lilith is pre-destined.

'Talk to me about your childhood,' she says, and I tell her about Momma and Daddy. About building tiny snowmen out of the thin gatherings of white flakes we'd find at the bottom of the trees in our neighbourhood on a cold winter's day. About collard greens and pumpkin pie and my mother's fluffy, buttery cornbread. I detail my journey into school – two yellow buses and sliding down in my brown leather seat to avoid the jibes of the bullies in the back. I tell her of the joy I felt upon receiving my first pair of crisp, white Air Force 1s on the morning of my fourteenth birthday, about the family squabbles that broke out over every Thanksgiving dinner. About the sound of cicadas and punishing yard work under the scorching Georgia sun. About my brother, seven years older, who joined the army aged eighteen, did four tours of Afghanistan and was never quite the same again. I tell her that I wish Elijah and I spoke more. That our relationship stretched beyond Christmas and birthday cards with photos of my niece and nephew tucked inside.

I tell her about Daddy. Not about his illness, though, because I don't want him to be defined by that. Instead I tell her about his life. How he never kept the same job for long. Yet, right up until his recent retirement, he worked consistently for decades. He can count the total number of days off he's taken in those years on his caramel-coloured hands. And each one of those days off was taken with great reluctance, when, and only when, he was physically too sick to move.

He started at sixteen, on the production line in a candy factory in South Carolina. It's where, he says, he got his habit of licking his lips between every sentence, searching for the sweet, white, powdery residue that covered his face, just like it did everybody who worked there. The place was a death trap, he told me, and he witnessed real horrors during his time there. Workers burned by molten sugar, at least a dozen severed fingers and one colleague of his getting jammed between two machines, where he remained for seven whole minutes before they managed to wrestle him free. He died moments later, of course.

Then, Daddy moved on to a cereal factory, which was safer and paid far better. There was a bonus every few months too – 'Cash money, you know. Not just a heap of candy that happened to be the wrong shape for us to sell!'

But his favourite job of all was making gothic windows for churches that wanted a little bit of 'European charm'. He'd create gigantic wooden constructions that he'd carve beautiful designs into, then use to make a mould that would be taken to the foundry to be cast. His favourite part was the stained glass. That was where his creative spirit truly sprouted wings.

Now that he's retired, he pours that passion into his garden.

'I'm fighting a war, you know,' he tells me one day. 'It's me versus the slugs. And I'm outnumbered.'

The problem with my dad is that he genuinely couldn't hurt a fly – at least not without a little coercion, and so it took a while for us to stumble upon the most humane way of killing his slimy little nemeses.

'At least they havin' a good time before they die, I suppose,' Daddy sighed, after collecting another tray of beer-covered slugs, who had quickly discovered alcoholism kills.

On the all-too-rare occasions I was able to visit, Momma and I would sit by the window inside, drinking iced tea and staring out at him, while he pruned petunias and uprooted weeds.

'I'm a magnolia widow,' my mother announced one day, theatrically. 'He loves them flowers more than he do me. I lose him for entire weekends sometimes. He only remembers the time when he starts getting hungry.'

I didn't disagree. Around seven o'clock, as the sun disappeared behind the trees, Daddy would throw open the back door and the sound of cicadas and birdsong would drift into the kitchen. He'd hobble in, wiping his moistened brow with the backs of his wrists, where his gardening gloves didn't quite reach.

'You girls have a good chance to gossip?' he'd ask, a warm, toothy grin spreading across his face.

'I came to see you too, Daddy!' I'd say, and he'd invite me out to the yard, to show me its latest developments.

I tell Lilith how much I miss Momma and Daddy. What a visceral discomfort that is. How it is a feeling that sits below my sternum and is almost impossible to shift. What I don't say is that we only speak once a week these days, sometimes less, and that I've barely visited in years. When I do, we chat and smile like we always have, sharing jokes and stories. But, beneath all that, is a sound not unlike radio static, an atmosphere that hangs between us like a dense, grey fog. A giant cloud full of unspoken truths that, if pierced, will surely implode and drown us all.

And then I tell Lilith about ballet. I keep it to one sentence and, when she pushes further, I am dismissive.

'It wasn't for me in the end,' I say, and when it becomes clear I won't say more she holds my hand in hers.

'I'm glad you have been reunited with your body here,' she says. 'Reminded of what it can do.'

I nod, a lump in my throat. I force myself to hold back tears, but I'm not even sure why I want to cry. Perhaps it is because I am overwhelmed by the kindness Lilith has shown me since the day we met. While I know I am paying for her time, the way in which we spend it is almost entirely up to her, and she chooses to use it to be gentle, to encourage me to feel good about myself, about my body and about this fragile little life I have built for myself.

A silk ribbon of gratitude snakes its way out of my chest and unfurls towards her, tying the two of us together – a bond that I never want to break. Without Lilith and Deep Flow, I would be home alone, waiting for Derek to return from shoots and networking events, going through the motions in my studio, unable to truly connect with my work.

There were times, during our first weeks in LA, when I wondered if it might be possible to die of loneliness. For that feeling to envelope me, gnawing the meat off my bones and discarding them before heaving its fattened belly away, ready to claim its next victim.

Life felt smaller in those days spent painting in the grey of twilight. And yet twice as overwhelming. I was more aware than ever that I am merely a tiny speck in a universe of billions.

But Lilith makes me feel like I matter. Better than that. She makes me *know* it. Believe wholeheartedly that I am part of something: a circle that will break if I am not there to hold up my side of it. It's a responsibility that brings me a sense of peace. Of completion. And I understand why so many of my fellow Deep Workers, as Lilith calls them, squeeze tears down their cheeks as they close their eyes and sway along with Lilith in class. The work we do here is transformative and has helped me understand that perhaps I don't need to fix my past at all. Not if I can become a whole new person in the present.

I float home to Derek and we decide to go out for dinner for the first time in a while.

'You seem so chill!' he says, and I know that, for someone as highly strung as I am, he means that as a huge compliment. 'Good session today?'

I smile. 'The best.'

'Man, this woman is like a therapist, PT and meditation guide all rolled into one! I gotta meet her.'

For some reason, this idea frightens me. It feels important to keep these two worlds of mine separate. As if breaching the thin membrane between the two will result in them both falling apart, unable to co-exist. I say as much but frame it as if it is a joke. Derek laughs and I'm able to safely divert the conversation.

We laugh a lot through dinner and then decide to cap the night off with a drink. In the bar he takes me to, we sit close together on stools, ordering mocktails for me and Scotch for him, my legs pressed against his. I giggle through my sugar high, recounting what had happened in the restaurant: the junior waiter's dismayed face after he dropped a bowl of soup down another guest's front and how Derek had valiantly assisted in the clean-up effort.

'Aren't you just everyone's knight in shining armour?' I joke, rubbing my foot up and down his calf.

The music in the bar grows louder and the DJ starts to play a Stevie Wonder track we've always loved.

'We *have* to dance to this!' I shout over the music, already getting up. Derek raises his eyebrows and smiles – it's usually him dragging me onto the dance floor, but it seems I'm not quite so self-conscious any more. I'm happy to move even if few others are out of their seats doing the same.

. . . When you believe in things you don't understand, then you suffer . . .

We're singing along, pulling out all our best moves, a friendly competitiveness growing between us before we begin to move in perfect tandem, like two cogs in a machine. The vibration of the bassline pulsates through our bodies as we dance, growing closer and closer. His fingers skip along the curve of my waist before his hand eventually settles on the small of my back, pulling me closer. My hair, now loose, brushes against his face as I lean in, my lips softly teasing his.

The DJ mixes in another track, something without lyrics this time, but we don't mind. We seem to have found a language beyond words and, at last, we dissolve into one another, enclosed in a perfect kiss.

In the cab, we touch and whisper what we intend to do to one another when we arrive home, but by the time we actually reach our bedroom, the fizz in our blood seems to have gone flat. Tiredness hits like a wave and, instead of acting out our fantasies, we simply melt, together, into our bed.

'Married life, huh?' Derek jests, and I give him a playful slap before succumbing to a chuckle. It's only funny because I know that neither of us minds. That, sometimes, the intimacy of lying wrapped up in one another, talking until we fall asleep, is enough.

EIGHT

'I just feel as if your work ethic isn't what it was, Sadie,' my agent Sarah says, squinting at me from the other side of a Zoom call. 'Quite a few things have slipped through the net and I'm wondering what's going on and how I can support you in it.'

It's all I can do not to snort. Sarah does a brilliant job at flying the feminist flag on social media and at networking events, but when it comes to *actually* supporting female clients much of her behaviour feels performative. Even the word 'client' feels strange. It suggests Sarah works for me and, in some ways, she does. She brings in around eighty-five per cent of my freelance graphic design work in exchange for her ten per cent cut. But, sometimes, her micro-managing style makes me feel as if she's my boss and her *real* clients are the companies we're designing for.

Later, on WhatsApp, Raheem pops up and I send him multiple eyeroll emojis to illustrate exactly that point. He's well aware Sarah and I have clashed on a few issues recently and I appreciate him taking my side. After all, it was him who got me signed to the agency in the first place, a mere two months after we started working side by side in the shared studio space.

Since then, he's remained one of the few people I feel like I can bitch to about work stuff. Sarah is his agent too, and we're both grateful for the freelance work and the space it gives us to continue creating our passion projects. But that doesn't mean we've not considered jumping ship in favour of other graphic design agencies once or twice.

'You think she's gonna dump you?' Raheem types.

'IDK,' I write back. 'I guess my focus has been elsewhere recently. And it's not like designing logos for surfer-dude start-ups is exactly my dream job.'

'Girrrrl,' Raheem types back, and I think about how that word can be used as a response in such a myriad of different scenarios and yet, somehow, I will always know what it implies.

Annoyingly, one thing I also know is that Sarah isn't wrong. The further I've moved into the Deep Flow community and my own self-work, the less time I've wanted to spend doing my boring day job. After class or a private session with Lilith, I come home, head straight to the studio and paint. There's a point, every day, when I know I should stop and work on my commissions, but, like a rebellious child unable to resist a jar of cookies, I stare for a moment at the clock on my studio wall and defiantly choose to stay exactly where I am.

One day, Derek comes home hours early and tells me that he isn't actually early at all. My clock is slow. Days later, it stops altogether and I don't bother to replace the batteries. Painting, unencumbered, is all that matters now. That and Deep Flow, of course.

It's exactly three months to the day since I joined the community and, in class, we're focusing on the fourth element:

air. Ironically, summer has arrived in Los Angeles and, outside, there is barely a breeze. I arrive with sweat already lacing my upper lip.

Lilith 'opens the container' by teaching us how to 'balance our *prana*'. Then we move into further balancing poses before our movement develops into a dance. She tells us to unclutter our minds and embrace the simple joy of breath. Thank our lungs for all they do for us as they fill up and send oxygen round our bodies. I think of Jeremy the Love Guru's pyramid scheme air purifiers and wonder if Lilith has been at all inspired by her husband's side-hustle.

Don't laugh, I tell myself, as I try not to imagine the two of them sharing notes on the respiratory system before he heads off to another conference and she comes to teach class.

As we move, Lilith guides us through an intense cycle of breathwork and I begin to feel dizzy. Beside me, Debbie is more flushed and sweaty than I've ever seen her, her hair plastered to her forehead. Eventually, she succumbs to her mat, desperately sucking the straw of her water bottle before sinking her head between her knees. *Not everyone's cut out for this*, I think. But I know I am. As Lilith ups the ante, I am determined to stay with her.

Then, out of nowhere, I am somehow thrust into one of my nightmares as I hear the sound of glass shattering. At first, I'm disoriented. How can it be possible to find myself here during my waking life? Or is it that I've been dreaming all along? Within seconds, though, I am snapped back into the present, and reality is confirmed by the almost tangible screams of my classmates. In front of me, Lilith looks terrified.

'He's got a gun!' I hear someone cry and, through the space where the window used to be, there's a flurry of activity. I can't make out where the shooter is, but I'm not taking any chances. I jump into action, pushing Lilith out of the way, just as another shot rings out.

Lying with Lilith on the cool, parquet flooring, I feel a warmth begin to spread through me as I continue to hold on to her, her arms wrapped tightly around me too. A moment of gratitude passes, as if time has stood still for us both, and then the noise and panic begins again. From where we are, I can make out a figure dressed in black struggling beneath what looks like a mountain of men – brave bystanders, I'm guessing, forcing a citizen's arrest.

'Sadie? Sadie!' A panicked Lilith whimpers from underneath me and I wonder if she can feel the rage emanating from me. I want her to feel safe, but the idea of a man taking something so precious from me again is almost too much.

Nonetheless, I take a breath.

'It's okay,' I tell her. 'I've got you.'

But then she shows me her hand and my eyes widen, heart sinking: blood.

'We need to get you help,' I say, before shouting for someone, *anyone* to call 9-1-1.

Lilith gently peels me off her by my shoulders.

'Not me,' she says. 'You.'

And then, suddenly, I realise where the blood is coming from.

PART TWO

TRUST

NINE

The world is ending. While barren wastelands swirl with sand-storms and starving people scramble for what is left of the world's resources, Lilith stands in the epicentre of it all. She will surely be the last survivor. Aside from her mildly windswept hair and the broken sandals that imply she has walked for miles to get wherever she is, she looks relatively untouched by the apocalypse.

As I grow closer to her, I realise I am airborne. Floating. Small and powerless. Lilith cups her hands and I feel her warmth envelop me as I land inside them, blue and yellow wings folding in against my sides. My tiny beak quivers and I sink my head into my body, attempting to retain as much heat as possible.

This feeling of safety lasts a mere second or two before I become aware of what is about to happen. That, between us, we will save the world, but it will come at a huge cost.

'Eat me,' I whisper, surrendering to my self-sacrifice.

And, with barely a moment's hesitation, Lilith puts me in her mouth and swallows me whole.

I wake to find an anxious Derek sitting beside me, the smell of antiseptic in my nostrils, a nurse standing at the end of my bed. She says something clichéd like, 'You gave us all a real fright there,' but it barely registers as Derek jumps to his feet and grabs my hand.

Memories of the attack on the studio come rushing back. My mouth feels dry. I can barely summon a syllable, but, somehow, I manage two: 'Lilith?'

'Forget about *her*. What about *you*?' Derek retorts, but the look on my face softens him. 'She's fine. Everyone's saying she's fine.'

Relief cascades over me and I smile as much as my dry, cracked lips will allow.

But Derek isn't done yet.

'What the hell were you thinking, Sadie?' he practically growls.

The truth is that I wasn't thinking and I tell Derek as much. I acted on instinct, I say. Anyone would've done the same.

Probably.

Derek disagrees. Seems disappointed. Says something about how we still don't have health insurance and I'm lucky to be alive.

'What's the damage?' I ask.

The nurse fetches a doctor, who also keeps using the word 'lucky' to describe my situation. He tells me that the fragment of bullet that landed me here only gave me a flesh wound, explaining they've done some scans to make sure there's no internal bleeding. I'd been hoping for a ball-park financial figure rather than a health report, but I nod in gratitude, nonetheless.

'And you're satisfied?' Derek asks. 'There's nothing more to worry about?'

The doctor confirms this and prescribes a bunch of pain

killers and a 'care plan' that will aim to stave off infection and keep scarring to a minimum. He tells me again how lucky I've been and then leaves Derek and me to indulge in a tense moment of silence.

I reach for my phone, expecting a grateful message from Lilith or at least a few missed calls.

Nothing. Just a message from Raheem with a cute cat video he thinks I'll like and a voicenote from Ashley. It's likely to be an update on her life that I'll almost definitely ignore.

My phone goes back on the nightstand and I pull the bed covers up further, wishing I could hide underneath.

'I just don't get it,' Derek eventually says. 'Do you not care about your life? Have you any idea how worried I was when I got the call?'

I say nothing for a few seconds and then burst into tears.

Derek's face runs the gamut of facial expressions: annoyance, shock and then sympathy. He attempts to hug me without hurting me, but the wound is right at the bottom of my ribs and so this is almost impossible.

'I'm sorry. I'm so sorry, honey. I didn't mean . . . It was just so scary. I'm so relieved you're okay. Thank God. *Thank God*. We should call your parents.'

'No!' I say, emphatically. 'I don't want to worry them.'

Derek looks unsure.

'Please?' I beg, and I'm grateful when he acquiesces.

Later, he heads home to shower and get a change of clothes. Shortly after, Lilith arrives and I'm gutted Derek isn't still around to meet her. If he spent even a minute or two with her, I know he'd understand what I did.

'Sorry I haven't called,' Lilith says. 'I try to stay off my phone as much as possible especially during times that could be mentally . . . taxing. It's important to have that space for yourself. For recovery. Up here.'

She taps her temple softly and delivers a sad smile.

'Are you okay?' I ask.

'My people are hurt,' she replies. 'Of course, there is grace and growth in suffering, but this . . . It isn't what I wanted for any of you.'

Everyone is alive, she tells me, but Andrea, one of the Puerto Rican girls, ended up having to have surgery to remove shrapnel trapped in the side of her skull.

'It's awful. Just awful,' Lilith says, perching next to me on the bed. 'To me, you are all my children, my sisters, my life. I want to protect you. Always. But the world out there is so dangerous. So full of ill intent.'

'Who was the shooter?'

It's all I've wanted to know these last few hours, the image of our attacker, shrouded in black, at the forefront of my thoughts.

Lilith shakes her head.

'There's been an arrest. So maybe the police will get us some answers. That's really all I want now. We are such a peace-loving community. Those bullets could not have been meant for any of you.'

She tells me that we must all find a way of moving on. Together. Unlike Derek, she doesn't try to hug me. Instead, she just holds my hand. Traces the blue-green veins that run from the inside of my wrist up into the crook of my elbow, disappearing before they reach it. I realise her face is wet with tears and I am gripped with the overwhelming urge to kiss her cheeks and mouth. Stroke her neck and push her hair back so I can see her more clearly. I lean forward in my bed, ignoring the pain, and am pleasantly surprised when she too leans in. Her hands on the back of my neck, she presses our foreheads together.

'You saved my life, Sadie,' she whispers.

I think of Deep Flow and, for a moment, I am back in the studio, leaping through the air. Hands to the sky. Joy flowing through me.

In my hospital bed, surrounded by bleeping machines, I smile through the pain at the bottom of my ribs.

'You saved mine too,' I tell her. And I really mean every word.

'It's a privilege, don't you think?' Emily says, peering over a cappuccino so large I'm afraid she might drown in it. 'Saving a life. Any life. But Lilith's? Wow.'

'I'm sure anyone in that position would've done the same, though, right?' Ruby counters. 'Right place, right time.'

When I ask why she wasn't in class that fateful day, she stares down at her nails, muttering something about feeling 'out of alignment'. Today, her hair lacks its usual lustre and, while Natalia and Emily lean forward, desperate for information, Ruby leans as far back in her chair as possible, staring daggers every time I begin to speak. It's like being in the dock, a place all too familiar to me, and this grilling is the last thing I need. It's not even been two weeks since I got shot. Sure, it was only a flesh wound, but I can't pretend the incident didn't knock me sideways.

Natalia and Emily had been at the very back of the class the day of the shooting, having arrived a couple of minutes late. Emily had taken Natalia for a surf lesson that had run longer than expected that morning. The two of them had shown up with damp hair and traces of sand all over their tanned, toned bodies. They'd taken cover in the changing rooms a mere yard or two from their mats the moment the first shot had rung out, leaving them physically unscathed but, apparently, wracked with survivor's guilt.

'Do you think things will be different now? Between you two? Like . . . Lilith kind of owes you now, doesn't she?'

Emily and Ruby look at Natalia as if she has just volleyed a baby off the roof of a skyscraper.

'Lilith doesn't owe anyone anything,' Ruby snaps. 'She has given so much to so many. The world is *always* in her debt.'

'No . . . of course,' Natalia stammers. 'I just meant . . .'

She doesn't finish her sentence and I watch her slowly sink into herself.

'Kinda weird, dude,' Emily says, shaking her head – perhaps in an attempt to rid herself of Natalia's stupidity. I realise this is a habit of Emily's, this head shake of disbelief, as if life is an endless source of surprise. It seems a quick way to move on, forgiving others their foibles while also expressing a vague sense of disagreement. It's perfectly neither here nor there and I decide I might adopt it myself.

'Don't you think it's strange that they haven't released the shooter's name yet?' I ask.

'There's gonna be a political reason for that, mark my words,' Emily says.

'What does *that* mean?' I demand to know, as I frown over my mug.

'She means it'll be someone who is connected to someone important. Someone big enough to keep their name out of the press,' Ruby says, leaning in. She's back in the room now, knowing her insight on this is currency. 'My bet is the shooter was a kid. Sixteen . . . seventeen, maybe. Rich parents never paid him enough attention so he spends his life playing video games in his room and trawling incel forums. Debbie did say the shooter was on the smaller side.'

'What?!' Emily says, almost spitting out her coffee. 'He wasn't small. That's bullshit.'

'How do you know? You said you were at the back,' Ruby retorts.

'Yeah, but I still got a look at him. And he was big. Like ex-military, I think.'

I turn to Natalia, who has been quiet since her earlier embarrassment. 'Um . . . I dunno. I think he was pretty stocky.'

Ruby glowers at her.

'But . . . um . . . short. Definitely short.' Natalia adds, nervously. 'Wearing all black. Face mask, everything. At least . . . I . . . think so. Sherri and Annette both said they thought he was wearing green. Like a khaki green.'

Emily sits back in her chair, a satisfied smile creeping across her face. 'Well, khaki would certainly track with my ex-military theory, wouldn't it?'

'Oh, this is ridiculous,' Ruby snaps. 'No wonder you were

all so useless with the police. How can you be credible witnesses if none of you can even remember what the shooter looked like?'

I instantly regret telling Ruby about how stupid I'd felt during questioning. But the others had echoed my thoughts.

'I think it's a trauma thing,' I offer. 'Happens all the time. Witnesses to a crime disagreeing on the details of what happened. I think it's our brain's way of protecting us.'

'Yeah,' Natalia says, suddenly brightening. 'Maybe the memories will come back one day.'

I nod, wishing that weren't true. As useful as it would be for us all to remember more about the shooting, the shards of traumatic memory that have pierced my subconscious on a regular basis for nearly two decades are already more than I can handle.

Ruby looks at us in a way that makes it clear she thinks we have failed somehow. If *she'd* been there, *she'd* remember. *She'd* remember every tiny detail. *Obviously.*

I'm grateful when my phone pings and I'm delivered a sudden excuse to look away.

'My husband,' I lie.

I hold the phone just under the table so the others can't see the message: 'Hey, Ms Perkins,' it reads. 'You doing okay? If you're finally allowed out of the house, I would love to see you!'

Veronica ends the message with a pink heart emoji and another tiny blue one of two faceless blobs hugging. Her genuine concern for my welfare makes me realise it's been about three days since anyone other than Derek has asked me how

I'm doing. If I'm honest, I'm both surprised and disappointed by how little I've heard from Lilith. And the girls from class seem more interested in gossiping than actually checking in on me.

I type back: 'You're not by any chance free now, are you? I'm stuck at the worst group coffee meet-up and could use an escape route!'

My fingers hover over various emojis before indecision makes me chicken out and I end up signing off with a simple 'x'.

'Derek . . . he's . . . um . . . doing some work on the house,' I tell the girls, who haven't said a single word since my last lie. Ruby looks as if she is answering work emails on her phone and Natalia is now distracted by a suddenly encroaching zit on her chin. Emily is the only one who bothers to pretend to be vaguely interested in what I have to say.

We both jump slightly as my phone rings: a private number. I pick up quickly.

'Ms Perkins, I'm calling you to let you know there is an emergency situation that requires your immediate and full attention.'

'Emergency?' I say into the phone, as panic creeps across my face.

'Would you be able to abandon your awkward coffee date and be at the Nacho Mamas taco stand by Venice Beach in the next twenty minutes? Or as soon as LA's hellish traffic will allow?'

'Well, if it's urgent, of course I'll be there,' I say, continuing to feign concern.

Moments later, I'm power walking down the sidewalk towards where my car is parked, laughing into my phone.

'Veronica, you saved me!' I exclaim. She giggles down the phone and tells me she'll already be in line when I arrive.

'This place does the best burritos, honey. If you haven't tried them yet, it *is* an emergency, for real!'

Veronica grabs my wrist and pulls me, urgently, out of the way as two roller-skaters career down Venice Beach Boardwalk and nearly knock me over.

'Sorry!' one of them yells, and Veronica laughs.

'Gotta have your wits about you here, baby.'

We throw our now empty burrito wrappers in the nearest trash can and I compliment Veronica on her choice of food. 'Best I've tasted in years,' I tell her. And the company is pretty great too. I've laughed more in the last thirty minutes than I have in the last four months.

Veronica tells me about how she first moved here from Sacramento almost ten years ago. 'I needed to be somewhere people didn't know me. Start afresh. As the new me.'

I tell her I relate and she feigns shock. '*What?* You're trans too?'

She laughs before I can clarify, clutching my hand as she does.

Given Veronica was a pastor in a Methodist church in her previous life, her transition wasn't exactly easy. However, she tells me how grateful she is to be able to joke about it now, to live her life 'loud and proud' as her 'full self'.

'Before I transitioned, I felt like an imposter in my own

body. Like I was always looking over my shoulder, waiting to get found out. I thought by getting as close as possible to God I'd find some answers. But so often I'd stand in front of my congregation and feel like God was gonna strike me down for being such a fraud.'

I ask her what her relationship is with God now and she, unexpectedly, smiles broadly.

'Oh, we good. *Real* good. I get to be honest now. We talk every day and I thank Him for giving me the courage I needed to be who I really am. I've had to be really intentional about the kind of life I want to live, you know? And sometimes the fight for that life has been unbelievably hard. So I don't take a single thing for granted.'

She talks about her former body simply being the house her soul first lived in when she was younger. She remembers the wallpaper, the floorboards, the feeling of living there and speaks of the gratitude she has to God for giving her that experience.

'But I live in a new house now. One that suits me better. One that God helped me find. I'm lucky to be able to hang on to the most important things God gave me. My heart, my mind, my spirit. None of that shit got lost in the move, baby.'

She smiles again and delivers a wink that makes me feel as if she has already taken me under her wing.

'I know I'm now in my flirty forties . . .'

I interrupt to tell her she doesn't look it.

'Well, only just, girl,' she caveats, before continuing her thought. '. . . And you're early on in your dirty thirties, but, I don't know . . . Emotionally, it feels like we're the same age. Like you've been through shit too.'

Her words echo through me and I think of metal on metal. Unwanted hands sliding beneath my clothes. An empty crib.

I use Emily's affectation – the head shake – to shudder the memories away.

'You saying I look tired?' I joke. Veronica laughs and it's enough to move the conversation on.

Before I know it, it's dusk and I realise we've been walking and talking for hours. I've heard all about how fascinating yet unfulfilling her chemistry degree was, how she was lost for a few years but then met a perfumer at an event and realised that was what she wanted to do. She's told me about her mini-trampoline and her obsession with YouTube rebounding workouts. She loves rollerskating and spends way too much money on skincare. Fine dining is her thing but dating is 'just not a priority' for her right now. In turn, I've told her all about my art, my favourite TV shows, how I met Derek and our former life in New York, my interior design plans for our new home and, of course, Deep Flow.

As we decide to go our separate ways for the evening, I think of Lilith, always encouraging us to bring more women into the fold.

'You should come to class sometime,' I say to V, as I've already begun to affectionately call her. 'It's such a transformative experience.'

'Baby, I've had about enough transformation to last me a lifetime.'

I blush, managing a chuckle.

'It's also . . . fun? I guess.'

'You don't sound so convinced,' she counters.

'I dunno. Maybe because "fun" feels like such a reductive word to use for Deep Flow. I guess what I'm trying to say is . . . I've never felt so present in my body before. And that's a good feeling.'

V raises one perfectly arched eyebrow in response.

'Just think about it, okay?'

'Okay, girl,' she says, and, moments after we hug goodbye, my phone pings with a message from Raheem.

In the two weeks since I was released from hospital, I've failed miserably at keeping in contact with old friends. It took until this morning for me to leave a long voice note to Raheem, explaining my absence from both work and social media. I also had to fill him in on my Deep Flow journey so far, realising it's about time I share my new obsession with him. In previous conversations about how distracted I've been from design com- missions lately, he'd assumed it was by my personal projects and, since he wasn't entirely wrong, I hadn't corrected him.

My message ended up being almost thirteen minutes long and I ended it by apologising for dumping so much on him in one go. As I swipe across my phone screen to read his response, I picture him seeing my mini-podcast arrive and waiting until he left the studio to listen to it on his journey home.

'So, let me get this straight,' his reply reads. 'You actually took a bullet for your yoga lady? That's CRAZY, Sadie! Even by your standards!!'

Another few messages pop up: 'I'm so glad you're okay but . . . hospitalised? Lawd. Do you know who the shooter was yet? Why they did it?'

I send Raheem a shrugging emoji that implies I only really

care about getting better. But that couldn't be further from the truth. With the house to myself, thanks to Derek being out for the day with Mehdi, I finally have the time and space to do some digging.

I start by calling the local police department, but, despite the fact I am one of the victims of the shooter, they can't tell me anything about the man they arrested, only that they've been bailed, which is, quite frankly, terrifying.

'How do I know he won't come after us again?' I ask.

'That won't happen,' I'm told. 'There's very strict bail conditions in place.'

I don't feel particularly confident that someone who would shoot up a studio like ours in broad daylight would worry too much about rules and regulations. However, it's clear I'm getting nowhere with the cops, so I mumble a goodbye and hang up.

My next step is to see if I can figure out for myself who might've had beef with Lilith and Deep Flow. I hit the message boards, forums and social media: Instagram, TrustPilot, Facebook, Twitter, Quora and, finally, Reddit. One username pops up over and over again: CCraw86. From the very first post, it's abundantly clear they have a vendetta. They claim Deep Flow is, at best, a pyramid scheme, at worst, a cult. They use the word 'scam' repeatedly and refer to Lilith as a 'fucking bitch-whore' and an 'evil Svengali'. Both of these labels make me feel physically sick. It's obvious what type of man has written these posts. Almost certainly the type of man who would turn to violence to prove a point, I decide.

What if Lilith has seen these posts? I imagine they must've

really scared her. But, knowing Lilith, I also reckon she'd meet this person with compassion, despite their behaviour. I wonder if it's possible that this man is the partner or ex of a Deep Flow member. Maybe someone she had a toxic relationship with before Lilith made her see the light.

It's a long shot, but I decide to search through the social-media followers of all three of my new friends and discover that Emily, Ruby and Natalia are all followed by someone called Mackenzie Crawford.

I scroll all the way through hundreds of her posts. And it's only when I get two and a half years back that I spot it: Mackenzie dressed head to toe in form-fitting white clothing like we wear in class, arm in arm with Debbie, Andrea, Ruby and two other women I don't recognise. The caption reads: 'Enlightening weekend with my soul sisters. Love my Deep Flow family! #Obsidian'. I feel a rush of blood to the head as my suspicions are confirmed: this woman *was* part of the Deep Flow community and a high paying member at that.

Within ten minutes, I learn this Mackenzie ('Kenzie' to her husband, 'Mac' to everyone else) is a middle-class homemaker who originally hails from Tennessee. In one Instagram post, she celebrates fifteen years with her husband, Caleb, who she married straight out of high school. In the post, she mentions how her plans to go to college on a full ride to study International Relations were 'happily derailed' after she met her 'greatest love'. Three kids and two dogs later, life seemed pretty good for her until about three years ago, when her posts on both Facebook and Instagram became far less frequent. Could this be when she first got involved with Deep Flow?

Perhaps going inwards and figuring out who she was beyond her roles as wife and mom made her less interested in the external validation we so often seek from social media. It's certainly been the case for me, I've found.

Twelve months ago, Mac's posts stopped entirely. She does, however, have a single highlights collection of Instagram stories saved under the title 'Quotes'. I click through about twenty impassioned pleas: 'I don't know who needs to hear this but . . .', 'Don't let someone else's fiction become your truth', 'Keep healing, growing, loving, going' and 'If you don't take care of yourself, how can you show up for anyone else?'. This type of content isn't new to me, but it's hard not to read into her last saved Instastory. Unlike the others, this one isn't on a pretty pastel background. Instead, Mackenzie has opted for white text on black: 'If it's destroying you, it isn't love.'

I let out an audible gasp.

What if her Deep Flow family was the only family Mac felt safe with? What if she refused to give them up, despite her husband's demands, and he did something to her? Even if he didn't and she's physically okay, it's entirely possible Caleb forced his wife to leave Deep Flow. It would certainly explain why she's no longer with us.

I discover that Mac started a candle-making business almost three years ago and the only posts on her accounts from back then are links to the now defunct website. I decide to plough through her business profiles, but am disappointed to find she doesn't have LinkedIn. There is, however, a small write-up on her from her local newspaper in Tennessee with a headline that reads: 'Smart student gains full scholarship to Vassar'. I marvel at how she threw away the opportunity to go to such a good school and then quickly realise it's the sort of thing so many women do when they are still unaware that they've fallen into the clutches of a controlling man.

I start work on Caleb.

Mackenzie's 'proud hubby' works in tech sales and is an LA native, having attended Beverly Hills High in the early noughties. Lacrosse. Rowing team. Swim team. Mathletes. Science Club. This guy somehow managed to be both a massive jock and a total geek. I find a digital copy of his high-school yearbook and scroll through to find his senior quote. In a whispered wager with the universe, I bet everything I own that he's chosen Emerson or Thoreau, just as millions of other graduates have done for decades. I'm satisfied to discover he's plumped for the latter and I cringe a little as I spy the words 'It's not what you look at that matters, it's what you see' scrawled in comic sans next to his photo. He might be scientific and sporty, but he's certainly lacking in imagination. But maybe this is what psychopaths do, choose the quote that gives virtually nothing away about who they actually are.

I soon discover his LinkedIn, then type the words 'Prisma Tech Solutions', the company he works for, into Google. And there it is – the business address and its opening hours. I check the time: 16:03. If I leave now, I might make it before the work day is over. Is it crazy to drive over there? Would I even recognise him if I saw him? I trace my thoughts back to that fleeting moment, right before I threw myself in the line of fire. I barely saw a thing, but I can't help consider the idea that seeing him again might trigger a memory.

I grab my car keys and am almost out of the door when Derek arrives home.

'We wrapped early!' he announces, as I struggle to hide my disappointment.

Months ago, I'd have given anything for a few extra day-time hours with him, but, right now, he is just an obstacle. I thought I would be satisfied if I had a clearer idea of who the shooter might be, but my discoveries so far have brought me little peace. The more I know, the more I want to know. I need to look this guy in the eyes.

I tell Derek we're out of milk and pray he doesn't check the refrigerator before I'm safely in my car.

'Just don't overdo it!' he shouts after me. 'You're still recovering, remember?'

Twenty-five minutes later, I pull onto the lot of a business park, sunlight reflecting off the puddles on the tarmac. It's only when I'm reaching for my shades that it occurs to me: I have no game plan. No idea what I'm going to say to this perfect stranger.

I tilt my rear-view mirror towards me and practise introducing myself. I'm doing this when I spot Caleb, late lunch in hand, heading into the building. But, instead of seeing this as the perfect opportunity to instigate a meet-cute of sorts, I panic, sliding down in my seat, as if back on the school bus trying to avoid the attention of bullies.

Part of me is amazed he's still going to work. I hadn't thought of it on the way over, but surely anyone is his shoes would elect to work from home, given the circumstances. Even if his bail conditions allow, surely the man would have *some* shame. Yet here he is, head held high, preparing to tuck into a fried fillet and salty side dish. The audacity of it infuriates me.

Heart pounding, I consider heading home. Maybe stopping to pick up milk on the way in order to allay Derek's suspicions. But my curiosity gets the better of me. This might be the best opportunity I get to speak to Caleb. At least for a while.

I get out of the car and follow him into the building.

At reception, a blonde woman in her early forties nervously brushes her hair. There's a stack of fliers on her desk advertising the pizza joint across the parking lot and another for the veterinarian's two doors down. The rest of her desk is immaculate. When she spots Caleb, she slips the brush into a drawer by her knees and plasters a smile across her face. There's a dash of red lipstick on her teeth that instantly makes me feel sorry for her.

'Mmmm. Smells good, Caleb!' she chimes, pushing up her bra moments after he passes. I notice he isn't very tall. Maybe five foot eight at a push. He's broad chested, but kind of slight everywhere else. I can understand why, entirely covered in black, Debbie thought he might be a teenage boy.

'Just the usual,' he smiles, and sits in the waiting area just by reception. There's a kitchenette with tables and chairs just beyond where he is, so I can only assume he's chosen his position for the sake of company. There's an old TV high up in the corner of the wall and Caleb pretends to watch it as he begins to unpack his lunch on the coffee table in front of him.

This is fucking *wild*, I think. Andrea had to have shrapnel removed from her skull. He could've killed one of us. He could've killed Lilith. And yet here he is somehow, business as usual, eating a *fucking sandwich* like nothing has happened at all.

'Can I help you?' the receptionist asks, and I realise I've been staring for at least a moment or two longer than social norms typically allow.

'I'm . . . er . . . here about a job,' I say, acting on instinct.

Caleb pipes up. 'Is that the marketing position we advertised?' he asks, between mouthfuls.

I thank my lucky stars it's a role that falls somewhere in the realm of my experience and nod enthusiastically. 'I just had a few questions, if you have time to talk?'

Caleb wipes his mouth with a napkin, then wipes both hands on his pants. It's an act that's both mildly disgusting and lacking in common sense, but I'm grateful when he invites me through to the back office and asks Cindy on reception to grab me a drink.

So far, so easy. Worryingly so, in fact. If it's this simple to track someone down and worm your way into meeting them face to face, it's a miracle no one has done this to me yet. Caleb sits me down and I remind myself that I still have a long way to go. Right now, I'm here to discuss a job I know nothing about. I'm nowhere close to figuring out how I'll be able to leverage that or shoehorn in a conversation about his wife and Deep Flow. What am I even hoping to gain from all this? Answers? Revenge? Both?

The homemade soup I had for lunch lurches in my belly and the pounding in my chest is now so loud I worry he may be able to hear it. Any moment now, the fat-fingered hand of a security guard will surely clamp down on my shoulder. I look at Caleb's hand, a mere inch or two from his cell phone, and picture him calling the police when he finds out I'm not who I say I am. I've watched enough true crime to know that it's small mistakes that so often lead to the collapse of the suspect's delicately balanced house of cards. Only I am not the suspect, am I? He is.

'So! Marketing!' Caleb says, leaning back in his chair. I notice something green trapped between his two front teeth.

'Yeah,' I say. 'I'm . . . um . . . really interested in the job and . . . well, I have a wealth of experience I believe I could bring to the table. I just . . . want to understand a little more about what, exactly, that table is.'

He looks at me, quizzically. I've lost him. Luckily, Cindy buys me time by clumsily entering and almost spilling a glass of iced water into my lap. After apologising profusely, she leaves and I resume.

'Prisma. I'd love to learn more about who you are. Your vision. Your . . . history. Is it a . . . family business?'

Caleb cracks a smile.

'I like your chutzpah,' he says. 'Takes real initiative, coming down here. Asking those important questions. I can see why you're good at what you do. At least, I assume you're good at what you do. Tell me about this "experience" you mentioned.'

He uses air quotes and it doesn't escape me that he's answered my question with a question.

'Well, I've been freelance for a long time now and I've worked with some huge brands over the years.'

I reel off a dozen of my graphic-design clients. If Caleb does any digging, at least their marketing teams will know who I am. I drop multiple buzzwords like 'pivot', 'newsjacking' and 'app fatigue' and, before long, I'm certain he believes I know what I'm talking about. My heart starts to return to its normal pace and the sweat that's accumulated on my upper lip starts to evaporate.

When I've finished my spiel, Caleb begins his: the company started in Silicon Valley, originally launched by his uncle, who eventually decided to branch out and needed someone to head up the LA office. Usually, I'd be forced to stifle a snort at the transparency of the nepotism that secured Caleb the job, but I'm so focused on how to continue my ruse I barely even register Uncle Crawford's incestuous passing of the baton.

'Look, in all honesty, I've had some . . . personal stuff to deal with recently and I'm looking to wrap up this recruitment process as quickly as possible,' Caleb says, leaning forward. 'You seem to really share our values and, like I said earlier, I admire your gumption. So, how would you feel about preparing a mock marketing presentation for say . . . Monday? If we like what we see, the job is yours.'

Driving home, my hands feel sweaty as they grip the wheel. The palpitations are back as I marvel at what I've just pulled off. And yet, despite successfully conning Caleb, I have learned a sum total of nothing about the shooting, nor confirmed beyond all doubt that he is even the culprit. In order to find out more, I'd have to go back and that means actually doing the presentation Caleb requested. It's a dangerous plan, but it's the only way to get a foot in the door, which in turn could lead to vital information. Past experience has proven to me countless times that if I rely on cops to do their jobs and the legal system to serve up justice, I will be severely disappointed. This time, I won't just sit and hope for the best.

I stop at the local gas station and pick up some milk so that I don't arrive home empty handed. After some small talk with the clerk, I'm on my way, arriving home less than two hours after I left. Mission complete.

'We have plenty of milk,' Derek says, emerging from behind the refrigerator door with a half full container in his hand.

'Oh?' I say, feigning ignorance. 'I must've stared right through it.'

'You were gone for ages.'

'Traffic.' I shrug, swerving past him to put our freshly bought milk away. 'I might take a bath.'

He frowns, then pulls me towards him, breathing me in as he does.

'What?'

'Nothing,' he says, seemingly satisfied. 'Just checking you're not having an affair.'

I laugh. Almost too loudly. He joins in.

'I'm joking, obviously,' he says. 'I know you're way too honest for that.'

In the bathroom, I take off my dressing and pull at one of my stitches. They're due out tomorrow anyway and I'm keen to bleed out a few drops of my guilt. I clench my teeth and start to tear at the biggest before quickly snapping out of it and picking up my phone instead.

Astrid Michaelson has a new boyfriend, I learn. Her mother, Katie-May, on the other hand, is on vacation in Hawaii with Jim, her partner of seven years. They are sitting beside a sun-soaked beach, in a small café with a wooden roof, and both hold brightly-coloured cocktails up towards the person taking the photo. I stare at them, frozen in time, and instantly feel so much better and also so much worse. The bleeding happens on the inside this time.

TEN

There's something moving in our garden bushes. Something so small that, at first, I think it might be a large beetle. Or a cockroach. I hate cockroaches. I poke at it with a stick and soon regret it. It drops several feet into the dirt below and reveals itself to be a tiny baby bird, no bigger than the palm of my hand.

It is half asleep and so delicate I can barely believe it's real. Am I dreaming? I grab the soft flesh just below my armpit and squeeze hard to prove to myself that I am, indeed, awake. I look around for signs of its mother or a nest of siblings, but my knowledge of nature is so woefully thin. I don't even know if this bird is the nesting kind.

The days are shorter at this time of year and the nights grow cold. What if there were a sudden storm? How would this fragile thing survive it? I spend a few minutes agonising over what to do before eventually scooping it up and carrying it inside.

'What if it carries diseases?' Derek asks, tearing a chunk out of his ciabatta and dipping it into the oil and balsamic vinegar the waiter has left on the table.

I shrug. 'It's a baby. I couldn't just leave it.'

Derek shifts uncomfortably in his seat.

'Are you sure you're not . . . . you know . . . projecting.'

'What?'

'It's almost two years to the day since . . . And there is such a thing as transference, isn't there? "Grief is love made homeless", isn't it? Maybe you're trying to find something to, like . . . pour your love into."

I stiffen and stare at him, attempting to ascertain if he is serious.

'I just think that most people would've left the bird there, that's all. Let nature take its course.'

'You used to like the fact that I'm kind. Now you act like it's some sort of affliction.'

'Oh, gimme a break, Sadie.'

He throws down his napkin and stares across the restaurant, his eyes landing on an older couple quietly eating without looking at each other, without conversation.

'We used to look at people like them and say, "Jesus, I hope we never end up like that." Now I look at them and think, "How close are we to becoming them? How many years do we have left?"'

'Derek, come on. We're fine. We're both just busy, that's all. Maybe a little stressed.'

His gaze returns to me and he is quiet for a moment. Then—

'When was the last time we had sex?'

'Derek—'

'It's like you're disappearing.'

I laugh. 'I'm right here. And it's date night. Let's just have a good time.'

114

But it's too late. The mood is set. We eat, munching our way through salad starters and meaty mains, both electing to skip dessert and only managing a thin veil of small talk before we pay up and head out.

In the car home I try to get him talking. Ask him to tell me more about the movie he's working on. He makes an effort. Even cracks a smile. But before the night is done I realise he is right: the distance between us stretches for miles.

We get into the house and I check on my new feathered friend.

'Selma,' I whisper, through the bars of the bird cage I picked up at the pet store shortly after I found her. 'Stay alive for me, Selma.'

I watch her tiny body inflate and deflate with each breath, over and over until I can barely keep my eyes open.

The next morning, on the way to Deep Flow, I call Raheem and spill my guts out to him, detailing my encounter with Caleb and my plan to see him again. I've already started work on the presentation.

'This is fucking crazy, Sadie. You know that, right?'

'Every idea is crazy until it works,' I retort.

'Okay, Harriet the Spy,' Raheem says, his derision crackling through my car's speakerphone. 'Say he is the shooter. That means this guy is *seriously* dangerous. If he finds out what you're up to, he could—'

'He won't,' I say firmly, refusing to admit that I, too, am worried about the danger I might be in. 'He's on bail. I bet the police are watching him very closely.'

'Not as closely as you are,' Raheem huffs. 'Look, if you're so sure of the feds, why don't you just leave this to them?'

'I *meant* that I'm sure Caleb wouldn't do anything stupid. I'm *obviously* not saying I have confidence in the police. In my experience, if you want a job doing, you do it yourself.'

'I just hope you know what you're doing, girl,' he says, sighing deeply.

I almost regret telling him, but I needed to talk to someone. It's too early on in my blossoming friendship with Veronica to reveal this side of me and everyone else I know in LA is connected to Deep Flow. I can't imagine Ruby, Natalia or Emily reacting well to me digging around for the truth. I can already picture Ruby telling me that what Lilith has told us so far should be enough for me. That my curiosity is an act of betrayal.

'So, tell me more about Lilith,' Raheem says, and I'm only too happy to oblige, spending the next fifteen minutes of my drive talking almost without a pause.

The sun shines brightly the morning I'm due to give my presentation. I tell myself that this is, in fact, the reason why I'm sweating. Not because I'm doing anything wrong. Not because I'm nervous. And *definitely* not because I'm going to fuck this up.

I'm wearing a green cashmere sweater Momma passed down to me years ago, a black A-line skirt with buttons down the front and polished black boots. Earlier, I dedicated half an hour to deciding which earrings to wear.

'I just don't think any of them say what I need them to say,' I message Raheem, after sending him six different selfies.

'What you tryna say? I'm a crazy-ass bitch stalker who should probably be arrested?' he claps back. I send him a meme of a school kid falling asleep at his desk. I'm tired of him picking holes in this plan without offering me a better one. Eventually, my phone pings again.

'The first ones,' he tells me, sending me an eye roll emoji.

'Really?'

'REALLY.'

I manage a chuckle, which, momentarily, quells the butterflies having a party in my belly. Despite him annoying the hell out of me, I know Raheem is right. This is *completely* unhinged behaviour. But, as my brother used to say, 'Ima do it anyway.' After all, I don't have any other ideas.

My first Deep Flow session since the incident has only strengthened my resolve to do something about Caleb. No doubt the trauma has bonded us all, but our precious safe space no longer feels quite so safe. I found myself jumping out of my skin at the mere sound of a floorboard creaking under a fellow member's weight. And I wasn't the only one.

There's a new joiner whose name is Bridget. She's actually quite lovely and it seems desperately unfair that she's joined at time when everyone is on edge. She deserves better. We all do.

Sitting in the parking lot outside Prisma Tech Solutions, however, I almost lose my nerve. In the board room, my flashcards are held by shaking hands and I pray Caleb doesn't notice. When he does, I blame it on one too many coffees and he seems to buy it. For a guy who was such a high achiever in high school, he is remarkably easy to deceive.

My presentation features three ideas for a company rebrand – no change to the name but there are new logo designs, guides to the corresponding aesthetics, details of a bespoke social-media strategy and a deck pitching three different events based on the aforementioned logos and aesthetics. I've done serious research on Prisma Tech's client base and the market as a whole, but I still worry that none of it will be enough. Because, of course, this isn't just a case of Imposter Syndrome. I am literally an imposter.

Throughout the presentation, I can feel sweat sliding down my spine. My heart is beating so hard, I'm almost surprised it can't be seen through my blouse. Yet, somehow, I make it through and Caleb seems impressed. He sits me down and starts asking questions – first, about my ideas, then, about my experience. Before long, the questions turn personal as he asks why I moved to LA.

'My husband, Derek, he's a director. He's actually making a movie out here right now.'

'I didn't think any movies still filmed in LA. Too expensive. Georgia seems to be the hotspot these days.'

I swallow hard. The mention of my home state immediately bothers me and I wonder how much digging he's done into my background. Unlike him, I don't have LinkedIn and my social media gives very little away, so it's entirely possible his comment is innocent. A lot of things *are* shot in Georgia. Nonetheless, I can't help but question if he's testing me to see how I'll react.

'Well, that's true, but a lot of the networking opportunities still seem to be here. He got the job on the movie and, of course, we could have moved out here temporarily, but, after a while, we decided that maybe we should try and make a life here. See what happens.'

Caleb smiles, seemingly satisfied with my response. It's enough for me to take a punt.

'How about you? How long have you lived in LA?'

'All my life.'

'You sound very settled.'

'Couldn't imagine living anywhere else.'

'And what about your family?' I ask.

He hesitates. It's clear he's reluctant to discuss his family. I press on, nonetheless.

'Are you . . . married? Kids? I've been curious about what it might be like to raise a family here. Derek and I are at the stage where we're thinking more seriously about it.'

My tone doesn't give away the fact that we have done far more than think about it. That we have an attic full of toys and baby clothes that were never used. We'd packed them in silence back in Savannah, both knowing that a debate about whether we should bring them from our old attic to our new one would only cause upset.

'Uh . . . yeah. We have three,' Caleb tells me. 'Twelve, eight, and sixteen months old.'

'Wow!' I exclaim. 'Big gap between the last two. How's that working out?'

'I think Jessie genuinely believes India is a living baby doll. She keeps trying to take over mothering duties.'

I laugh. 'That's adorable. Bet your wife is only too happy to share the load!'

Caleb's smile fades. 'She's . . .'

He doesn't finish his sentence, just clears his throat as if he's going to change the subject. I can't risk that and so quickly interject with another question.

'Is she in the tech industry too?'

It's clear he's weary of keeping up the façade now, but I pretend to be oblivious to his social cues, plastering on a smile and feigning genuine interest.

'Uh . . . she's a stay-at-home mom right now.'

'Oh cool! My mother was a homemaker too,' I lie. 'They're the real heroes of society, I think. And, if your wife is anything like my momma, I'll bet she's got a busload of hobbies to keep her busy.'

'A few,' Caleb says, looking down at his hands.

'What's she into these days? Or . . . what has she been into in the last few years?'

Caleb frowns. Pauses. I hold my breath.

'You seem *very* interested in my wife, Sadie.'

Fuck. I've gone too far too fast.

'Sorry,' I say, employing the Emily headshake. 'People always tell me I ask a lot of questions. By-product of a curious mind. Although, I'll admit, I do have a *bit* of an agenda.'

I'm met with silence and decide to launch into part two of my charm offensive.

'Look, maybe this isn't something you can relate to, having lived here your whole life, but . . . LA is pretty new to me and it's so much harder than I thought to make friends here. Find my people. Find my thing.'

Remembering Caleb is no stranger to air quotes, I use them myself on the word 'thing'.

'So I guess when I start prying into the lives of others,

asking about hobbies and all of that, I'm really looking for ideas. For myself.'

Like all good lies, it's not *that* far from the truth, but Caleb's face takes a whole ten seconds to change. Ten seconds that feel unbearably long.

Finally, he smiles, warmly.

'I might not know what it is to move to a new city, but I do know a thing or two about feeling lost and lonely.' He stops himself, realising how much vulnerability he's shown. 'I mean . . . everyone does, right? They're universal feelings. So, I get it. Just . . . whatever you get into, make sure you're careful with your money.'

Now we're getting somewhere.

'What do you mean?' I ask, innocently. He shifts around in his seat while he tries to conjure the right words.

'Well, LA is a funny place. Some people here are outright conmen. And women.'

The irony of him telling *me* this is far from wasted on me.

'You sound like you speak from experience.'

It's a question that sounds like a statement – an opportunity for me to get more answers without seeming like I'm further interrogating him. I notice my sweat has dissipated, and my heart is no longer pounding. Instead, the hair on my arms bristles slightly with excitement and I imagine my pupils dilating as I soak up Caleb's words. I'm pulling off what feels like a world-class heist and it's a hit of dopamine I didn't know I'd been craving.

He breathes in through his teeth and tilts his head as if recalling a painful memory. I wait for him to spill, to finally give me the information I've been desperately pursuing since the moment I first walked into his office.

Instead, he simply says, 'You live and learn,' and gets up, changing the subject so quickly there is nothing I can do to pull it back.

'Anyway,' he says. 'The job is yours, if you want it? Course I understand we'll need to talk contracts and negotiate your salary, but if, in principle, you're interested, then—'

'Yes!' I say. 'I'm interested.'

We both smile, but deep down I am panicking. What the hell am I doing? This wasn't the plan. Problem is, I now feel so close to the truth that I can't just let it go.

It's only when I'm heading into the parking lot that I begin to question how I'll be able to juggle a sixteen-hours-per-week job on top of freelance design work, my own art and, of course, Deep Flow. What started as a tiny twisting of the truth now feels like a snowball rolling down a hill, out of control and growing bigger by the second.

Then there's also the fact that Caleb seems . . . nice. Really, *really* nice. In fact, not at all the sort of person who could shoot up a building full of women. But monsters always do hide in plain sight, don't they?

Seventeen Years Earlier

The day Daddy got the all-clear, his lungs were still rattling like an old car engine and the skin on his hands and elbows, no matter what lotions and home remedies Momma tried, were cracked and peeling, as if recovering from being caught in a house fire. His eyebrows had been reduced to thin wisps and the hair on his head had disappeared entirely. The doctors told us it may never grow back, but today, at breakfast, I spy a soft, fuzzy layer of reddish fur coating the top of his skull like eiderdown. It's been less than three months since he rang the bell, signalling the end of his chemotherapy. Trust him to beat the odds again.

He makes a joke about looking like Malcolm X and Momma smiles through watery eyes, grateful to still have him with us, but exhausted at what it took to get him here. Bills stack high and I decide not to mention the hole in the bottom of my shoe that's gaping wider and wider every day.

I finish every scrap of food on my plate, excuse myself from the table and head upstairs to get ready for class. I'm half dressed when I spot the mailman do his drop off at our box next to the driveway and, although checking for any letters when I need to leave for ballet seems like the least sensible thing, I can't wait that long for answers. I'd been expecting it to arrive yesterday and had since spent a miserable twenty-four hours on pins, doing intermittent silent prayers and nervously biting my nails down to the quick. Waiting any longer would be torture, and so I throw some jogging bottoms on over my leotard, shove on my sliders and make my way to the mailbox. I find what I've been waiting for buried in between some red letters and a flyer for a local window-cleaning company – an envelope addressed to my parents but written in the unmistakable handwriting of the secretary at my dance academy. I tear it open and yank out the contents.

Dear Mr and Mrs Calhoun,

We sincerely hope this finds you well. We are happy to have had another successful year at the academy and are writing to inform you of your daughter's progress and scholarship status ahead of the beginning of the new semester.

Throughout the next year, we will be continuing to focus on the RAD syllabus, allowing students to further study ballet at a pre-professional level in preparation for their dance career. This will include further explorations of pointe work, free movement and character dance, as well as the opportunity to delve deeper into ballet history and theory.

Whilst we agree that Sadie is a remarkable, hardworking student and an accomplished dancer, the need for financial support at the academy far exceeds our current capacity. This means we have had to make some very difficult decisions. Since Sadie has received support for a total of five years now, it seems only fair that we give another student the chance to grow their dance career in the same way.

Of course, we are aware of the health issues that have troubled your family in recent years and are glad to have been able to help with Sadie's dance education during that time. We hope that, since Mr Calhoun has thankfully received the all-clear, you are now better placed to carry the cost of Sadie's next year with us. We very much look forward to working with her further.

May God continue to bless your family.

Annaliese Wilkins, Roberta Chen and Gaultier Fontaine
(Dictated to Marjorie Waterson, Academy Secretary)

I let out a tiny gasp as my heart sinks into the depths of my stomach and I am possessed by a singular thought: I have to talk to Gaultier. He loves me. He'll fix this. He has to find a way. The final words of the letter burn through my subconscious: 'May God continue to bless your family.' These people seriously have no *fucking* clue.

As Elijah's car swings into the driveway, I screw up the letter and shove it into the pocket of my jogging bottoms. I have no intention of telling any of my family what I've just read.

'You ready to go?' Elijah shouts out of the window of his rusty orange pick-up truck. It's got nothing on the beautiful navy blue Pontiac he used to drive. Selling his pride and joy so he could give a few grand to Momma and Daddy truly broke his heart. But he did it. Daddy being cancer-free is all that matters now, but I'll bet the pain of Elijah's sacrifice rides shotgun in that Chevy every time my brother drives it.

'Almost!' I yell back at him, and run inside to finish getting ready. In my room, I compartmentalise: just get through this afternoon, I tell myself. Gaultier will fix this. I know he will.

I throw on my old Mellow Mushroom t-shirt from a birthday trip to Hilton Head and check myself out in the mirror. I got my braces off shortly before Daddy got the all-clear and I have real boobs now, so it's frustrating that Gaultier and I have struggled to find the time to meet these last few weeks. I've never felt more confident. More sexy. I'm blossoming into a woman and I don't doubt that this has made being too busy to see me so much harder on him. His busyness must be why my scholarship renewal slipped through the net.

'He'll fix it,' I say out loud to my reflection.

'SAY-DEEEEEE!' Momma sings up the stairs. 'Your brother's waiting on you!'

I shout back that I'm coming and shove on a purple-pink hoodie and my battered old Nikes. There's a berry-red Lip Smacker in my pocket that I'll use on my lips and cheeks in the gap between jumping out of Elijah's pick-up and arriving in class. I need to show Gaultier my best face, today of all days.

But, when I walk into the studio, it's not Gaultier teaching.

'Hi, Ms Chen,' I say, the last in a canon of several girls who have also just shown up. 'Is Mr Fontaine sick?'

'No, he's taking a personal day to work on his pool house,' she replies, breezily. 'He's redecorating.'

I'm only too aware of Gaultier's little project. It seems to be consuming his entire life right now, leaving no time for me or anything else.

Pushing through class is painful. All I want is for it to be over so I can go and see Gaultier. Persuade him to talk to the board and the other teachers while I help him work on his pool house.

It's been over a year since we started seeing each other and we haven't celebrated our anniversary yet. Maybe I'll speak to him about making a plan. We could go away, perhaps. To Myrtle Beach or Charleston. Somewhere where no one knows us. We'll stay in a little hotel that serves breakfast and we'll hold hands as we walk along the beach together. Just like he always used to talk about us doing. He might need reminding, but I know his dreams are still the same as mine.

Ms Chen tells me to remember to squeeze my glutes as I rise up onto pointe. A searing discomfort darts through my toes, into the arches of my feet and up both of my legs. Roberta must sense it as she walks by us, one by one, observing our form: 'Pain for beauty, girls,' she says. 'Pain for beauty.'

Perhaps that's what love is, I think.

'Can you drop me at Abby's?' I ask Elijah, as I slide into the car seat, after class.

'Oh, hey, Elijah. How's your day going? So far, so good. Thanks for asking, sis.'

I roll my eyes and groan at my brother's sarcasm.

'Please?' I whine, knowing he'll say yes, the same way he has the last two dozen times I've asked him to give me a ride to Abby's place. He's found it hard to resist since he discovered Abby lives only a street away from his high-school buddy Antonio. The lure of pot and video games is too strong a temptation.

Despite always dumping his car in the spot just outside of Abby's house, Elijah hasn't yet discovered that 'Abby' doesn't exist.

Maybe he suspects that Abby is a boy. But he definitely has no idea Abby is a teacher.

'Call me on my new number when you're done, yeah?'

I shrug and he takes out a pen and scrawls it up my arm. His writing is needlessly large, and he's done it in permanent marker, but I don't complain. I can't risk him asking me why I care so much. Can't risk him digging around in my lies.

As I watch my brother round the corner at the end of the street, I pull out the wrinkled letter and knock on Gaultier's door.

Nothing. I sigh and walk round his beautifully designed

bungalow to where he is almost certainly working away in the pool house. Sure enough, I soon hear the echoey sound of a record playing: The Beach Boys' 'God Only Knows'.

The door is slightly ajar and I slip inside, admiring the deep blue and green walls and dark wood of the new flooring as I move towards the guest room, where I can hear a fragment of human noise beneath the music. He's always had such good taste, I think.

In the guest room, Gaultier is shirtless, bent over his work, perspiration trickling down his back. I start to say his name but then my eyes suddenly make sense of what they are seeing and I stop in my tracks.

He turns his head towards me as a floorboard beneath me creaks and the girl lying underneath him reaches for a blanket. Vinyl crackles and continues to spin on the record player in the corner and I realise I recognise this girl. She was there that first day I came here. April's younger sister. She can't be more than eleven years old.

Horrified, Gaultier pulls up his shorts and lunges towards me. I recoil in disgust and the girl pulls her knees up to her chest and starts to cry.

'Darling,' he says, but I don't wait around to hear what he might say next.

He comes after me, shouting my name, claiming he loves me and that this girl has been a mistake, but I don't stop. He chases me round the side of the house, back the way I came, and, at first, I think I'm faster than him. That what he's done is terrible but he'd never hurt me. Not physically, anyway. Then, suddenly, he grabs me, pushes me against the wall and puts his hand in my pants, his other hand is a vice-like grip around my wrist. He pushes it hard into the brick.

'See? We can go back to the way it was, Sadie. None of this matters. It's just a . . . how you say . . . *lover's tiff.* You love me, remember? And you love me touching you.'

I say no, over and over, but he keeps talking.

'Love conquers all, *non?*' he says, as if hamming up his French accent will paint him in a more romantic light. He releases my wrist and presses his left hand into my neck before leaning in for a kiss. In a flash, I take my chance, simultaneously spitting in his face and kicking him between the legs before squirming free.

I run towards Elijah's pick-up truck, thanking God for his habit of keeping a spare key lodged in the gap between the windscreen and the top of the hood.

Fumbling with the key, I somehow manage to unlock the car and climb into the driver's side. I shove it into the ignition and fire up the engine. Thoughts of leaving Elijah with no way to get home and the fact I only have my provisional licence aren't enough to deter me; I have to get away. My only real regret is that I can't take April's little sister with me.

A wounded Gaultier slams himself against the window on the driver's side, screaming that he'll kill me if I tell anyone what I've seen.

I notice he has never sounded more American.

ELEVEN

'I want things to be good again with us, Sadie,' Derek says. 'That's all I want in the world right now.'

I snort.

'So, gun to head, if you had to choose between that and an Oscar . . .'

Derek kisses his teeth loudly, then gets up to walk away.

'If you're not gonna take this conversation seriously—'

'What gives you the impression I'm not being serious?'

Part of me is. Part of me would love to know just how important to him I am. But, in my heart of hearts, I also know I'm being deliberately antagonistic. And, in fairness to him, I've spent the last fifteen minutes feeding water to a baby bird with a bottle intended for a newborn human, while mopping up her dribble with a monogrammed handkerchief. If he's finding it weird, he's been kind enough not to say. Maybe I should cut him some slack.

'Look, I'm sorry. About everything. I didn't tell you about the job because I didn't see any point unless I actually got it.'

Derek sighs. 'It's not even that. It's . . . marketing? I had no idea that was in your realm of interests. And that makes me feel like I don't know you any more.'

'Don't be so dramatic,' I say, feeing mildly smug about how the tables have turned. It's nice to be the calm one these days, and watching Derek freak out feels ever so slightly satisfying.

'I'm not being—'

He sighs and gets up again, this time mumbling curse words under his breath. I realise I've pushed this as far as it can go before it breaks entirely. If I'm going to salvage the rest of the day, I'll need to do it now.

'Listen, why don't we have some one-on-one time tonight? Watch a movie. Order takeout. Maybe from that Chinese place we used a lot when we first moved in? It's been a long time since we've curled up on the couch together.'

He nods, wearily, and suddenly, I feel tired of fighting too.

'Will it just be the two of us?' he asks. 'Or will your little friend be hogging a seat?'

I chuckle, even though I doubt his question is intended as a joke.

'We could get a sitter,' I say.

He looks appalled.

'I'm *kidding.*'

He manages half a smile and leaves me wondering when he lost his sense of humour. Lilith would've laughed, I think. I bet Lilith would've died laughing.

The sun is barely up when I check the joint account and see a second payment of two and a half thousand dollars has made its way to Deep Flow. A disgusting wave of bilious dread surges upwards from my stomach and I'm forced to reassure myself that it's worth it. My first quarter is now complete, and I'm hopeful that quarter two will enable me to delve deeper. Maybe I'll be able to upgrade to a Carnelian membership in quarter three. If I work on manifesting the money. Things might seem messy right now, but Lilith has told me repeatedly that this is the hill I must climb to get where I want to be.

'It's like clearing out your closet. The only real way to do it is by making piles of things that you've pulled out and sorting through them. If someone were to walk in on you doing this, of course it would look like chaos. But the end result will be a smoother, happier, more efficient life.'

In class, Andrea's return is heralded with a massive round of applause from all of us. She looks exhausted, like she's been to hell and back. She's also got a scar on her head and a patch of hair missing. I think about Caleb, swanning about the office like butter wouldn't melt. If he'd been Black or Brown, I do not doubt for a second that he'd be spending months in jail awaiting his trial. But he obviously had the money and connections to be granted bail, no matter the suffering he's caused.

The smallest, unexpected sound still sends a shudder around the class. Nervous laughter each time a car backfires in the street or someone slams a door too loudly. Annette's brother, who owns a jewellery store, put Lilith in touch with someone who came to replace the window with bullet-proof glass, and Debbie has taken it upon herself to lock the door after the last student arrives. There's no room for latecomers any more and our safe space no longer feels quite so . . . safe.

At the end of today's session, Lilith reminds us about next weekend's big event: two nights of 'awakening the soul', with a day of workshops sandwiched in between. Then, a Sunday 'confessional', which will start with two hours of breathwork and ninety minutes of chanting before we allow the group (or just Lilith) the opportunity to 'bear witness to our truth'.

Two nights without sleep sounds like torture to me, but Debbie jokes about how she's had many sleepless nights since becoming a mom and I decide that, if she can do it, I sure as hell can.

I do worry about leaving Selma for two whole nights, however, since I found her, bare flesh and peach fuzz have turned into beautiful gray-green and yellow feathers. The research I've done online tells me she is a Yellow Warbler and that, despite not being much larger than my thumb, she's about as big as she's going to get now. I contemplate leaving her with a supply of insects from the fishing shop down the road, some berries from the yard and plenty of water to see her through. Maybe going away *is* possible. Even if I will miss her like hell.

As we ready ourselves to leave the studio, Ruby and Natalia give a glowing review of last year's Soul Awakening weekend.

'It was like all the bullshit of daily life melted away and there I was – the real me, you know?'

I don't know. Not really. But I've already been on the receiving end of Ruby's patronising tone when she's had to suffer the indignity of explaining something twice, and I'm keen not to ever go there again. Thankfully, Natalia is eager to expand on Ruby's point.

'The mask we all wear, the armory, the walls we put up – all that stuff is stripped away. You're forced to be your most authentic self. Which feels totally bat-shit at first. You know, that hysteria you feel when you're really tired? But, when you move past that, it's this intense, natural high.'

There's an excited twinkle in Natalia's eyes as she speaks. Over and over, she uses words like 'lifechanging' and 'transformative' and, given the seismic shift I've already experienced because of Deep Flow, I strongly believe she's being anything but hyperbolic.

'The feeling of unburdening yourself at the end of the final session is incredible. I wish we could do it more than once a year.'

'You don't do it in your one-to-ones with Lilith?' I ask.

'Oh, totally. But this is different. There's this amazing support system around you and you're all vibing on the same frequency. Obviously, the lack of sleep is fucking intense, but it's all about emptying out your vessel so you can fill it up with new energy. When you're asleep, you're basically sedated, and this is all about waking *up*. Your mind, heart, soul. Plus, we all pull each other through the exhaustion and share every part of it together. It's really special.'

Ruby nods along and, when Emily catches us up, she also gets the sales pitch.

'I dunno, guys. Sleep deprivation can *literally* make you go insane. I've read articles about it.'

'Of course you have!' Ruby shrieks. 'Because the media doesn't *want* you to know how powerful you are. They don't *want* us to tap into our psyche or go deeper. They want us to remain mindless sheeple that blindly follow *their* agenda and never get to tap into our true selves. Lilith's husband, Jeremy, talks about this *a lot*.'

I feel my eyes narrow. 'Have you met him, Ruby?'

'Yeah! I've been for dinner at their house several times, actually. He makes a mean beef stew.'

And here I was thinking the man was surviving on steak alone.

I'm hit by a pang of jealousy as I think of Ruby being invited into Lilith's inner sanctum. I picture her sitting at her dinner table, laughing at Jeremy's jokes, and begin to feel nauseous.

'I've been too,' Natalia says. 'It was around the time I became an Altostratus.'

'Excuse me?' I say.

'Oh, I'm in Elements. Jeremy's affiliate marketing group. As you achieve more and more, your cloud status gets bigger and better. Cirrus is the next one for me. Then Nimbo.'

Natalia did mention her work in 'sales' when we'd first met, but I'd never been interested enough to dig deeper. Now I knew she was part of Jeremy's pyramid scheme, a lot of things about her made so much more sense.

'I've never been to Lilith's place,' Emily pipes up, putting the conversation back on track. 'Kind of seems like a couple's thing, really.'

'I guess I haven't been since me and Eddie separated,' Ruby says, as if having an upsetting epiphany she's desperate to hide.

'I haven't been since Chris and I broke up either. Not that they ever thought he was good enough for me. They're . . . protective, I guess. It's kind of sweet.' Natalia smiles, but there's a sadness in her eyes and a modicum of empathy rises in me before I return to feeling sorry for myself.

I *am* in a couple. And Derek and I are fantastic conversationalists. That's one thing I am sure of. So, why haven't we been invited for dinner yet?

Over the course of the next few days, this question becomes an obsession and I decide to make a list of all the reasons Lilith might not like me as much as the others.

It's not the first time I've made a list like this, and the exercise feels like a hugely triggering instrument of self-torture, but I push through. I have to get to the bottom of this. Especially since, no matter how many negative things I write down about myself, one fact continually prevails: *I saved her life*, and I've still got a large scab on my side to show for it. Surely that's enough to warrant a dinner invitation.

Maybe I shouldn't have let her pay my medical bill? She *had* insisted. But what if that was some kind of test? What if she now thinks I'm only trying to get close to her because I'm some kind of grifter?

If that's the case, I *have* to prove her wrong.

Back at my new job, I anxiously peel the plastic design off the old, unused mousepad sat on my desk. Caleb notices and asks if I'm all right. I nearly snap at him, nearly reveal all: 'No, I'm not all right. I'm here, in your office, wasting my fucking time when I could be at home painting. All so I can figure out why a nutcase like you would want to harm the most perfect person I've ever met. Yet, despite all that, despite how much I care and how much I'm willing to give up for our community, Lilith doesn't even value me enough to invite me round for food.'

Of course, I don't say any of this. I simply smile through gritted teeth and offer to discuss the company's SEO with him. The ruse continues, day by day, and I feel Caleb becoming more and more relaxed around me. I join him for lunch in reception and we talk about NFL, his kids and Derek's moviemaking. And, every now and then, I get the tiniest glimpse into his family life and it makes it feel worthwhile carrying on.

Then, I get a call. It's Sarah, graphic-design agent extraordinaire.

'Sadie, sweetheart!' she coos down the phone. I roll my eyes, glad she can't see me.

'What's up?'

'Exactly what I wanted to ask *you*, actually,' Sarah continues, perky tone unwavering. 'What's going on, Sadie? Two of your clients have said you've missed deadlines and left emails unanswered. You've not replied to my emails either.'

I can't blame the clients for being pissed – I was paid a sizeable advance for both logos and I haven't done a lick of work on either. Juggling the work with my new marketing role, the odd bit of painting I still get to do and, of course, class, is almost impossible. Truth be told, I probably should've turned down both commissions, but I needed the money to cover Deep Flow's fees. The meagre paycheck I get from Prisma Tech barely touches the sides.

'I just need to know where your head is at, Sadie-girl. There's been a real shift in commitment since you moved out to LA and, going forward, we're gonna need that to change. Or . . .'

'Or what?'

'Look, you will need to honour both of these contracts and I'll support you as best I can to get them over the line, but, when these projects are complete, maybe we should have an honest conversation about whether you're in the right headspace to have representation right now.'

My heart sinks. Being dropped from the agency would feel like a huge failure, and my income stream would quickly slow to a trickle without any further commissions. I have to plead my case, but, just as I'm about to launch a protest, Caleb walks back into the office and I'm forced to wrap up the call.

'Look, I don't have time for this,' I say, hanging up.

'Who was that?' Caleb asks.

'Sales call,' I lie. 'I made it clear I wasn't interested.'

'Good for you,' he smiles.

Then, suddenly, a burst of inspiration hits me.

'Caleb, would you and your wife like to come for dinner on Thursday night?'

I've caught him off guard and, this time, he's barely able to hide it.

'Oh. That is so kind. But we already have plans.'

'No worries. Short notice, I guess. How about next week? My husband would love to meet you both.'

I see his Adam's apple move up and down as he swallows hard, trying to think up his next excuse. I know what he's thinking: 'How can she not know I've been arrested and charged with a major crime? Even if I've managed to keep my name out of the press, isn't everyone gossiping about it?'

I continue to feign ignorance.

'My wife . . . she's . . . unwell . . . at the moment.'

There are tears in his eyes now and I suddenly feel terrible. There's no excuse for what Caleb did, but I've got no idea what he and Mac have been through. Sure, they've unjustifiably blamed Lilith for their troubles, but, if Mac is mentally ill, I totally get why Caleb might be looking for someone to point the finger at, even if it isn't really anyone's fault.

For a while, I'd forgotten Caleb was a real person and the expression on his face is a sobering reminder of the potential impact of what I'm doing. How sneaky it is. What a betrayal it might seem if I ever get found out.

I resolve to quit while I'm ahead. What at first seemed a victimless crime now feels like a cruel prank. I'll hand in my notice next Monday, I decide. Tell him I've been headhunted or something. Too good an opportunity to pass up. Huge apologies etc.

After Caleb leaves the room, I check my bank balance on my phone and silently wish I'd known I was skating on such thin ice with Sarah before I'd paid the deposit for the Soul Awakening weekend. Without any further commissions and my job at Prisma to keep me going, I'd have to tap into the joint account again for any further Deep Flow expenses.

I write Sarah an email, apologising for the abrupt end to our call and my lack of client communication. I've been dealing with a lot of stress recently, I tell her. It won't happen again.

Moments later, the bell rings at reception. I wait for Cindy to deal with it, but the bell rings again and again. Eventually, I sigh and make my way through the open door to the front desk. A short, round woman stands there with a stack of flyers. Her cheeks are pink and mousy wisps of hair float in front of her watery blue eyes.

'June,' she says. 'From the veterinarians? Just dropping off some more flyers.'

I glance at the barely touched stack already sitting on Cindy's desk.

'These have updated opening hours on them,' June says, barely moving her lips as she does. 'Of course, we have flyers for your business at our reception too.'

She smiles, almost sarcastically. I can't imagine the use a tech company would have for advertising in a veterinarian's, but I don't want to ruin the relationships they've clearly established with the locals.

'Diminished responsibility then, huh?' June says, as I graciously accept the flyers.

'Excuse me?'

'Your boss's wife? I heard that's what they're arguing. In court. Thought *you'd* know all about it.'

She looks at me suspiciously. 'You do work here, don't you?'

Then, she holds her hand out, as if expecting me to heap further information into her palm. Instead, I simply stand there, mouth agape.

'The shooting?' she says, letting out a huge sigh of frustration. It's obvious to me now that she was hoping to squeeze me for more information and yet, here I am, bewildered.

It wasn't Caleb who shot up the studio at all.

It was Mac.

'Of course,' I say, struggling to find the words. 'Have you . . . heard anything else? Like maybe an explanation of why she did it?'

June tuts. 'I told you. She's cray-cray. Now, are you gonna give me any of your flyers or what? I got ten cages to muck out this morning. Can't be stood here flapping my gums all day. Especially since you don't know anything anyway.'

I remain dumbstruck. How could I have missed this? What little information I've been able to find via online news outlets has been keenly noted down in a little journal I keep in my nightstand, along with other research and mini mind maps where I've attempted to make sense of my findings. Not once has the shooter ever been referred to as a 'she'. But, I realise now, they were never referred to as a 'he' either.

'How do you know about this?' I eventually ask.

'My neighbour's sister works at the court,' June says, before swiftly changing the subject. 'You got anything you want us to put out in our reception or what?'

'I . . . I don't think we have any more flyers,' I stammer.

'Okay.' June shrugs, and, within moments, she is out the door.

I stand alone for all of ten seconds before I follow her.

'Hey, June!' I shout after her. 'Can I ask you something?'

She keeps walking. 'If it's about Mrs Crawford, I've told you all I know.'

'It's about an animal,' I say, and she stops, whirling round to face me, mildly annoyed but definitely intrigued.

'Make it fast.'

'If someone were to rescue a baby yellow warbler, what's the best way to take care of it?'

June's eyes narrow. 'There isn't one. Warblers are meant to live in the wild. Doctor McGill would tell you that too.'

'But if . . . *if* you had one and you were looking after it and it seemed healthy . . . how long before you could . . . or *should* let it go? Could it return to its mother?'

Hands on her hips, June stares at me.

'Are you telling me you have a yellow warbler in your home?'

'No. I'm speaking hypothetically. It's research. For my son's school project.'

I decide June has no way of knowing I don't have a son. She issues an exaggerated sigh.

'How long have you had it?'

I say nothing and June starts to walk away, talking as she does.

'Its immune system won't be strong enough to survive in the wild if you've had it a while. And it won't have learned the skills necessary for survival either. You let it go, it dies. But you shouldn't be keeping it in your home either. It's illegal. Seriously, is everyone close to Mr Crawford cray-cray? Mrs Crawford shooting up them hippies, Cindy always brushing her goddamn hair . . .'

She's speaking to nobody, ranting all the way across the parking lot until she's out of my earshot. I watch her as she goes, considering just how I've managed to fool Caleb so easily, when the likes of June manage to see through me in an instant.

TWELVE

Late afternoon on a Saturday, Derek and I walk up a honeysuckle-hazed hill towards what can only be described as a mansion of medium size. The sun is already hanging low in the orange-streaked sky, teasing us with the balmy evening ahead as our shadows grow long on the sidewalk. On either side of the teal-painted front door an ornate tiger sits with a golden apple clenched in its jaw. Jeremy receives us, all broad shoulders and bravado. His teeth are perfect, but also slightly menacing, as if they've been sharply chiselled, ready to sink into flesh. He gives Derek a good, firm handshake: 'Nice to meet you, bro.'

I'm almost vibrating with excitement, unable to believe I'm actually here, that Lilith pulling me to the side at the end of the last class and inviting me to dinner *genuinely* happened. Even if I do think that it's about fucking time, all things considered.

'You should come around for dinner sometime,' she'd said, casually. 'It would be great for Jeremy to meet you. And bring your husband. I'd love to finally connect with him. With that part of your life.'

It was as if she'd somehow sensed the blistering resentment building within me. As if she knew I might start to pull away if that wound grew much bigger. She'd been preoccupied after the shooting, and who could blame her? But she valued me too much to let our burgeoning friendship fizzle out. She'd value me even *more* if she knew I was going above and beyond to get to the bottom of what happened that day, in the hope that finding out the truth would protect her from anything like this occurring again. But I can't tell her about Mac yet, not when all I have to go on is hearsay.

The hallway is instantly intimidating. High ceilings, marble flooring, paintings (not prints) hanging on every wall. Jeremy gives us the tour, reeling off obscure artists even I haven't heard of as he gestures towards his 'investments'. We drift casually in and out of rooms: the living space, his office, the snug. There's a library that's pocket-sized but teeming with books that jostle for space in the floor-to-ceiling shelves. Then, the perfect reading chair in the perfect nook by a window that looks out onto their yard, or rather 'the gardens', as Jeremy puts it.

'These people must be multi-*multi*-millionaires,' Derek whispers, the moment our tour guide is slightly out of earshot. I, myself, am open mouthed in awe. This house represents a level of luxury I've never before had the privilege of coming into close contact with.

We reach the kitchen, where we find Lilith loading up plates. It's an incredible spread and Lilith is quick to notice my amazement.

'Of course, we got caterers to handle tonight for us,' she laughs. 'As much as I'd like to claim this is all my handiwork!'

She pulls us both close, a level of familiarity I feel Derek subconsciously stiffen against. I'm used to Lilith by now, but

Derek may need a little more bedding in. Jeremy is prattling on about how, despite the rest of the cooking being outsourced, he will be preparing his famous steak for us and has a barbecue already set up just outside the kitchen door.

'Great,' I say, as earnestly as possible, already dreading having to pretend his salt and oil 'method' is anything but dull.

In the dining room there's an open fire raging below a Native American headdress that's hung up on the stone wall.

'That's . . . controversial,' Derek says, uneasily.

'As in, you don't think I should I have it in my home?' Jeremy says, a slight smirk playing across his face. It occurs to me that the headdress might be a provocation – an opportunity for Jeremy to engage in a verbal sparring match with anyone who dares criticise.

'Well, it's kind of culturally inappropriate, given the mass murder and marginalisation of indigenous people in this country. Not to mention the continual theft of their culture. Like . . . do you eat Thanksgiving dinner in here, with that hanging in the background?'

I'm reminded of the conversation Mumtaz and I had around the same topic, when we first started to get to know each other all those years ago. But, while I understand Derek's prickliness, we've only been in the house for twenty minutes. It feels way too soon to launch into a socio-political diatribe.

'I hear you, bro,' Jeremy says, and I wonder if that's what he calls all male friends of his or just the Black men he meets. 'You're actually kind of right to be offended. Although, some might say a *little* snowflakey. But what you don't know is that I was actually Native American in a past life. So was Lilith. We did a past life regression years ago and discovered that I was a chieftain and she and I were lovers back then too.'

Derek laughs and then his smile freezes as Jeremy's sincerity dawns on him.

'Wait. Are you serious?'

Jeremy nods. 'Whatever life we've lived, she and I have always been two souls intertwined. And when we leave this life and move on to the next, we'll find each other again. That's why I don't fear death, bro.'

'Isn't that beautiful?' Lilith says, carrying in some canapés. Derek shoots me a sideways glance and I give him a surreptitious shrug. Admittedly, these two *are* a little woo-woo, but who are we to say that what they believe isn't real?

We sit down for dinner and, as the conversation drifts from subject to subject, I spy Derek, on numerous occasions, valiantly attempting to hold in what will surely be an acerbically derisive laugh if he lets it out. When Jeremy starts to discuss his new business venture, however, the dam breaks.

'Grass-fed butter?' Derek chuckles.

'Ghee,' I clarify, attempting to quell any confusion.

'Call it whatever you want. *I'm* gonna call it Winters' Wonder,' Jeremy says. 'It's clarified. It's Ayurvedic. And it'll come in thirty flavours.'

'Wow. Nearly as many as Baskin Robbins,' Derek responds. Only I know him well enough to recognise that his words are tinged with contempt.

'Sweet chili, truffle oil, parmesan, rosemary, Chinese all spice, orange neroli, English butter, pink sea salt and cracked black pepper, jalapeno, caramelised onion . . . the list goes on.

I'm also working to formulate an Italian pesto flavour that's infused with basil oil. It's gonna be the next big thing, I'm telling you. I honestly can't believe no one has done this before.'

'Maybe because you shouldn't?' Derek offers.

'Excuse me?' says Jeremy. He blinks hard and the atmosphere of the room suddenly changes, as if the cold air of a hidden draft has blown between us.

'Well, ghee is something that's woven into the fabric of South Asian culture. It has been for centuries. So, it feels kind of weird to brand it as your own product and corrupt it with all these Western ideas. Like, sure, people use it for cooking, but I also know South Asians who use it for medicine and religious rituals too.'

'You seem to know a lot about South Asian culture for someone who isn't South Asian,' Jeremy says, steadily.

'True, I can't speak on behalf of a community that isn't my own, but I am close friends with a few Indian and Pakistani people, so they've taught me a thing or two. Look, I'm not trying to cause trouble here, okay? I'm just saying that a certain subsection of the people you'll be marketing this product towards might find it at little . . . offensive.'

'There's that word again, bro!' Jeremy says, laughing with his mouth but not his eyes. I'm almost positive Derek hasn't previously used that word at all tonight. 'Listen, I'm not out here living my life according to the laws of these snowflakes, okay? There are many Westerners who have made millions by bringing products they discovered in the East to a broader audience. Look at Wim Hof. He rebranded Tai Chi as the Hof Dance! Genius! The whole cold-water immersion thing? Tibetan monks were doing it for centuries before he was! But, now, everyone knows it as the Wim Hof Method and the guy's made millions out of it. Changed people's lives. Screw the monks!'

He raises his wine glass high as he says this, as if toasting the demise of anyone who might get in the way of his ambitions. Genuinely curious, I finally pipe up. 'Could he not just own the fact that he's borrowed ideas from other cultures? Maybe actually give them credit and, I dunno, point people in the direction of those cultures, if people using these methods want to find out more?'

Jeremy looks at me like I'm two inches tall. 'Okay. But if you wanna make money, *real* money, you gotta make these things your own. It's not about the product, it's about you. It's about the *branding*. About making something a trend.'

'You want to make other cultures *a trend*?' Derek asks. He's throwing down the gauntlet, but Jeremy misses the point he's making entirely.

'Yeah! And isn't that great for them?'

'No. No, it's not. Trends go out of fashion. But the people who actually belong to those cultures can't *choose* to opt out the moment that happens. For us it's in our DNA. It's not something we can just pick up and drop. And creating a watered-down version of something we own to make it more palatable to white people is . . .'

'Offensive!' Jeremy cries, as if catching Derek out in a game he didn't even know he was playing.

'I was going to say problematic, but, sure, go off. I am curious to know, though . . . *bro* . . . have you actually spoken to any South Asian people about this?'

The worst arguments are always the ones that take place from behind smiles.

'Why don't we move on?' says Lilith, who has been notably quiet throughout this entire debate. She spits out the words quickly, but her voice is typically calm. 'I don't doubt that these challenging questions are important. And, of course, we invite criticism. It's how we grow, how we evolve. How we shore up our investments. But I think this particular conversation might be plateauing. At least enough for us to perhaps be ready to move on to something a little more . . . productive. And, of course, we have dessert.'

She says the word 'dessert' as if we are about to be presented with something made of melted gold and adorned with rubies – a thing of such beauty it will, undoubtedly, make our disagreement fade to dust. Instead, we are given a dense chocolate brownie, served warm with a generous scoop of vanilla ice cream and drizzled with caramel sauce.

'You're getting a cab home, right?' Lilith checks, before filling our glasses with dessert wine. For a moment, I worry about being drunk. About feeling out of control. But Lilith always manages to make me feel safe somehow.

Two glasses in and both Derek and Jeremy begin to mellow. I find myself feeling a little spaced out, but cosier than I've felt in this grand old house since we arrived. It is as if the edges of everything have softened and the conversation, once fraught with tension, becomes easy. Together we giggle and leave sentences unfinished, only for them to be picked up by someone else. In the snug, Jeremy lights another fire and puts a record on the vintage turntable in the corner. Extending an arm to

Lilith, he invites her up to dance with him. Soon Derek and I are up on our feet too, our shadows cast onto the walls as we slow-dance in the firelight. Then there's Scotch and cigars for the men and Lilith grabs my hand to take me on a tour of the upstairs rooms. A stag's head furnishes the wall at the top of the stairs and I'm convinced, for a moment, that it winked at me. A trick of the light, surely.

Drinking as infrequently as I do has given me the lowest of tolerance levels when it comes to alcohol, but I'm shocked to discover just how smashed I really feel. Anxious about embarrassing myself in front of Lilith, I lock myself in the first bathroom we come to and allow myself to slide down the wall, into a seated position on the floor. If the room could stop spinning for a minute, I'd have a chance of regaining my grip on reality. But sitting down makes things feel even fuzzier.

'Sadie? Are you okay?' calls Lilith from the other side of the door. The bathroom wallpaper is covered in tiny monkeys swinging from branch to branch amid a jungle exploding with blooming tropical flowers. One monkey looks like it is smiling and the grin I offer in return turns into a giggle.

'Sadie?'

'I think I'm just gonna stay here,' I call back. 'It's comfy in here. So relaxing!'

'We could lie on the bed, sweetheart,' Lilith says. 'Imagine how relaxing that would be. Soft blankets and pillows. Better than that hard tiled floor.'

I get up and unlock the door, opening it a crack and staring into the hall where Lilith stands. She reaches her hand through and settles it on my hip, drawing me into the corridor and deep into an embrace.

Next thing I know, I'm on the bed in Lilith and Jeremy's room. This is it, I think. As close to Lilith as it gets. Lying next to me, she interlaces her fingers with mine and we stare up at the intricate, celestial pattern on the ceiling. It is as if it is designed specifically for moments like this.

'I feel like a smudge,' I say, dreamily. 'Like I am the tiniest dot in the universe. Like I might disappear altogether. Turn to dust and float away.'

'That's just the pot talking,' says Lilith.

'The what?'

'The marijuana.'

'I didn't smoke any marijuana,' I protest, weakly.

'Of course you didn't. But what did you think was in the brownie, you silly thing?'

Lilith laughs and suddenly it all makes sense: the rippling walls, the blurred edges, the winking stag. I'm stoned. Gently, yet completely, stoned.

A long hum escapes from my mouth, softly buzzing between my lips, and Lilith giggles again.

'I don't think I can afford to come to the Soul Awakening Weekender,' I confess. 'I know I've paid my deposit and I really wanna come, but money is bad, bad, bad right now.'

Each utterance of the word 'bad' is slightly longer than its predecessor, the pot loosening my tongue and pushing my inhibitions aside. I'd been wrestling with this embarrassing truth for days, worried about what Lilith might think of me if I confessed.

Now I realise that I need not have been concerned. Lilith

shifts her body even closer to mine. She stares in to my eyes and strokes the side of my face. When she presses her lips to mine, I'm so stoned that I think for moment I must be dreaming. She pulls away and gives me a look that feels like something close to admiration. It baffles me and yet I have never felt so seen.

'You don't need to worry about anything, my angel,' Lilith says. 'We'll work something out.'

'We will?'

'Absolutely. It's about time you learned more about our community and how we keep it strong. Honestly, I'm so excited for you to take a deeper dive into what we do.'

I smile, woozily. *We'll work it out,* I think to myself. *It's all going to work out.*

Later, as our cab speeds silently down the street, taking us home, Derek and I begin our debrief. We're slowly starting to come down from our chocolate and cannabis high and Derek is, unsurprisingly, appalled.

'I can't believe they fucking drugged us,' Derek says. 'Those people are wild.'

'It was just pot,' I say. 'We took far worse back in our New York City party days.'

'Yeah, but we *chose* to take it. We had agency in the situation. What they did, it's spiking.'

When I'd confronted Jeremy about our dessert's secret ingredient, he told us he'd wanted us to 'loosen up' and that the pot brownies provided us with 'a rare opportunity to relax'.

'It kind of is spiking. I don't disagree,' I tell Derek. 'But I do think it came from a good place. In a weird, twisted kind of way. And don't pretend you didn't have a good time in the end. We *did* loosen up. And that was definitely necessary, given the tension over dinner.'

Derek tries to fight the smile that's spreading across his face. 'I did have a good time, I guess. Eventually. But now I see that was probably the drugs. Not the company.'

'I do appreciate you giving them a chance,' I say, resting my head on his shoulder.

'Lilith does seem . . . sweet, I guess,' Derek says, magnanimously. 'But Jeremy. My God, his opinions are so whack. And all that woo-woo shit about past lives—'

'You don't know that past lives aren't real. Plenty of religions and spiritual systems all over the world believe in the validity of reincarnation. And even science tells us that energy can neither be created nor destroyed. It has to go somewhere.'

'Okay, fine,' Derek sighs. 'I'll agree there's something convincing about that concept, but . . . actually *remembering* past lives? And the idea that they just so happen to have been lucky enough to be reincarnated as humans each and every time? Nah. That's some *bull*shit.'

I'm still light-headed and only half listening as Derek launches into a tirade detailing how he suspects it was Jeremy's idea to spike us. I let his voice fade into the background as I do a little internal inventory, reflecting on how the night went. Sure, there were hiccups in conversation, but I'm still able to enjoy luxuriating in my newfound insight into how Lilith lives. It's a life people dream of and I find myself wondering if a more committed and long-term exploration into my Deep Flow practice is what will provide me with the tools I need to one day make it my reality too.

THIRTEEN

Monday. I stare at my outfit, hung up, ironed and ready to wear: A white blouse, grey pencil skirt and thick blue belt with a large gold buckle. I've even laid out the chunky gold earrings I'll wear with it. I'm still in bed, though, dreading what the day holds. The magic of our beautiful dinner with Lilith has faded fast and there's no nice way to tell Caleb I'm quitting. Worse still, I'm none the wiser about exactly why his wife decided to shoot up Deep Flow, which makes me feel like all of this deception has been for nothing.

I haven't had a dream I can remember for weeks now, however, which is a small miracle, given how stressed and guilty I've felt. With this in mind, I decide to make a pledge to myself: this week, I will be grateful for every tiny step forward, every sliver of joy, every stroke of good fortune. And it's with this thought that I finally slide out of bed, right leg first.

In the office, there's a contractor tinkering away with the air-conditioning unit while a watchful Caleb eats what looks like a chicken buttermilk biscuit at his desk. His predilection for fast food will surely kill him one day, I think.

'Pepper jack cheese,' he tells me, when he notices me looking. 'Sets the whole thing right off. You should try it.'

'I will . . . take that under advisement,' I reply, managing a smile. 'What's wrong with the AC?'

I can already feel sweat prickling across my brow.

'I believe the technical term is "it's fucked", 'scuse my French. But Bertie here is gonna fix it for us, aren't you, Bertie?'

Bertie shakes his head. 'Not any time this week, sir. Need to order in a part. Reckon it won't get here 'til next Monday.'

'We can't wait that long,' Caleb says, appalled. 'Look. My cheese is melting.'

'I could always fit you a whole new system,' Bertie says, clearly uninterested in his client's Monterey.

Caleb twitches. 'Just . . . order the part. We'll keep the windows open.'

Sitting down, I begin to regret the pencil skirt as sweat starts to gather where my thighs touch. This is all I need. I'm already nervous and Caleb is pausing between bites of his breakfast to stare off into the middle distance, noticeably worried. If only I could offer him words of comfort instead of another dollop of stress to add to his highly stacked plate.

'Can I talk to you about something?' I finally say, snapping him out of his stupor.

'Of course,' Caleb smiles, crumbs dotted down his shirt.

'I've had a really great time working here and I'm so grateful for the opportunity. The last thing I want to do is leave you in the lurch and I know I've not been here long. It's just—'

'Is this about the AC?' Caleb interrupts. 'Because you can work from home 'til it's fixed, if you want?'

'No. No, not at all . . . I wouldn't quit over something like that. It's . . . another job. An offer I just can't refuse.'

'Whatever they're paying you, I'll double it!' Caleb announces, then laughs, awkwardly. 'A little joke. I can't actually afford . . .'

'I didn't expect . . .'

We both trail off and then sit in silence for a moment. Then, Caleb clears his throat.

'Is this about . . . my wife? Have you . . . heard about our . . . troubles?'

I falter. 'Uh . . . June from the veterinarian's mentioned something about her being in court. That's really all I know.'

'Oh, come on, Sadie. It's all over town. Moms talking about it at the school gates. People staring in the store. To be honest, part of me hired you because you seemed like the one person who hadn't already made a judgement about me. About us. But you can't still be in the dark. I don't buy that.'

Inside my blouse, a bead of sweat runs down between my breasts. My palms feel sticky, my feet swollen inside my poorly chosen penny loafers. Of course I know everything. There isn't a scrap of information in the public domain that I haven't eaten up, processed and regurgitated into my little green notebook. And yet I continue to lie.

'It really is very hot in here,' I say.

'I'm sorry. I don't mean to put you on the spot,' Caleb responds, now staring at his hands. His glance downwards gives me a chance to regroup. I wipe my face on a napkin I find discarded on my desk and pick up a paperclip so my hands have something to do. As he begins to talk again, I pinch and fold the metal between my fingers.

'There's stuff you don't know, Sadie. Stuff no one knows.

They judge us. Gossip about us. Middle-class family, fallen on hard times. "Oh, it's so *embarrassing*," they say, behind our backs. But then they show up on my doorstep with casseroles and lasagnes and half-baked sympathy. And I don't want any of it. I just want this horrible nightmare to be over.'

This is an experience I know all too well. Except for the 'middle-class' part. When Daddy was diagnosed with cancer, we ate nothing but lasagne for what felt like months. And then people got tired. Compassion fatigue, I've heard it called since. No one likes it when your pain lasts too long. When it starts to become an inconvenience to them or begins to make them uncomfortable because it's so hard to look at.

'It sounds like you're at the beginning of a long and difficult journey,' I say. 'But every journey has an end. Every problem, a solution. And one day this whole mess will just be a story you tell your kids about what you survived and how your family stuck together, against all odds.'

It's a short speech stolen right from my Aunt Sheila – one of the few useful things anyone managed to say when our family was going through hell.

Caleb looks up at me and smiles through tears. He sniffs, trying to keep his emotions in check, but the tears keep coming at an alarming rate.

'Thank you, Sadie,' he says. 'That's beautiful.'

He takes another bite of his biscuit and I realise it's comfort food. That he's probably been eating to dull the pain almost every day since Mackenzie did what she did. That it's his way of coping with it all.

'Is that blood?' Caleb asks, nodding towards my hands and

I realise I've been clenching the metal paperclip so hard the tip of it has pierced my index finger, dripping blood onto the paperwork stacked on my desk in front of me. I suck at the wound, the taste of metal and salt lingering on my tongue afterwards. I think of my razor blade, neatly taped under my bathroom cabinet. After a day like this, it might be too hard to resist when I get home.

Later on, Caleb apologises for 'losing his cool' and asks if I'll work my two weeks' notice despite the AC issue. I tell him I absolutely will and that I'm happy to come into the office so he can make the most of me while I'm here. It is, after all, the least I can do.

In the early hours of the morning, on the day the Soul Awakening weekend is due to start, I dream that I am escaping from a burning building. At first, it seems as if there is no way out – hot flames are licking my ankles, there's a smell of burning hair and skin. Then, a door appears and I thrust it open. On the other side I find a suburban street where Veronica sits at a lemonade stand. She tells me she plans to invest the money she makes into a bigger, better business venture, but I tell her I don't have time to talk further. There, on the side of the road, lies a discarded bike. I pick it up and climb on, but, bizarrely, it seems so much smaller than I thought it would be. I start pedalling only to find the wheels are stiff and the bike moves painfully slowly. But it's all I have and I am sure someone or something will soon burst out of the fiery house and drag me back inside if I don't flee. Eventually, Veronica brings me a cup of her lemonade. I've barely moved since I told her I didn't have time for her and, embarrassingly, I'm only a few yards up the street. I take the cup, drink the sugary sweet liquid and wake up sweating, my sheets wrapped around me as if attempting to tie me to the bed.

There's a momentary panic as I search for Derek, but then I realise it is him closing the door on his return from the bathroom that has woken me.

'Sorry, sweetheart,' he whispers, slipping into bed next to me. He helps me untangle myself and then pulls me close, gathering me into his arms. We fall asleep like this.

Shortly after sunrise, I wake and spend a few precious minutes watching Derek sleep, his eyelashes gently vibrating as he breathes in and out. His deep brown skin is virtually unblemished and his hair is cut to the perfect fade. We've spent little time together lately, bickered more than I would like and yet I still feel connected to him, still feel as if I am his and he is mine. But he will never understand this world I live within now. Deep Flow has fed my soul and given me the sense of community I've craved for such a long time. I won't let anything or anyone jeopardise it – not a crazed random shooter, not boring freelance work and not my husband, however much I love him.

I've left him strict instructions on how to take care of Selma, both verbal and written. I've decided that soon I'll have to invest in a larger home for her. It seems wrong to be keeping her in a cage at all and I've already let her loose around the house for a few hours at a time, much to Derek's dismay.

'What if I sit on her? Or step on her? I keep having to duck. In my own home.'

Every part of me wants to send her back into the garden, so that she can live a more fulfilling life, but June's words still ring in my ears. Right now, it feels like keeping Selma imprisoned is the only way of keeping her safe.

I clock watch all the way through my workday, wishing the time away, excited to be reunited with my Deep Flow 'sisters'. I'm surer than ever that we are on a journey together and that every penny I've spent thus far has been a real investment in myself and my future. Lilith talks about this idea of a cocoon, explaining that we need a period of incubation before we can be fully realised. It's a concept that connects so perfectly to my dream about the electric indigo butterfly that I latch on to it and think about it multiple times a day. Encased in this shell, I can feel myself growing, evolving, changing beyond all recognition, the Sadie of the past slowly disappearing, unable to taint who I am now with her shame and trauma. After years of contemplating my death, Lilith has helped me discover that I don't need to take my own life to feel a sense of peace. Instead, I can be reborn. I tell her over and over that that's what I want and she promises to get me there. The Soul Awakening weekend is the next crucial step.

I message Veronica: 'Hey, beautiful! I dreamed about you last night! Think my subconscious is telling me we need to hang soon, ha. I have a big weekend with Deep Flow but free after that. Let me know when's good for you. Xx.'

I still haven't heard back from her when I show up at the converted warehouse Lilith has rented for the weekender. From the outside, it looks like a factory – cold and industrial. But inside is an expansive yet warm space, strung with fairy lights and coloured fabric. There are candles and lanterns everywhere and the familiar smell of burning Palo Santo fills my lungs. As I move through the room, I notice several of the Deep Flow regulars standing or sitting together in small groups. But there are also several women I don't recognise. Then, suddenly, Lilith appears.

'Welcome, Sadie,' she says, taking my hands. 'Let's get a one-to-one in the diary soon, shall we? It's been a while.'

She's right – it's been almost three weeks. Juggling regular classes, attempting to get started on my freelance commissions *and* working at Prisma has been intense. However, I'm hopeful the Soul Awakening weekend will give me the chance to show Lilith how committed I am to Deep Flow.

Lilith notices me looking at the new additions to our group.

'They've come from our sister studios in the mid-west,' she says. 'We currently have a network of eight studios altogether, led by other lightworkers that I know and trained in our methods. So if you're ever travelling for work or pleasure, let me know. There might be somewhere you can practise Deep Flow nearby. We're always expanding.'

She gives my hand a final squeeze and heads off to mingle with my fellow attendees. However trained they are in Deep Flow's methods, there can't possibly be seven more people like Lilith. She is surely one in a million. I make a note to find out more about these 'lightworkers' after the weekend is over. Then I push through the crowd in search of Ruby, Natalia and Emily.

I soon find them in a corner, excitedly chatting away. They receive me with broad grins and draw me into a group hug.

'This is gonna change your lives,' Ruby says to me and Emily.

Emily looks at me, a little nervous. I grab her hand, remembering that, even though she's been attending Deep Flow sessions for years, this is her first weekender too.

'We're in this together,' I tell her. 'It'll be great. I just know it.'

At the front of the room, Lilith claps. It's time to begin.

FOURTEEN

I push my fingertips into the corners of the wooden box to see if I can prise it open. No joy. As I stand in the dark, I contemplate, once again, whether there is enough room to crouch down or if I might risk knocking the box over onto its side if I attempt it. I think of my fellow Deep Workers, alone inside each of their individual boxes. Are they struggling as much as I am? For a moment I think I hear the sound of someone crying and then I remember that this is a sensory deprivation box – the reality is that I can't hear a single thing.

It feels as if it's been at least two hours since Lilith unveiled the boxes to us. They are rectangular, around seven feet tall and painted entirely black. We've been assured there are holes punched through the wood so that we don't suffocate, but, as I stand inside what feels like a coffin, I can't help but question if that's true. I don't see any holes. And if there are holes, how can these boxes be soundproof?

Before we stepped into the boxes, Lilith waxed lyrical about what we'd learn from removing everything external with the aim of 'pouring ourselves back into our inner worlds'. She tells us sensory deprivation will enable us to 'dive deeper into

167

the psyche' and insists it will teach us patience, gratitude and who we are outside of our typical context.

I looked at the box, full of fear. The idea of being in a dark, enclosed space without any real perception of time wasn't something that appealed. Then Lilith added something else to the mix, telling us to 'strip ourselves of outside influences'. Literally.

Out of my peripheral vision, I saw the other women removing their clothes, some more reluctantly than others. Natalia nodded encouragement my way and I felt my face burn red as I became desperate to remain covered. Lilith seemed to sense this and gently approached. 'You don't need to hide any more, Sadie. We are your sisters. Be open. Be vulnerable. Embrace who you are.'

Too tired to protest, I took off my hoody, then my t-shirt, then my leggings. Standing in my bra and panties, conscious of the naked bodies around me, I knew that, if I didn't go all the way, I'd look as if I wasn't committed to the process or like I was undermining Lilith. Neither were viable options and so I took a deep breath before taking the final plunge. Then, I stepped into the box.

At first, it felt liberating, but now I'm cold and exhausted. It's Saturday afternoon and, after a night spent chanting, dancing, beating on drums, painting on huge sheets of paper with our fingers, feet, limbs, I have little else to give. Lilith told us we'd spend a total of thirty minutes in the box, but it already feels as if hours have passed. Every part of me aches, desperate to be enveloped in the warmth and comfort of my bed.

I think about Ruby and wonder how she is coping in her

box. Surely someone so used to a life of luxury would find this an almost insurmountable challenge? But then I remember that weird 'rawdogging' craze that swept social media not so long ago. An expression that used to be associated with sex became something new entirely, as white, cis-het, middle-class men began claiming they'd 'rawdogged' entire eight-hour flights – no water, no food, no phone use, bathroom breaks or entertainment (beyond staring at the flight map). But, what could've been construed as a form of meditation, an act that would pull people away from the trappings of modern life, drawing them closer to something deeper and more purposeful, was quickly clarified as a competitive act of machismo, in part, by the insatiable desire these men had to document their 'accomplishment'. It wasn't long before making fun of the rawdogging trend became more of a trend than rawdogging itself.

We spent breakfast this morning nibbling on dried fruit and nuts before a bowl of something not unlike porridge was passed around and we were each invited to dribble a sliver of it onto a plate. All in all, it was less food than I'd give to Selma in a single sitting. Then, we were told to strip down to our underwear before we were each given a cloth, asked to form a circle and turn towards the person on our left. As urns of cold water were handed to us by a select few women who seem to be volunteering for Lilith, we were instructed to wash the person in front of us, cleaning paint and dirt from our neighbour's skin as Lilith read aloud a passage discussing the importance of intimacy.

A lightning bolt of a memory broke through my

169

consciousness as I was cleaned by a stranger. Suddenly, I felt small again as I remembered being sat on a couch, a shirtless man bending over me. I successfully pushed the feeling down but, hours later, trapped inside my dark, quiet prison, I am haunted by it again.

Something wet drips onto my naked feet and, for a second, I fear I have wet myself, but then I realise my face is soaked with tears.

'Please,' I start to whisper. 'Please, let me go.'

Then, louder: 'I can't . . . I can't do this any more. Please. Let me out.'

I knock on the inside of the box. But no one seems to hear. I try pushing hard at the door again and again, until the box begins to rock and I am so terrified it will fall over with me inside that I stop immediately. Once I'm sure the box is stable, I settle for sliding down to the bottom and finding myself in a small squat, knees pressed against the corners of the box, heels raised, spine slammed against wood. I risk grazing my back as I slide my butt down to the bottom of the box. My knees push up in the opposite direction, pressing my shins against the door, my toes pointing down. I'm in the foetal position but sat up, unable to truly rest, yet slipping in and out of consciousness, flickers of dreams dancing at the edge of my somnambulist state. I remain like this, quietly weeping and audibly begging to be set free, until, inevitably my legs begin to go numb. Then, I panic.

How will I get up? What will happen to my legs if I don't restore the blood flow soon? I start to shout.

'Help! Please! I don't want to do this any more! Please!'

I think I hear a voice for a moment. Then a few others.

Paranoia creeps into the box beside me as I envision all of the women crowded around my wooden cell, listening to my cries of distress, watching me through the holes and laughing.

'How weak,' one of them says, and I'm sure I recognise Emily's voice.

'Pathetic!' cries another. 'She'll never be one of us.'

Lilith, meanwhile, says nothing. Just sighs disappointedly and folds the other women into group hug.

'Shut up,' I tell myself. 'It's not real. You're imagining things. It's not real.'

I begin to bring my mind back from the brink, but my body is in trouble too, and, as my panic grows, I realise there is only one thing I can do to help myself. I take a breath and begin to push as much weight as I can into one side of the box. It takes a few attempts but, eventually, I feel the entire unit rock over and there is an almighty bang as it crashes onto its side.

For a moment, I lie there, battered and bruised. Then, survival mode kicks in and I wriggle towards the top end of the box, finally able to stretch out my legs. I flail them about in the small amount of space I'm afforded, accidentally kicking at the walls more than once. I'm so desperate to regain feeling in my legs, I barely even register the damage I might be doing to them. More cuts and bruises, I suppose.

Perhaps this isn't so bad, I start to think. Perhaps I can just rest here now. Complete the remainder of this trial lying on my side. But then, just as I start to relax, the door to the box is thrust open and blinding light pours in. I am suddenly grabbed and dragged out and I become aware of a voice, Lilith's, shouting.

'What were you thinking?' she yells. 'Your selfishness, your laziness, has put your sisters at risk! How could you?'

Confusion consumes me as I squint into the light. I become aware of a handful of other women standing around watching me. It's far from the entire cohort, but enough to make me feel as if my worst fear has been realised. I make a vague attempt to cover the parts of myself I wish to keep private and start to stammer a response.

'I . . . I don't . . .'

'You toppled your box,' Lilith snaps. 'We're all *very* lucky the boxes to the left of you didn't all go down like dominoes. Never . . . *never* . . . in all my years of running retreats has anyone ever been so *selfish*.'

I'm startled by Lilith's raised voice and overwhelmed by self-disgust. But how could she think me selfish when I literally took a bullet for her? When everyone can see the scar just below my ribcage that proves it?

'I'm sorry,' I say, as I start to pick out faces in the crowd surrounding Lilith. Ruby. Debbie. Natalia. Andrea, who I'm surprised is medically allowed to be here. Bridget, who seems far too new to Deep Flow to be attending this baptism by fire. They are all mostly clothed now and I feel full of shame and horrendously self-conscious.

'I was about to let you out,' Lilith says. 'I was working my way along the line. All you had to do was wait your turn.'

'I didn't know you were . . . I . . . I panicked,' I say. 'My legs were . . . I felt . . .'

'It's scary for everyone,' Ruby pipes up. 'But that's how you know it's working.'

'I'm hurt that you couldn't just trust the process, Sadie,' Lilith says. 'You chose giving in to your own fear over protecting your sisters.'

'It's disgusting!' one of the women I don't know shouts.

'Really selfish,' I hear another say, as the others nod vigorously. Then, out of nowhere, Debbie muscles her way through the crowd of women and slaps me in the face. It's so unexpected that it almost knocks me off my feet. She hits me again, but, this time, I retaliate, going straight for her neck.

'Sisters!' Lilith screams. 'Stop this!'

'How dare you,' Lilith says, staring angrily at Debbie. 'Whatever her crimes, Sadie is one of us. She must be forgiven. Protected. It is up to us to help her grow beyond what we have witnessed in her today. It is up to us to surround her with love until she sees that there is no other way.'

As the women form a circle around me, I discover my t-shirt and panties only a few feet away. I'm not sure which I'm more grateful for: Lilith's forgiveness or being reunited with my clothes.

Lilith scoops me into her arms and begins to stroke my hair and rock me like a child. I start to cry, overflowing with gratitude.

'I'm sorry. I'm sorry. I'm sorry,' I say.

'My darling girl,' Lilith says. 'My sweet, sweet child. I love you so much. More than you could ever know. Surrender yourself, darling. Here, with us, there is nothing but love. We cradle you.'

As she says the last three words, the entire room, now all free of their boxes, speak in unison, repeating after their leader.

'We cradle you,' they say. And part of me believes them.

*   *   *

Sunday. The third day of the Soul Awakening weekend and I have not slept since Thursday night. The exhaustion is all consuming and I feel nauseous and dizzy. Praying silently to God, I hope I won't actually vomit. There's so little in my stomach, I doubt I'd regurgitate anything of substance, but the energy it would take to retch might finish me off.

There's talk of a 'cacao ceremony' and I tremble like an addict at the thought of anything that could give me much-needed fuel. Cacao is just hot chocolate, right? And, at this stage, even that could help keep me sane.

The stony silences and appalled looks of my fellow attendees melted away soon after Lilith demanded they be kind and held me so gently in front of them all. But, today, my body bears the scars of my ordeal. I am beaten and bruised from my time in the box, and, in my mind, I keep replaying Debbie's attack. It's clear any one of my so-called 'soul sisters' could turn on me at any moment and yet I wouldn't be without them. Deep Flow has become such a part of my life that I'm not sure if I'd know how to be outside of it. Beyond this community is a cold, hard world that I have no wish to navigate alone.

I catch Bridget staring at my grazed arm, an alarmed look on her face.

'It's not always like this,' I say, smiling, despite the lump in my throat.

'Are you sure you don't want to get checked over?' she whispers back. I shake my head and smile again. I can tell she wants to say more, but we are interrupted by the sound of a gong as the cacao ceremony begins.

As I suspected, it consists of hot chocolate and chanting. I barely register Lilith's words as she talks about consuming the drink mindfully and repeats the same mantra about pouring ourselves back into our inner worlds, 'nourishing the soul' as we do. I feel jittery one minute and totally drained the next. Is this what growth is meant to feel like? I don't feel nourished or cradled. Despite now being fully clothed again, I feel naked and seem to be continually ricocheting between a sparseness of feelings and a tsunami of emotion.

After the ceremony, we eat, just as we did yesterday: a palm full of dried fruit and nuts and a dribble of cold porridge. I obliterate it all within seconds and feel no different afterwards than I did before it arrived. I try to catch the eye of someone I know, but Natalia and Emily are at the furthest corners of the room and Ruby seems totally consumed by her own experience.

Music starts and we are encouraged to move, slowly at first. A voice inside me screams that I have nothing left to give, yet I push through dizziness and find a way to dance, my feet beating patterns into the hardwood floor as the music builds towards a more frenzied rhythm. Some members of our cohort manage some whoops and yells, but I am not one of them. My own voice is an empty husk lying at the bottom of my throat. I feel barely in control of my body as we move in tandem and then begin to freestyle, sweat covering our skin, many choosing to strip down to the bare essentials, some even choosing to wear nothing at all. This, especially, seems to please Lilith.

'Yes!' she shouts, smiling. 'Strip away the nonsense! Show me who you truly are!'

Is this who I truly am? My body feels almost useless, starved of food and sleep, beaten black and blue. What clothes still cling to me are basic, devoid of statements, slogans and personality. Yet still I move. Is it my soul that keeps me going? Beyond everything I have endured?

This epiphany is like a ray of light. Perhaps *this* is awakening, I realise. *This* is the self-knowledge I would've spent thousands to come here and discover, had I been able to afford to pay. Yes, I've suffered, but perhaps that suffering has merely been the hewing of a rough diamond.

The idea of this, surprisingly, propels me into laughter, a giggle that erupts from deep within and grows and grows until I can't control it. Hot tears stream down my face as I laugh hysterically. And then I am no longer laughing at all, and loud, shuddering sobs take over. Soon, I'm on my knees, hands pressed into the floorboards as I continue to cry. I notice I am not the only one.

A piece of fabric is dropped in front of me and I realise it's a white smock. I look around. The other women each have one too, likely one-size-fits-all given how baggy and long they are on the more petite members of the class. I slip on mine. It fits like a glove and I wonder how larger women would manage. I notice Debbie, who would barely be considered plus-sized, struggling to fit into her smock. Then I realise that she is the largest woman I've ever seen in the Deep Flow community. I'd feel sorry for her if she hadn't smacked the shit out of me yesterday. Despite wondering if she only did that because she feels she has a point to prove, right now I don't have the energy to sympathise with anyone but myself.

We're finally brought to rest and the sound of waves filters through the room as Lilith leads us all in a guided meditation. We ohm and ahh while Lilith taps the side of a Tibetan bowl and then, just as I start to feel as if I might fall asleep, she asks us to open our eyes.

'We're now ready for our closing circle,' Lilith says. 'And a final opportunity to stand in your truth and allow your sisters to witness it.'

I watch as, one by one, women from the group take their place in the centre of the circle, next to Lilith, and confess all manner of sins out loud. Everything from accidentally poisoning a neighbour's cat to breaking the arm of a high school bully to mild embezzlement. Several women, likely those with more harrowing truths to bring to light, are invited out of the circle to whisper their secrets to Lilith in a quiet corner hung with a makeshift silk curtain and a few dream catchers.

After each admission, Lilith places a thumb print of 'Ayurvedic oil' in the centre of the confessor's forehead, in order to 'cleanse the third eye', before stroking a little more across each of their hands, absolving them of all guilt.

As it gets closer and closer to my turn, my heart starts to pound. Part of me is desperate to let it all out. Tell the whole room who I am and what I did all those years ago. But a bigger part of me, the part of me that wants to run, is busy trying to think of another, lesser crime I can confess to. Big enough to get the others off my back, small enough for them to think I'm still a good person. A person worthy of being in the Deep Flow community.

'Sadie?' Lilith says, ushering me to my feet.

I stumble into the circle. The incantation Lilith is speaking aloud in order to bless my forthcoming confession sounds as if it is coming from underwater. I open my mouth, but nothing comes out. Next thing I know, Lilith takes me by the shoulders and guides me out of the circle towards the curtained corner.

When we arrive, Lilith holds both my hands and stares into my eyes.

'You can tell me anything,' she says. 'Let me carry the weight of your secrets for you. Let's rinse your body clean so you can move forward feeling lighter. Freer.'

I try to force the words from my mouth, but all that tumbles out is a raspy breath.

'I . . . I . . .'

Lilith leans closer.

'I . . . can't,' I finally say.

She swallows, clearly disappointed, and I hate myself for letting her down. But then she pulls me close, breathing into my hair, and I am reminded of her lips against mine.

'Whenever you're ready,' she says. 'I'm here, Sadie. I'm always here.'

FIFTEEN

It's almost four in the morning when I finally arrive home. Shaky and exhausted, I now understand why Lilith advised we get a taxi to and from the Soul Awakening Weekend and I'm grateful to not have to drive. I share my cab with Andrea and we barely say a word to one another the entire journey, but, somehow, the silence feels comfortable.

This means that getting out of the car is like emerging from the safety of a cocoon. It's late summer and so dawn is already breaking and I feel totally exposed beneath the bright light of the sun. The inside of the house, however, is shrouded in darkness. I move silently through the hallway, careful not to wake Derek. Selma is tapping on the side of her cage in the living room and I softly approach her and whisper hello. Derek's done a great job. Her cage is clean and Selma looks happy and well fed.

It's only two hours before I need to be up and getting ready for work, and I worry that if I attempt to sleep, I won't wake up in time. My body is exhausted, but my brain is wired, a strange energy running through me as if I've taken a stimulant of some kind. My awareness of everything around me is heightened: the sound of tree branches brushing against the exterior wall of the house as a slight breeze slips through them. A muffled conversation as two people leave their home and step into the street before heading to their car. The buzz of the refrigerator. The whir of the bedroom fan. The tick of the clock on the wall. The house is alive. A living, breathing entity that merely allows me to coexist alongside the other beings currently thriving within its ecosystem. I am insignificant. A guest in my own home. Transient.

There's a note on the table, written in Derek's scrawling cursive: 'Back in a few hours. Gone to pick up a surprise. Love you. X'

I'm completely mystified. What kind of surprise would he need to leave the house before 4 a.m. to collect?

I reach for my phone and then remember Lilith advising us against using technology for as long as we can after the retreat. I'll just have to trust that Derek is fine.

My eyes are too tired to read and a nap will surely drag me under for days. Still mindful of Lilith's words, I decide I should stay away from my phone and the digital junk food of social media, so, in the end, television feels like the lesser evil.

I close the door firmly and switch it on, the volume lowered to ten. After flitting around channels for a few minutes, I settle on a televangelist. I'm reminded of Sundays spent in church during my childhood. I'd learned to sing there. Met Raheem. Attended countless events. It made me feel as if I were a part of an extended family for a very long time and, while church is no longer a part of my life, there's a comforting familiarity in this TV preacher's ranting. And, unlike the perfectly mani-cured women encouraging me to shop for things I don't need on every other channel, I can, at least, rest assured this guy won't try to sell me anything.

I snack on some crackers in an attempt to gently bring my stomach back into a normal eating pattern. It growls loudly with hunger, but starving it for almost three days seems to have destroyed my appetite. One of the front teeth on my bottom row is a little wobbly and I can't resist wiggling it around. Then, to my dismay, it falls out. I hold it in my hand. Blood and spittle dotted across my palm.

Setting it down on the table beside me, I reach into my mouth to feel for the cavity it has left behind, only to notice the tooth next to it is also far less stable than it should be. I attempt to push it into my gum. *Not you as well*, I think. I can't afford to have two teeth replaced right now. One is bad enough. Is this the consequence of my rigorous weekend? The price I must pay for an awakened soul?

I'm wondering this when a loud commercial wakes me. I'm not sure how long I've been dozing and I discover that, while I slept, my phone battery died. I check the side table. No crackers. No tooth. No mouthful of blood. I'm relieved and then horrified that I've slept long enough to dream. While I scramble for a phone charger, the TV noise starts feeling aggressive, as if someone is kicking at the sides of my skull. I switch a lamp on and turn the TV off, thankful when its flickering light disappears from the wall opposite.

A slice of daybreak pierces through the gap in the curtains and, when my phone charges up enough, the display reveals I've been out for a couple of hours. Somehow I feel worse than I did before I slept. I'm even more jittery and dizzy with exhaustion.

But I have to go to work. Given my abrupt resignation and the guilt I feel for continuing to deceive him, I can't let Caleb down again.

In the shower, I let the heat cleanse me of everything the weekend has put me through. Lilith swears by cold water and ice baths, encouraging us to do the same, but, right now, I need to feel truly clean. I crank the temperature up until its almost scalding and scrub away at my skin with citrus and lavender foam.

I step out of the shower and slather myself with lotion before donning my bathrobe. With each layer of skincare, I feel more alive.

'You can do this, Sadie,' I say into the mirror, as I comb my edges into perfect little waves and ready myself for the breakfast of champions. It's not even seven thirty yet. I've got almost an hour to give my churning stomach a proper meal.

After throwing on some clothes, I check on Selma on the way to the kitchen. I'm already fantasising about gorging myself on scrambled eggs and maple syrup pancakes, raiding the refrigerator for fruit and dosing up on caffeine.

But my heart stops as I approach Selma's cage.

She's not moving. Her tiny chest is still, her eyes clamped shut as if in pain.

No. Not this. Not now.

I'm not ready.

I open the cage and scoop her out, cradling her tiny body in one hand. I lie her down on the couch and use my index finger to pump at her chest – a desperate bid to get her heart going again. But the truth is that I have no idea what I'm doing.

I grab the car keys, put Selma back in her cage and take it with me. Gripped by panic, I start up the car engine. It's only when I put my foot down on the accelerator that I realise I've forgotten to put on my shoes. No time to run back inside, I decide. Selma's body is still warm. If there's any chance of saving her, I have to go now.

As I take off, it happens again. Another flash of a memory. My body tenses for a moment as it remembers the feeling of impact, of being thrown forward and then shunted back, my seatbelt cutting into my neck. I shake my head, shake the feeling out of me as best I can, but my jaw is tight, teeth clenching as if my mouth is wired shut. Tears sting the backs of my eyes and my sweaty palms slip slightly on the steering wheel. I shouldn't be driving like this. But what choice do I have?

I almost skip a red light and am forced to slam on the brakes, but, aside from that, I make it to the veterinarian's without incident. Please God, let them be open, I pray, as I pull into the parking lot. I jump out of the car and pull the cage out of the passenger seat. The building is dark inside and I knock on the window, hoping for signs of life. Eventually, I spot movement in the back: June.

She waddles to the door and opens it for me.

'We don't open 'til—

I barge past her, putting the cage on the reception countertop.

'I knew it,' June says, pointing at my bare feet. 'Cray-cray.'

'It's Selma,' I say, ignoring her.

'Who?'

'The warbler I told you about. She's not breathing.'

'You left the house with no shoes on for a bird?'

'Please,' I say, clasping my hands together in front of me. 'Just help her, will you?'

June tuts, sighs and walks towards the cage. She pulls some blue latex gloves out of a box stuck to the wall and proceeds to put them on. I notice Selma's yellow chest is barely visible now, her grey wings folded neatly in, as if she has been drained of all colour.

'You know I'm not an actual, fully qualified vet, right? I'm still in school.'

I nod. Not because I knew that, but because, whatever her qualifications, June surely knows more than me and is, currently, the only hope I have.

'Is she still alive?' I ask, as June pokes and prods her tiny body.

'Barely,' June says. 'What do you want me to do?'

'*Help her*, obviously.'

'Well, there are lots of ways we could do that. We could euthanise her—'

'No!' I snap. 'I'll pay you. Whatever you want. I want you to save her.'

'Okay, cray-cray. I'll do my best. But Doc McGill ain't here for another thirty minutes and, like I said . . .'

She looks at me and sighs.

'You got work today?'

I nod.

'There's a Shoe City on the other side of the parking lot.'

'Okay. Thank you,' I say. 'You'll . . . do everything you can, right?'

She rolls her eyes. 'Everything I can,' she says, sounding bored.

I'm halfway out the door before I realise.

'I don't have my phone. Or my wallet.'

June rolls her eyes and groans. 'You said you had money. How you gonna pay for the bird?'

'I'll bring the money later. I promise.'

June disappears into the back for a moment and then returns with her purse. It's a big brown thing made of fake crocodile skin. She fishes around inside it before producing a fifty-dollar bill and handing it to me.

'Here,' she says. 'Can't have you proving that Southern stereotype of going around barefoot now, can we?'

She doesn't smile. If anything, she looks mildly annoyed, but I am still bowled over by her kindness. I thank her profusely and then jot down my Prisma office extension number on a lime green Post-It note.

'If anything happens . . .'

'I'll call,' June replies.

Eighteen minutes later, I arrive at Prisma's office, wearing a pair of cheap black ballet flats, hoping to dash into the bathroom and clean up my face before I'm put to work.

But, when I arrive, Cindy and Caleb are standing together in reception speaking in hushed tones. Caleb spots me and smiles broadly and I wonder what further bad news he's about to dispense regarding the broken AC.

'Sadie!' he says, and then, suddenly, his smile vanishes. 'If that's even your real name.'

'What?'

'Did Lilith send you here? To spy?' Cindy has her hand on her hip, her mouth set as if she is crunching down on a wasp.

'I don't know what you're—'

'Stop pretending, Sadie. We know you're part of the Deep Flow "*community*".'

Cindy does air quotes as Caleb grows pink with rage, struggling to speak. Cindy takes her tablet out of his hands and hands it to me, tapping the screen with a red-painted nail to reveal a group photo on social media.

Then, I remember: the flash of a phone camera at the very end of our Soul Awakening weekend as we were all made to gather round. I'd been so tired that the moment had scarcely registered with me.

'How did you . . . ?'

'My cousin posted it,' Cindy says, her top lip curling upwards. 'Debbie?'

I feel as if I've been kicked in the stomach. 'Debbie's your cousin?'

'Uh huh. I've been trying to get her out of that nasty little cult for years.'

'Deep Flow isn't a cult,' I say, defensive.

Caleb steps in. 'I assure you it very much is. My wife fell victim to it too. But then you know that already, don't you? You've known it from the moment you first stepped foot in here.'

My words dissolve in my throat.

'I spoke to Debbie,' Cindy tells me. 'She says you were there the day of the shooting. That you took a bullet for Lilith.'

'It was . . . just a graze,' I mutter.

My tongue feels paralysed, feet rooted to the spot.

'What is it you want, Sadie?' Caleb asks me. He seems weary now and my own fatigue begins to catch up with me too. As the room starts to spin, I fight the urge to collapse. With the AC still broken, the heat is immense. An electric fan they've set up points directly towards Caleb and Cindy, but I'm standing behind it, the sun shining through the reception window and directly onto my back.

'I said, what do you want?' Caleb repeats, angrier this time.

The truth is that I don't know what I want. But I have a hunch that getting as close to Lilith as possible, close enough to bask in the glow of her reflective glory, might bring me somewhere near to getting it. The information I hoped to bring back from this mad mission was supposed to be currency. Something I could trade for love.

'This is all just a big misunderstanding,' I say. 'A coincidence.'

'You really think I'm stupid, don't you?' Caleb spits. 'You don't think I noticed all those questions you asked about my wife?'

'I was just getting to know you.'

'No. You were digging for dirt. So you could report it back to Lilith.'

Cindy walks into the open-plan office and picks up a box full of my things. She returns, face like thunder, and shoves it into my chest.

'I let you in,' Caleb continues. 'Gave you a job. Showed you nothing but kindness. And the whole time you were taking advantage of me. Feeding off my pain for your own personal . . . I don't know what.'

'It wasn't like that,' I say, with the intention of attempting to explain further. But Cindy quickly bulldozes me.

'He's a good man. He doesn't deserve anything that's happened to him. And you . . . . you're evil. Twisted in the head. I should've known it from the start.'

Something clangs in my heart as her words hit home. This isn't the first time I've been called evil. Twisted. Sick. Broken.

'I'm sure I don't need to say this, because no doubt it's pretty fucking obvious, but just in case it's *not* abundantly clear to you . . . you're fired, Sadie. Now get out before I call the cops.'

He doesn't need to tell me twice, and I head for the door, stopping only to issue one more parting apology.

'I'm truly sorry,' I say. 'This all just got so out of hand. And, for what it's worth, I really did love working with you.'

'OUT!' Cindy screams, so loudly I think her eyeballs might pop out. Her feet almost certainly leave the floor for a moment.

After leaving, I head straight for McGill's. I notice June looking bored at reception as I grow close enough to see through the front window. She's scrolling through something on her phone with one hand while her other cradles her chin, elbow resting on the countertop. When I enter, she immediately looks nervous – strange for someone who so clearly doesn't give a shit about anything. I decide, within a split second, that she's merely been startled by the bell on the door jangling on my way in and ask her how Selma is getting on.

She puts her phone down and shakes her head gravely.

'We did all we could.'

'We?'

'Well . . . Me. It was just me. Dr McGill is stuck in traffic.'

For a while I don't say a word.

'Do you understand what I'm saying?' June asks eventually.

'I . . .'

There's another silence until June smacks her gums loudly and adds an almost imperceptible eye roll to the conversation.

'Um . . . she's . . . . your warbler has . . . *expired*. She's . . . dead. She's dead. I'm sorry.'

I am immediately hit by a cascade of grief. It's unbearable and, feeling as if the floor might give way beneath me, I crumple into a nearby chair.

June says something about not charging me and not to worry about the body, they'd take care of it, but it sounds as if she is speaking to me from the side of a pool and I am sinking into blue. And then, suddenly, I am underwater, Gaultier swimming towards me, arms outstretched.

'Hey. Hey!' June yells into my face, snapping me out of my stupor. 'I get that you're sad and all, but can we keep it moving? Dr McGill will be here soon and I don't want her nine-fifteen seeing you here, miserable. It's not a good look for the business.'

I hear the loud drip of a water cooler I haven't noticed before and, weirdly, it grounds me. Reminds me of what's important.

'The body. What did you say you'd done with the body?'

'Oh. We can get rid of—'

'I'll take it.'

'You sure?'

I nod, never surer of anything in my life.

I didn't get to bury my daughter.

This would be different.

June hands me the cage with Selma inside and I thank her before carrying it out into the parking lot.

'I'll . . . make sure I bring you back the money for the shoes,' I say, as the bell on the door chimes again, signalling my departure.

Tears swirl within me, threatening to bubble over and spill out onto the tarmac. Fighting to push them down, I count the steps to my car, count the seconds until I'm no longer in public and able to grieve in peace.

'Sadie?'

If it's at all possible for my heart to sink any lower, it does. The hairs on the back of my neck prickle at the sound of this all-too-familiar voice and I turn around.

'What are you doing here?' Mumtaz asks. It's the first time I've seen her in months, since that awful dinner party that led to Derek and I going to bed on a fight.

'I'm . . . the veterinarian's. What are *you* doing . . .'

Thankfully, she doesn't need me to finish my sentence. 'Caleb Crawford. You know, the guy whose wife . . .' She mimes shooting a gun and makes a little 'pew pew' sound. 'His office is in this retail plaza. Look, I hope you don't feel it's a conflict of interest, given our friendship and the fact that she attacked *your* yoga studio . . . or whatever it is, but I *am* working on the case. It's pretty fascinating, actually.'

'You're his lawyer?' I say. Given it's meant to be a sprawling metropolis, LA can really feel like the smallest town in the world sometimes.

'Oh, Sadie. I *really* hope that's cool.'

190

She drags the word 'really' out for several seconds. It's like nails on a chalkboard.

I say nothing.

'It's just a job. I have a very neutral view on it all.'

I stare at her, still unable to fathom how any of this could be happening.

'So, what *is* that anyway?' Mumtaz says, trying to get a better a look inside the cage. She takes it out of my hands and holds it up for closer inspection. 'Is it a rat?'

Anger flushes through me, like a cloud of blood spreading through a pool of water. I picture a pot of rage soup boiling over, its contents sizzling as they splash across the stove top.

'SHE'S A BIRD, YOU FUCKING BITCH!' I scream, yanking the cage out of her arms. Mumtaz pales and her mouth opens slightly in shock. As I get into my car, slamming the door behind me, I realise it's the first time I've ever seen her speechless. I dread to think what Derek will make of our interaction when word of this gets back to him, but, right now, I am past caring what anyone else thinks of me.

Tyres screeching and the cage strapped into the passenger seat, I gun it down the road towards home, envisioning being in my armchair with Selma in my lap as I prepare to see her out of this world properly. But when I arrive home there's a car I don't recognise parked in the driveway alongside Derek's and I'm forced to pull up on the road. On closer inspection, I realise the car is a rental, but the furry dice hung on the rear-view mirror are unmistakable – I've seen them in every car Raheem has ever had. He's said for years now that it's 'bad juju' to drive without them.

Bewildered, I head into the house, putting Selma's cage down on the chair by the door as I slip quietly through the hallway. I can hear Derek and Raheem's voices in the kitchen. Their conversation comes to an abrupt halt the moment they see me. The table in front of them is laden with pancakes, syrup, cups of coffee and fresh fruit. My angry stomach growls loudly.

'Not talking about me, are you?' I say, with a nervous laugh.

'Hey, girl!' Raheem says, weakly. His voice cracks and his smile is somehow sad. 'What's going on?'

'You tell me,' I say, defensively. 'You didn't say you were coming to LA.'

He raises both hands half-heartedly. 'Surprise.'

Derek gets up and draws me in for a hug.

'I missed you this weekend,' he says.

I nod. 'Missed you too.'

It almost sounds true. He pulls away and sits back down.

'Raheem's been filling me in on a few things. Kind of seems like there's a lot I don't know about, baby.'

'What?' I ask, eyeballing Raheem, accusations of betrayal etched across my face.

'I've just been telling him about some of our conversations since you moved to LA. You know, before you quit replying to my messages,' Raheem says, his eyes meeting mine.

My heart slows to a slightly more normal rate. Maybe this means he hasn't *completely* ratted me out.

'I leave you on read for a few days and you fly all the way out here to . . . what? Tell me off?'

'It's been way more than a few days, Sadie,' Raheem says, a hard edge to his voice.

'We're concerned that Deep Flow is controlling aspects of your life that maybe it shouldn't,' Derek tells me.

I scoff.

'Aren't you supposed to be in the edit today?'

'Day off,' Derek replies, without batting an eyelid, and I couldn't be more disappointed. Or more desperate to be left to my own devices, without the pressure of having to explain myself to people who couldn't possibly understand.

'It's a community. A way of life. A support system,' I tell him. 'I've never felt so protected or accepted or . . . seen. Lilith, she sees me. And, even though I'm flawed, she loves me anyway.'

'*I* love you anyway,' Derek says, as if he has some sort of monopoly over it.

'We both do,' Raheem follows up.

'Yeah, so much that you've both been sat here for God knows how long talking smack about me behind my back.'

'It wasn't like that. We—'

'What *is* this? Some kind of intervention? Some plan to take me away from the one thing in LA that has made me feel like something other than just your plus one?'

'You're not my . . . Sadie, I honestly had no idea you were feeling this way.'

'Why would you?' I ask. 'When was the last time you asked me how my day was and actually wanted a genuine answer?'

Derek's mouth moves but no words come out.

It doesn't matter. There's nothing he can say to change the way I feel anyway. Or change my mind about what I plan to do next.

I grab my phone from where it was charging in the living room, leave the house and press the button on my keys to unlock my car. There's a satisfying double beep.

'Sadie, sweetie, don't do this,' Raheem says, following me out onto the driveway. 'We just want to help. Have some breakfast with us, at least. Come on.'

'No,' I say, practically spitting the word into his face. 'I don't feel like I can trust you any more, Raheem. You're the one person, the *one* person other than my family who knows about my past. Do you have any idea what it's taken for me to not just cut you off so I can have a clean break? For me to trust that you won't ruin this new life I've made for myself?'

'I know. I *know*,' Raheem says. 'I wasn't gonna come. Even when Jenna and Ashley told me you haven't spoken to them in months. That you've been ignoring their messages. I thought, maybe you're just doing you. But then I saw your mother in the grocery store and *she* said you'd barely spoken to her since you moved to LA. And that's not you, Sadie. Something's wrong here.'

'I've spoken to her plenty,' I snap, so sure of my words, but then, suddenly forced to think about it, I realise I can't remember the last time I called home.

Tears well up inside, but I refuse to break. Not yet. Not until I'm sure I'm safe.

And then Raheem makes a huge mistake.

'Please,' he says. 'Just come back inside and talk.'

He reaches towards me and grabs my wrist and it is as if time slows down. My body stiffens and I can almost feel my pupils dilate. He looks into my eyes and immediately realises his error. But it's too late. My dam of tears crumbles and, within seconds, I twist myself out of his grip and jump into my car.

'Sadie! Sadie, please!' he shouts, tapping on the side window of my car. 'Sadie, come on! I didn't mean to . . . You know I'm not . . . Sadie, this is *me*. Please!'

I do a screeching, too-fast U-turn in the street and speed away, leaving a crestfallen Raheem standing on the sidewalk.

My escape and the adrenaline that comes with it leave me feeling as if I've just been on a rollercoaster and I begin to laugh through my tears.

Let Derek and Raheem talk about me. They can do it until the cows come home and eat their dinner and go to bed for all I care. I know now exactly where I need to be.

Fifteen minutes into my drive, my phone rings: no caller ID.

I pick up and Sarah's voice is filtered through my car speakers.

'Sadie-girl!' she says, jubilantly. 'How are you?'

Fuck. This is all I need.

'I'm fine,' I reply, my tone clipped. 'Look, it's not really the best time, Sarah.'

'Well, it never seems to be these days, hun. Which, I guess, is why you don't often pick up my calls. So here I am! No caller ID! Gotcha!'

She giggles as if she's pulled off the heist of the century. Then she takes a breath.

'Um . . . so look, there's no easy way to say this, but I've been reviewing my roster of clients in the hope of trimming a little fat here and there. You know, just so that I have the time and space to be the best agent possible for my *most committed* clients. And, well, it's absolutely nothing personal, but I don't feel that you're currently in a place where you're able to offer what the companies we work with need. That's no reflection on your talent or skill or . . .'

Her words fade away as if someone has slowly turned the volume down on my speakers and, suddenly, I am underwater again. I feel myself slide out of my body entirely and someone else, I'm not sure who, takes the reins long enough to keep my car moving safely forward.

I'm not sure how far or for how long my inner being drifts this time, just that, when I snap out of it, I'm more sure than ever of what I need to do.

'I have to go,' I tell Sarah, hanging up on her just as she begins a new sentence.

One of the perks of being an Amber member is that Lilith has given me access to the key store by the studio, so that I have 'a sanctuary. A place to just *be* whenever the stress of the outside world becomes too much'. Once inside the safety of the studio, I can heap the pillows and blankets into a pile and finally get some rest. A vital chance to recalibrate.

But, when I arrive, Lilith is there, preparing the room for this evening's class. She spots me – mascara-smudged, messy hair, ill-fitting shoes – and stops in her tracks.

'Hey, you,' she says. And there's that sparkling smile again.

'I . . . didn't think you'd be here,' I say, genuinely surprised she's not still sleeping off the weekend as I imagine everyone else is.

'I don't need that much sleep,' she tells me, revealing yet another superpower. 'And nothing brings me more joy than making the most of a morning.'

Lilith loops an arm round my waist, then guides me deeper into the studio. The incense is already burning and there are fresh flowers in a vase by the window. She sets down some cushions and then envelopes me in a blanket.

For a while, we sit in silence, our eyes shut, foreheads pressed together. It is like a sort of prayer, one all our own, and soon my chaotic thoughts begin to calm, like choppy ocean waves finally brought to rest.

Eventually, she asks me to tell her what's going on with me and, unlike before with Derek and Raheem, I don't feel as if this is an interrogation at all. Instead, it is more like Lilith has softly opened a door that was always there and gently offered me a chance to walk through it.

And so I do. I tell her everything. Right from the very beginning.

Seventeen Years Earlier

I slam my foot down on the accelerator and speed off, a roaring, raging Gaultier growing smaller and smaller in my rear-view mirror as he stands, half-naked, in the road behind me.

There's a moment where it occurs to me that, after months of practice, I'm actually, successfully driving alone and it's about sixty seconds after this thought that everything starts to go wrong.

Two cars that seem to be driving in convoy overtake me just before the lights turn red. They make it, I don't, and I'm left stuck, waiting, terrified that Gaultier will jump in his own vehicle and catch up to me. I picture him, hot on my tail for block after block, until we reach a twisted, country lane and he forces me off the road.

I drum on the steering wheel, silently praying the lights will change and trying not to think of the horrors I saw in Gaultier's pool house. How long had this been going on? And could there be other girls younger than me?

After what seems like hours, the lights finally change and I'm racing through traffic now, weaving in and out of lanes like I've driven for years. Maybe I get too confident. Or maybe my concentration lapses, another flash of Gaultier penetrating my subconscious. Whatever it is, I take my eye of the ball for just a split second.

And then I see what I think is a dog dart out in front of me. I swerve to miss it, but feel a thud against the bumper as it rebounds off the corner of the car. Then I'm spinning out of control, desperately pulling at the steering wheel in an attempt to stop the inevitable. The car smashes into another parked vehicle at the side of the road and Elijah's windscreen cracks and starts to cave in before the airbag explodes into my face. As I lift my head up, there's a ringing in my ears and the sound of people screaming. The wing mirror is, thankfully, still intact and I squint into it to see what's going on behind me.

A tiny multicoloured clump lies in the road, a woman bent over it, inconsolable, as another woman attempts to calm her down. There's a man stood nearby on a cell phone. He keeps running his hand through his hair and then putting his hand over his mouth as he looks nervously back at the scene. And then he stares straight at me and starts to approach.

Panic takes hold and I force the truck into reverse, marvelling at how it's able to move at all given how busted the front is.

The man starts shouting, 'Hey! What the hell are you— No! No, don't you dare leave! No!'

But I know he doesn't understand. I *have* to go. Because the moment I get out of the car and look at what I've done, it becomes real.

'You sure you don't want a drink, sweetie?' the woman asks. 'Not even water?'

Maybe they'd be able to track me down through the DNA I've left on the glass, I think. But, then again, I have already dripped blood on her vinyl flooring and my fingerprints are all over her house phone now. The horse has well and truly bolted.

'Um . . . okay. Water would be good, thank you.'

She smiles, satisfied. 'Lemme get you a bandage for that cut on your head too,' she says, having already given me a pack of cotton pads and some Neosporin to work with.

I tell my brother to come quickly and ask no questions, the black ink of his Sharpie now smudged on my arm but, mercifully, his new cell number is still legible. After knocking on the door of a random house fifteen minutes' drive from where the accident happened, I'm careful not to arouse suspicion. I attempt to communicate with Elijah in code, explaining that I had to take his truck, but can't tell him why and now he needs to find a way to come get me.

'What the fuck, Sadie?' he yells down the phone. 'You better be glad Antonio has a car I can borrow.'

The woman stands a mere two yards away from me during

the entire course of the phone call and, as Elijah's voice increases in volume, I fear my cover will be blown. I parked the Chevy around the corner and lied that I'd fallen over and hit my head on a fence. Now that I've hung up the phone, however, she's attempting to help me clean out the wound and it's clear she's suspicious.

'You've got all these little bits of something in here,' she says, pulling out a pair of tweezers. On further investigation, she tells me she has discovered tiny shards of glass trapped inside the cut.

'How did these happen to be here, do you think?'

I shrug my shoulders. The woman puts her tools down and sighs.

'You know, if you're in trouble, you can tell me. I might be able to help.'

'You *are* helping,' I reply, managing a smile. 'Thank you for letting me use your phone.'

She stares at me for a moment and I hope she will relent, but have no such luck.

'Is it your dad? Is he . . . does he have a temper?'

'No!' I say, alarmed. 'He's not like that at all. Neither's my momma. They're both good people. Promise.'

'And your brother? Sounded like he was pretty mad on the phone.'

I look directly into her eyes in the hope this will make her believe me.

'I really did just fall.'

She moves away, still not quite convinced.

'How about some cookies?' she says. I couldn't stand to eat

a thing but I nod enthusiastically anyway, in a bid to change the subject. Hopefully, my brother will arrive before they hit the plate.

Ten minutes later, I'm trying not to gag on a chocolate chip and, suddenly, there's a loud banging on the door. My first thought is that the police have found me, so I'm grateful to see my brother step over the threshold. His face is like thunder, but the moment he claps eyes on me his anger dissolves into concern.

We issue polite niceties before heading out of the door and, as we round the street corner, Elijah spots his rusty orange pick-up truck. The windscreen is broken, the front fog light smashed in and the bumper hangs by a thread.

'Tell me everything,' he says. We go and sit in Antonio's Cadillac and I start from the beginning, watching my brother's eyes widen in horror. At several points in the story he punches the steering wheel or curses under his breath. Part of me is scared he'll go over to Gaultier's and tear him to pieces. Another part of me is so angry that I'm not sure I'll mind if he does.

When I tell him about the clump in the road, Elijah starts asking questions. Lots of them. But the truth is, I don't know for sure what it was. Only that what I hope it was and what my gut tells me happen to be two different things.

'We need to find out,' he says. 'We gotta go back there.'

I cry and beg and plead, but, in the end, I relent. He drives me to a nearby Chuckie Cheese, hands me a ten-dollar bill and tells me to wait inside until he's back. I do as I'm told and spend forty minutes staring at a strawberry milkshake

I can't stomach. When he returns, he is ghost-like. It is as if something has broken inside him, something essential that can never be repaired. There would need to be a whole new Elijah after this.

As soon as I see him, I start to cry, tears splashing all over the table in big, salty drops. He grabs me and speaks through his teeth.

'Don't you do that. We can't do that now. Not here.'

He drags me into the parking lot, and on the leather front seats of Antonio's Cadillac, I hear the news that my life is over.

'Okay. Here's what we're gonna do,' my brother tells me. 'We're gonna say I was driving. That you weren't even there.'

'No. No, no, no. We can't do that,' I sob.

'We can. I'm military. They'll go easy on me—'

'You're Black!' I scream, tears and snot now covering my face. 'You'll die in jail.'

'Well, better me than you!' He roars back, and I realise he is crying now too. 'You're smart, Sadie. You got a chance to make something of your life. I ain't letting you throw all that away just because some nasty old pervert took advantage of you.'

'He's not a pervert,' I say, quietly.

Elijah laughs through his tears. 'You reckon not, huh? Reckon you still love him and he really loves you? Even after that shit you just saw?'

He shakes his head and then lays it on the steering wheel.

'Crazy to me how smart you are in so many ways, but so *fucking* stupid in others. Book smart, ain't you? But no god-damn common sense. You wouldn't last a second in jail, kid.'

And my gut, the same gut that knew right from the beginning

that I had killed a child out there on the road, rises up once more and tells me that Elijah is absolutely right.

My one condition is that we tell Momma and Daddy the truth and Elijah fights me on this all the way home. I tell him that, if he refuses, I'll go straight to the cops and turn myself in. When we arrive home, Elijah pulls the car into the driveway and looks me square in the eye.

'You know that, if we gonna tell them the truth 'bout the accident, you gonna have to talk to them 'bout all that stuff before, right? That stuff with your dance teacher.'

The idea of sitting across from Momma and Daddy and talking about Gaultier makes an ugly, two-headed monster of shame and fear begin to squirm in my belly. But I also know that it's the only way. If Momma and Daddy know the truth, there's a little hope that they might have a better idea of how to resolve this mess than Elijah does. An idea that keeps us both out of jail.

My brother tells me to go to my room as he closes the door to the kitchen and sits Momma and Daddy down. A hushed conversation follows and I hear something smash before Momma comes running into my room. She says nothing, just hugs me while Daddy stands in the doorway, uncomfortable in his own skin.

An hour later, however, and they have so much to say their words trip over one another. I listen to them arguing through the walls of my bedroom before I eventually get up and open my door a crack, allowing fragments of their debate to drift in.

'. . . I don't wanna have to choose between my kids . . .'

'. . . Maybe Sadie would only get juvie . . .'

'. . . Her life would still be over. What's she gonna do with that on her record? Work at the Chicken Shack?'

I slip into the hall and sit on the floor outside the kitchen, drawing my knees up to my chest the way the girl in Gaultier's pool house did when our eyes met. Maybe she and I aren't so different, I realise. Maybe I'm still a kid after all.

'We have to tell the truth,' Daddy says. 'It's the only way Fontaine will get what's coming to him.'

'Don't be so naïve,' Momma says. 'He's a wealthy white man. You really think they gonna believe a little Black girl over him? Your white mom and my white dad might mean you and me light-skinned enough to get a bigger slice of life that most folk round here. But you best believe our privilege don't stretch that far.'

'Don't you talk to me like I don't know nothin'!' Daddy shouts, slamming his fist down on the kitchen table and making me jump out of my skin. I can count on one hand the number of times he's raised his voice at Momma. 'My father was *lynched* for taking my momma out one too many times and you well aware of that. I *ain't* stupid.'

'I know, Curtis, I know,' Momma says, softer now. 'I'm just reminding you that change is slow round these parts. My Mom and Pops couldn't get married 'til nearly twelve years after I was born.'

'You told this story a hundred times, Dee. And I seen the pictures of you at the wedding. I don't need to hear it again,' Daddy says, sounding tired.

'I'm telling you 'cos I'm trying to make a point. Point being

that all that wasn't that long ago now, was it? Sadie goes to a
forced integration school. Elijah went to the same one. Our
little girl's best friend still gets bullied for being too dark.'

'Kirby?'

'Yeah! You ask me, that's why she stopped dancing.'

Daddy snorts and his rage-filled retort sounds as if it comes
from between clenched teeth: 'Or maybe she quit dancing 'cos
her teacher was a fiddling, trifling, nasty little . . . *fuck.*'

It's the first time I've ever heard Daddy curse and he spits
the word out with such violence and vitriol I feel sweat start
to prickle in my armpits. It's becoming more and more clear
that Momma and Daddy have as little idea as me and Elijah
about what we should do.

'They won't believe her,' Momma says, so quietly I almost
miss it.

'What makes you so sure?'

Momma says nothing for a while and then sighs.

'Because it happened to me. Not in the same way. I was
grown at the time. But . . . . this colleague of mine, years ago,
before you and I met . . . he . . . grabbed me. In the supply
closet. And . . . well. I reported him. He tried to convince
them I wanted it. I told them I didn't. Eventually, they said
they had "grounds to believe I'd led him on" and they moved
me to another department.'

Momma tells the second half of the story quickly, her words
pouring out like the rapid fire of a machine gun, as if talking
fast will help her escape the past.

'Denise. Baby. I didn't know. How could I have not known?
All these years and I never knew that about you.'

'That's because it *ain't* about me,' Momma tells him. 'It's *never* about us, Curtis. It's about *them* and their ego and their violence and their Lord knows what else. Me? I moved on. Put it in a box and left that box in a cupboard in the old building I used to work in. And when I left I chose not to take it with me. But trust me when I tell you that we Black women have to fight *every day* to prove ourselves. With every damn thing. And it's almost never enough.'

Daddy says nothing for a while. I'm old enough to understand that he already knows everything Momma is telling him about the world. But he's doing exactly what I did when I persuaded Elijah to talk to them – grasping on to the desperate hope that the truth might help us somehow.

'I'll kill him,' Daddy says.

'Which one?' Momma fires back. 'You can't kill 'em all.'

There's a silence. I imagine them reaching for each other across the table, but their hands not quite connecting, instead resting on the table, inches and whole worlds apart.

'Is it really too much to ask to be able to trust that your child is safe when you drop them off at school?' Daddy says, voice cracking.

Momma scoffs. 'Maybe you should ask the NRA that question.'

He sighs, long and deep. 'Feels like there's threats coming at our kids from every direction these days, huh. And I don't know how to protect them. But with Elijah in Iraq most of the time I just thought Sadie was the one we *didn't* have to worry about.'

There's a silence and, when Momma speaks, I realise that quiet moment was her thinking time. Her planning time.

'I could say I was driving.'

'Or I could,' Daddy says.

As if being fired out of a cannon, Elijah storms out of his room, past me, and into the kitchen.

'Y'all need to stop,' he says. 'The decision's been made. It's my truck. It's me who's been giving her a ride to Fontaine's house nearly every week for the past year being stupid enough to believe she was seeing her friend Abby. None of this would've happened if I'd asked a few more questions. So it's me. It's my fault. All of it. It's my fault.'

I'm sobbing now and I step into the kitchen just in time to see Momma scoop my brother into her arms. She rocks him and strokes his hair and we all cry together.

'I'm gonna turn myself in,' Elijah says. 'You need to work and take care of Sadie and run this house. You don't need me. You've already proved that every time I've been on tour. This family is good without me. And I'm okay with that.'

Momma starts to wail at this point, the way I always expected her to if we ever opened our door to two military men with a folded American flag in their hands and the worst possible news. And, despite Elijah's mea culpa and all of those questions he never asked, I know that it really is all my fault. That I have torn the fabric of my family apart at the seams and the damage I've caused is irreparable.

It isn't until later on that night that I turn on the TV and the guilt I feel for destroying my family shifts.

On the local news there is a photo montage of a little boy. The reporter states that he was barely three years old, 'his young life stolen from him by a reckless and cowardly driver, who didn't even stop to see if he was okay'.

The final picture of him shows him being held up to the camera by his young mother, joy sparkling in her eyes. He's a truly cherubic child, smiling in every photo, chubby cheeks and limbs, curly chestnut hair. How could I have snuffed out this perfect little life? How can any of this be real?

Cody Michaelson's image permanently seared into my retina, I let the guilt consume me, wave after wave of it, clawing and gnawing at me from the inside out. I scream and cry and hit myself until Momma comes in and embraces me from behind and Daddy grabs my fists and forces me to stop. The pain is unbearable. And, yet, I want it. I want to suffer. It's what I deserve. The only way I'll come close to balancing out the universe again.

'No,' I say to Momma and Daddy. 'I can't do this. I wanna go to jail. I need to be punished for what I've done.'

'You can't,' Daddy says. 'Not now.'

'He's already at the police station,' Momma tells me. 'Antonio dropped him there after Elijah took him his car.'

Inconsolable to the point of madness, I cry out more pleas. Begging my parents, God, anyone who will listen to make this not so. To allow me the chance to go back and stop all this from happening, from the moment I got into Elijah's truck and asked him to take me to Gaultier's. I beg for it all to be a dream. Attempt to make a bargain with anyone who'll accept what little I have to give in exchange for this nightmare to end. But it all falls on deaf ears and, as the hours drag on and Elijah fails to return home, it starts to sink in. There is no going back.

PART THREE

COMMITMENT

SIXTEEN

Lilith presses another hot mug of herbal tea into my hands. We've been sat on the floor of the studio for almost two hours now and my back aches. I shift towards the wall and feel sweet relief as my spine relaxes against it. Lilith joins me, her body language mimicking mine beautifully as we both lean back and take our first sip.

'You have to forgive yourself, Sadie,' Lilith tells me. 'What happened was a terrible accident.'

'It doesn't matter if it was an accident or not,' I reply. 'I killed that little boy. And I destroyed two families in the process. His and mine. How can I ever move on from that? I'm not sure I even deserve to.'

'Every day of life that you are given on this earth is a gift,' Lilith says. 'And you are not given that gift just so you can use it to continue to suffer. You are meant to experience joy and reflect that joy back out into the world. *That* is how you make amends.'

These words entirely dismantle me and I burst into tears. I picture myself shattered into a million tiny pieces, each smaller than a grain of salt, little heaps of me gathered on the floor. *Maybe I need to be reduced to nothing in order to start again*, I think. Lilith's view on this is one I've never before considered.

Cody wasn't afforded the privilege of living to my age and, in the years that have been gifted to me, I have done little more than punish myself. My fingers dance across the tiny scars on my inner thighs, so numerous that Derek has never been able to tell which are new and which ones were created before we met. I've become remarkably skilled at excusing myself from intimacy while I heal between self-harming binges, navigating the inconvenience of wearing my secrets on my body. But, when I was pregnant, I stopped. Fully aware of how important a vessel I suddenly was. Hurting myself might, in turn, hurt the baby somehow, I thought. It was a risk I couldn't take. My restraint, however, did not pay off.

When I lost the genetic lottery and the pregnancy failed, I swiftly went back to my old ways. *If only I'd cut deeper, punished myself harder*, I remember thinking. Maybe then I would've been worthy of carrying this baby into the world. Perhaps it would've been the penance required for taking away someone else's child.

One day, though, I went too far and Derek found me in a pool of blood, staining the white grout between the bathroom floor tiles. He took me to the ER and made me swear never to cut again.

What's one more lie? I thought to myself, crossing my heart. *I'll just have to be more careful next time.*

But the closer Derek and I became, the tougher it was to hide. And so I found other ways to punish myself. First, comparing myself to my peers on social media and then, when that didn't cut deep enough, I resorted to repeatedly checking in on Cody's grieving family.

Reminding myself of what I've done, sometimes multiple times a day, gives me a strange sense of relief. As if I'm taking charge of my own punishment. The biggest relief, however, is seeing one of them happy, because then, for a moment, I get to fool myself that there might be some sort of redemption for me someday. If they can move on, then maybe I can too.

Having unloaded my biggest secret, I'm surprised at how unfazed Lilith is. She seems more appalled by my guilt than by my crime. She rubs my back, holds my hand, lets me cry on her shoulder and through it all tells me that I am still of value, that I am still loved.

'You should come to our next retreat. It's at Joshua Tree,' she says to me. 'I think it will be good for you. A real opportunity for you to work through some of these issues.'

'I dunno, Lilith,' I say. 'I hate to admit it, but I really struggled with Soul Awakening. It was actually kind of brutal.'

A few days ago, I would've been embarrassed if she knew this, but now that I've confessed everything else to her, there's a new sense of intimacy between us. She knows all my secrets and, thankfully, this one makes her laugh.

'The Joshua Tree retreat is very different,' she says. 'The Soul Awakening weekender was to strip away all the external crap to lay yourself bare. The Joshua Tree retreat, on the other hand, is about nourishing ourselves and tightening the bonds between us all. There's physical and emotional work from early morning until about four o'clock, which is all about team building and picking through latent trauma together. But then the rest of the day focuses on self-soothing activities – mud baths and hot tubs. There's a sauna on site and cold water

immersion. There'll be creativity workshops and the food –
don't get me started on the food! Now that our souls are
awake, they deserve to be fed! So what do you think, Sadie?
Will you come eat with us?'

I grin. Despite everything, it seems she still accepts me and
wants to keep me close. It's a feeling that flies in the face of
all that I've believed for the longest time. All I have to do now
is figure out how to pay for another retreat when I'm already
indebted to Lilith for the last one, I've lost two jobs in twenty-
four hours, and I've got Derek and Raheem questioning my
every move.

The house is empty. On the kitchen table is another hastily
scribbled note from my husband that reads, 'We've gone
looking for you. Please call when you're home. I'm so sorry
about Selma. Hope you're okay.'

I've ignored the calls to my cell. Not out of malice, of
course. I love them both beyond words, but dealing with an
inquisition is too much for me right now. I send them both a
message on WhatsApp: 'Safe and sound. Going to get some
sleep.'

I look through the thin metal bars of Selma's cage, now
returned to its place in the living room. Derek must've moved
it, but I'm thankful he knew not to mess with her body. June
has placed her on her front and she kind of looks as if she is
sleeping. Later, I'll bury her under the rose bush in our back
yard.

First, however, I need to eat. I down a protein shake, make
a turkey sandwich and, while I take hungry bites, I allow my

feet to carry me wherever they want to go. They land me in my studio and I realise it's been weeks since I last spent any time here. I've barely produced anything since before I started working for Caleb.

A thin layer of dust is beginning to gather on everything. Discarded paintbrushes, a filthy palette streaked with orange and blues, my dancer series propped up against the wall, unfinished. I feel so distant from my work that being surrounded by it is like standing in the house of a stranger thinking about how we were once lovers. Paramours who tore at one another's clothes, desperate to be closer, and who christened every inch of this place with paint and promises. The previously booming heartbeat of my life's passion is quieter these days. Background noise. I stand for a moment, finishing my sandwich, unsure of where to put myself, of what to touch. In the end, I'm grateful for the sound of the doorbell, saving me from attempting to return to something that now feels so far behind me.

Mumtaz stands on the doorstep. The memory of our parking lot interaction crashes down upon me. I expect a look of cold contempt to crawl across her face, but she looks genuinely concerned.

'Are you okay?' I ask.

'Are *you*?' she says, pushing past me and into the house, uninvited.

'Uh . . . Derek's not here,' I say to her back.

'Well, I'm not here to see him, am I? I'm here to see you. Shall I make us some tea? I'll make some tea.'

She moves with a nervous energy and I watch as she busies herself in the kitchen, stopping only to ask me where a few

215

things are. I gesture towards cupboards and pastel-coloured storage containers, too exhausted to push back. Eventually, I find myself on the couch beside her, nursing a mug of what must be my seventh dose of herbal tea today.

'Brought you something,' Mumtaz says, rifling through her purse before handing me a small but beautiful cardboard box. 'It's for your pet. Thought you might like something nice to bury him in.'

'It was a girl, I think,' I say, turning the paper sarcophagus over in my hands, inspecting the intricate folds that make up its perfect structure. 'This is . . . lovely. Thank you.'

'I got really into origami tutorials on YouTube during the pandemic. Kind of a useless skill. I probably should have learned another language or the guitar or something. But I found it quite calming. Building stuff while the world fell apart. Therapeutic, I suppose.'

I nod, thinking about how I'd tried, unsuccessfully, to start a vegetable patch in our garden back in Savannah. Turns out Daddy's green fingers are not genetic.

'I can't believe you made this for me,' I say.

'Maybe I made it for me. Needed to chill myself out after you shouted at me in the car park, didn't I?' Mumtaz looks like she's trying to stifle a laugh.

'I'm sorry I called you a bitch,' I tell her.

'I'm not,' she replies. 'I kind of am a bitch. Sometimes. I often think the thing that makes me exceptionally good at my job also makes me sort of shit at life.'

There's a silence as my opportunity to disagree with her comes and goes.

'I treated you badly, Sadie. And, for what it's worth, I am genuinely sorry. I was going through some stuff at the time and, well, I guess I kind of used you as an emotional shield. If I could deflect some of my shit onto you, I wouldn't have to face up to it all.'

Her regret is surprising. I half expect her to tell me that this entire conversation is actually a joke, a prank that she's been live filming or something. But the more she talks, the more I find myself struck by her sincerity.

'Yeah, well, I definitely didn't appreciate being covered in all your shit,' I say, and we both chuckle. 'But the apology means a lot. I was pretty confused at the time. We were friends, I thought.'

'And I mucked it up, didn't I?'

I tilt my head to one side and grimace, once again failing to disagree with her.

'Look, you have every reason to never trust me again. And I wouldn't blame you. But I would like to be on better terms with you one day. I'm not saying we should be bosom buddies again or anything like that, but it would be nice to be able to sit in a room together and not want to tear each other's hair out.'

'How do I know you've actually changed?' I ask.

She drops something round and plastic onto the table. Coin-like, it spins for a few rounds before settling with a satisfying click.

'My sobriety chip,' Mumtaz says. 'Two months now. It means nothing unless I stick with it, I know, but it's proof that I'm trying. To be better.'

I marvel at it. At her. The honesty and determination and

217

humility. All things I never expected and yet none of it means I can totally trust her. We've a long way to go before any of that.

'Mackenzie Crawford,' I say, and Mumtaz retrieves her sobriety chip and looks down at it, rubbing it between her fingers as if it's a reminder to do no wrong in all aspects of her life.

'You know I can't talk about her, Sadie. Client privilege.'

'I figured,' I tell her, attempting to push my curiosity back down my throat.

'One thing I will say, though, is that you should watch out for that Lilith. Deep Flow seems like this harmless, hippy community specialising in Westernised New Age wellness. But it's dangerous.'

I snort. '*Anything* is dangerous in the wrong hands.'

I'm referencing Mackenzie, of course. If she really is struggling with her sanity, it's not Deep Flow that's the problem. It's her mental health.

Mumtaz picks up her bag and stands up. 'You don't know how true that is.'

She hugs me goodbye before she heads for the door. A parting gesture.

'Just be careful, yeah? If anything doesn't seem quite right, you can talk to me. Any time.'

I close the door behind her. Perhaps she *is* genuine? But, on the other hand, there is the possibility that her sudden urge to make amends is just an attempt to swindle information out of me. Intel she can use to win her big court case.

Tossing the cardboard coffin into a storage box, I head to the bedroom for a nap. Hours later I sense Derek come in. He slinks into the bed next to me and pulls me close, as if finding a missing treasure he won't let out of his sight again. His warmth is comforting, the smell of his aftershave enveloping me as he nuzzles the nape of my neck. I put my hand on his thigh and draw him closer, right before I drift back into sleep.

Alone again in the early hours, I gaze out of our bedroom window and watch a swoop of swallows flit across the sky as the rosy glow of sunrise dwindles into the blue of a fresh new day. I must've slept for over sixteen hours and our bed is empty again, except for the vague imprints of our bodies, wrinkles left on the sheets where we lay. The house is silent, and being alone with my thoughts is troubling. After lifting the heavy weight of my secrets onto Lilith's shoulders, I did not expect to feel like this. I thought I'd feel lighter, breathe a little easier.

I trust Lilith entirely – I'm sure of that. And yet I feel a creeping sense of dread that my confession may have been a terrible mistake. Eventually, I decide that it isn't sharing my truth that has led to these feelings. It's having to live through my past again in order to convey all that happened. It felt exposing. Vulnerable. Triggering. And why wouldn't it? What else could I expect? This is the first time I've spoken to anyone other than a therapist since spilling out all the details to Raheem when we were teenagers.

The solution to salving the horrible feeling in my stomach is food, I resolve, and, twenty minutes later, I'm sitting at the kitchen table with two plates full. Hot buttered toast, waffles and eggs with runny yellow yolks, half a blueberry muffin that Derek must've left in the fridge, chunks of mango and blood-red pomegranate seeds, Greek yogurt dribbled with golden honey and scattered with granola and pumpkin seeds. I eat and eat, but it seems as if nothing will fill my belly or quench my thirst. I gulp down water and, even when it feels like I've drunk gallons, I still want more. I make a cappuccino in Derek's highly prized coffee machine and then, after drinking it down in seconds, I make another.

I'm standing by the refrigerator, slurping grape juice right out of the carton when Derek and Raheem walk in, laden with paper bags full of groceries.

'We didn't think there was much in the house,' Derek says, eyeing the mess I've made. 'But it looks like you've managed to eat something.'

'I'm cooking dinner for you both tonight,' Raheem says. 'My famous pasta al pomodoro. And then . . . maybe we can all talk.'

I nod, sullenly, and swallow the last dregs of the juice before throwing the empty carton into the trash and announcing my intentions to take a shower.

'Or I could run you a bath?' Derek says. 'We've barely used that tub since we moved in. Why don't I fill it with bubbles and light some candles? You could put some music on. Have a bit of "you" time.'

He's making such an effort I almost burst into tears. Instead, I manage to mumble a thank you and start to clear up the kitchen.

'Don't worry about that. I can clean up later,' Derek tells me. It's evident he's not going to take no for an answer and

I am full of gratitude. Even the smallest tasks feel suddenly overwhelming. Peeling myself away from the sink, I follow him to the bathroom.

'How are you feeling?' he asks. It's as loaded a question as it gets.

I shrug. 'Fine.'

'I'm really sorry about Selma,' he says, sincerely. 'I know she meant a lot to you.'

Derek turns the faucet on and I watch as a tiny waterfall cascades into the bathtub.

'Have you thought about how you'd like to bury her?' he asks, gingerly. 'Because I know that things were complicated with Ramona and it meant we couldn't . . .'

I flinch at the mention of our daughter's name. He notices. Backs off.

'Mumtaz came over,' I say, watching as his eyebrows drift upwards in surprise.

'That's . . . unexpected,' he says. 'What did she want?'

Half a bag of Dead Sea salt goes into the water, followed by a large dollop of bubble bath.

'I ran into her. Outside the veterinarian's. Did you know she's representing the woman who shot up the studio?'

Derek looks away, his silence speaking volumes.

'You didn't think I deserved to know that?' My question isn't aggressive. Merely inquisitive. Curious. Years ago, this kind of information would've been hot gossip. A conversational piece that would have been meticulously dissected over dinner.

'Since when did you start keeping secrets from me?' I ask.

Derek laughs, sardonically. 'You're kidding, right? Your

whole life is a secret these days, Sadie. Or maybe it always has been. I dunno.'

'What does *that* mean?' I counter. Has Raheem said something?

'You don't think I've noticed all the money disappearing from our joint account?' He says these words softly, but the revelation that he knows still runs through me like a hot knife.

'I . . .'

'Look, I'm not mad at you. Although I probably should be. I'm just worried.'

He turns off the water as foam rises beyond the rim of the tub, creating a bed of soft bubbling clouds for me to slip into. I fantasise about the bath being bottomless, allowing me to climb in and sink beneath its watery shallows, escaping from reality and all the questions I don't know how to answer.

'Why didn't you tell me about Mumtaz?' I ask again.

Derek sighs. 'Mehdi told me on one of our golf meet-ups. I thought about letting you know, but I guess I didn't want to make the issues between you two worse. These people are two of my oldest friends and all this bad blood is the last thing I wanna have to deal with.'

'I'm sorry it's so inconvenient for you,' I retort, petulantly.

'Put yourself in my shoes,' he says. 'Imagine if me and Raheem hated each other.'

'It might not be as bad as the two of you colluding behind my back and staging this weird intervention.'

'It's not an intervention. It's just two people who care about you rallying round at a time where it seems like you're struggling.' He moves towards me, running his hands down my arms reassuringly. 'I know you find it hard to accept love sometimes, Sadie. But I promise you, that's all this is. We're on your side. Always.'

The force field around me breaks and I melt into his arms, allowing him to hold me, telling him that I love him too. While we kiss, I stroke the back of his neck and he rubs the small of my back, our defaults for so many years now. Then, he undresses me slowly and guides me towards the bath.

'Relax, okay? Take as long as you need. We'll talk when you're ready to.'

Landing a final kiss on my forehead, he lights a candle by the door and leaves me to it. I rest my head on the rim of the tub and close my eyes, exhaustion taking hold again.

When I wake, the bath is tepid and the candle has gone out. The bubbles have dissipated and I'm now pruney and lying in murky water, the light of the moon casting an eerie glow through the slats in our Georgian blinds. The dream I was having comes back to me: an enormous old tree, covered in twisting tendrils, its roots bursting through the earth around it. Lilith stands beneath it, holding something in her hands. The thing casts a warm, yellow light onto her golden face. When I attempt to approach her, I realise my foot is caught under one of the roots and, looking down, I see that they are writhing around beneath me, as if alive. Pulling myself free, I make my way towards her, snake-like vines pulling at me all the way. I'm almost there when a large, thick root suddenly rises up and wraps itself round my waist. As it attempts to pull me down, Lilith reaches out, proving she is stronger as she yanks me towards her. The plantlife proves no match and recoils back into the ground. I grin conspiratorially at Lilith and she smiles back. But, when she opens her mouth to speak, she has no tongue. Instead, a swollen serpent of a tendril spirals out towards me. It is my own gasp that wakes me with a jump.

'You're letting Mumtaz get to you,' I say out loud. 'Idiot.'

At dinner, I stare at my plate of tomato-sauce-covered spaghetti and think of the coiling, curling creepers I saw in my dream. It's enough to make me gag. I grab my wine and sip it quickly to keep the food down.

'I just think you've got Deep Flow all wrong,' I tell Derek and Raheem. 'And that comes from not knowing enough about it.'

'Well, why don't I check out a class while I'm here?' Raheem suggests.

'It's women only.'

'Convenient,' he replies, raising a single eyebrow.

'Exclusive, more like,' Derek says. 'Lilith is . . . sweet but kind of pretentious, you know? And her husband . . . *well* . . .'

I roll my eyes. 'Derek, you barely know them. Yes, they are a highly successful couple, but I'm sure they're just like us deep down.'

Raheem starts to sing, 'Celebrities! They're just like you and me!', while voguing with the salad spoons.

'You're *so* annoying,' I tell him. I am, however, secretly thankful for the lighter mood and for my surrogate brother's presence at the table. 'Enough about Lilith and Deep Flow. I wanna know how it's all going with you and the delectable Harry Chang.'

'Can you believe I'm dating a guy who wears a suit to work?' Raheem says. 'And not just dating any more either.'

'Hold up. Are you saying we can finally start using the word "boyfriend"?' I ask.

Raheem smiles and nods enthusiastically. 'I honestly can't wait to get back to him.'

'Damn, I would've gotten the Prosecco out if I'd known about all this!' Derek says, and for the rest of the evening we giggle and gossip and tell stories and drink wine and it's wonderful.

SEVENTEEN

Thursday evening rolls around fast and a day of hot, sticky sunshine ends with a large, milky grey rain cloud hanging over our back yard.

'Shame,' I say wistfully, as I stare through the window at the rose bush, in full bloom but now sadly marred by the melancholy light. 'It's been lovely out there recently.'

Veronica stands behind me, sipping a glass of homemade peach iced tea.

'I'm not mad at it,' she says. 'We've been crying out for rain around here for so long now I was getting ready to do my rain dance. When the alternative is bush fires, miserable weather is a small price to pay.'

It's the first time I've invited her over since we met and it feels like a valuable next step for our fledgling friendship. With Derek's long hours on set and business trips away, the prospect of having someone else to do things with leaves me fizzing with excitement. But I also have another agenda. With Lilith newly aware of my financial woes, she's given me the task of bringing more women into our community as another means of paying my way. Bringing a couple of newbies into Deep Flow will pay off the debt I accrued during the Soul Awakening

Weekender. A few more and I'll have enough credit to go to the Joshua Tree retreat too.

'Outreach is a vital part of what we do here. As cosy as our sisterhood is, we never want it to be closed off. Of course, in order to protect our precious container, we have to be selective about who we bring in. But making sure we extend the invitation so as many women as possible can find out more about our practice is really important.'

Veronica absent-mindedly leafs through a glossy interior design magazine I've left on the table and asks if I'm still going to my 'hippy dippy classes', as she likes to call them. This time, I don't mind. She's provided me with the perfect segue.

'I really think you should come along sometime,' I say. 'There's a four-week trial you can do before you would have to stump up anything. But, I promise, if, after three classes, you hate it, you won't ever have to return and I will one hundred per cent get off your back.'

'You'll never mention it again?' V asks, reluctant but softening. I mime locking up my lips and throwing away the key. She rolls her eyes, groans, but, inevitably, agrees to come to class next week.

Internally, I celebrate my victory. Lilith has given me a target of five, which seems like a fairly lofty aspiration, given I don't even know five people here in LA who aren't already Deep Workers. But, now I've managed to secure Veronica, my target doesn't feel quite so impossible.

I pick up my own glass of peach iced tea and follow V through to the living room, just as the rain cloud finally bursts, soaking everything that lives beneath it.

*   *   *

'I look like a snake,' I tell Derek, examining the green dress I've poured myself into for tonight's wrap party. 'Are you sure this isn't too much?'

'Not at all, honey. You look perfect.'

Swivelling left and right, I admire the iridescent shimmer that covers the dress as it hugs my every curve. Perhaps it *was* worth renting. I can't think of what I would've worn otherwise.

'Proud of you,' I say, leaving behind a rosy imprint as I kiss Derek on the cheek. 'Must feel so good to know you finally have this film in the can.'

'It does. And I'm cautiously optimistic about how it'll be received. I'm happy.'

He smiles and tiny fireworks explode inside me. Sometimes I forget how much I love him. How far we've come.

'We have a good life here, don't we?' I say, reaching for his hands and pulling him towards me.

'We do. And you know what? I've given it a lot of thought and if Deep Flow is an essential thing for you, something that makes *you* happy, you should keep doing it. Just . . . try not to spend *all* of our savings in the process, yeah?'

My smile matching his, we pull each other close again. I breathe him in, growing suddenly serious. It's now or never.

'Derek, my agency dropped me.'

He pulls away. 'What?'

'Sarah said something about it being the wrong culture fit.'

I, of course, leave out the fact that all this happened weeks ago. He doesn't need to know that.

'Well, she's an idiot,' he replies, annoyed. 'How could she do that to you?'

I shrug. 'Maybe she's right. Designing logos for start-up companies isn't exactly a lifelong ambition of mine. It's lined my pockets for a while, but the truth is, I was bored. Focusing on my own art is what I want now.'

'You sure about that?' Derek asks. 'You're barely in your studio these days. I kind of thought you'd lost your inspiration.'

'I have,' I concede. 'But I'll find it again. Somehow.'

'That's the spirit,' he says, drawing me in for a kiss.

At the party, he thanks me for coming along, unaware that my presence there is an attempt to kill two birds with one stone. Casting my gaze around the room, I count the women I feel I might be able to approach tonight – the kind of women who wouldn't look out of place in a Deep Flow class.

Determined not to let Lilith down, I head towards my first mark, a frothy blonde woman in her twenties.

'Sadie,' I say, holding out my hand. 'I'm Derek's wife.'

She bypasses the handshake and pulls me in for a hug. 'So nice to meet you at last! We've heard so much about you, *obviously*. I'm Shaylene. I play Jessie in the movie.'

Having read the script a hundred times, I'm aware of exactly how many scenes each actor has. Shaylene sits at a modest yet respectable six, two of which may end up on the cutting room floor. She's certainly not a heavy hitter, but her expensive jewellery and designer handbag give the impression she works often enough to earn a good living. Or, at the very least, she has a well-paying day job.

'Do I detect a Southern accent, Shaylene?'

'Oh my gosh, yes! I'm from South Carolina! How about you?'

As a rule, I try to avoid telling people where I'm originally from, preferring to pretend my life started after the accident, when, following months of torment from the locals and a battle to avoid bankruptcy, we'd moved into a two-bedroom bungalow near Savannah. More than two and a half hours drive from my hometown, it was liberating to be somewhere no one knew us.

'Savannah!' Shaylene gushes. 'We vacationed there once or twice. What a cool place to grow up. No wonder you're an artist.'

I tell her about how I'd persuaded Derek to move back to Savannah with me a few years after we'd finished college in New York, and how continually inspiring it had been to be surrounded by the incredible artistic community there.

'You must miss that,' Shaylene says, looking genuinely sympathetic and playing right into my hands.

'Well, I'm lucky enough to have found a whole new community here,' I begin. Within twenty minutes, I convince Shaylene to sign up to the four-week Deep Flow trial on her phone. Another one down, three to go.

In the bathroom an hour later, I get talking to a beautiful, raven-haired woman as we both reapply our lipstick in the mirror. It turns out her name is Constance and she worked in wardrobe on the film.

'Derek's the nicest guy, isn't he?' she says. 'You're so lucky.'

Deciding not to interpret her words as a slight, I plough on with my mission, complimenting her figure, asking her what she does for exercise and, eventually, teasing a confession out of her: 'I go to the gym regularly. And I've worked with a personal trainer. But the truth is, I wanna do exercise that doesn't feel like exercise.' Like a spider awakening to a delicate tug as a fly lands on one of its silken threads, I realise this is my chance to reel Constance in.

Astounded by how easy it's been to snare my first two new joiners, I start to get confident, only to be shut down by a slightly older woman at the bar and then again by a mousy brunette I'm introduced to by Derek. I'm halfway across the room, ready to approach a new mark when my husband pulls me aside.

'Hey, Mary from production just told me you were trying to sell her some wellness programme at the bar earlier. Is that true?'

'I may have recommended Deep Flow to her, yeah. But I wasn't trying to *sell* anything.'

I look into his eyes, defiant. This woman has nothing on me. I didn't say a single thing that could be proved to be anything more than simply making polite conversation.

'Okay,' Derek says, at least a little satisfied. 'I just don't want people getting the wrong impression of you, that's all. Everyone here might seem cool and progressive, but a lot of them are actually pretty old school.'

'Got it,' I say, pushing the corners of my mouth into a grin in a bid to sweeten the deal. 'I won't mention Deep Flow again. Or religion. Or politics.'

No longer feeling the need to keep such a close eye on my behaviour, Derek takes a small step away and is instantly scooped up by another suit and tie eager to schmooze him. It seems I've convinced him I don't have an ulterior motive, but further pursuit is too risky and I will, unfortunately, have to down tools for tonight. After all, it's not as if I'm at this party under my own steam. I am merely an extension of Derek. Here to bask in the glow of his reflective glory and nothing else.

'I wouldn't if I were you,' I say, mimicking the first words Lilith ever said to me as I watch a woman reaching for a box of Crunchy Wheats on the top shelf. 'Full of preservatives.'

The woman gives me a filthy look, takes her cereal and walks away, most likely cursing me under her breath and wondering why I'm such a nosy creep. Shit. How the hell did Lilith charm me with that line? Maybe it's that she's better at knowing what people need than I am. When she'd started speaking to me all those months ago, I probably radiated loneliness. She knew I needed to be welcomed into her flock.

I leave the store, disappointed, embarrassed and out of ideas.

In class, we move as one, except for Constance and Shaylene, who have taken up a couple of mats in the row behind me, having both seemed glad to see one another. Veronica is beside me and is proving to be a real natural. It's as if she's been doing this for years. At the end of the session, Lilith tells me how impressed she is that I've already managed to get three new people to sign up.

'About that,' I say, sheepishly. 'I think I might've maxed out my contacts.'

'Already?' says Lilith. Her eyebrows shoot up in surprise, but her forehead does not move with them.

'Honestly, I don't know many people here in LA that aren't already part of the Deep Flow community. Obviously, I really want to come to Joshua Tree and I'm glad I've managed to introduce some new people to what we do here, but I don't think I can do any more.'

Lilith puts a sympathetic arm round my shoulders and I watch as Veronica rescues her stuff from one of the cubbies on the other side of the room before pulling on her boots.

'How about I offer you a significantly reduced rate for the retreat?' Lilith says. 'You've brought in three out of five. That's sixty per cent of what I was hoping for. So how about you pay forty per cent of the retreat fee?'

Forty per cent is still a stretch, but it's such a big discount, and such a wonderful opportunity, I'd be stupid to say no. Especially since Lilith seems to have forgotten all about the fact that I still owe her for the Soul Awakening weekender.

'Can I think about it?' I ask. 'I'd need to square it with Derek before I can commit.'

'Of course!' Lilith pulls me close. 'Do what you need to do, angel. Please just know I'd massively value your presence there. I think this is a real opportunity for you to continue on your spiritual journey and truly evolve. And, if you really can't get the money together, I do have another option we can discuss. Just keep me posted.'

I assure Lilith that I will and head over to the cubbies to grab my shoes and purse.

Since Soul Awakening, things have been weird with the Deep Flow regulars. Debbie and I mostly avoid one another. Ruby glares but rarely says hello. Natalia and Emily issue awkward pleasantries when we cross paths before quickly excusing themselves at the first opportunity. Arriving today with three new friends feels good. Perhaps I don't need the others at all. And perhaps them realising that will make them want to come back to me. With several other new people joining in the last few weeks, forgetting about my old pals and moving on to fresh blood feels a lot less impossible these days.

'You ready to go?' Veronica asks, jacket and bag now in hand. Shaylene and Constance, who have been chatting in the corner since the end of class, turn to greet us.

'We were thinking of getting tacos for lunch. You wanna come?' Constance says, and Veronica and I turn to one another and smile. I notice Bridget just a few feet away. She's alone, grabbing her things from her cubby and busying herself on her phone. I remember what it is to be new to Deep Flow and how exclusionary the other women can be. After the shooting, I felt like I was really *in*. There was a smattering of jealousy from the others, but I could tell it was tinged with admiration. When people got word I'd been to dinner with Lilith and Jeremy, that only increased. But my behaviour at the Soul Awakening Weekender instantly smashed the social capital I'd built to smithereens.

'Hey, Bridget!' I call over. 'Tacos?'

She smiles and nods, clearly grateful to be included at long last.

The restaurant is packed and would be overheated if it weren't for its large open windows, the kind that allow you to rest your arm on the ledge so you feel as if you are half inside, half outside. Neither Veronica nor I have been to this place before, but Shaylene seems to know the menu by heart. We let her order for us.

'I loved that class,' Constance says. 'The whole vibe is just . . . different, isn't it?'

'It's definitely different,' Shaylene says. 'Feel like I might need a few sessions to get into it, though.'

'What did you think, V?' I ask.

'Girl, that class is a mess. Not in a bad way, necessarily. Like . . . it is fun and sweaty and I feel great. But it's such a strange hodge podge of disciplines all thrown into one. When Lilith was doing all that crazy chanting at the end, I was like . . . *girl, really?*'

Constance laughs. 'Yeah, that was the only part of the class I wasn't feeling, to be honest. I'm totally going back, though. Feels like I've been looking for something like that for the longest time.'

'I like the community vibe,' Shaylene says, in between sips of her strawberry milkshake.

'Give it a chance,' I tell them. 'I wasn't sure at first either. In fact, after my first session, I was like, "thanks, but no thanks!" And look at me now. I'm obsessed. It's changed my life.'

'For the better?' Veronica asks, dubiously, and the others laugh before agreeing they'd commit to the four-week trial and then decide how they felt.

Bridget asks me a few questions about how long I've been going to class and what my relationship with Lilith and the others has been like.

'The Soul Awakening Weekender was pretty full on, don't you think? I mean, you didn't exactly have the best time there, did you?'

'It was tough,' I say. 'Challenging. But that's kind of the point.'

I can tell she's in two minds about whether to continue, but, by the end of the meal, it feels like I've convinced her to keep going. If only I could get a referral credit for *her*, I think. Too bad she joined Deep Flow before I got the chance to give her my sales pitch.

Already, things with this group feel different to how it was with Ruby, Natalia and Emily. I feel as if I can breathe more freely and genuinely be myself. Silently, I pray Deep Flow will win them round. I could really use friends like these.

We eat dinner in the backyard. Derek has made a large salad and honey-roasted some salmon fillets. The sun has not yet dropped behind the trees and I am bare shouldered and uncharacteristically talkative.

I tell him all about my day: the grocery store (minus my attempt to recruit that woman in the cereal aisle), Deep Flow, tacos and then, best of all, time spent in the studio.

'Wow. Seems like you're getting your mojo back,' Derek says. He's currently doing nine-to-five days in the edit suite but is home more now that filming has wrapped. He knows five dishes and cooks them well. I joke that he may have to learn a few more if he plans to cook more often.

'I need inspiration,' he tells me. 'A new cookbook. Or a cooking show I can get into. Can you find me something?'

Later, as the sun sets and I am forced to cover up with a shawl, I choose my moment to talk to him about the retreat, reminding him of the generous declaration he made before the wrap party: if Deep Flow makes me happy, I should do it. I start by telling him the full price, then reveal that Lilith is giving me a whole sixty per cent off.

'Why?'

'I guess she just likes me,' I lie. 'We've bonded. Especially after we went over there for dinner. Guess we're friends now.'

I want, so desperately, for that to be true. For my whopping discount to not have been quite so transactional. Even the closest friends return each other's favours, don't they? Perhaps it's not such a lie after all.

'We're good, at the moment. Financially,' Derek says. 'Not excellent. But we're okay. So it's cool. If this is what you want, we can make it work. Have you thought about when you might get another job, though? Or if you're gonna try selling your work soon?'

My choice not to display or attempt to sell my work has been a bone of contention for as long as I can remember. It's a choice dominated by fear, admittedly. But, nonetheless, it has always been my choice to make. Hiding from the past has kept me safe for years. The repercussions of my crime ran me and my family out of town once. I don't want it to happen again. Thing is, though, I told Derek I didn't care about being dumped by the agency because I wanted to focus on my own work. If I refuse to attempt to sell it, he'll undoubtedly think I've made a false promise, and then he might start to feel like Sarah and I parting ways is more catastrophic than I'm letting on.

'I'm working on it,' I say, vaguely, before collecting the dishes from the table and carrying them inside.

Later, we put on a movie and curl up on the couch together. As we watch I think about how much things have improved since Raheem was here. Did his presence make me feel triggered? A remnant of my past permeating my new life? I shake my head. No. I'd felt bad before that.

Then, it hits me like a swinging brick: Selma.

Two days after Mumtaz had come over, I'd rescued the origami sarcophagus she'd made from the storage basket. Derek was working late and Raheem was getting an early night, so I'd taken the opportunity to give Selma a burial by candlelight. A poem I'd copied down off the internet in my trembling hands, I'd read aloud over a tiny mound of dirt, then snuffed out the flame. Back in the house, I'd pulled an old shoe box out from under the bed. Inside was an ultrasound printout with the words 'Baby Perkins' written underneath. Staring at it for the first time in years made something collapse inside me, a waterfall of grief spilling out into my lap.

'We never talk about her,' I say to Derek, pressing pause on the movie.

'Who?'

'Our daughter.'

'Come on, Sadie. I'm tired. Let's just—'

'That's what you always say,' I tell him, more weary than confrontational. 'And then you promise me we'll talk about it another time. And then that conversation never comes. Because when you're not tired, you're busy.'

He's quiet for a minute and then—

'Sometimes I feel like I've said all I can say. Like there aren't any other words that could describe our pain or make things better. And, for the record, I don't talk to *anyone* about what happened. Because it's not useful. They don't know what to say either. So they say the wrong thing. Like . . . well, you can try again. Or something about it being God's will or not meant to be. Or they say nothing at all. As if she never existed. And maybe, in their eyes, she didn't. And I don't know what's worse. The wrong thing. Or nothing. So I don't talk about it.'

I put his hands in mine and land a kiss on his shoulder.

'You can talk to me,' I tell him. 'You can always talk to me. In fact, I want you to. I'm the only one who understands you. And you're the only one who understands me.'

'Except I don't, do I? Sure, it happened to both of us. But I didn't have to carry her around for nine days knowing she was already dead. And you . . . you nearly died because of that. They made you into a human coffin and there was nothing I could do about it except sit and watch you suffer.'

I try to put his mind at rest. Tell him that none of that was his fault. That I know he tried. And I watch as his eyes glaze over with tears.

'We don't have to just bury all this. We can talk. Whenever you want,' I say.

'But that's where we're also different,' Derek says. 'Because I don't want to talk. I want to move on and I want you to move on with me. Maybe you can't because your experience of losing her was so different. But I also feel like you carry around this sense of guilt. You said it at the time. That it was your fault. Even though the doctors said it wasn't. Even though I never blamed you. And I don't think you've ever let go of that.'

I think of the multi-coloured clump lying in the road. Of Elijah in an orange jumpsuit, his palm pressed against mine through a pane of prison glass, an old-fashioned phone receiver resting against his ear.

'It *was* my fault,' I mumble. 'But that doesn't mean we just pretend she didn't exist.'

Derek sighs. 'I love you. And I loved Ramona. But I'm not gonna let you use talking about her as an opportunity to self-flagellate, Sadie. I won't be a part of that.'

He leaves the room and I hear him clattering around in the kitchen while I sit in silence on the couch. We go to bed without finishing the movie.

EIGHTEEN

I let the beads slip through my palm, watching as they reflect the light of the studio. A river of sparkling black onyx and marbled red and grey jasper flows through my fingers before Constance gently takes the necklace out of my hands, replacing it with the one she has been musing over: rose quartz and jade with a beautiful section of mother of pearl preceding a white tassel that's held on with silver beads.

'They're all incredibly stunning,' Constance breathes, as Lilith hands her another.

'Clear quartz, black obsidian and tiger eye. Crystals for healing and protection.'

'I could do with a whole heap of that right now,' Constance says, with a sigh.

'You wanna talk about it?' I ask, both curious and concerned.

'The hair,' she says, pointing at her head. 'It's a wig.'

She pauses, allowing us a moment or two to process the first piece of information, carefully studying our reactions before dropping her second bombshell.

'I have cancer,' she says, and offers us an uneasy smile.

'Damn, girl. That's a really good wig!' Veronica says, appearing behind us. The three of us are the last to approach the stall Lilith has set up at the front of the studio. When she announced she had new stock of her 'Mala beads', I genuinely had no idea what she was talking about. But the long-time Deep Flow devotees certainly did and the rest of us were almost trampled in a stampede to stock up at the end of class. Constance's confession comes as we pore over the last few necklaces and Veronica's words break through the weighty silence that follows, leaving Constance giggling.

'My dad had cancer when I was a teenager,' I tell Constance. 'He got through it, though. Even though it was real bad at one point. It's amazing what doctors can do these days.'

'Not that big pharma is necessarily the way to go,' Lilith interrupts.

'Maybe not the *only* way,' I say. 'A holistic approach of chemo or radiotherapy and then more alternative treatments to deal with the pain could be . . .'

I trail off as Lilith rolls her eyes. It's the first time I've seen her do that. She's usually open to the opinions of others, almost to a fault. But, today, I feel child-like and small under her gaze.

'Don't let yourself be sucked in, Sadie,' she says. 'There's proof that sticking with an entirely alternative route promotes long-term recovery and wellbeing.'

'I'm not . . .' I flounder for a second then find myself again. 'Look, I am all too aware of the fact that one of the brands that is most famous for causing cancer is also the biggest provider of chemotherapy in this country. And it's a fucking outrage. People should be protesting in the streets about it. But we also can't ignore the science.'

'Science is the same as any belief system,' Lilith says, a vein of condescension pulsating through her words. 'It's only right until it's proven wrong.'

'Then the burden of proof is on you,' I counter, feeling the thin veil of hairs that cover my body begin to prickle. 'My dad would not be alive today if it weren't for chemo. Yes, my mom regularly baked pot into his apple pie – a concept I know you're all too familiar with – in order to help manage his pain. And it did make a real difference. But I don't believe for a second he could've beat cancer just by using crystals and positive thinking.'

Veronica puts a reassuring hand on my arm. Constance looks aghast, clearly wishing she hadn't said anything.

'I understand your concerns,' Lilith says, shrugging. 'There's years of societal conditioning to detangle here. But, Constance, can I ask, do you feel your current treatment plan is working for you?'

Constance looks at me apologetically and then shakes her head. 'Not really. It's kind of the reason I missed the last couple of classes. The chemo makes me feel terrible. There's the nausea, the way it makes the skin on my hands and feet peel, the headaches, the dry mouth. It feels like I'm trying to fight poison with poison and my body is collateral damage.'

Lilith draws her in. 'What if I could put you on a wellness programme? Very low commitment. Something you could try for just a few weeks and see how you feel. A series of alternative therapies that I think could genuinely help you feel better, shrink your tumours and enable you to get your life back?'

I look at Constance in horror, trying to telepathically communicate the words: 'Please, no.' But it seems they cannot permeate the mystical bubble Lilith has trapped her inside.

The moment we are out of earshot, V makes it clear that she shares my trepidation.

'What the fuck? Did that actually just happen?'

'Honestly, it's the first time I've seen a side to Lilith I'm not sure I like,' I say.

'I mean, nobody's perfect, but that's one hell of a fatal flaw. Is it bad that we left Constance there with her?' Veronica wonders. I share her guilt, but, deep down, I know there isn't much we could've done. Constance was entranced in a way that I identify with wholeheartedly, having lived under Lilith's spell for so many months now. For a split second, I picture Mackenzie again, lying on the floor outside the studio, surrounded by smashed glass, a police officer's knee pressed into her back, her eyes almost meeting mine. Then I get a grip. Snap back to the present moment. Remind myself I can't afford to think about her. Can't afford to consider the reasons why she did what she did. Can't afford to turn my life upside down in an attempt to get answers. That way madness lies.

'She definitely bought that necklace, didn't she?' Veronica huffs. 'They were pretty. But three hundred bucks for some beads? They best be doing miracles for that price.'

Later, we go to a market stall along Venice Beach and buy some crystals of our own from a stall run by an Indian American woman with sparkling eyes and hands laced with henna. I already have a few at home and Veronica reels off an exhaustive list of what she has dotted around her place. I buy tiger's eye for luck and mental clarity, moonstone for calming and manifesting, amber for grounding and moss agate for transformation. In all, I spend less than twenty bucks.

'You going to the Joshua Tree retreat?' I ask Veronica. 'I saw you take a flyer.'

'I don't think so. I'm not deep enough into this shit to make a commitment like that yet. But I *do* wanna hear all about it when you're back.'

The next day, I find out that Shaylene has booked a last-minute acting job in New York and may be gone for months. The news hits me hard, despite only knowing her for a short period of time. Not having my new group of friends around me could lead to the retreat being a far more solitary experience than I had hoped. I remind myself I'll still have Constance, but I also wish I hadn't already paid my non-refundable deposit.

At the end of the next class, Lilith reminds us we need to pay off the balance by the end of the following week if we're serious. I hesitate, wondering for a moment if it's worth cutting my losses. But then Lilith mentions something that makes a feeling churn inside me for the first time in years.

'I'll be doing fertility readings at the retreat too, for those of you who are interested. I know some of you have begun your journey through motherhood already, but I'm also aware that some of you are still attempting to harness the divine feminine in order to create the necessary energy to achieve what you desire. I'm also aware that some of you have experienced loss and frustration and would perhaps like to find out what your future holds. Because, of course, the more you know, the more you'll be able to manage your expectations. Natalia, would you like to talk about your journey so far?'

Natalia is glowing and while I, personally, would hate for

a studio full of people to know anything about my fertility, she rises to the occasion, as if being asked is a great honour.

'So, I've been trying to get pregnant for a while.'

Has she? How have I not known about this?

'I'm currently single, which means it's a solo mission,' she continues. 'And, at first, I found that incredibly daunting. After the breakdown of my last relationship, I felt like my dream of having a baby was further away than ever. But then I had a reading with Lilith and she helped me realise that wasn't the case, reminding me of how the original divine feminine, the Virgin Mary, brought a baby into this world alone.'

Pretty sure she had Joseph and God on her side, I think. But okay.

'And so, using a sperm donor—'

As the Virgin Mary famously did.

'—I decided to move forward. Lilith's reading told me that I would fall pregnant while the weather was warm and give birth in a cooler climate to a perfect baby boy. And I'm pleased to tell you all that I am now three months pregnant and the baby is due in late February.'

There's a gasp around the room. Despite my initial cynicism, even I have to admit that Lilith's clairvoyancy is impressive.

'Part of me wonders if the reading somehow called this baby into existence,' Natalia muses. 'Could it be that by speaking my heart's desire out loud and exploring it through tarot, I made it clear to the universe that this was what I wanted? Did it help me manifest this? I don't know. But two hours after we did the reading I went to the store and bought this adorable little hat for the baby. The baby I didn't even know for certain I would have. And now my son will wear that hat!'

The entire class bursts into rapturous applause and the thing stirring at the pit of my stomach bubbles to the surface. *I want what she has*, I think. *I have mourned and I have suffered and, now, I am ready to try again.*

The second class is over, I pull my phone out of my bag and pay off the balance, fully committing myself to the Joshua Tree retreat. I'm halfway out the door before Lilith calls after me. When I turn back, she beckons me closer.

'I see Veronica isn't here today,' she says.

'Oh no, she has a hair appointment. But she'll be back.'

Lilith looks awkward for a moment. 'I was thinking it might be best if that weren't the case.'

Frowning, I try to read Lilith's face. 'I don't understand. Did she do something to upset you?'

She pauses, attempting to navigate what is becoming an increasingly awkward conversation. 'I wasn't aware of Veronica's . . . status. Not until yesterday anyway.'

'Status?'

She sighs.

'Look, Sadie. Deep Flow is, and always has been, an inclusive, safe space. But the way that we keep it that way is by being intentional about who we allow into that space. This is a women only class. A strong, female community. A precious container. Veronica is . . . a beautiful being and I am glad to have met . . .'

She searches for the word. I finish her sentence: 'Her.'

'But I'm afraid we need to keep this space safe for the women here.'

'You think Veronica's not safe? Because she's trans?'

I can hear my heartbeat. Blood pulsating in my ears. The back of my jaw tightens as my teeth begin to grind against each other. This can't be happening.

'It's not about that, *per se*. More that some of the women who come here are victims of sexual violence. Some have experienced domestic abuse at the hands of men. One of the founding principles of Deep Flow is that women come here to explore themselves fully and that requires a huge amount of vulnerability. I just can't risk my members being triggered by the presence of someone who has lived as a male. Nor can I risk them feeling oppressed due to being viewed through the male gaze.'

For a second I am speechless, the pit of my stomach suddenly weighty, as if I have swallowed several pounds of lead.

'This is discrimination,' I say. 'TERFism.'

'You can call it what you want,' Lilith says, defiant. 'But I won't apologise for protecting the women under my care. Including you.'

'I can't believe you're saying all this. You've always seemed so open-minded. So full of compassion and love. I don't get it.'

'Sadie, I'm still all of those things,' Lilith replies. 'I believe in trans rights and that trans rights are human rights. And I advocate for them to have their spaces. I just want us to have ours too.'

Furious, I pick up my bag and I head for the door. I'm almost out of it before I decide to turn back and issue a parting shot: 'You know, Lilith, there is no us and them. There's just us.'

Her sharp intake of breath comes just as the door swings shut behind me.

Later, she messages me: 'You've opened up to me such a lot, Sadie. Told me all there is to know about your past. I'd hate for our difference of opinion today to be a relationship deal breaker. You'll speak to Veronica, won't you?'

As the night wears on, I read and re-read the message what must be over twenty times, wondering if her bringing up my confession should be interpreted as some kind of veiled threat. She knows where the bodies are buried, of course.

I begin to slowly drift away from the sense of relief that came with finally telling someone and start to move towards something that feels like abject terror. If she were to unleash the secrets of my past, my life in LA would be completely untenable, all friendships and my relationship likely lost in the process.

Shivering with shame at the thought of Derek knowing everything I've been keeping from him for all these years, I picture him never being able to look at me in the same way ever again, judgement and disgust where love and joy used to be. My imagination runs riot. My own brain providing the purest torture.

Phone slippery in my clammy hands, I try to imagine how Lilith would want me to reply. Swallowing my values, I type a message back: 'Of course it's not a deal breaker. People can have different opinions, I guess. I'll speak to her.' I stare at the word 'her' before I press send. Refusing to misgender Veronica feels like a final attempt to cling to a sense of loyalty. But I know it's pathetic, that there's a special place in hell for people like me. Those who talk the talk, but, ultimately, fail in their allyship right when it matters most.

*   *   *

Allowing my spoon to run rings around the edge of my coffee cup, I wait, steeped in fear and attempting to keep my hands, my mind, as busy as possible. Devil's Ivy climbs the walls of the café, gnarly green vines growing over one another, twisting round metal pipes along shelves. I am reminded of my dream and of Lilith calling out to me, foliage snaking out of her mouth.

An elderly couple sit several feet away. His wrinkled hand reaches across the table to meet hers, happiness dancing in her watery eyes as they chat and laugh together. I imagine that they've known each other all their lives, but things only got romantic a few years ago. Both widowed or divorced. Both still in need of love and intimacy. Both looking for a different type of marriage. A marriage that is all about companionship now as they journey through their twilight years.

Eating a caesar salad and staring out of the window, a man in a suit sits alone. I notice his briefcase and wonder if what he does for a living is worth this loneliness. Worth eating a solitary lunch here and then maybe dinner at home by himself later on. I imagine a meal for one in front of his giant plasma television screen. Not even a pet to keep him company on account of his hours being too long for him to be able to adequately take care of anything. On Sunday nights he calls his mom. Tells her that one day soon he'll introduce her to his girlfriend. His girlfriend who doesn't actually exist.

Another solo diner sits two tables away from this guy, nervously twirling her flame-red hair round her finger. She wears scuffed sneakers and flared jeans that fray at the bottom. She kicks the leg of the chair in front of her: *duff, duff, duff, duff.* She's on the phone, attempting to make plans with a flaky friend who she, perhaps, sees as a little more than that. She chews her lip when she's thinking and wrinkles her freckle-dotted nose when she's irritated. I picture her finally meeting up with him or her, sitting down next to them on a park bench, leaves swirling about their feet. A hand on a knee turning into a kiss that has, until this moment, felt forbidden. For now, though, she settles for a hot chocolate with whipped cream and a plate of smashed avocado on toasted rye.

Four girlfriends in their late forties sit at the table in the corner, all giggling and talking just a little too loudly. They are exactly who I dreamed I could be with Shaylene, Bridget, Veronica and Constance. Natalia, Ruby and Emily before them. Jenna and Ashley back in Savannah, and Kirby and Marianne back in high school. None of these groups have stuck and so I envy these women. Envy their friendship. How light they seem. As if the perils of life have rolled off their skin like droplets of rainwater. Perhaps that's what happens when you have a strong group of female friends supporting you through thick and thin. I fantasise about them running track in high school, first as individuals, each achieving moderate success, before coming together and discovering the joys of racing as a relay team. Inseparable ever since.

I'm studying a terse exchange between a man and a woman who look like they could be siblings when Veronica walks in. The dread lying dormant in my gut springs to life again.

'Am I late?' she asks, noticing my near empty coffee cup.

'I was early,' I say. 'Overestimated the time I needed to get here.'

Either that or I was subconsciously trying to get this

nerve-wracking encounter over and done with as soon as humanly possible.

Veronica looks like a Black Barbie doll, dressed head to toe in pink, a sniffling little chihuahua draped over her arm. She perches herself on the edge of her seat and reaches her other, currently unoccupied, hand into her gigantic purse. Elbow deep, she rummages around for a few seconds before producing an empty dog bowl and a packet of treats that, even closed, immediately send the dog into a state of mania.

'Is that yours?' I ask.

'Dog sitting. For a friend,' she clarifies, feigning exhaustion with an exaggerated flutter of her eyelashes. 'Girl, I thought *I* was needy, but my *God*.'

'He suits you,' I say, as she scoops him up and holds him at eye level.

'You hear that, LaDarian? Maybe I won't send you back to your momma after all.'

I smile. Attempt to gather up the courage required to do the awful thing I need to do. I remind myself that I've spent half my life living in a perpetual state of guilt and shame. By now there should be a comforting sense of familiarity in it. Instead, I feel like I might throw up all over the table, rivers of vomit carrying my coffee cup into Veronica's lap and spilling out onto the floor. The elderly couple stopping to look in my direction. The flame-haired girl wrinkling her nose more than ever while the lonely businessman makes a mental note to lunch elsewhere in future.

'Sadie,' Veronica says, snapping me out of my daydream, 'what did you wanna speak to me about?'

I pause. How can I possibly do this? What if I just . . . don't? What if, instead, we hail the waiter and simply have a nice lunch together? I follow this possibility all the way through to the point where I am forced to imagine Veronica turning up to another Deep Flow session. Lilith staring daggers at me. The air being sucked out of the room as she berates me after class. The prospect of her ejecting me from the community altogether. I picture her showing up at my house when I'm out shopping for groceries. Doorstepping Derek and telling him who his wife really is. What she's done.

'We need to talk about Deep Flow,' I say to Veronica. Her face contorts into a frown and I think about lying. *There's not enough room*, I'd say. *The class is massively oversubscribed right now*. Maybe she'd buy that. But she started coming before both Constance and Shaylene. What if she finds out that they're still going?

'What about Deep Flow?' she asks.

'Um. I . . . I guess what I want to say before anything else is that Lilith is progressive. In a lot of ways. And maybe more old school in other ways. Like . . . um . . . I really believe that she's created something incredible in Deep Flow. But even our biggest heroes can be problematic, right? I mean, you said it yourself, didn't you? Nobody's perfect. And two things can be true at once, can't they?'

At this stage, I'm unsure of who I'm trying to convince here: Veronica or me.

Veronica rolls her eyes like she's been through this a million times before and tells me to 'cut to the chase'.

'I . . . I guess she's one of those people who would describe themselves as . . . uh . . . *gender critical*,' I stammer.

Veronica laughs bitterly. 'Of course she is. Of course she *fucking* is.'

'I mean I think she genuinely *believes* herself to be a feminist . . . It's just . . . complicated.'

Veronica sighs. 'Feminism isn't complicated, Sadie. You either believe in equality or you don't.'

The waiter returns with a now full bowl of water and Veronica sets LaDarian down. She watches for a second as his tiny, thirsty tongue goes to work and then clears her throat loudly.

'So. What does this mean?'

'She said something about . . . um . . . being concerned that some of the women in the class might not be . . . comfortable . . . with your presence. And so—'

'No,' Veronica interrupts, brusquely. 'I meant what does it mean for you, Sadie? *I'm* obviously not going back there. I'm asking what it means for you.'

My mouth opens and closes, but no words come out. The flame-haired girl's friend arrives and I watch them embrace out of the corner of my eye.

'I don't understand.'

'Well. Are you gonna keep going? Or are you done?'

The elderly couple pay their bill and start to gather their things. Veronica's chair scrapes the floor as she gets up.

'Are you . . . leaving?' I ask, as she scoops LaDarian up and empties what's left of his water into my coffee cup.

'Listen, Sadie, I don't know what spell that witch cast on you, but if, after all of this, you're still not done with her, I'm sorry, girl, but I'm sure as *hell* done with you.'

She elongates the word 'hell' as if she has never been more certain of anything in her life and exits, head held high, before I can say another word.

What V doesn't know is that I have no choice. Even if I think shutting her out of Deep Flow is wrong, Lilith knows everything about me now. And who knows what she'll do with that information if I don't play by her rules.

Seventeen Years Earlier

'Here. Take this one out to your daddy too, will you?' Momma says, handing me another bucket of hot, soapy water. 'He looks like he could do with all the help he can get.'

I take it from her hands and head out to the front yard where, this time, Daddy is attempting to scrape eggs off the front door and outside wall of the house.

I set the bucket down beside him.

'I'm sorry, Daddy,' I say, staring down at my feet.

'Why? Was it you who got up in the middle of the night and threw these at our door?'

I shake my head and he cracks a smile. 'Didn't think so.'

'All this is happening because of me, though,' I reply.

He puts down his sponge and sits on the porch steps. 'All this is happening cos of that bastard Fontaine. You want somebody to blame, blame him.'

Elijah called from prison last night. I could hear in his voice that he was putting on a brave face. He told us they finally set a date for the trial. Three months away. Three months that

257

he'd spend languishing in jail if our lawyer's bail appeal didn't land how we hoped.

'Don't worry,' Elijah told us. 'Sounds like I'm probably better off here anyway. Safer.'

Momma had cried when a boy on a bike had thrown a can of red paint over our front door two weeks ago. But her tears were short-lived.

'They put a burning cross in my parent's front yard, you know,' she told me. 'I think we can handle a little red paint.'

Our door had needed repainting though and, thinking shrewdly in case of any further attacks, Momma and Daddy decided to paint the door a shiny shade of strawberry. The eggs, on the other hand, are proving less inspiring.

'They smell so bad,' I tell Daddy, scraping a hardened drop of yolk off the porch steps with my nail.

'It'll blow over,' he replies. 'Once the trial is done and your brother gets his sentence, it'll be old news. You wait.'

I say the idea of a little boy's death being old news any time soon makes me sad, and Daddy suddenly decides he needs to cut the lawn and goes to the garage to fetch the mower.

Later, after the sun sets and I head to bed, there's a knocking at the door. At my window, I look down and see two of Daddy's friends arrive, both looking a little worse for wear. Fred carries a baseball bat and Arthur has a black eye. Mystified, I slip out of my room and lurk in the corridor.

'It's done,' says Fred.

'Did he struggle?' Daddy asks.

'He tried to run,' Arthur tells him. 'But we were faster.'

'Thought you said he was French?'

My heart pounds. Gaultier. Even now, the idea he could be hurt feels torturous.

'He is,' Daddy says, confused. 'You sure you got the right guy?'

Fred delivers the most accurate description of Gaultier possible, right down to the birthmark on his neck. Arthur chuckles. 'He don't look too much like that no more, though.'

Daddy asks if he can keep the baseball bat and, after his friends leave, I head to the bathroom window overlooking the back yard and watch as he digs a hole in the dark and buries it.

At church, no one looks at us. It's as if we have become invisible. The three of us sit together and no one sits too close, a ring of emptiness surrounding us on all sides. The news of my brother's arrest and the death of Cody Michaelson is inescapable. At school, I eat lunch alone in the cafeteria, people slip cruel notes inside my locker and someone pushes me over in the hall. I find myself speculating on how much worse it would be if everyone knew it was me who had killed Cody.

I cry myself to sleep almost every night and am haunted by horrible dreams. Sometimes I don't sleep at all. I lie awake, staring at the ceiling, thinking about all the people I've lost and wondering if I might die of loneliness. The only people who reach out to me are Kirby and Marianne. One night, after forcing me to swear on everything that I won't breathe a word about Gaultier or my involvement in the accident, my parents allow them to sleep over.

'You know he's left the academy, right?' Marianne says. 'Mr Fontaine. Around the time you stopped coming, actually. Like, a week or two later.'

My cheeks burn and I try to get my heart rate under control.

'Do you know why?' I ask.

'Something about his mother being sick. He's gone back to Paris to take care of her. It was all very sudden.'

I picture him making a shaky phone call to the school after being beaten to a pulp by Arthur and Fred. Making up an excuse to avoid explaining his predicament. But had he really left town? Would I never see him again?

Kirby braids my hair and asks about Elijah.

'It's sad what happened,' she says, sympathetically. 'Everyone knows he didn't mean to kill that little boy. It was an accident, wasn't it?'

I nod and say nothing, just like my parents instructed. Kirby tells me to keep my head still until she finishes.

'He should've stopped, though,' Marianne says. 'I can't imagine how you could drive away and leave someone to die in the road like that.'

I can feel the heat of Kirby's fiery gaze over my shoulder.

'*What?*' Marianne bleats. 'I'm just *saying.*'

After that night, I never speak to her again.

The following weekend there's a church cookout and a boy I've not spoken to before puts his arm on my shoulder and asks if I want a piece of the cornbread his grandma made.

'You sure you wanna speak to me?' I ask. 'Momma says we're "social pariahs" now.'

'I know,' the boy says, sitting down next to me. 'Your dad's fried fish was the best thing here last year, though, so I'm still keen to trade.'

I smile. It's a free-for-all, really, no bartering required, and

I know he's just being nice. But kindness towards our family is so hard to come by these days, I'll take what I can get. Raheem introduces himself and we talk about everything *but* my brother and the accident. Raheem wants to be an artist, 'or maybe a fashion designer', and tells me it's just been him and his Grammy for as long as he can remember. He likes it that way and she's taught him how to cook 'near every recipe she knows'.

He's different in a way I can't quite put my finger on. It's like he understands what it is to be on the outside looking in, and it feels as if he recognises that in me too and knows how important it is to not make a big deal about it. We sit on the ground, backs against a gigantic magnolia tree that is currently in bloom, and eat his grandma's jalapeño cornbread with Momma's red-bean chili and a fillet of Daddy's fish. The cornbread is buttery and soft, salty and a little sweet. As it melts in my mouth, I realise it's the first time I've been able to stomach a proper meal since the accident.

Suddenly, Daddy approaches, sweat on his brow, anger in his eyes.

'Come on. We're going.'

'What? Why?'

Several yards away, I spot Momma having an altercation with Agnes who plays the church piano and Johnnie Franklin who sings in the choir. Daddy holds his hand out and I use it to leverage myself up before scooping the final bite of chili into my mouth and crumpling my paper plate into a nearby trash can.

We leave in a hurry and Raheem must have a sixth sense

that this may be the last church gathering we'll attend, because he comes running after us.

'Do you have a MySpace account?' he asks. 'I just got one. Thought we could message and stuff, if you want?'

Momma and Daddy must be grateful I'm exchanging details with a boy my own age. Or perhaps it's that they also sense Raheem is different from most of the other church boys. Either way, they don't bat an eyelid when I tell him I'll set up an account so we can keep talking.

Seconds later, we're in the car and there's a stony silence for a while before Daddy pipes up.

'So *that's* done, huh?' he says.

And Momma says, 'Yes, the hell it is,' before cranking up the radio loud. There's a sticker on the bumper of the car in front of us that reads: 'God wants spiritual fruits, not religious nuts', and I contemplate how many church attendees genuinely fit into the first category. Certainly not Johnnie or Agnes. They'd be a lot more forgiving if they did.

I open the window and float my arm through the breeze. *Elijah may never have this feeling again*, I think. *Cody definitely won't.* I've stolen something from both of them that, no matter what, I can never give back and no amount of praying will change that.

But then, one day, the police come to our door.

Two nights previously, someone smashed the window on the driver's side of Momma's car and threw in a bottle with a flaming vodka-soaked napkin stuffed inside. It burned out the entire interior before anyone was able to put out the fire and so, when the cops arrive on our doorstep, we assume they've caught the culprit. Instead, they ask for one of my parents to accompany me down to the station and tell Daddy he needs to call a lawyer.

It turns out the woman who fed me cookies and allowed me to use her house phone has come forward after seeing my brother's face on the news. She remembers meeting him ever so briefly and, more importantly, she remembers meeting me. How shaken I was. The bloody laceration on my forehead. How it seemed as if I had been lying about how I'd gotten it. And the police would've perhaps thought nothing of all this if it weren't for the man. The man who had been at the scene and had seen my face reflected in my wing mirror, if only for a split second, before I'd driven away.

'I'm sure it was a female driver,' the man had said, at the time. But then Elijah came forward and, despite writing down the man's statement in full, the Black police officer in charge had dismissed this part of it. We all look the same to them, he probably thought, after years of being treated as such.

In the cold, grey interrogation room, I listen as the detectives explain how they've begun to put the pieces together and I decide I don't want to pretend any more. I ask for a recess, and while they're out of the room and the tape recorder is switched off, I beg Momma and our lawyer to allow me to put a stop to all this.

'If I don't tell the truth, I'll go crazy,' I say. 'All these lies, every day, what it's doing to you, to Elijah . . . I wanna die, Momma. I feel so guilty. In church, we talk about forgiveness being the road to redemption, but how can I start that journey if Cody's parents still don't know what really happened to their little boy?'

Momma holds my face in her hands and then draws me into her, squeezing me tight.

'We could tell them about Fontaine,' our lawyer says. 'Use that as part of our defence when it goes to court. If he's out of the country, we may not be able to get him to stand trial himself, unless the French government are willing to extradite him. But, if we discuss your accusations against him in court, the judge might be more lenient.'

'Is this really want you want, Sadie?' Momma asks, peeling back so she can look at me again. What I want is to press a rewind button that reverses everything that's happened these past couple of months. The flame of a Molotov cocktail disappearing back into the match that lit it. Red paint that covered our porch being sucked back into its can. Shells of smashed eggs repaired and made whole again. Elijah walking backwards out of the police station. The multicoloured clump in the road springing back to life. Me, never knocking on Gaultier's door in the first place.

But I can't have that. Any of that. So instead I just nod.

NINETEEN

The dance studio looks brand new. The floor a polished black vinyl, absent of any imperfection. I'm the first to arrive and I'm wondering, already, if this has all been a huge mistake. Barely remembering the ride here, I realise I must have driven on autopilot, my head in the clouds the whole way. The thought of this scares me. Not being absolutely present when I am behind the wheel is a wickedly unforgiveable crime given my history.

My hair is scraped into a bun. I'm wearing a black leotard, pale pink tights and flesh-coloured ballet shoes. White flesh, of course. Not mine. Never mine, I think.

But then I remember something. They *do* make shoes in more shades these days. Why didn't I try to find them?

This thought is quickly replaced by another: my age. What am I doing dressed like this? Taking a ballet class after all these years? I'll stick out like a sore thumb. The other students will surely notice me. Notice how much less flexible I am compared to them, the younger, slimmer dancers. How I don't, can't, jump nearly as high as they can. How my sense of balance often fails me when I need it most.

And yet, as I approach the barre, I see how the light flatters me, making me look so much younger than my years. In fact, almost exactly how I looked the last time I danced, as a teen. There's a crackle as a speaker somewhere in the room springs to life and music filters in. Quiet. Almost imperceptible at first. But then it grows louder.

God only knows what I'd be without you.

The song sounds slower than I remember, the acoustics of the room making it echo as it bounces off the breeze-blocked walls. Gripping the barre with my left hand, I float my right arm out to the side, shoulder height, my right foot drifting out to the side along with it.

And then I see him in my peripheral vision, reflected in the mirror. *Feel* him leaning in to whisper something in my left ear. I whirl round to face him, but . . .

Nothing. No one. The music stops abruptly and only my own warped reflection stares back at me through the black as I look down at my feet. I slide my toe against the vinyl and it feels cold underfoot, as if I am standing on the surface of a dark, frozen lake. And then, without warning, it caves in beneath me and I am suddenly sinking into blue, flailing, desperate for breath. Gaultier swims towards me and the music starts again, distorted here in the deep end. I scream, but only bubbles come out, chlorine rushing in to fill my lungs. Water in my eyes and hair and dribbling down my neck.

Dribbling down my neck?

'Sadie!' Derek shouts, and I open my eyes to find myself sitting up in bed, my face and hair wet, my husband holding an empty glass.

'What . . . what the fuck?' I pant.

'I couldn't get you wake up,' he says. 'You were having one of your nightmares again.'

I nod, wipe my face with my hands and get out of bed, taking my phone with me. On the toilet, my attempt to get back to reality by scrolling social media is thwarted by an ad posted halfway down my feed: 'Have you had a bad experience with wellness and movement community Deep Flow? A lawsuit is currently being brought against its founder and you might be entitled to damages. Call Cavill's Legal now for more information.' I click the ad and land on the law firm's page. It takes me all of five seconds before I find what I'm looking for – or, rather, who. A post with an all too familiar face smiling back at me: Mumtaz.

'Sure you don't wanna take the kitchen sink with you too?' Derek jokes as I drop the last of my luggage by the front door. I make a face, tell him he's not as funny as he thinks and then throw my arms around him.

'I will miss you,' I say. 'Even though you're the worst.'

He laughs and reminds me that he's been away from me for far longer periods on his numerous work-related trips. Surely I'm used to us being apart by now.

'It's different when you're the one leaving,' I say, even though deep down I suspect it's harder to be the one left behind. Each time I've bade Derek goodbye, I've had to go on living the same life while navigating the gaping hole he's left in his wake. Meanwhile, he has undoubtedly had the opportunity to replace my energy with that of new and exciting people, and our home with interesting and culture-filled locales.

'Make sure you keep a regular bedtime,' I tell him. 'No binging Netflix 'til four in the morning. It'll fuck up your internal clock and throw off everything else in your life.'

He rolls his eyes. It's excessive mothering and I know that. But I also know I'm right and he knows himself well enough to be aware of exactly the kind of slippery slope he runs the risk of sliding down.

'You just make sure you come back to me, okay?' he says.

'What do you mean?' I ask, frowning.

'I dunno. I guess I've watched enough true-crime documentaries to know that sometimes people go off to the desert and never come back.'

I stare at him, then kiss my teeth. 'See. This is what I mean about watching too much late-night Netflix, Derek.'

He playfully swats my ass and then pulls me in for a deep, long kiss – our last until we are reunited.

'I love you,' he says, when we finally pull apart.

'I love you too,' I smile, the warmth of all he is spreading through me. Right on cue, we hear the double honk of a horn – the van hired to transport us to the retreat. I land little kisses all over Derek's face and squeeze him one last time before, together, we gather up my things and head out to the van. He tells me to jump inside and I climb into the empty seat next to Emily. She says hi and Constance, who is sitting in front of me, does the same. Through the back window, I watch Derek load my stuff into the trunk of the van, all long limbs and smiles. He knows it's the last thing he'll get to do for me for a while and, when he's done, he taps on the window round Lilith's side of the vehicle. She rolls it down.

'You look after her, okay?' he says.

Lilith twinkles, tells him I'm in the safest hands, but not to expect me to come back unchanged. 'Imagine a snake shedding its skin,' she says. 'We will all leave things behind. Things that no longer serve us. Maybe people too!'

Derek stares at her for a moment, unsure of what to make of her statement. Eventually, he just yells his goodbyes into the van and taps the side of the door, letting the driver know he's happy for us to go. Even if I could see past the heads of the other women packed into the vehicle, I choose not to look back. I am almost certain, however, that Derek's eyes are on us, watching until we disappear over the horizon.

When we arrive at the park, the air is sticky and shimmering with heat. All nine of us disembark and the driver helps us unpack our luggage. He tells us this is as far as he can take us in the van. We'll have to walk the rest of the way to the retreat centre.

'It's not far,' Lilith says. 'And I'm sure you were all wise enough to travel light.'

Staring at my three bags and large suitcase, I realise I've fucked up. Already. But, just as I'm beginning to grapple with my various belongings, Emily comes to my rescue, picking up two of my smaller bags. I thank her and we share a grin. Perhaps our friendship isn't dead in the water after all. The driver takes off, leaving a cloud of reddish-brown dirt in his wake. No turning back now.

With Ruby, Natalia and Lilith leading the crowd, Constance, Emily and I bring up the rear while Debbie, Andrea and Bridget chat away in the middle of the cluster. Given how unsure Bridget seemed about continuing with Deep Flow that day we all went for tacos, it's certainly a pleasant surprise that she's made the commitment to come to the retreat.

'I just need a massive life overhaul,' I hear her saying to Andrea. 'My job hasn't been making me happy for a long time and things aren't great in my relationship either. Coming away with you guys felt like an obvious choice in the end.'

'What is it you do for a living?' Debbie asks.

'Uh . . . recruitment,' Bridget replies, cringing slightly as she does. 'I know it's not very cool. I bet you're all creatives or media types.'

'Sadie is,' Emily says, as we start to gain on Bridget and the others. 'She's an artist.'

'Yes! I remember you mentioning. Is there anywhere I can see your work?'

It's a question I'm used to and one I've always struggled to navigate.

'I'm . . . getting some work together for a show. I'll keep you posted.'

'And Constance works in costume design, don't you?' Emily continues.

'Wardrobe. On movie sets,' Constance says, gently correcting her. Emily does her famous headshake, clearly a little embarrassed: oops! 'Easy mistake to make,' Constance kindly caveats.

'What about you, Debbie?' Bridget asks.

'Four kids! They're a full time job, let me tell you.'

'And you, Emily?'

'Still trying to find my thing, but I'm doing some sports modelling at the moment. I surf and social media endorsements pay the bills. Not that I'm an influencer or anything.'

I try not to scoff. Emily *absolutely* is an influencer and, given she is heir to a huge family fortune, I highly doubt her endorsements are necessary for anything other than pocket money.

'Have you ever heard of Elements?' I hear Natalia ask Bridget and I choose that moment to purposely zone out of the conversation.

Beneath my skirt, my thighs start to rub together and, inside my shoes, my toes begin to swell in the heat.

'Is it much further?' Debbie asks, and a few of us echo her sentiment.

'It'll be worth it,' Lilith says simply, leaving all of us unsatisfied. It feels like hours before the building becomes visible, and our sore feet and aching calves only just carry us over the threshold. Each of us caked in sweat and eager for a shower. We peel off into two separate groups that will stay in two adjoining dorm-style rooms: Debbie, Andrea, Ruby and Constance in one and the rest of us in the other.

On arrival, we're all asked to hand over our phones, with the aim of 'protecting our sacred container', keeping our 'safe space' as safe as possible. I give mine willingly. Mostly because I've felt so tethered to it recently, my habit of repeatedly checking in on the Michaelsons still very much an issue. Not to mention the fact that, each time my phone rings these days, bad news seems to follow. Tapping out of reality and going off grid for a while feels like an attractive prospect.

The showers are cold but none of us mind. All we want is

to feel clean again. The last in our dorm to shower, Bridget reappears after ten minutes with her hair wrapped in a towel, still dripping and trailing soap suds across the stone floor of our room.

'So, how long have each of you been part of the Deep Flow community?' she asks, breezily. She already knows my story but the others answer and Bridget then fishes for information on why we might've joined. 'Feels like we all want to change our lives,' she says, wistfully, after hearing our stories.

'Are things that bad?' Natalia asks, sympathetically.

'Honestly, I just feel kind of . . . stuck,' Bridget replies.

'Well, then,' Natalia smiles. 'You're in exactly the right place.'

For the opening circle, we filter into a huge space with an entirely wooden interior and a gigantic domed ceiling. Already, there are mats laid out, bolsters and blankets strewn every-where. Lilith and Natalia quickly set about lighting dozens of candles and sticks of incense before placing the latter in burners of all different styles. The identifiable scent of Californian white sage reaches my nostrils and reminds me of home. My recent insistence on saging the place each morning is a source of much amusement for Derek, but even he has to admit the aroma is comforting. As I find my place in the room, I notice more women pouring in. Women that aren't from our original party. I recognise several of them from the Soul Awakening Weekender. These are the women Lilith mentioned might be coming – Deep Flow devotees from studios elsewhere in America, along with the studio hosts Lilith has trained up herself to be conduits for her work.

Once we are all in and settled, I do a quick internal head

count and surmise that there are around fifty of us present. I consider that, if we are those who managed to make it to the retreat, there must be at least a hundred more who couldn't afford it or weren't available. Deep Flow is growing in numbers and I feel so lucky to be among the privileged few that get to connect with it in a more profound way over the coming days.

That doesn't mean, however, that I'm not a little apprehensive. Especially after the Soul Awakening Weekender and the unfortunate ramifications of my fatigue. Not that my tiredness was entirely to blame, of course, but I may have dealt with things that happened in a better way had I not been so exhausted.

When I finally had the opportunity to speak to Lilith about it all, taking care to leave out my firing from Prisma Tech Solutions, she put my mind at rest. 'Perhaps fate drew these challenges to you at that particular time *because* you were at your rawest and most vulnerable. Not in spite of that. The universe clearly wanted you to feel things fully. Maybe doing so released some emotional blocks.'

This thought helps me swat away the other one, that ugly, terrible thing lurking in the corner of my eye: Lilith's treatment of Veronica. *How much more incredible could this beautiful space be if she let all women in?* I wonder.

After her opening speech, we start to work our way around what is now an enormous circle of people. One after another, we introduce ourselves and sum up why we are here in three words. When it's my turn, I pause. Looking around the room, I spot Constance, offering a warm smile, Bridget giving me a nod of encouragement. Even Natalia graces me with a wink.

'Belonging,' I say. 'Acceptance. Hope.'

There's a thin ripple of applause that tells me many of the women here identify with what I've said. It's enough to make me feel validated, comfortable here at last.

During the tour of the building, we are shown around the kitchen, which is laden with fruit and vegetables, the refrigerator packed to overflowing with meat and fish, cupboards fit to burst with grains and bread and cans of beans and chopped tomatoes. Lilith's San Diego counterpart, Isla, explains that we'll be taking it in turns to cook, in groups of five. 'It'll be the perfect opportunity for you to get to know your sisters within a different context and for you to experience the joy of serving others,' she tells us.

When dinner comes, it is piping hot and plentiful – a far cry from what we experienced at Soul Awakening. Two members of the Denver contingent and three others who practise Deep Flow in Milwaukee and the brand-new Omaha studio are in charge of cooking and serving this evening. What they have achieved amongst them is astonishing: fillets of salmon that are crispy on the skin side but flaky and melt-in-the-mouth on the other, served on a bed of cannellini beans cooked with spinach in some kind of spicy tomato passata. Then there's bread and potatoes baked to perfection, cherry strudel for dessert, served with buckets of ice cream passed along the table, and washed down with gallons of herbal tea. We end the night outside, chatting around three different camp fires. Devon, the facilitator of the Hamptons branch of Deep Flow, tells me she used to be a girl scout: 'I could build a fire anywhere,' she boasts. 'From literally nothing.'

Lilith overhears her and laughs. 'That's because you're a lightworker. Not because you're a former girl scout.'

An hour later, I decide to extract myself from a conversation about how the Rockefellers and the royal family are most definitely lizards, in favour of dragging my aching limbs, tired feet and heavy belly back towards the dorms. Bedtime beckons and I silently pray for a long, dreamless slumber from which I'll wake up refreshed, remembering nothing but black. I realise sleep might have to wait, however, when I spot Emily sitting on Bridget's bed, holding what looks like a diary.

'You okay?' I ask.

'I dunno, Sadie,' Emily says. 'I . . . I don't wanna throw accusations around, but . . . I think Bridget's a journalist.'

'What?'

I rush over to sit beside her and she hands me the notebook. The pages are covered in scrawled handwriting, as if each sentence has been written hurriedly. Both mine and Emily's names are mentioned repeatedly and I also spot the names of the rest of our cohort, detailing things we've said and what Bridget thinks of us. She describes me as 'sweet but directionless', Emily as much the same. Ruby is 'cruel but beautiful. The kind of girl that might've bullied you at school.'

'How do you know this isn't just a diary?' I ask.

Emily shrugs. 'I don't. But I've had this weird feeling about her since we got in the van. All the questions. The fishing comments. The fact that she's come from nowhere and all of a sudden decided to come on this trip.'

'She hasn't come from nowhere. She's been attending classes for weeks,' I snort.

Emily grabs the notebook back and waves it in my face. 'Don't you think she writes a little too well for someone who just works in recruitment?'

'I dunno. I don't know what people in recruitment write like. All I'm trying to do is caution you against jumping to conclusions. And look – say she *is* a journalist, would it really matter that much?'

'Please. I know you of all people wouldn't want anyone publishing an article about you.'

My face prickles with heat. Has Lilith said something?

'What is that supposed to mean?' I ask, dreading the answer.

'That you're super secretive. You don't get close to anyone. You . . . keep yourself to yourself, don't you? Not in like a serial killer kind of way. But like . . . it's obvious you're hiding *something*, Sadie.'

Keen to deflect, I pull the journal out of Emily's hands and skip to a random page. 'Natalia seems to believe Lilith has powers that extend into the realm of fertility,' I read aloud. 'While she hasn't explicitly attributed her pregnancy to her, she's certainly implied Lilith might've had a part to play.'

Emily gives me a 'told-you-so' look, but I refuse to bite. 'I really think this is just a diary, Em. Let's not blow things out of proportion.'

Getting up to start my bedtime routine, I toss the book onto the bed, dismissively.

'You're saying I should just forget I ever saw anything?'

'Well, you can't exactly confront her, can you? What would you say? Sorry I read your diary, but despite the fact I had no discernible proof – and still don't – I suspected you might be a hack?'

Emily looks deflated. 'I guess, when you put it like that . . .'

I return to my seat and put a comforting hand on her knee. 'You're just trying to protect us. I get that. But . . . even if she is a journalist, she'd have to change all our names anyway. That's, like, a legal requirement. Unless we gave our permission. And she'd be writing about Deep Flow. Not about us as individuals. With Lilith and the others wanting to expand, that can only be a good thing, right? It's free press for our community.'

My bed is looking all too irresistible now. I get up and move towards it.

'Besides,' I continue, fluffing my pillow. 'It's not like Deep Flow has anything to hide.'

TWENTY

Derek and I spent our honeymoon in Italy, hopping from Florence to Lake Garda and then on to Venice, where an old woman on a street corner insisted on telling us our fortunes in exchange for ten euros each. We'd walked what felt like miles that day, so our calves were like bricks, my lower back pulsating with pain. It had been worth it, though, of course. The sights we'd seen. The stores we'd overspent in. The food, glorious. It was only three thirty, according to Derek's vintage gold Casio, and already we were exhausted and sun-baked enough to be grateful for the offer of a chair and a sit down at the end of the cobbled street we'd just walked along. We almost didn't mind what we were paying for.

I'd expected tarot cards. Maybe a crystal ball. Instead, the woman poured hot tea into chipped china, loose leaves filling the bottom of the cup. She stirred and, in a thick Italian accent, told us each to ask a question about our future.

'Will I make it?' Derek wondered out loud, before clarifying how keen he was to know what may be in store for his directing career. The woman poured the tea out onto the cobbles and then gazed so deeply into the cup at the remaining leaves I feared she might fall in.

'You will be frustrated for long time first. And you will never be happy with your success. Never enough for you. Big, big highs. Also, lows. But always you will have a . . . *carriera*. Eh . . . what is the word?'

'Career?' I suggest, helpfully.

'Yes, as I say. A career you will have. Now, you.' She nodded towards me and put down the cup, leaving Derek slightly shell shocked. She rinsed the china out with sparkling water straight from the bottle and then filled it up with tea again. The steaming liquid came from a very pragmatic -looking metal flask. No-frills mysticism at its best.

'What is the question you have for me to ask?'

'I dunno. Um . . . I guess I just wanna know what will make me happy?'

She looks at me, seemingly displeased. 'You Americans always want to find shortcut. I tell fortune, not help you be lazy.'

Confused, I stammer a sort of apology. 'Should I ask a different question? I . . . I don't understand.'

'Life is about discovering for yourself your happy thing, no? My thinking is this. But . . . I will answer your question,' she says, tipping the cup onto the ground with even more vigour than she had when she'd read Derek's fortune. The dark water splashed onto the wall of the house behind her, staining the yellow stone brown.

'I see a bird,' she says, after a minute or two. 'Wings big like flying. This means freedom, I think.'

Then, before either of us could ask any further questions, she looked up from the cup and abruptly told us to 'have nice life'.

'Well. She was . . . delightful,' Derek said, once we were

both safely round the corner. And, in an instant, we were both laughing so hard we could barely stand up.

Since then, however, I've always questioned what the bird might've meant. Wondered what freedom is to me and how I can attain it. Years later, as I wait to have my fortune read again, this time via tarot, that thought returns.

Esther, who leads Deep Flow in Omaha, sits surrounded by a circle of her cards, which look to be from multiple different decks. Informed by my first experience, I'm determined to get things right. As the old Italian lady proved, happiness is too broad a subject for any definitive answers and, the truth is, I've always known that art is what makes me feel joy. That whatever and wherever I'm creating feels like home. But putting it out into the world is another thing entirely. So, when my turn arrives, I keep a different question in mind. The same question that, at twelve years old, I saw Laurence Olivier's evil Nazi character repeatedly ask Dustin Hoffman's beleaguered runner in the film *Marathon Man*: 'Is it safe?'

'You can go ahead and pull a card,' Esther says. 'Or even as many as three, if you'd like?'

Waving my hands over the decks in the hope of generating some sort of magical energy, I carefully choose three cards and Esther tells me to turn them over when I'm ready. The first is the Garden of Delights, and the image on the card reminds me of Daddy's perfectly curated garden back in Savannah. Verdant, with glimpses of red and blue flowers gleaming like rubies and sapphires amongst the shrubbery. The one good thing that came from being forced to move. The second card presents another outdoor scene: a bronzed, naked woman pouring water into a pool, a giant yellow star hanging above her head.

Turning over the third and final card, I feel myself recoil at the sight of a skeleton clad in iron, riding a horse and carrying a black flag. A golden king awaits him, a blazing sun beyond the horizon, but neither of these things mitigate the word written in block capitals across the top of the card: DEATH. Esther senses my worry and reaches for my hand, giving it a comforting squeeze.

'Death isn't always a bad thing,' she says. 'It's natural and inevitable. It's beyond our control and that's scary. This card often means the death of something you hold dear. But that thing is often replaced by something better. So, really, it's about change.'

Reassured, I nod. 'Let's talk about the other cards,' Esther says, picking one up. 'The Star is a very hopeful card. It's all about creativity and healing. The possibility of achieving one's goals, but that being dependent on you having the faith to continue, even through hard times. It's a reminder that you are blessed and the universe will bring forth everything you need.'

'Okay,' I say, grinning. 'That's a great card to pull. We're on the up.'

Esther chuckles. 'Seriously. Trust me when I say that the Death card is not a bad card. I remember pulling it at a really significant time in my life, years ago. I'd grown up Mormon in Salt Lake City and decided to leave my community. It was a tough decision and for months afterwards I felt so lost. And then I met Lilith. She was doing tarot readings at a convention I stumbled into and I pulled the Death card. At first, I was terrified, but when Lilith explained what it meant, it made total sense. Something dear to me was no longer a part of my life.

But that reading gave me hope that there were better things to come. And there were!'

Struck by Esther's story, I consider what I might need to lose in favour of something better. 'What if I lost something a few years ago and I'm still waiting for the good stuff to replace it? Does that count?'

'Far be it for me to speak on behalf of the universe, but I think it would have to be more recent. Perhaps something you still have to lose.'

Like a rolodex, my mind flips through all the things I hold dear: Derek, Momma and Daddy, Elijah and his little family, Raheem. My thoughts drift to Veronica. It was still early days when our friendship ended, but the connection we had felt very real and the loss of her has been painful. Could she be the blood sacrifice that has been necessary to make way for whatever comes next?

'You're an Amber member now, right? Do you ever dream of becoming a Carnelian or Obsidian?'

'I don't think I could afford it,' I say.

'It's an investment,' Esther nods, 'and that comes with sacrifice.'

Esther picks up my final card: the Garden of Delights.

'So this card is from one of my oracle decks and it's about allowing yourself to live a life of beauty, love and abundance. But first that needs to come with the realisation that you deserve those things. You've been stuck living a limited life under a false illusion of security for a long time now. But living like that it not truly living. Stepping into the garden is risky, but the rewards are fruitful if you are ready and open enough to receive them.'

Realising my face is wet with tears, I wrap my arms around myself and press my chin towards my chest. Esther reaches out and wipes my cheeks.

'Does this resonate?'

'Yeah,' I say, sniffing loudly. 'I'm definitely fearful of stepping into that garden. And I absolutely question whether I'm deserving of any of the things in it.'

'But you are, dear one,' Esther says. 'You are so deserving. Your choice to come here, to be a part of what we do and the community we've built, proves that you want to continue to work on yourself. Which makes you even more deserving. You don't need to be this tightly wound. Those walls you think are protecting you are just barriers to what you want. Open your hands and accept what's yours.'

She holds both my wrists, encouraging me to physically open my hands, and I bawl like a baby as light pours in through the cracks for the first time in years.

'So, my hair is starting to grow back,' Constance says, whipping off her wig for a moment to show us the layer of fuzz underneath. 'And I'm feeling better than I have for ages. Chemo was sucking the life out of me and *crippling* me financially. Lilith's regime is cheaper and I actually feel like me again!'

While the rest of the women at the lunch table clap, I occupy my hands by tearing another hunk of bread from the loaf in front of me. I can't deny that Constance is glowing, but I also can't endorse her quitting Western medicine entirely. Not when the stakes are so high. Plagued with guilt at having been the person who introduced her to Lilith in the first place, I've repeatedly tried to talk sense into her over the last few weeks. But every time it seems as if I'm getting somewhere, Lilith's methods manage to convince Constance all over again. The word 'miracle' comes up in conversation more than I would like and, with big pharma being almost impossible to defend, I've ended up feeling entirely rudderless. It's not hard to see how Constance has been pushed towards this.

I allow my ears to pick up another nearby conversation. Isla, from the San Diego branch, is holding court further down the table, talking about the time the San Diego studio was burned almost to the ground.

'If the trauma of it all didn't bond us for life, the rebuild sure did. There was something so special about starting again. About building a studio that represents and caters for the community we'd already established. We were given such bitter lemons and yet, together, we still made the most beautiful lemonade. Years later, our little hive is stronger than ever.'

Someone, who I assume is a member of the San Diego studio, leans in to hug Isla, announcing how much she loves her as she does. Isla is their Lilith, I think, just as Esther is the Lilith of Omaha and Marie and Janine fill the role for the Milwaukee and Denver contingents, with Devon covering the Hamptons. Like Esther, they will all likely have Deep Flow origin stories of their own and, after lunch, I get some insight into why dozens of the women attending the retreat have found solace in this community.

We sit in a circle, all of us cross-legged, some of us eyes closed, others looking into the centre. Too curious to close my eyes, I allow them to gently scan the room in nervous anticipation. A woman suddenly raises both hands to the sky and proclaims, 'I practise Deep Flow to forget my abusive ex-husband!'

The effect is like dominoes. Another woman not far from her puts her hands up in the air and closes her eyes: 'I practise Deep Flow to cope with grief.' Then another: 'I practise Deep Flow because I hate my job, but feel like I can't quit.'

The annunciations go on and on.

'I practise so I don't leave my wife and children.'

'I practise so the agony of my *apparently incurable* endometriosis doesn't drive me insane.'

'I practise Deep Flow because I'm lonely and need connection.'

'I practise Deep Flow to deal with my anxiety.'

'I practise to deal with depression.'

'I practise because my husband left me for my best friend.'

'I practise because my twin died in a shooting last year and left a gaping hole behind.'

'I practise Deep Flow because motherhood made me forget who I was.'

'I practise to restore a sense of empowerment and safety within my life after a home invasion stole that from me.'

'I practise Deep Flow because my son went missing four years ago and not having to think about where he is and if he might be dead for even five minutes is a mercy.'

'I practise to deal with my addiction issues.'

'I practise because I was sexually assaulted during my first year of college and I've never gotten over it.'

As we continue to purge our secrets, the declarations get heavier and more detailed. I realise that, eventually, I'll have to speak up.

'I practise Deep Flow to manage my guilt,' I yelp, casting my eyes towards the wooden roof. Somehow, it doesn't cave in. Somehow, despite the pressure within me bursting upwards and outwards, everything around me stays intact.

When everyone is finished, Lilith tells us we'll keep the container open for a minute or two, 'in case anyone wants to say anything else, then we'll close the practice'. We wait in silence for a while and then Lilith signals for us all to hold hands. There's an intensity to it, though, as if we are each about to give birth. All clenched fists and gritted teeth. And then the moaning starts. At first, it sounds as if the women who started it are in serious pain, but, by the time this noisy little virus reaches me, I realise we are attempting to release pain from experiences past.

'We have all suffered,' Lilith shouts over us all, her typically calm voice suddenly booming. 'It is human to suffer. But I am proud to be able to give you special access to the spirit of the universe. And it gladdens my heart to know that I am, along with sisters Esther, Isla, Marie, Devon and Janine, your conduit to self-discovery. We are the middlemen – or women,' she chuckles at this, and her counterparts laugh along with her. 'The middlewomen between you and the light, and I feel such gratitude for that. It is my greatest privilege. Now, let us close with an ohm, and as you let this sound travel out of you, let all tension and worry leave your body too.'

The groans gently subside into silence. Then we open our mouths again and hum together, sending soundwaves bouncing across every surface once more.

'With this ohm, we are one,' Lilith says, when the noise of it fades away. I notice a few session members have tears dribbling down their faces. The whole experience has been cathartic. Freeing, almost. I think of the bird at the bottom of the tea cup. Then of the dream I had where I was airborne and tiny, floating towards Lilith, alighting in her hands only for her to consume me whole. Maybe allowing oneself to be consumed, surrendering entirely, handing over control to someone who knows better, maybe that's what freedom is. No need to think. No need to decide on anything. A true escape from mistakes and, therefore, regret. Space to just *be*.

We filter out of the room for snacks and bathroom breaks. I'm about to head back to the dorm when I get a tap on the shoulder.

'Manage your guilt about what?' Ruby wants to know. Natalia is by her side, twirling a lock of her flame red hair around her finger like a high schooler.

'Just . . . past mistakes,' I say, deftly parrying her overstep. '*You* never do anything you wish you hadn't?'

'Sure.' Ruby shrugs. 'But feeling guilty about it isn't useful to anybody.'

'I think feeling guilty, especially if you've wronged someone else, shows you have compassion,' a steely Constance says, as she joins the conversation.

'How useful do you think your guilt actually is to that person, though? People want explanations. Truth. For situations to be resolved, if that's possible. Guilt is self-indulgent. It's for you. Because you think that self-flagellating somehow redeems you. It doesn't.'

'Maybe you should just give Sadie room to feel whatever

288

she needs to feel, okay?' Constance says, before wheeling me away from Ruby and Natalia protectively. 'I *really* don't like her,' she says, lowering her voice, conspiratorially. 'She thinks that, just because she's an Obsidian, she can talk to us lowly Carnelians like shit.'

'Yeah, I do kind of feel like I've dodged a bullet in not having to room with her,' I say, deciding not to mention I'm still only an Amber.

Constance mimes shooting herself in the head, making a little splat noise as her imaginary brains hit the wall next to us before the top half of her body slumps forward theatrically. I giggle and then drift into silence for a moment, considering Ruby's comments.

'What if there is some truth in what she was saying, though?'

Constance makes a face as if she has drunk sour milk, then shifts the focus to Ruby's sidekick.

'Wild that Lilith helped her get pregnant, isn't it?'

I stare after Natalia wistfully. 'Yeah.'

'Do you and Derek want kids?' Constance follows up.

'We tried. I had a miscarriage,' I blurt out. 'A few years ago. It was quite far into the pregnancy so . . . I thought we were . . .' I trail off. Constance's eyes widen and I realise I'm as surprised as she is that I've suddenly shared this information.

'Sorry,' I mutter, without really knowing why.

'What?' Constance exclaims. 'You have nothing to be sorry about. I'm so glad you told me. People need to talk about this stuff more. So many people go through it.'

'I know,' I say. 'It's just . . . well . . . you've got enough of your own stuff going on.'

'Hey,' Constance says, punching me in the arm, playfully. 'Just because I have cancer doesn't mean I can't empathise with what other people are going through.'

I smile, comforted by her kindness.

'I don't know if you can tell – the genetic lottery being what it is – but I'm actually half-Japanese. On my mom's side. And in our culture, we talk about "mizuko" – water babies. Ever heard of that?'

I shake my head and she continues.

'The idea is that the unborn child's soul lives in this in-between place. At conception it starts to get to know its parents and get a sense of the world and then it decides if it's the right time to be born. If it doesn't feel right, the pregnancy ends and the soul returns at another time. So no soul is ever really lost.'

I feel my eyes begin to well up as something inside me shifts. 'Thank you,' I half-whisper. 'People never usually know what to say but that was lovely.'

She shakes her head with a grin. 'Don't sweat it. I'd wager, like, ninety-nine per cent of people have no idea what to say to me half the time either. When they find out I'm sick, I mean. Veronica, she's great, though, huh? Always knows how to make me feel like a person again. You know, instead of a human pill box. How come I haven't seen her in a while?'

Inside my head, I venture down a corridor of possibilities. Possible lies I could tell to mask my guilt and embarrassment and keep my loyalty to Lilith intact. But as I move down the hall, each door swings shut, one by one, until I arrive at the only one that remains open. A painful inevitability: the truth.

'Lilith felt Veronica wasn't a good fit for the Deep Flow

community. And she felt that I'd be the best person to tell her that. So I don't think Veronica is all too happy with me right now.'

'What do you mean "not a good fit"?' Constance asks, her brow furrowing.

'Well, she had a bit of a problem with—'

'Vulvas!' Lilith suddenly says into a microphone now set up on a platform at the front of the room. My conversation with Constance will have to wait. 'Gather round, gather round, my angels. Our Female Sexuality workshop is about to begin. It's time to make friends with your vulva.'

Constance and I exchange a look as we both try not to laugh. The itinerary of the retreat has been shrouded in mystery since the start, so every event has been a surprise thus far.

'Okay then,' Constance says, and, arm in arm, we head over to where the crowd is gathering.

We start by removing our underwear. This morning we'd all, without explanation, been told to wear dresses or skirts. Now I realise the instruction was designed to make this moment easier. Marie sits up front with Lilith and Janine, playing a drum, while Janine sings a sweetly ethereal, lyricless song, floating her melody below Lilith's words. We start to move and Lilith tells us to enjoy our unharnessed bodies, feeling the freedom between our legs. Later, I find myself sat with dozens of other women, staring at the reflections of our nether regions in hand mirrors we've all been given. No one is less than about eight feet away from me and yet I still feel self-conscious, particularly when Lilith begins to instruct us on how to 'have a conversation with' our vulvas. If Derek could see me now.

Repeating Lilith's affirmations, I tell my vulva she is beautiful.

That she is a unique and celebrated flower. That she is the gateway to my womanhood. My sexuality. The last two snag. The idea of being defined as a woman based on my sexual organs doesn't sit right with me. It *sounds* like feminism, but surely I'm more than that? And as for my vulva being the gateway to my sexuality . . .

I remember my third date with Derek. How he'd told me he was 'obsessed' with my mind. How my creativity and intelligence was what he found most sexy about me. I'd thought it was all game. But, years later, I get the same compliments from him.

Then there was that women and non-binary-folks-only club night I became a regular at while in college. Where dressing up only for myself, entirely outside of the male gaze, had made me feel more empowered and sexier than ever.

'Stay out of your head and return to your body,' Lilith says, as if she can hear my thoughts. I steal a glance in her direction. Her eyes are closed and she is swaying to Marie and Janine's music as if in a trance. 'The past does not define you. The future is of no consequence. Remain in the present moment. Remain in your body.'

My mind whirrs again: how can the future be of no consequence? Isn't the future entirely about consequences? What is the present moment without the context of my past if my past is how I got here in the first place?

Shut up, Sadie, I tell myself. *Stop thinking and just focus.*

Attempting push away my doubts, I lock into the music, focusing on the rhythm of the drum, synchronising my breath to every beat. Then, I turn my eyes back to the mirror.

'You are not to be ashamed of. I carry you between my legs and I feel proud!'

Lilith then encourages us all to touch ourselves down there while still looking in the mirror. 'Repeat after me, sisters: you are perfect. You are perfect. You are perfect. Forgive me for how I have wronged you. I am sorry. I am sorry. You are perfect.'

I follow her instruction, pushing through my discomfort. And, at first, it's fine. But then, a few minutes in, my stomach really starts to churn and, suddenly, it's *his* hands touching me, *his* words telling me he's sorry, that I'm perfect. Whispering in my ear, his French accent dripping sweet nothings, and I can almost feel the weight of him on top of me, suffocating me.

The mirror clatters onto the floor as I pull down my dress, jump up and run out of the room, bare feet on hot, red dirt as the door slams shut behind me. I allow my body to carry my faltering mind several yards away from the retreat to a group of rocks under a tree. Grateful for the shade, I sink down onto one of the stones, head in my hands.

'Get a grip, Sadie,' I say to myself, under my breath.

'You okay?' a voice asks, and I look up, squinting into the sunlight. Bridget and Emily are standing over me, at first silhouetted against the searing yellow light of the mid-afternoon sun. Touched that they've both followed me out, I'm unsure of what to say. All they get in return for their concern is a nod.

Bridget sits down next to me.

'Did you . . . feel triggered?'

Another nod.

'They should've issued a warning. I think this workshop might be quite challenging for a lot of sexual-abuse or sexual-assault survivors. Would you say that label might be one you relate to?'

293

Emily tuts loudly. 'Why are you asking her that?'

'Sorry. I didn't mean to overstep.'

Finally managing to find a few words, I tell her it's fine. That she's right. I do relate.

There's a long silence and I half expect cracks to appear in the ground as the carefully constructed world I've created for myself begins to fall apart. But there is nothing. Just Emily sitting down on the other side of me and saying the words: 'Me too.'

I stare at her in shock. 'My uncle,' she clarifies. 'I was thirteen. It went on for a while. Then my parents found out and sent me to boarding school in New England. About as far away from them as they could get me.'

'That's appalling,' Bridget says, and I open and close my mouth a few times, speechless.

Emily shrugs. 'My father and uncle inherited the family business. Things could've gotten messy if my dad had kicked up a fuss. So he didn't. He kind of chose to believe I'd sort of . . . Lolita-ed my uncle.'

'What the fuck?' Bridget says.

'I'm really sorry that happened to you,' I eventually tell Emily, wishing I could say more. She leans her head on my shoulder affectionately and then, unexpectedly, I do say more. 'It was my dance teacher.'

A sharp intake of breath from Emily as she raises her head and stares Bridget out. 'You're not gonna publish any of this, are you?'

'Emily, come on,' I say. Coping with the awkwardness of her wild accusations and conspiracy theories on top of what I'm already feeling would be too much for me.

'What d'you mean?' Bridget asks.

'I know you're a journalist,' Emily says, deadpan.

Bridget emits a tiny sigh, like a miniature balloon deflating. And then she says nothing. My eyes widen as I turn to look at her.

'Wait. You're not . . .'

'Okay, so let me just clarify—'

'You're a fucking journalist?'

'It's not how it sounds.'

Emily snorts. 'I think it fucking is. I think you lied about what you did for a living so you could infiltrate our group and harvest personal information with the intent of publishing an article that aims to destroy our community. How am I doing?'

'If you really believed all that, why would you share such a personal story about your childhood?' Bridget asks.

'Because you have no way of proving it. And because if you dare to publish it anyway you'll look like an evil bitch from hell and my family will come after you. And they will not stop until you are sleeping in a cardboard box under the freeway. And because I'll use the settlement fee I get out of whatever mediocre paper or online platform you write for to launch my own swimwear line. And I don't believe anything would make me happier than being able to do that.'

We are all quiet then. Emily has always seemed so mild-mannered before this.

'I won't publish anything about your childhood,' Bridget says. 'Or yours, Sadie.'

'You better fucking mean that,' I say, angrier than I intend to sound as something small inside me shatters. 'And you better tell us what you're trying to do here too, or I'll go straight to Lilith and tell her to expel you.'

This seems threatening. Deadly serious. But the truth is that I don't actually mean it. Ratting Bridget out could have consequences for her that are far more dire than expulsion. It would take the most extreme circumstances for me to want to be responsible for that.

'Can you both sit down? Please?' she asks. I don't even remember standing up, but her question makes me realise that we've been towering over her rather intimidatingly for most of the conversation now. I sit down right away. Emily is slightly more reluctant, but eventually joins me.

'The first thing I want to make clear is that the article I'm writing isn't about trashing Deep Flow. But it isn't a puff piece either. There's been gossip and speculation bandied about LA for years now in regard to Lilith, her husband and, of course, Deep Flow. I just want to get to the bottom of it all. I'm only interested in the truth.'

'For someone who claims to prioritise the truth, you've sure as hell told a lot of lies to get here,' Emily sniffs.

'And I can understand why that might make you feel like you can't trust me. But I'm not here to report on any of you individually. I'll change all your names in the article, unless you don't want me to, and I won't share any personal stories that aren't relevant. What would be useful, however, is if either of you wanted to share anything about your Deep Flow experience. Good stuff. Bad stuff. Everything and anything in between? I want to get a rounded idea of what being inside this community is really like. That's why I came in undercover.'

Emily gets up. 'You can write whatever you want. But none of it will come from me. I won't say anything about you. But

I won't sell Lilith and the others down the river either. Not after all they've done for me.'

She leaves me alone with Bridget and I'm unsure of what to say. Part of me is terrified that she'll take all she knows about me, dig through my past to find out more, and then write an exposé that will bring unwanted attention to my door, with my life imploding in the process. But another part of me is possessed with the same curiosity that led me to take the job at Prisma Tech Solutions and stick it out despite the risk. What is it that Bridget knows that has led her to believe Deep Flow is a worthy subject matter for her article?

At least once during every session, Lilith tells us the work we are doing in class, on ourselves, is revolutionary. I've always doubted it. Always wondered if revolutions can begin by looking inside ourselves when the trouble is out there, in systems and institutions and government. Lilith has never once talked about politics or social issues. Only told us that a shift is happening and we are somehow part of it. Maybe Lilith's been right all along. Maybe Bridget is here to explore just how disruptive our community might end up being. Maybe rebellion is quiet sometimes.

'Will you talk to me, Sadie?' Bridget asks softly.

Twelve Years Earlier

'This could be a chance for you to tell your story,' the woman says before lighting another cigarette. She's been chain-smoking since she arrived, red lipstick-stained butts piling up in the makeshift ashtray next to her. The dish is blue and painted with red and yellow flowers. When a friend brought it back for us from Mexico during freshman year, Derek and I had marvelled at its beauty, but ultimately decided its awkward size made it impractical for anything other than the dead ends of doobies.

The woman is managing a tremendous juggling act and it's hard not be impressed. Drinking black coffee from a mug with a car dealership advertisement printed on it while puffing away and scribbling down notes in her pad, she is a well-oiled machine who has likely worked like this for decades. Neither Derek nor I have visited the car dealership printed on the mug as far as I'm aware, and I have no idea how it got into our apartment. Come to think of it, I don't really know how this woman did either.

'Sorry, what was your name again?' I ask.

'Barb,' she says, in a husky voice. 'Barb Horowitz.'

'Yes. Of course,' I reply. 'Look, I moved on from all this years ago. I'm not sure I'm the right person to—'

'Don't you care? That he's on trial?' she interrupts, staring me out. Her glasses are oversized with clear plastic rims that make her look like a bug. She casts her eye around our loft conversion, which, when you call it that, makes it sound way cooler than it actually is. In truth, it's just a huge, empty, open-plan space above what was once a car repairs shop. So maybe that's how the mug came to be here. Maybe the mug was always here. Even before we were.

'I can see you got a nice life these days, kid,' Barb continues, in a New York accent so broad that, at first, I wasn't sure it was real. 'Betcha think you're real punk rock living like this, huh?'

She nods at a giant Kandinsky-inspired canvas I'm halfway through. 'And you've gotcha self another talent. Which is great. I'm happy for you. It's important to be able to move on. From trauma, I mean.'

'I'm in therapy,' I say. 'Have been for years, actually. On and off. It's helped.'

'I'll bet,' Barb says, and draws a deep breath as if she's about to ask me another question. I cut her off before she does.

'How did you find me?'

'One of the computer geeks at the paper. He's a real whizz with Facebook.'

'No. I mean how did you *find* me? Like, how did you find out about what happened? With me and Gaultier? I was a minor. All that stuff wasn't public.'

Barb stubs out her cigarette. Takes a gulp out of the mug. 'I'm a journalist. It's my job. Plus it's amazing what fucking someone who works at the DA's office can get you.'

Internally, I squirm and start to grind my teeth.

'Listen, Ms Horowitz—'

'Barb, for Chrissake.'

'Barb. I'm glad Gaultier finally got caught out. And I hope he goes to jail. But I don't see how me talking about what he did to me – you know, publicly like this – will help anything.'

Her slender, wiry fingers prise open another pack of slims. Nails perfectly manicured, a dark bloody burgundy, the colour of red wine, so shiny the tips of her fingers look like tiny little beetles. As they glint in the soft light of the retro lamp that stands close by, she uses a fresh, unlit cigarette to point at my half-baked painting again.

'You're an artist. So I know you care more than you're making out. Because artists care about stuff. They have empathy. They got things to say about the world.'

I scoff. 'I could name you *at least* twenty famous artists that didn't give a shit about anyone but themselves. Francis Bacon. Ted Hughes. Hemingway. Dickens. Picasso—'

'All right, all right, I get it. You're smart,' Barb concedes, gesticulating enough for her smoke to waft into my face. 'Too smart for this tactic to work anyway, huh? So, lemme level with you. I'm an artist too. A storyteller, if you like. And call me old fashioned, but even in an age of bullshit tabloids and shitty little magazines, I still think this job of mine means something. I still believe that good, investigative reporting can change things. Because even if that loser abuser gets off, people will know about him. Sure, I'll have to caveat every accusation with words like "allegedly", but people know there's no smoke without fire.'

I watch Barb's own fumes curl towards the ceiling and I think of Derek, away in the Catskills, shooting a short film for his final year project. He isn't back for three days, but I'm already worrying the smell of this conversation will linger long enough for me to have to sell him a lie. Explain I had an impromptu gathering. A swirl of drinking and smoking and dancing with friends until the early hours. 'What friends?' he'd say. He knows all of them, I realise. They're his friends too.

'Sadie?' Barb prods, attempting to regain my attention as she flicks the remnants of her latest cigarette into the ashtray, leaving the embers to burn. Her subtext reads: *Wake up.* But I say nothing as my eyes catch on our unmade bed in the corner and I cringe at what a mess the place is. It's not as if I was expecting company, though, and we aren't doing too badly considering our low-income backgrounds and how crazy expensive New York is. So why do I feel so self-conscious? So exposed?

'You know, we don't have to talk about the boy. It's not relevant to the article. This is about Fontaine. Nothing else.'

For a moment it feels like all the oxygen has gone out of the room and I am being suffocated by Barb's cigarette smoke.

'I don't know what you're talking about,' I say, a noticeable quiver in my voice.

'Sadie, you were a kid. And what happened to Cody Michaelson was not your fault.'

Don't, a voice inside me begs at the mention of my victim's name. But it's too late. My shoulders shudder and I start to sob. Barb puts a comforting hand on my shoulder before getting up to pour me a glass of water.

I sip it slowly and she patiently waits for me to calm down before saying anything else.

'What happened to your brother in the end?' she asks, eventually.

'He got six months for perverting the course of justice. Half of which he'd already served in the run-up to the trial. I always thought the name of his conviction was pretty ironic given the only real pervert was Gaultier.'

After we'd downsized and moved close to Savannah, Daddy converted the garage of our two-bedroom house into a bedroom for Elijah, ready for when he got out of jail. But the lack of windows and a particularly cold winter led to him moving out only a few months later. Despite its diminutive size, however, Daddy's adoration of the beautiful back garden means that, even now he and Momma are financially a little better off, I doubt he'd ever want to abandon it for new pastures.

Elijah got kicked out of the military. Struggled to find a job for a while thanks to his criminal record. Then, eventually, he moved out of state. Followed the work he could get. I remember him saying to me once that he loved me, all of us, but couldn't help being full of resentment every time he looked at me. Even though confessing to killing Cody was his idea. Even though he felt like he had no right to feel any type of way about it. He said he could love me better from a distance. He'd never say it, but I know he blames me for the way his life turned out. And that's okay. I blame me too.

'You have to forgive yourself, Sadie,' Barb says. 'You did not murder that child. It was an accident.'

'That's what they ruled it in the end. An accident.'

But in some ways the verdict actually made me feel worse.

It had been both terrifying and humiliating to know that everything that went on between me and Gaultier was going to be laid bare in court. As a minor, I gave my testimony via video link so I wasn't privy to most of it. But even knowing it was happening made me feel nauseous and ashamed. Our lawyer kept using the word 'groomed' in relation to what Gaultier did to me. It took years before I could accept that was the case. When my mitigating circumstances failed to give my lawyer much leverage in court, though, she had to change tack.

'I was right,' Momma had said. 'They don't believe her.

Her word against his and, even though he ain't here, they still believe him over my Sadie.'

In the end, it all came down to the coroner's belief that I hadn't actually been driving dangerously, despite being underage. Cody had toddled into the road while his mother had turned her back for a moment to pick up some groceries that had fallen out of a split plastic bag. It was no one person's fault. Just a series of calamitous events. If the bag had been stronger. If her husband had been around to help. If Cody had run towards the house instead of away from it. If I hadn't been rounding the corner at that exact moment . . .

Since then, I've lived my life dreaming of every parallel universe where what happened never did. Imagining all the Sadies who live guilt-free and happy. All the lives I could've had. Because no matter the technicalities that led to me receiving a slap on the wrist and a five-year driving ban, there will always be blood on my hands.

'Do you still love him?' Barb asks, the most tentative she's sounded since she arrived. 'Fontaine. Are there still . . . residual . . . feelings?'

'No,' I say, almost too quickly. 'I hate him. Gaultier is . . .'

I flounder, then reassert myself. 'I *hate* him.'

'If only love and hate were mutually exclusive emotions, kiddo. Life would be a whole lot simpler,' she says, before writing something down.

'What do you mean?'

The backs of my eyes start to sting and I feel a lump in my throat as my face starts to burn beet red.

'That two things can be true at the same time. You recognise that what he did was damaging. But maybe there are also times he made you feel real good too. Helped you with your dance. Taught you things that shaped who you are. Maybe he was a shoulder to cry on when you were going through stuff. But, ultimately, he groomed you and abused you. And maybe you're even starting to realise why he chose you in the first place and that disgusts you.'

She watches me slowly process what's she said as so many new things dawn on me, tiny epiphanies exploding in my mind like fireworks. Then she asks me what the hell kind of crackpot therapist I'm seeing if this is the first time I've been made to consider these things.

'You should get your money back, kiddo,' she says. 'Ask for a refund.'

When I eventually speak, it's to express, once again, how mystified I am that she found me. I don't even use my real name on Facebook.

'Like I said, the kid at the paper's a real geek. No one's that hard to find. Least, that's what he always says.'

She grinds her last menthol into the ashtray and stands up. 'Listen, sweetheart. I ain't gonna make you talk if you don't want to. No thumbtacks or water torture here. But I do hope you change your mind. Not just for my story either. For you. I reckon it could genuinely help you move forward. Here's my card. My personal number is on the back and you can call whenever you want. Twenty-four seven. But, if my husband picks up, do me a favour, will you? Don't tell him I'm smoking, okay? I'm supposed to have quit four years ago.'

The card reads *Barb Horowitz* in embossed, italicised black lettering. There's her number and email address, which, as she heads for the door, she tells me she never checks.

'You know, you and the other girls have a lot in common. All from working-class backgrounds. Almost all of you, Black or Hispanic. And you know what I reckon? I reckon he's banking on the idea that girls like you won't talk. Because when you do, people are less inclined to believe you. But I believe you. And if you talk to me I'll do everything in my power to make sure other people do too.'

I tell her thanks. That I'll honestly consider reaching out if it ever feels right.

'Oh, and, Barb?' I say, just as she gets to the door. 'You know your husband probably knows, right? About the smoking?'

She nods. 'I know. But as long as neither of us says it out loud, we don't have to deal with it. Some things are better that way, kid.'

And, as she closes the door behind her, I decide I agree.

Derek shouts something along the length of the bar, but I can't hear him over the music. The lights flash violet and magenta in time to the beat and a stinging green laser beam slices through simulated smoke. Ribs jammed against the bar, I find myself sandwiched between two drunk girls with a guy built like a refrigerator standing directly behind me.

'What?' I yell towards Derek.

'What did you say you wanted again?' he yells back.

Splitting up to see who would get served first had seemed like a good idea at the time. I flash some pathetic hand signals and internally curse the school system for not teaching us all ASL from elementary onwards. 'Pineapple juice!' I shout.

I end up with apple juice instead, and make my peace with it as we push through a crowd of sweaty, writhing bodies towards where our friends are. There's Amal, a theatre student from Wisconsin; Teddy, a business major from England; Kezia, a freshman who is still undeclared; and, of course, Raheem, who is here for the weekend to 'party, party, party'. Tonight is about having fun.

It's with this in mind that we leave the others to chat near a table and head off to dance together. The floor is already sticky with spilled drinks and we hold ours aloft as we move to the beat, shimmying and shaking and grinding and twirling, our bodies casting glorious shapes onto the walls as the strobe lights shine down upon us. Raheem and I pull each other close, tiny flecks of my apple juice and his gin and tonic landing on our clothes and skin as we collide. But we don't care. Both of us clad in Air Force 1s, his orange and white, mine purple and red, our feet pound the floor as if in attempt to puncture it. He grabs my hand, flipping me under his arm and I spin and spin before making him do the same. Looking up at the DJ booth, I spot tonight's selector dripping with sweat, waving a bottle of water above his head as the hi-hat of the track he's just mixed in starts to come to the fore. Raheem crushes something up in his hand and slips it into my juice. I moan about not having planned to get too crazy tonight, but he tells me to shut up – 'How often do we get to party together, baby? Come *on!*'

The vocals kick in. The word 'ecstasy' whispered over and over again as we dance faster and faster. I lift my arms towards the ceiling and close my eyes, trusting my body to move how it needs to and, when I hear the strings begin to melt into the music, it feels like I'm flying.

Through the backdoor of the club is a garden. Although Daddy would say calling it that is a *real* stretch of the English language. There's AstroTurf, fake plastic trees and blush-pink and butter-yellow fabric flowers glued to a wooden trellis that's wound with fairy lights. Sweaty and breathless, Raheem and I stumble into this warped Eden, desperate for fresh air, only to find ourselves surrounded by smokers. We laugh, shrug and find a spot to sit, cross-legged, on the faux grass. My tight black dress rides up the moment I sit down so I untie my jacket from round my waist and put it in my lap to cover me up.

'Prickly,' Raheem observes of the AstroTurf. I agree, but my legs need a break now if I'm going to stay out much longer. Not to mention the fact that my entire body feels like it's made of Jell-O.

'Aww,' he says, sweeping a spiralling ringlet out of my face in order to get a better look at me. 'Did baby come up?'

I roll my eyes and then start giggling. 'I guess I'm having fun.'

'Yeah, girl. Even if I did have to drag you into it kicking and screaming.'

'So, what's going on with Riley?' I ask, as I slurp my drink through a straw.

'Sweetie, I am so done with dating straight boys.'

'Well, he's obviously not straight if he's dating you.'

'Closeted, then. Closeted with a capital C. Girl, I am *bored* of it. I need to be with someone who wants to parade me around.'

'Like a horse?' I laugh. He slaps me playfully on the leg and tells me it's all very simple: he wants a guy that's proud to be with him and I tell him he deserves that. That really that should be the *bare minimum*.

'I don't wanna be a dirty little secret any more,' he says, and there's a pregnant pause as his eyes meet mine and he takes a long sip of his drink. 'Speaking of secrets, have you told Derek about your visitor yet?'

'Nope,' I say. 'Because then I'd have to tell him everything else, wouldn't I?'

Raheem sighs. 'Would that be such a bad thing? You guys have been together for ever now, Sadie. He loves you. Can't you just trust that?'

'He loves the story of me I've sold him—'

'Sadie—'

'It's true! If he knew the real me, things might change. And I can't risk that. I never thought I'd be able to . . . you know . . . *be* with someone. Comfortably. After Gaultier, I never thought I'd feel . . . safe. Derek makes me feel safe. And I might not ever find that again.'

Raheem grows visibly smaller as he slowly deflates, muttering as he does. I tut loudly. 'What?'

'I just think it's sad, that's all. Isn't the whole point of love, of finding your person, about having someone know you completely? And having the chance to know everything about them too?'

I laugh. 'You're such a romantic. And I get it. I do. I've seen all the same movies you have.'

Raheem chucks his straw at me and it's probably exactly what I deserve. I'm aware I might be coming across as condescending, but the truth is that even if I didn't have secrets as damaging as mine, I'd still believe in a version of love that doesn't involve sharing everything. That allows each partner to keep something of themselves for themselves.

'Okay,' Raheem says, surreptitiously slipping more crumbled crystals into his drink. 'You don't want to talk to Derek about it. But have you thought about speaking to her? Barb Horowitz? She did say she'd keep you anonymous if you did.'

I inhale through my teeth before telling Raheem that, yes, I have thought about it and, no, I'm not going to.

'I have a life now. And I like it. It's fresh and new and no one looks at me like I'm dirty or as if they pity me. I wanna hang on to that for as long as I can.'

'Who says you can't do that *and* talk to Barb?'

'Maybe I can. But having to talk about it all again, from the beginning, it puts me back there. In that old life.'

Raheem looks like he is finally starting to understand. He offers me a sip of his drink and, impulsively, I take it. 'Do you ever think about getting closure?'

Nodding, I confess that I think about it all the time. 'I don't think I'll get it from talking to a journalist, though.'

'In a dream world, how *would* you get it?'

In a dream world, none of this would've happened in the first place. Gaultier would've just been a nice, normal teacher. And maybe I would've lusted after him still. A twisted, teenage fantasy I'd laugh at years later. But nothing more. At the time, I'd felt all grown up, but, looking back at old pictures, I'm horrified by how small I am. Baby fat and braces. Blinking naivety and blind faith.

'I think I'd need to see him again,' I say. Raheem's eyes widen. 'Not like that. I don't . . .'

Struggling to articulate the wild spectrum of emotion that suddenly manifests when I think of Gaultier, I take a moment. Then, I tell Raheem I want to see Gaultier in jail. Or, at least, in court. I want to see him convicted. Maybe publicly named and shamed. Because maybe then I would finally feel the vaguest sense of vindication.

Raheem says nothing, instead choosing to pull me into his arms, squeezing me close.

Later, in the unisex bathrooms, Raheem puts his hand around my waist after I emerge from a cubicle and join him at the mirrors.

'I'll drive you,' he says. 'If you wanna go see that nasty old childfucker in court, I'll drive you.'

'You're kidding,' I say to Raheem, when he drives up in a vintage BMW E30 M3, cherry red and clean as a whistle, furry dice hanging from the rear-view mirror. 'Where the hell did you get this?'

'A very attractive older man I met when I was in New York a while ago. Let's just say he owed me favour.' Raheem winks, and I assume the car has been handed over in return for some sort of sexual act, but I can't imagine what. 'Girl, if we gonna do a road trip, we gonna do it in style!'

Half an hour later, I'm vomiting my lunch out of the window on the passenger's side.

'I can't do this,' I tell Raheem, as he pulls his sugar daddy's pride and joy into the layby. 'I thought I could, but now it's real and I feel like there's a roller coaster inside me.'

Unsure of what else to do, he reaches for the cooler in the

back seat and hands me a 7Up. 'Here, drink this. It'll make you feel better. When we get to the motel, we'll watch a funny movie and take your mind off things.'

The liquid fizzes in my mouth as I force it down, grateful to taste something other than my own bile. But I still feel on edge. The idea of getting any sleep tonight when I know I have to face Gaultier in the morning feels impossible. Particularly given the fact I'll be lying on a shitty motel mattress instead of in my own bed. None of this feels right and yet I know it's now or never.

'Think about all the reasons you wanted to do this in the first place, Sadie,' Raheem says. We lean against the car and there's a snap and a hiss as he opens his own can. 'You're the bravest person I know. Been through stuff I can only imagine.'

Bubbles sting the back of my throat as I gulp down my drink, desperate for it be the miracle elixir I need to start to feel normal again. Then, I crunch the empty can beneath my black Doc Marten boot and pull my hair out of my face, tying it back with a black band I've been carrying on my wrist.

'Okay,' I say. 'Let's do this.'

My voice implies confidence, but I'm still jittery and unable to think clearly, my brain fogging up like the warm inside of a window on a cold winter's day. We make it twenty minutes up the road before I crumble again. Tell Raheem to stop. That I want to go home. Or, at least, I want to go anywhere Gaultier isn't.

'Because what if he isn't convicted?' I say. 'What if I have to watch him walk away from this? Big smug smirk on his face. What if he sees me? He'd enjoy that, I think. Showing me how powerful he is. Showing me he can do whatever he wants and get away with it.'

Raheem takes about five seconds to process this and then he does a full U-turn in the middle of the road, taking us back the way we came. Except we don't go home. Not yet, anyway. Instead, we end up at a roadside diner. Crimson and silver exterior with turquoise leather seated booths inside.

We order milkshakes, caramel for Raheem and banana for me. At first, we sip them in silence while I watch the softly spoken waitress flit from customer to customer. There are only five here, apart from us. A pot-bellied trucker who seems like a regular, given he's on first-name terms with the staff. A weedy guy, who looks like a farmer, and his anxious wife, who sits across from him twisting a napkin in her hands. Then there's two high-school students, one dressed in a cheerleading outfit, both stuffing their faces with waffles and talking animatedly. They look like children and yet I estimate they are at least two years older than I was when things started with Gaultier.

Raheem pipes up suddenly: 'At least I had an excuse to take that damn sexy car out for a drive.'

'Mmm hmm,' I nod. 'It is a damn sexy car.'

Staring out of the window into the parking lot where the BMW is sitting, I try to imagine what Raheem's sugar daddy might look like inside it.

'How old is he?' I ask. 'The owner?'

Raheem shrugs. 'Old enough to have a full head of pure white hair. But young enough to still be able to get it up.'

'Doesn't it bother you? The age gap?'

312

'I'm not gonna marry him, Sadie.'

He looks up from where he's poured several packets of salt onto the table, creating a sort of Japanese Zen garden that he's now drawing shapes in. 'You know it's not the same, right? I'm legal. I'm consenting.'

'I thought *I* was consenting,' I say. 'I thought I loved him.'

'Because he brainwashed you into thinking that. He was your teacher. And he totally abused his power.'

'You don't think this guy who is, I dunno, let's say twenty years older than you, maybe thirty, and has way more money than you, more cultural capital too, isn't doing the same on some level?'

Raheem shifts uncomfortably in his seat. 'It's different. I'm an adult. I'm old enough to make choices.'

Sniffing my disapproval, I look back out of the window and the tinny speaker in the corner of the room that's been playing eighties' music since we walked in changes from one song to another.

Don't you . . . forget about me . . .

'You know, someone somewhere, at some point in time, decided what the legal age was. And my guess is they decided that legal age based on what was convenient to them, not, like, science or anything. And at another point in time that age would've been different. Younger. Right? If Gaultier had lived at another point in time, everything he's done might be perfectly legal. And if the owner of that car had met you sooner, he'd be just as bad as Gaultier, if not worse.'

'Wait, are you defending Fontaine? Is that what this?'

'No,' I say. 'I think I'm just trying to explain how I got into this mess in the first place. I wasn't a stupid kid. I really thought about what I was doing. Really rationalised it. I was so, so sure of myself. Of all of it. Would've bet my life on it. But I was wrong. Now, when I look back, I can see how monumentally fucking wrong I really was.'

'That's a good thing, though, isn't it? It means his spell is broken,' Raheem says, reaching for my hand across the table.

'Maybe. Except it also makes me feel like I can't trust myself. That I'll never be able to trust myself. Because, if I was so sure back then and I was wrong, how can I ever be sure of anything ever again?'

A group of rowdy high-school students arrive at the diner and it's already getting dark outside, so we order French fries to go and eat them while sitting on the hood of the car.

'You know what really gets me?' Raheem says. 'The fact that he pretended to be from Paris. Like, how was he not exhausted putting on that fake-ass accent every day?'

I shrug. Barb's revelation that Gaultier was, in fact, Canadian had tumbled out of her mouth before I'd even made her coffee. 'And he's not even from the French part,' she'd exclaimed. 'His mother was. But he's from a part of Toronto that's so close to the Canadian border he's almost as American as apple pie.'

The idea that Gaultier has been a mere eight-hour drive away from me all this time fills me with nausea. I'd spent years believing there was an ocean between us and, somehow, that was almost as good as him being dead. Yet, the one thing I can't confess to Raheem is that I still feel a strange sense of loyalty towards Gaultier. I want him in jail, but I can't bear to be the person who sends him there. In the days between

Raheem offering to take me over the border to Canada and the moment I'd thrown up out of the car window, I'd fantasised about Gaultier seeing me again. Watching me look down on him in the dock and him being impressed. I want him to regret giving up on us. Regret treating me so badly. Finally see how well I'm doing without him. How much I'm worth.

Elsewhere in the parking lot, I spy empty paper cups, a discarded blanket, a child's left-behind left shoe. There's a rusty public phone savaged by the wind, the receiver dangling, hung by its own spiralling cord.

'My therapist says I have depression and anxiety,' I say, licking salt from my fingertips.

'Because of your past?' Raheem asks, crushing up the cardboard carton the fries came in and shooting it expertly into the nearest trash can. I tell him about how my therapist keeps trying to get me to talk about my childhood, and that I fight her tooth and nail every time. I had a good childhood. Kind and loving parents. Bad things happened to us but we were a good, strong family. She talks about abandonment and I protest, telling her that concept doesn't align with my experience.

'And she just says that even if my parents didn't mean to abandon me, Daddy getting sick and Momma having to focus her attention on him may have meant I was neglected. I get mad when she says shit like that, of course. Then she talks about how a lot of my friends abandoned me. My church. My community. And I guess I can see that.'

'It *was* pretty brutal,' Raheem says. 'You've been through more challenges than anyone I know. Honestly, it's kind of a miracle that you're not a complete lunatic.'

'Sometimes I feel like one,' I say. 'Thing is, I've Googled depression and anxiety and there's so much that I'm going through that I don't think those things really account for. I dunno. Maybe I just need to keep looking.'

'What does your therapist say the solution is if it is depression and anxiety?'

'She told me to relay her diagnosis to my doctor and he prescribed me Prozac.'

'Okay, girl,' Raheem says, his reservations etched across his face.

'Don't worry. I took it for three weeks and threw the rest away. All it did was make me feel numb. Like a ghost. It didn't solve anything.'

I scoop myself up off the car and tell him we should start heading back. Truth be told, going home isn't something that remotely appeals, but I know I have to tear the Band-Aid off sooner or later. Derek thinks Raheem and I are doing a road trip for fun. That we'll return from Toronto tomorrow night with hilarious stories and shit souvenirs. He'll be shocked when I arrive home before it's even bedtime.

I concoct a lie about the car breaking down as I dig a shallow hole into the dirt with the heel of my boot. It's a tiny, mildly pathetic attempt to show that I was here. That I tried. Raheem fumbles for the keys and I watch him drop into the driver's seat. Despite all my earlier comments, I know he's in a good place right now. That there's a growing chasm between us as he moves closer and closer towards living his most authentic life and I continue to go in the exact opposite direction.

TWENTY-ONE

The room is empty when Bridget and I return. No women deliberately up-skirting themselves. No Janine and Marie making music together. No Lilith. We can, however, hear voices coming from outside.

The two of us head over to the window on the other side of the giant wooden hut and are greeted by the sight of several dozen women lying on the ground outside with their legs up the air. I can just about make out what Lilith is now demanding of them: 'Embrace mother nature,' she cries. 'Let the sun kiss you between your thighs!'

Bridget and I exchange a chuckle.

'You don't know the effect that might be having,' I tell Bridget, railing against her obvious cynicism. 'Maybe it feels good. Liberating, even.'

There's a smile still playing across my face with these words, however. Even I am finding it hard to take all this entirely seriously. If Lilith forcing me to exclude Veronica from Deep Flow wasn't enough to make me worry about a misalignment of values, her promise to cure Constance's cancer certainly had. I know Natalia is pregnant, and maybe Lilith has somehow helped her on her way, but there's also a chance it could all be pure coincidence. Surely even Lilith can't be quite that magical.

'Did you feel liberated during the last exercise?' Bridget asks. 'Because you didn't look it. You looked scared.'

My smile fades and I say nothing. But, silently, I agree. Lilith should've given us all a trigger warning before thrusting us so far into the unknown.

'Look, I'm not saying the woo-woo practices she engages with are *all* bullshit,' Bridget says. Many of them can and will make you feel great. But what actually qualifies her to experiment with them? With you and your trauma? The wellness industry is almost entirely unregulated and you can become a "life coach" without any qualifications whatsoever. Which means you've got these totally random people being paid to guide others through big life choices despite probably knowing as little about life and success as their clients do.'

'Lilith's not like that,' I mumble. 'She's built an amazing life for herself. One that any of us would be incredibly lucky to have. She's inspiring.'

Bridget pauses, as if worried that the next thing she says could result in a level of destruction she might not know how to handle.

'What?' I snap, impatiently.

She takes a breath. 'Look, I've done extensive research already for this article and part of it is going to explore just how Lilith and her husband have come to have such a million-dollar lifestyle. Deep Flow works almost like a pyramid scheme, with her at the top. Then Jeremy also runs a more traditional pyramid scheme—'

'Elements,' I say.

Bridget nods. 'I actually have reason to believe he provided Lilith with the blueprint for Deep Flow. And then there's their origin stories.'

'What do you mean?' I ask, dreading the answer.

Bridget sighs. 'The stuff about Jeremy training with Buddhist monks? There's no evidence of it. And that Michelin-starred chef he says he worked with on his superfood brand says they met twice at most. The story about Jeremy and Lilith's meet-cute? Also bogus. I've got three separate people who were friends with them at the time happy to go on record and say they actually met on Raya.'

'The celebrity dating app?'

'Yep,' Bridget replies. 'They only had small followings at the time, but their love story playing out on social media the way it did and all the endorsements that followed made them go stratospheric.'

'You really think they lied about all this stuff?' I ask, already knowing the answer.

Bridget looks sympathetic. 'Look, I don't want to alarm you, Sadie, but I'd be remiss if I didn't give you the facts while I had the chance. These businesses, they all feed into one another. Lilith exploits women through Deep Flow, getting you all to pay extortionate amounts of money to be a part of the com-munity – the classes, the crystals, one-to-one sessions, retreats. And it feels *good* most of the time, so you want more and more, right? Then, if and when you end up struggling to pay or in debt, she swoops in and offers a number of ways out. One of them is recruitment. Getting more girls to join Deep

Flow. But if you're in financial crisis, that won't fill your bank account. It'll just keep you in the community. So then she'll suggest "helping Jeremy out" with his ventures. You know he runs a men-only love coaching business, right?'

I nod. Of course I do. Love Guru is both famous and highly exclusive.

'Well, part of it is giving the men real-world dating practice. With actual women. And I have it on good authority that a large percentage of these women—'

'Are funnelled in from Deep Flow,' I say, my blood running cold. 'It's escorting, isn't it?'

'And there's nothing wrong with that. Except that these women have no idea what they're getting themselves into. Not really, anyway. They're told they'll be safe, that it's all above board. It's all about female empowerment. And there's a chance to make a lot of money. Fast. But Jeremy, of course, makes the most money of all.'

My stomach churns.

'Surely people complain? When the clients go too far?'

'When they do, they get gaslit to fuck. Told it's their fault. Made to feel like they could get in trouble for soliciting. It's so messed up.'

I feel my way back onto the floor, dizziness taking hold. When I'd told Lilith I didn't think I could recruit more members in lieu of payment for the Joshua Tree retreat, she'd suggested a sixty per cent discount. Luckily, Derek gave me the money to cover it, but I remember Lilith saying there might be another way if I couldn't pay up. Was passing me over to Jeremy that other way? I feel nauseous, and, suddenly, I find myself back in Gaultier's pool house, the echoey sound of The Beach Boys playing on vinyl as I move through the corridor towards the inevitable. Blue walls and the vague smell of lemon leaves, patchouli and Gaultier's aftershave.

Bridget continues to talk, but I can only make out the odd word or phrase. It's all too much and, for a second, I feel like I might pass out. Slip out of reality altogether. But then Bridget mentions something that makes me snap back into the present: the shooting.

'You were there, weren't you? On the day?'

The most I can manage is a nod.

'Don't you think it's funny that every single one of the Deep Flow studios all over the country, except for the newest branch in Omaha, has experienced some sort of traumatic event? The shooting in LA. The fire in San Diego. The group boat trip in the Hamptons that led to the ship sinking and several members almost drowning. The hostage situation in Denver. The Milwaukee retreat, where the centre flooded while everyone was asleep. I don't have any solid evidence that any of these things are linked, but they can't all be coincidences, can they?'

I swallow. Hard. Other than the fire, I'd had no idea about any of these other incidents.

'Maybe people are jealous of what we have. Outsiders, I mean. It certainly sounds like we're under attack.'

Bridget stares at me for a long time. 'What if I told you I don't believe the people who are doing this *are* outsiders?'

This idea gives me pause. Could there be more Mackenzies out there?

'What if I told you that I think they're all former and maybe

321

even current members of Deep Flow?' Bridget offers. 'Because I believe Deep Flow has pissed off and hurt *a lot* of people.'

Bridget's words strike a chord, but I'm not ready to truly examine what it all might mean. Not yet anyway.

I wipe my face on the front of my dress and tell Bridget we should get outside. 'People will start wondering what we're doing.'

She grabs my hand and looks into my eyes. 'Don't you want to get to the bottom of all this?'

I pull my hand away, but not soon enough. A memory catches up with me. Someone else staring me out with the same intensity, cigarette smoke dancing in front of her face. I didn't speak up back then and I lived to regret it.

I'd typed Barb Horowitz's name into my Google search bar five years after her visit, only to discover she'd died of lung cancer. Hardly surprising, but no less devastating. She'd only managed to get two of Gaultier's victims to go on record. Her article, a mere footnote, published on the same day as the horrific news of the Sandy Hook Elementary school shooting. Nobody had even noticed it.

The memory of this stings and I reach for Bridget's hand. The very hand I'd sharply pulled away from a mere ten seconds before.

'I love Lilith,' I say. 'And I love Deep Flow. But I've found myself at the wrong end of what I thought was love before and it ruined my life. I don't want to go there again. So I will talk to you. But not now.'

Bridget nods. 'How about we sneak out when everyone else is asleep? Tonight?'

'Okay,' I agree. 'As long as you can guarantee I'll be completely anonymous. Lilith, she . . . she knows all my secrets. And she's leveraged them before to get me to do something terrible—'

'What . . . what did you do?'

Shame envelopes me and I can hardly bear to speak it out loud. 'She made me push my friend Veronica out of the community. Because she's trans. Actually, no. I *let* her make me. It was my fault. I was so weak, so pathetic, I barely even pushed back. I let my fear of everyone knowing my secret become greater than my sense of humanity. My grasp of my own morality. I . . . I fucked up.'

'It sounds to me like you want out, Sadie.'

'What would be the point of that?' I scoff. 'Veronica will never forgive me. And she shouldn't. I don't deserve it. My only other friends live in Georgia. Outside of Deep Flow, I have no one in LA. I have nothing.'

Bridget squeezes my hand and gives me a sympathetic smile.

'I'm sure that's not true,' she says. But it is. I have no job. A failing career as an artist. A husband who's away for work more than he's home. A fractured family and an ugly, broken past. Deep Flow *is* all I have. And yet I feel entirely conflicted. I see so many flaws in how we operate.

'Can I just ask you one question?'

Bridget nods. 'Anything.'

'Are you working with Mumtaz Nasir? Did she send you here?'

'She didn't. We have had a conversation, though. I know about her case. And she did say she had a friend in the community.'

'*Friend*' is a stretch, I think. But who knows how to describe what Mumtaz and I have?

'I won't talk to you if she knows anything about it,' I say. 'You have to promise me you won't tell her.'

Bridget nods again and I'm grateful she doesn't ask for an explanation, because the truth is petty and pitiful. The truth is that I simply can't bear the idea of giving Mumtaz the satisfaction.

'What happened to you earlier?' Ruby asks suspiciously, as she tears a hunk of bread off the loaf in the middle of the table and stuffs it into her mouth.

'I just needed a moment,' I say.

'A moment? You missed the whole of the second half of the session.'

I answer her with a shrug that I hope conveys the fact that it's actually none of her damn business.

I've only now sat down after spending the last two hours toiling in the kitchen alongside my dorm mates, Bridget, Natalia (who barely lifted a finger on account of her 'condition') and Emily, who is notably very quiet this evening. We've prepared a lamb stew for the meat eaters and a butterbean and lentil version for the vegetarians and vegans amongst us. There's copious amounts of freshly made bread, Hasselback potatoes and plenty of greens served with chili, garlic, lemon and smashed hazelnuts. After dinner, we work our way through vats of kombucha before Lilith invites us onto our feet for an evening of 'ecstatic dance'.

I'm amazed at how sluggish I feel and put it down to the hours spent in the sauna and hot tub before heading to the kitchen to begin cooking. While we relaxed, the other women talked of how 'transformational' the feminine sexuality workshop had been.

'I feel like I've made friends with my vagina,' one of the women from the Omaha branch told another.

'Same,' said the other. 'But, you know, I cried at the end of the session. All these years I could've spent truly getting to know her. Having these special conversations like we did today. I wasted them.'

'No, no. Don't blame yourself—'

'But it's true, I have—'

'It's not your fault, though! It's society.'

I listened quietly, almost voyeuristically, my head nodding only fractionally in silent agreement. How hard the patriarchy works to keep us at odds with our bodies. How powerful we would be if we didn't spend such a large part of our lives being forced into shame.

After joining everyone in an hour or so of moving my body to the beat of Marie's drum, I collapse by the fire. Attempting to throw myself into the remainder of the day's activities while simultaneously pushing down the feelings now eating away at me is beginning to take its toll. There could be women right here at the retreat who have been cajoled into working for Jeremy's Love Guru enterprise in order to keep their place in the community and survive financial ruin. And it's with this thought that images of Natalia, Emily, Andrea and the others begin to flash through my brain. Disgusting men in hotel rooms. Naked breasts and empty eyes.

It's hard to fathom how Lilith has allowed Jeremy to lead her so far astray and, while I don't want to misdirect my revulsion towards him, it's hard not to see her as spineless in the face of his dirty dealings. The Lilith I thought I knew would surely never stand for this.

Ruby stares at me through the flames as I sit sipping fermented lemon and ginger while feverishly fighting my imagination. Her eyes are narrowed. Lips set in a thin line. The hairs on my arms prickle despite my proximity to heat, my body alerting me to danger. She might be a woman, I think, but she is absolutely an agent of the patriarchy. Always making me feel as if I am wrong. As if I need to prove myself. As if I'm not good enough. Wearing her difficult personality proudly, like a gaudy fur coat: fashionable but cruel.

I scan the crowd in a bid to avoid her gaze, only for my eyes to snag on Andrea and then on Debbie. Bizarrely, the latter waves at me and then starts to come towards me.

'Sadie,' she says, sitting down beside me. 'Do you have space for me to share something with you?'

If it's another slap, then, no, thank you, I want to say. But I don't and she sees my silence as permission to offload.

'I wanted to acknowledge my behaviour at the Soul Awakening Weekender and let you know that I'm aware of the impact it may have had on you.'

'Oh. Okay,' I say, marvelling at her strange wording.

'Lilith and I have spoken extensively about the situation and, of course, I *could* offer apologies, but I decided in the end that I wanted to explore something of real substance with you. I want to have an honest conversation about growth and where I found myself before and after our interaction that day.'

'Uh . . . sure,' I shrug.

'So, as you heard me mention in the opening circle, a big part of the reason I practice Deep Flow is to remind myself that I'm a person outside of my kids. Of course, I love and cherish them and would never be without them. But I was a whole human being before they came into my life and remembering that is like walking a tightrope some days. Some days, I feel invisible. And, that weekend, I was holding a lot of that . . . I don't know . . . rage.'

'Rage?' I say, silently seething. '*You* feel a sense of rage?'

'I know. It is surprising. So many people look at me, at my life, and think, "Wow, she's got it all." But, you know, I still struggle.'

I think of her sweaty, red face in Deep Flow, the whispers of the other women behind her back, the way Lilith looks at her. I've always felt sorry for her, even after she attacked me at the Soul Awakening mini-retreat, but, as she continues to talk at me, I feel all my sympathy slowly begin to ebb away and something inside me snaps.

'This is so boring,' I say, interrupting her. 'Aren't you bored?'

'Excuse me?'

'Well, you're not actually saying anything, Debbie. You've come over here talking about how you're gonna offer me something of substance, I presume in lieu of the apology you know you owe me, but don't seem to want to hand out, and you've said exactly . . . nothing. I don't need you to acknowledge that what you did was wrong. I know that already. And, to be honest, I'm not exactly sure that merely acknowledging the fact you did something wrong counts as real accountability.'

Debbie's jaw hangs open and she looks at me as if she's seen a ghost. Her skin pales in the moonlight and she brings a fleshy hand up to sit softly on her chest.

'Where is this coming from?' she asks.

I sigh heavily. If she were wearing pearls, I don't doubt she'd be clutching them right now as if her life depended on it.

'I guess I'm just sick of people talking *around* things. All this flowery New Age language *sounds* good, but what does any of it really mean?'

Debbie gives me one last long look of astonishment and then starts to get to her feet.

'You have a very dark energy, Sadie Perkins,' she tells me, just before she walks away. And I am reminded of an old lady at my church back in Georgia who'd said something similar when news of my indiscretions had begun to spread through town.

Carrying the weight of my shame feels exhausting tonight, however, and my conversation with Bridget has made me feel reckless. As if I might burn everything to the ground and start my life anew again. I've done it multiple times before with varying degrees of success, I realise. Why should this be any different?

I lie in bed, grateful that the evening has now drawn to a close and everyone is finally tucked away. All I have to do now is wait for the others to fall asleep and then make sure I stay awake long enough to slip out into the darkness with Bridget. I spend what feels like hours listening to a whispered conversation between Emily and Natalia about the validity of vaccines and the potential pointlessness of protest.

Derek and I had gone to countless protests during college. It had been one of the things that had bonded us, our passion for dismantling the system.

Unlike me, he'd had a relatively smooth journey through high school and the transition to college, where he'd been funded by a basketball scholarship. His life had for ever been stable. That is until an incident in sophomore year, where a cop had pinned him to a wall near our campus, scraping the skin off one side of his face.

Derek had been on his way to meet me and tried to call just as he was confronted. The cop roared at him to hang up before knocking his phone out of his hand. On the other end of the line, I'd heard everything. Unexpectedly, though, when I arrived on the scene, I suddenly felt a strange quiet within me. My skin prickling, hair bristling, it was as if the air changed the moment I caught sight of Derek pressed hard against bricks, the weight of the police officer's body squeezing the breath out of him.

The cop had wanted to know what was in his backpack and why Derek, late to meet me, had been jogging along the sidewalk. Hands in the air, I'd asked the cop if I could approach the backpack and show him the contents. He'd barked orders at me throughout and yet, somehow, I'd found myself possessed by an eerie sense of calm as I pulled out Derek's laptop and schoolbooks.

It was afterwards that I'd crumbled. Rivers of hot tears snaking down my face, dripping waterfalls off my chin, as my shoulders shook. At the time, though, navigating this terrifying man's colossal ego, appeasing him in a bid to survive, had felt familiar, as if I'd done it dozens of times before.

Almost a decade later, Derek and I marched side by side, waving banners, while others shouted through megaphones: 'No justice, no peace!' All of us determined to take a stand against police brutality. Because we knew that *we* were America too. That America had been built on the backs of our ancestors and, after two centuries of abuse and oppression, enough was enough.

Of course, it so often felt as if nothing we could say or do would make anything better. But that didn't stop us trying. Didn't stop us posting stuff on social media and creating art we hoped would spark systemic change or, at the very least, make people like us feel *seen*.

'I know you're tired. But there's a warrior within you, Sadie,' an old therapist had once told me, when I'd talked about how exhausting constantly shouting about the wrongs of the world often felt.

Lying in bed now, listening to the passive aggression passing between Natalia and Emily as I fight fatigue, I attempt to summon that warrior again. Begging her to keep my eyes open. *Use toothpicks if you have to,* I tell her. *Pinch me awake if I start to drift off. This conversation is important. I cannot fuck this up.*

Eventually, the women in the two beds beside me descend into silence. I hear Natalia snoring faintly and notice Emily is almost corpse-like, she is so sound asleep. I look over to where Bridget's bed is on the opposite side of the dorm and I'm about to make my move when I hear footsteps and the door creaks open. Two figures enter and tiptoe towards Bridget's bed. She doesn't stir and I question whether she has dozed off. I clamp my hand over my mouth to stop me yelping as

I watch the figures put something over Bridget's head. She wakes, struggles, but ultimately acquiesces as they bind her wrists and ankles and carry her out.

It's then that I do scream. Loud enough to wake myself up.

'Thank God,' I whisper into the dark. *A dream*, I tell myself. But when I look over at Bridget's bed, she is gone.

Careful not to wake the others, I open the door to the dorm and head outside to see if I can find her. Perhaps she got up only a few minutes ago, expecting me to follow. Perhaps she's waiting by the same tree we had our first honest conversation under. But, as I step out into the cold night air, I realise there is no one. Just a vast expanse of desert beneath a ceiling of deep, midnight blue.

'Such a shame,' Esther says, sucking honey from her spoon absent-mindedly. 'We have so much more in store that she's going to miss out on.'

'It's odd that she left in the middle of the night,' I say, frowning my suspicions across the breakfast table. 'It must've been one hell of a family emergency.'

Esther drops her spoon back into her porridge bowl with a clatter and takes the hands of the two women beside her. 'Let's pray that she's okay, shall we?'

'How did she leave anyway?' Constance asks. 'We're in the middle of nowhere.'

This question seems to stump Esther for a moment, but Janine, who's sitting further up the table, helpfully pipes up. 'I arranged transport for her. The driver came and picked her up.'

There's something slightly unconvincing about the cool,

calm way in which Janine responded and, while Constance goes back to her breakfast, seemingly satisfied, a horrifying sense of dread begins to sink into my bones. Bridget wouldn't have left. Not without her story. I can't imagine what kind of emergency would have led her to depart without saying goodbye, mere minutes before I was due to tell her everything I know.

Back in the dorm, I open the drawer in her bedside table and am disappointed to find it empty. Her unmade bed gives nothing away and I drop to my knees to look underneath. But when I hear approaching footsteps and voices, I am pushed into sudden panic, choosing, instinctively, to roll under the bed. The large comforters, most likely intended for a double, swamp the single dorm room beds. Already embarrassed by my snap decision, I'm grateful for this, the curtain-like extra bedding dangling to the floor, sealing me safely inside my hiding place, as if I am a child encased in a homemade fort.

The voices belong to Lilith and Emily and, as one of them picks Bridget's bed to sit down on, I watch it dip slightly in the middle, the mattress springs squeaking as it moves threateningly towards me.

'You did the right thing telling us,' Lilith says. 'Our container is precious. We can't have that kind of energy here disrupting it.'

'Thanks, Lilith,' Emily responds, and I smart at her betrayal. 'I've found the whole situation really challenging, to be honest.'

I wonder if they can hear my heart pounding.

'Do you think Sadie shared much with her?' Lilith asks, and, at this question, my heart seems to stop beating altogether, instead catching in my throat. Terrified they'll hear me breathing, I choose this moment to hold my breath.

'I dunno,' Emily replies. 'But if she hasn't already, I think she would've eventually.'

'We can't risk her spreading worry and discord throughout the camp,' Lilith sighs. 'I'll speak to the others. See if we can figure out what to do about her.'

The bed squeaks again as Lilith gets to her feet and the mattress starts to return to its former shape. 'Thanks again, Emily,' she says. 'What you've done is a true act of love. You really are such an essential part of this community.'

'I feel bad, though. About Bridget,' Emily whines.

'Stop it, Emily. We can't have a *journalist* creeping about amongst us,' Lilith spits. 'This is a space to be vulnerable. And she compromised that.'

I let out the stale breath I've been holding in my chest and dare to gulp in some fresher air as I hear Lilith open the dorm room door. Emily's voice stops her.

'Bridget was right, though, wasn't she? About Mac. And the other . . . events. I'm okay with it all, obviously. I get it. But not everyone will.'

'I know that,' Lilith says, tersely. 'That's exactly why there is the inner circle and then there is everyone else. Only my most valued, most enlightened sisters have the privilege of getting to see the mechanisms of our magic. I'm so glad that you continue to prove how right I've been to trust you. We should certainly speak more about you graduating from Obsidian to Bloodstone.'

Emily says nothing as Lilith leaves, but I can practically feel the warm glow she's emanating and, despite being horrified by all I've just heard, I can't help but envy her. I've never even heard of a Bloodstone membership, but it sounds worth more than money can buy.

I turn their conversation over in my mind. It's a miracle I didn't let out an audible gasp when Lilith all but confirmed the incidents were linked.

Eventually, Emily leaves the room too, and I roll out from under the bed, ready to continue my search. Now, there's an added sense of urgency. Surely Bridget's kidnappers wouldn't have known her every hiding place. She was stealthy. Secretive. Smart. This might've been her first time undercover for all I know, but I'm certain of her professionalism. She knew exactly what she was doing.

I move on to the shared bathroom. Her toiletries bag is still stowed in the cupboard, so I pull it out and unzip it. This time, I do gasp out loud. Deep Flow underestimated Bridget. Perhaps they've underestimated me too.

I hide the recorder between my breasts and hope the part of my bra that usually presses into my sternum will hold it in. Then, I walk far enough away from the retreat centre to get some privacy. The whole charade reminds me of when I used to sneak tiny bottles of spirits into clubs in my twenties, only the stakes are much higher this time.

I find a place near an old tumbledown shed and pull the recorder out to listen, only too aware of how little time I have before people might come looking for me. I press play and am startled to hear Ruby's voice.

'I dunno,' she whinges. 'I sort of feel like Lilith has favourites. But they change. Like the seasons change, you know?'

'Does it feel important to be one of her favourites?' Bridget wonders out loud.

'Kind of.'

'Why?'

'You get to go to her house. There's more time spent one-on-one. I dunno. I just feel like she shares more with her favourites. Like . . . I was one of them for a long time. But since some of the new arrivals have gotten close to her, I feel like I'm out in the cold. As if she has less time for me. And that's a strange feeling after being such a part of her core group.'

I fast forward, then hear Debbie's voice. 'Things are tough. Financially, I mean. Spiritually, everything's great.'

'But don't your money worries impact on your spiritual wellbeing?' Bridget asks.

Debbie ums and ahs about this for a few seconds, then changes the subject entirely. I fast forward again. Natalia: 'Oh yeah, I owe her big time. I wouldn't have been able to get pregnant without her guidance.'

'Did you honestly not feel like you'd meet anyone who'd be a suitable co-parent?' Bridget asks. 'You're still young.'

'Nah. Lilith made me realise that life is too short to waste not doing the thing I'm destined to do.'

Each one of these conversations is a muffled recording, whole sections of speech often obscured by the sound of rustling clothes and leaves. Or of background hubbub and birdsong. It's clear she's recorded them without the speaker knowing, so there's no way she'd ever be able to make these recordings public. They would have certainly provided rich material for her article, though. If only she'd managed to take her note-taking device with her.

'I knew Mackenzie,' Andrea says, in her recording. 'In fact, there's a bunch of us still around who knew her when she was coming to sessions at the studio a few years back. I heard she got herself into some pretty bad debt. Didn't think she'd come back for revenge one day, though. She never seemed the type. It just doesn't make sense.'

Andrea's words shock me. I had no idea anyone else knew the shooter's identity and it's certainly surprising to hear Andrea talking about it so openly.

I listen for about twenty minutes before heading back to the retreat centre. During this time I discover that the majority of recordings offer little insight. Snatched conversations that don't tell much of a story individually, but, together, they paint an interesting picture. Enough for the tug of my gut to become too strong to ignore, while that tiny voice inside me, the one that I've been attempting to silence for months, grows louder.

I have to get out of here.

TWENTY-TWO

The first time I ever saw snow, I was six years old. I sat at the window and watched in awe as fat, white flakes fell quietly to the ground.

'It won't stick,' Daddy said from behind his newspaper. 'Not in Georgia, it won't. No, ma'am. No way.'

I begged Momma to take me to the park nonetheless. I wanted to build a snowman, I told her. Just like in the movies.

Reality was much different, however. The cold biting at my fingers, toes and nose. The searing pain around the edges of my ears. The novelty of snowflakes landing prettily on wool fading as soon as they melted into nothing, leaving icy, wet gloves behind.

My snowman was barely the size of a small cat, and gathering enough snow even for that was a painful, challenging experience. But I was determined, little legs marching back and forth between the same two trees, gathering the sleet that had caught between their roots. Then, a carrot for the nose, Oreo cookies for eyes, a slice of melon for the mouth. Daddy's contribution had been the advertising section of his paper, which he'd carefully fashioned into a hat before we left.

I stood back, admiring my work, and then realised my snowman didn't have arms.

'How will he eat?' I asked Momma, and she took my gloves off temporarily so she could rub and blow warm breath onto my frozen hands. Then, she helped me hunt for twigs and, luckily, we managed to find two that were roughly the same size. It would've been the perfect first foray into colder climes if it hadn't been for one of the twigs drawing blood as I pushed it into the side of my snow child. Momma decided to snap a photo of me standing next to him anyway, believing I'd want to look back on that moment someday. I crossed my arms, pressing my bleeding hand into my chest.

Click! The slush kid and me, tear-stained and frustrated, frozen in time for ever.

Since then, I've often questioned if I still would've developed such a hatred of snow if that unruly stick hadn't carved a C-shape into my palm that day.

'What's meant to be is meant to be,' Momma told me, when I cried and asked her why it had happened in the first place. She filled the bathroom sink and stuck my freezing hand into the warm depths of it. Then, fascinated, I watched the blood spread through the water like a blossoming rose.

'I was just trying to make a friend,' I said, snot gathering around my nostrils as she dried my hand and then cleaned the wound with antiseptic wipes.

Years later, Gaultier would examine my C-shaped scar and kiss the centre of my palm, telling me it was beautiful. He'd made me feel so special before he'd slowly dismantled me, and I wonder now if I was always destined to arrive here again. Finding myself in a familiar type of trouble. Caught up in the maelstrom of someone else's ego. A broken fragment floating through time, waiting to catch on something else jagged and sharp, a comforting familiarity anchoring me.

'I was just trying to make a friend.'

'Imagine this,' Lilith says. We are all gathered in a small auditorium at the back of the retreat centre. It's impressive the centre even has one, but it is lo-fi and not all of us have seats, instead sitting on stairs or leaning against walls while our leader speaks her grand vision aloud. We all sip orange and mango juice from the plastic cups we were given on the way in. I accept two, grateful for the sugar. I'll need all the energy I can get to execute my plan.

'Imagine getting to live like this all the time, free of the shackles of day-to-day life. Free of loved ones that let you down. Lack of community. Jobs that no longer fulfil you. An unnecessarily large carbon footprint. Imagine, instead, living within an ecosystem. Growing our own fruit and vegetables. Farming our own animals. Getting out what we put in, all while being safe from the economic impact of war, recession, pandemic. All while living with your sisters and practising Deep Flow every single day.'

Lilith signals for Devon to click onto the next slide in her presentation and the image of a large house is projected onto the wall behind her. 'This . . . is Arcadia. A commune *for* us, *by* us. Because I believe that to truly evolve into who you are supposed to be, you must leave the old you behind and cut ties with the dead weight holding you back from the life you are supposed to live. A simpler life. A more beautiful life. A life that is your own.'

Arcadia sounds like paradise. A dream within a dream. So much of what Lilith says makes sense. We *are* fucking up the planet. There is a real lack of community throughout so much of this country. Capitalism has us in a chokehold. But is Lilith's plan really an alternative to capitalism or just a new version of it? One where we are beholden to her and the money-driven hierarchy she has created?

Rapturous applause fills the auditorium as almost everyone sitting offers Lilith a standing ovation. No one claps louder or harder than Natalia, however. Today her pregnant belly appears rounder than ever, as if she's had a growth spurt in the night. Amid the fervour, I slip out of the back door.

Heading straight for the retreat centre's office, I pray Lilith's presentation will keep everyone entertained for long enough for me to complete my mission. There's a Deep Flow session directly afterwards and we've all been asked to dress accordingly, so it's entirely possible they'll all move seamlessly from one activity to the next without ever noticing I am gone.

I sprint across the yard to the dorms, then, I head up the adjoining staircase to the office. When I get there, I attempt to push the door open only to find it's locked. Okay, Plan B: head to Lilith's room and find the key. Back down the stairs and down the corridor, I find her annex opposite the two larger dorms that house Janine, Marie, Devon, Isla and Esther. Thankfully, the door is open and, inside, I find a bunch of keys in her bedside drawer. It all feels almost too easy, until I realise I have no idea which key is the key to the office. Not to mention the fact there's no guarantee the key is even within this set. But I have to try. I've gotten this far, after all.

I take the whole bunch and race back down the corridor and up the stairs. By now, my heartrate is peaking and my clammy hands fumble the keys as I try one after another in the lock.

Suddenly, there's a noise downstairs and I freeze before softly creeping over the window. A thin breeze is blowing an empty, discarded plastic bottle against the side of the building.

False alarm. I ignore the sweat gathering above my top lip, return to the office door and try another key. This one works, rendering a satisfying click as the door pops open. I squeeze inside, clambering over boxes of equipment and papers as I go, the detritus of retreats past as well as this one, I suspect. On the desk are two boxes. One is full of jade and rose quartz crystals, all of them oblong and softly pointed at one end. These are the 'cleansing crystals' Lilith tried to sell us at the end of the feminine sexuality workshop, telling us that sliding them inside ourselves would heal us of all manner of trauma, renewing our erotic energies.

'Isn't stone porous?' Constance had whispered to me. 'What if their pores are dirty? What if that dirt leaks into our vaginas?'

This, the first bit of doubt she had shown in regard to Lilith's medical expertise. I silently prayed she'd cling on to it.

In the other box are dozens and dozens of phones. Jackpot.

I rifle through them and soon find mine, hurriedly switching it on. How stupid had I been to so easily give up my only way of contacting the outside world. I've already decided what I'll message Derek. *S.O.S.* I'll say. *Mumtaz was right and I'm in danger. I love you. Come get me.*

My phone springs to life, its logo melting across the screen.

Shit. 'Update required'. Full of dread, I watch as the 'percentage complete' bar moves towards one hundred. It's quick but not quick enough and every second feels like torture. When it's done, my fingers flick through the options to find my recent contacts and I pull up Derek in my messenger. There's 4G and the tiniest sliver of signal. I start to type.

'Sadie? What are you doing?' says a voice behind me.

My blood curdles, my shoulders lifting towards my ears as my entire body tenses. I turn round, pressing send as I do, a mere fragment of my intended message hopefully making its way to Derek.

'You know we're not allowed phones here,' Esther says.

'I know,' I say, desperately trying to worm my way out of being caught so red-handed. 'I just . . . really miss my husband.'

'Why didn't you say? You could've talked to us about it,' Janine tells me, as she enters behind her fellow 'lightworker'. She is glacial and there is a sinister tone to her voice.

'You're right,' I say. 'I'm sorry. But, you know, while I have my phone and it's all switched on, I may as well go back to my room and just call him. You know, for five minutes. And then I'll give the phone back to you.'

'That would be a regrettable choice,' Janine says, steely.

'It's vital we protect our precious container,' Esther says. 'That means no technology.'

'Would you kindly put Sadie's phone away for her, Esther?' Janine asks and Esther begins to move towards me.

'I can put it away myself,' I snap. 'If I want to. And I don't want to.'

'Sadie, you knew the rules before you attended. Please, don't make this difficult.'

As she says this, I suddenly feel as if my senses have heightened. Is this my body flipping into survival mode? Ready to escape attack? But, as Esther lunges for the phone and I swerve her, I realise this is something else. Something familiar.

'It's *my* phone,' I say, as the colours in the room begin to pulsate and inanimate objects start to seem, somehow, alive.

'We don't have possessions in Deep Flow, Sadie. We share everything. All parts of ourselves. Heart and soul. Skin and bones.'

I swerve again, this time pushing Esther back as I do. As the edges of everything start to soften, I become convinced that I can see both Janine and Esther's auras. The latter's sparkling green glow grapples me to floor, upending the box of phones in the process. They spill across the carpet as we do the same, pulling clothes, hair, skin, anything we can get our hands on. Janine watches in the corner, effervescent with pale blue and pink light. It's clear she believes her comrade has this under control.

I manage to find my feet, but Esther does too, grabbing me by the throat and pinning me against the desk, her legs pressed hard into mine to stop me from kicking her. Gasping and panicked, I reach for the nearest object and hit her on the side of the head with it. She drops like a sack of sand and I open my hand to see one of the rose quartz dildos clasped inside.

Giggling hysterically, I run for it, taking my phone with me, but opting to leave the healing stick behind. Janine stands screaming for back up in the doorway as I shove her away and tear down the corridor. Isla runs up the stairs towards me, vibrating crimson red and fiery orange. I clatter past her, almost taking her down the stairs with me.

My giggles fade then, and I am terrified again, running out across the yard, where Ruby tackles me to the ground. Some of the other women stand outside the retreat centre, mouths gaping as I kick Ruby off me and run free.

I feel myself slipping in and out of my body, and it is as if my limbs are not my own. For a moment, I question if this is because warrior me has sprung to life and taken over. But then I think of the orange and mango juice we were given on the way into the presentation and, suddenly, only one explanation makes sense: Lilith has drugged me again. Only, this time, I don't feel warm, fuzzy and safe. Whatever she slipped into our drinks has me feeling totally out of control.

I trip, stumbling over a rock, grazing both my knees as I land face down in the dirt. As I attempt to get to my feet, a gust of wind sends the sand in front of me swirling. When it settles, I am astonished to see Lilith, standing alone, arms outstretched.

'Am I hallucinating?' I half whisper.

'No,' Lilith chuckles. 'The magic in your drink is psyche-delic, not hallucinogenic. I'm really here. For you. Just as I always have been.'

She steps towards me and is visibly shocked when I shrink away.

'Come on, Sadie. Take my hand. Let's not be silly, okay?'

'Why did you drug us?' I ask.

'You make it sound so . . .' Lilith sighs. 'I thought you

understood me. Understood Deep Flow and what I'm trying to create here. Has allowing you in been a mistake?'

Despite myself, I shake my head.

'I use things to help us bond, Sadie. To facilitate a sense of community. Our connection is everything. What it takes to get there shouldn't matter.'

'But it does matter,' I say. 'We didn't consent to being drugged. Manipulated. Financially exploited. Lied to. Trapped.'

'You signed a waiver,' Lilith says, as if I'm being ridiculous.

'And all that was in the small print, was it? Because I don't remember seeing it.'

'The wording is . . . broad.'

'Wow,' I say, genuinely stunned as I watch Lilith's mask begin to slip. 'You really don't give a shit about our wellbeing at all, do you?'

'Of course I do, darling one,' she replies. 'But, at the end of the day, I have to run a business.'

I laugh bitterly and get to my feet, my internal monologue roaring at me to ignore the quivering sky, the rippling landscape, the gold and indigo aura that surrounds Lilith. *You're high, Sadie,* I tell myself. *But you're okay. Just take one step at a time.*

'I'm going to go home now, Lilith,' I say out loud. 'And you're not gonna stop me.'

'Okay, Sadie,' she shrugs, seemingly unbothered. 'But, please know: you have as little chance of finding your way out of this desert on your own as you do of surviving this harsh, horrible world without me.

I scoff, then tell her I'll take my chances. As I start to walk past her, anger flickers across her face like lightning.

'If you leave now, you won't be able to come back to us. And, trust me, many women before you have tried.'

I turn on my heels and face her again.

'Is that what happened to Mackenzie?' I ask. 'Did she leave and then try to come back again? Did you reject her?'

Lilith laughs. 'You think you know so much, my love. And yet you still haven't put all the pieces together, have you?'

She glides towards me, silent as a desert snake.

'My followers will do *anything* for me. Risk *everything* for me. So when I told Mackenzie we needed something to create an unbreakable bond between us all, she understood. It was a chance for someone like you, Sadie, to be a hero. And a chance for Mac to repay her debts. Win–win. We never meant for anyone to get hurt, obviously.'

The truth hits me like a runaway train.

'Bridget was right. The shooting. The fire. That boat sinking. It wasn't all some big coincidence. You set it all up.'

Lilith smiles and holds her hands up: 'No comment.'

'When I get back to the city, I'm gonna—'

She chuckles as she interrupts me. 'Sadie, Sadie, Sadie. You're not gonna do anything. You've got too much to lose. Too much to hide. Your glass house is bigger than anyone else's in the whole of Deep Flow. Except maybe Judy from the Denver contingent. Pretty sure she killed her husband. But . . . I digress. *You*, Sadie, would be stupid to cross me. And you know it.'

I falter. Bridget said I could go on record anonymously. That I didn't need to expose myself in order to help take down Lilith. But where is Bridget now?

My silence appears to feed Lilith and, eventually, she seems sure that she's leveraged enough of my secrets to allow hers to remain safe. She thinks I'm weak because I've been through this before, but she's wrong. My past experience is how I know how to deal with this. How to deal with someone like her. I never got justice when it came to Gaultier. This time will be different.

'You're dismissed,' she says, coldly, and turns back towards the retreat centre. As she does, the invisible cord between us snaps.

'Thank you,' I say.

She whirls around, sensing the triumph in my voice.

'For what?' She asks

'For giving me a chance at a do over,' I say, offering her a grin that clearly catches her off guard. But, before she can say anything more, I sprint away from her, towards what I hope will be the road.

A wave of euphoria hits as I dart across the arid desert sands, skipping over rocks and brittle, thirsty plant life. *Don't look back*, I tell myself. *Don't ever look back*. But what feels like hours later, I realise I am lost. I feel sober now and my mouth is bone dry. I slide my tongue back and forth in an attempt to generate some saliva, but there is nothing there.

Think, Sadie, an insistent voice inside my head says, as I stare down at my useless phone. No signal. No internet services. I can't rely on the compass app or maps to work effectively. I can only rely on myself.

One thing I know for sure is the time: 18:43 PST.

'The sun sets in the west and rises in the east,' I murmur under my breath. Or is it the other way around?

The voice in my head returns: *Trust yourself, Sadie.*

I close my eyes and think of Elijah drawing lines in the dirt when I was a kid, teaching me north, south, east and west. I think of Daddy and me sitting on the porch together, watching the sun turn into orange and red streaks in the sky. Momma telling me my new room in Savannah would get plenty of natural light just like the repurposed garage I use as my studio in LA does now because—

'The sun rises in the east,' I say out loud, this time drawing a real sense of certainty from my muddled, dehydrated brain.

I look up. The sun is hours from setting, but has already begun its slow descent. The angle of my shadow across the sand feeds me information too. I picture a map in my head and I'm almost certain that, when we arrived on the bus, we approached Joshua Tree from the north side. I say a prayer, trust my gut and start to walk and, what feel like hours later, I spot a road sign on the horizon.

When I reach my destination, I am exhausted, filthy and at the brink of collapse. My joy at finally reaching something familiar is quickly mitigated by the fact that I am, once again, without a plan. The road is deserted and my lungs are shredded. I'd hoped my phone signal would grow stronger the closer I got to civilisation, but I have no such luck. Here, there is no signal at all. No 4G. No friendly neighbourhood café I can sponge Wi-Fi off of. No hope of survival.

Feeling faint, I sit at the side of the road, the skin on my lips peeling, my head pounding. I consider the idea of walking until I find a roadside diner or a gas station, but I can no longer summon the strength. I'm almost certain I'll be dead before I reach the door.

The worst part of all of this is that it's my own stupid fault. Mumtaz warned me. Veronica too. Even Derek had his suspicions. Yet, still, it took me this long to figure out what a complete charlatan Lilith is. Anyone would think, after everything I went through as a kid, that I'd take note of the giant red flags waving in my direction. But every time I saw one I ignored it. Explained it away. Told myself I was being irrationally triggered. Perhaps the truth is that I walked towards the danger because it felt strangely nostalgic. And now it might cost me my life.

I have a sudden surge of nausea, dizziness sending me spinning, and I know that, soon, I'll be unconscious. If I weren't so dehydrated, I might cry at the unfairness of it all. After all I've been through, dying on the side of the road like a dog feels . . . ridiculous. So ridiculous that, instead of crying, I start to laugh. It's a dry, rasping cackle that reminds me of the noise Daddy used to make when he was sick and I realise I may have teetered into insanity. Surely the final stage before death.

But then – a lime-green pick-up truck comes speeding along.

I flail helplessly, my screams drying up in my throat as the car zooms past me. Convinced the driver sped up at the sight of me, I collapse into hopelessness.

I picture Lilith's minions, now rabid with rage, catching up with me. Dragging me back to the retreat centre by my ankles, where they will surely skin me alive and serve me up as the perfect accompaniment to this evening's communal meal.

It's a sobering thought. And I'm thinking exactly this when I spot another car approaching in the distance. Could this be my way out of here? I ask the heavens. Then my heart sinks as I realise it's driving way too fast for me to flag it down. Yet another driver clearly not open to hitchhikers. They have places to go. People to see. Urgently. And yet I find myself waving my arms in desperate hope. Perhaps the drugs haven't worn off yet, after all.

Miraculously, the car screeches to a halt a few yards from where I stand, the smell of burning rubber instantly filling my nostrils. The driver rolls their window down and, when I see who it is, I realise that even if my church abandoned me all those years ago, right when I needed them most, maybe God never did.

'We found you! Oh, thank you, Jesus, we found you!' Veronica calls out.

I'm too paralysed with shock to move.

'Jump in the back, girl. Let's get you out of here!'

Am I dreaming? Hallucinating? Can this really be real?

'Hurry up!' she yells, impatiently, loud enough to jolt me into action. I dash towards the car and yank open the door before climbing inside. Next to me, LaDarian is yapping up a storm and, in the front passenger seat next to Veronica, is Mumtaz.

'Hello, darling,' she says, turning round to face me. I try to think of something to say, but my mouth is still bone dry and I am thunderstruck.

'Shut *up*, LaDarian!' Veronica shouts, saving me from my wordless stupor. 'No wonder your momma left town and dumped you on me again!'

And, with that, Mumtaz turns round and the hundred questions I have inside me are left on the tarmac as we speed off down the road.

TWENTY-THREE

Dirt swirls down the drain as I rinse away the day. If I could physically purge myself of everything that's happened since I met Lilith, I would gladly stick two fingers to the back of my throat and release it all. But, even if that *were* possible, it's not a form of self-harm I've ever engaged in. Strange, how I've always been too squeamish for vomit but am happy to slice tiny cuts into my flesh.

I do a sense check. Nope. I don't want, don't *need* to do that right now. In fact, I don't want anything other than to lie on the couch and have Derek feed me chicken soup while he strokes my hair.

Only, Derek isn't here. When I finally emerge from the bathroom, stinking of lavender and bergamot, it's Veronica and Mumtaz who greet me. LaDarian has, thankfully, found fun in chasing anything that moves around the back yard. A tiny bird. A butterfly. A fat, incredibly vocal bee.

'How you feeling?' Veronica asks.

'Okay,' I tell her. 'Like I could eat a horse, but, all things considered, I'm okay.'

Mumtaz pulls a store-bought lasagne out of the refrigerator and there's a pop-pop-pop as she pierces the film before shoving it into the microwave. I smile my thanks and sink into an armchair, pulling my cardigan around my shoulders.

'So, how the hell do you two know each other?' I ask.

Mumtaz and Veronica exchange a glance and an almost imperceptible smile.

'I put an ad on social media,' Mumtaz says. 'About Deep Flow. Asking if anyone with bad experiences would be interested in talking.'

I nod. I'd seen that ad.

'And it turns out I had *a lot* to say,' Veronica laughs. 'It was right after I saw you last, so . . .'

My entire body burns hot with shame.

'For the record, I'm disgusted with myself,' I say. 'The only way I can explain not following you out of Deep Flow the moment I realised what a bigot Lilith is . . . well . . . she's got something on me. Something big. And I guess I felt . . . trapped.'

'It's not the first time Lilith has leveraged people's secrets against them,' Mumtaz says, sympathetically. But it's not *her* forgiveness I want.

'I'm so sorry,' I say to Veronica, who simply sniffs and looks down at her shoes. 'I don't know why you came to rescue me. I really don't deserve anything from you.'

'No,' Veronica says. 'You don't. But after some big conversations with Mumtaz here, and Bridget too, I'm—'

'Bridget? You've spoken to Bridget? Is she okay?'

After she'd disappeared, my thoughts had become full of dark expectations: finding her dismembered head in the retreat centre refrigerator or her dead body left abandoned in the desert. Maybe they'd driven to the coast and dropped her into the sea, or forced her to walk a long way off a short cliff.

'She reached out to me after they sent her home from the retreat,' Mumtaz says, putting my fears to bed at last. 'We'd spoken before about the article she's writing. She was really concerned about you and, obviously, she knows we're friends.'

Friends, I think. That word again. My instinct is to disagree, but what else would you call people who drop everything to come and rescue you from a nightmare?

'How did you find me?' I ask.

'Derek, actually. We called him and told him what was going on, but he couldn't get a flight back in time to do something about it. He *was* able to access your Find My Phone, though. We jumped in the car and drove there right away.'

'Bridget's with her family,' Mumtaz tells me. 'Said she needed to take a moment after all that happened, but she does want to see you when you're ready.'

I nod, suddenly feeling incredibly tired.

'Are you sure you don't want to go to the hospital?' Mumtaz asks, frowning.

'Yeah, girl, I'm worried you're still dehydrated,' Veronica chimes. 'You must've been wandering around that desert for hours.'

Before I can push back again, I hear Derek's key in the lock and, within seconds, he is in the room, scooping me up into a hug. 'I'm so sorry I wasn't here,' he says, a crack in his voice. And I realise he's not just apologising for this time.

'It's okay,' I tell him. 'I survived.'

I am, also, not just talking about this time.

'We should talk,' I say, and Veronica and Mumtaz nod their approval as I lead Derek to the bedroom. They'll wait, they tell me. They're here if I need anything at all.

Derek and I sit down on the bed, and I hold his hands in mine.

'Firstly, I want to let you know that I love you and I understand if you feel you can't be with me after I tell you all this.'

'Sadie, don't be silly. Of course, I—'

'Don't,' I say, holding my hand up before resting it softly on his cheek. 'Don't make promises you can't keep. Because you don't know anything yet. Not really.'

'Are you self-harming again?' he asks.

I shake my head.

'If this is about your past, I've told you time and again that I don't need to know. It's who you are now that matters.'

I kiss his hand and smile through the tiny puddles forming at the edges of my eyes. 'Maybe you don't need to know. But I think I need to tell you.'

He nods. Acquiesces.

I clear my throat. Take a breath.

'Seventeen years ago, I killed someone. A little boy named Cody Michaelson.'

We'd talked about the name Ramona, like in the Beverly Cleary books, for our daughter would need to be brave in a world like this one. Then maybe Denise, after Momma, for her middle name. Lying awake at night, a cavity on Derek's side of the bed, I'd say her name out loud so I didn't feel so alone. 'Ramona,

Ramona. Ramona Denise. Ramona the Brave,' I'd say, hoping she'd offer a kick to tell me she was listening. 'I can't wait until you're here, little one.'

Five minutes before Derek came through the door after returning from another business trip, I'd found blood. I went to him in panic before he'd even put his cases in the hall.

'Something's wrong,' I told him, and all the way to the hospital he told me it would be fine.

'She's tough, our girl,' he'd said.

When he was wrong, I wanted to punch him. Wanted to blame him for everything. For not being around for so long. For tempting fate by being so confident *our* girl would survive. It lasted seconds, that feeling, but I've never forgotten it, how unforgiving and unforgivable it was.

The doctor spoke to us in a quiet voice. It was a tone I knew well. Conflicted. And laden with shame.

'We can't . . . um . . . we're *not allowed* to do anything to help. To help things along, I mean. It's . . . um . . . I'm so, so sorry. The law is . . . it's different now.'

'What do you mean?'

The doctor gathered his thoughts.

'Your baby will need to pass naturally.'

And then they sent me home to an excruciating blur of physical pain and torrential grief. It felt as if I might drown in it all. Like each wave, heavier than the last, might crush me. It was like my insides were being torn out, piece by piece. And all the time there was the memory of the doctor's parting words, reminding us both to come back immediately if my heart beat too fast. If I started shivering or sweating or losing my breath.

He never told me how to tell the difference between sepsis and grief.

It took nine days. Nine days before I was able to truly begin mourning my baby's life without having to fear for my own. And, sometimes, even as Derek gathered me up into his arms and pressed his lips against my forehead, I wondered if I wouldn't mind just slipping away after her. Following our little Ramy down a darkened corridor and towards the light. Knowing that, when I reached the end, I'd get to hold her hand for ever.

It's really only recently that I've stopped feeling like that, my conversation with Constance about the concept of mizuko giving me hope that, one day, our baby's soul might come back. When the time is right.

'When we lost Ramona I thought it was because I didn't deserve anything,' I tell Derek. 'Least of all a child of my own. I thought that God was punishing me.'

He hasn't moved a muscle except to blink since I started talking and it's been at least twenty minutes. I'd seen people have tiny, imperceptible seizures like this on TV medical dramas. Could I have provoked something like that in him? Shocked him into a waking coma?

'And I thought you'd blame me. For Ramona. For what happened. My bad karma ruining your life as well as mine.'

At this, he squeezes my hand and makes a noise as if he's about to say something. Instead, he gets up and stands at the window.

'I think I knew,' he says, eventually. 'I think I always knew it would be something like this. Because it was clear, you know.

That something had happened. That something was wrong. I probably thought about every scenario possible.'

'How do you feel now you know?' I ask.

He's quiet for minute or two, thinking.

'I don't know what I feel. But I know I love you. And I know I want to work on this. And it wasn't your fault. Ramona. Your ballet teacher. None of it. I'm sure of that. I just need time, I think.'

I consider the idea he might leave me. I want to work on this too, but, while the end of us might have shattered me years ago, I know now that, somehow, I'll find a way to cope.

I've spent most of the last year hanging my whole life on Lilith, and I did the same with Derek for years and Gaultier before that. But now I've told the person I care about most the truth about me and the world hasn't ended. So, perhaps now I can just belong to myself for a while. Perhaps that's okay.

TWENTY-FOUR

'Have you heard of an artist called Georges Seurat?' I ask Dr Angelina Kwan, my new therapist.

'It's a familiar name,' she says. 'He a big influence of yours?'

'A little. He's the guy who made Pointillism famous. Created these paintings, some of them huge, all made up of tiny dots of colour. If you stand too close, you can't tell what the image is meant to be. So you have to stand back. The further away you are, the clearer it is.'

Dr Kwan writes something down.

'I think, maybe, that's why I couldn't see what was going on with Deep Flow. I was too close to it all.'

She looks up at the ceiling. Three months in, I'm starting to learn that's what she does when she's thinking.

'Has it occurred to you that you *did* see what was going on? That your desire for love and community, for the affection and approval of someone so venerated, allowed you to ignore it?'

This is a hard thing to admit. I look down at my hands. Pick tracings of oil paint away from the edges of my nails.

'I understand why that idea might make you feel uncomfortable. But it is a pattern of behaviour that's consistent with your diagnosis.'

'A repeat pattern,' I say, directing my gaze out of the window. Not a single cloud in the azure sky. There is, however, a cluster of black birds, all turning shapes in tandem. I think of the bird at the bottom of the Italian tea-leaf reader's cup.

I'd thought that telling people about my past would make me feel that sense of freedom the old woman had told me would make me happy. But, while I do feel better, I'm not there yet. And I can't fathom why.

'Yes. A repeat pattern. I want you to realise, however, that repeating patterns does not make you a failure. It makes you human. It's how our brains are wired. You were groomed at an age where your brain was still developing. It makes sense that later in life you would again feel drawn to the kinds of people who attempt to control others – even though it's dangerous. And believe me when I say that these kinds of people are also looking for you. Doing everything they can to find vulnerable people with the aim of exploiting them.'

'I wish I wasn't one of them. I wish I wasn't vulnerable,' I say.

'Everyone is vulnerable in one way or another. And vulnerability can be powerful. If you know how to harness it. And you do, Sadie. That's how you make art.'

I smile at this. The last few months have been one of the most creatively productive periods I've ever had. Within weeks of leaving Deep Flow, I started therapy again and, with that, started painting again too. Shaylene returned from her acting job and, after insisting on a tour of my studio, commissioned me to paint something to hang above her fireplace. After an initial month of having to suck it up and let Derek finance my therapy, the money from my commission enabled me to commit to a few more months, covering the cost myself.

Admittedly, I was dubious at first. Therapy has never really stuck before. So often have I started sessions and been forced to drop them within a matter of months due to the financial strain. Eventually, I grew weary of having to tell my story from the beginning to each new therapist. It felt like I was reliving my trauma over and over and that so much time was taken up filling them in on my background, we rarely got as far as diagnosis or solutions.

Dr Kwan is different, however. She works through a charity that part-subsidises the care they offer, making it more affordable for those of us who have more sporadic incomes. It's almost an hour's drive to get to her, but she's worth it. It's a journey I never could've made when I was in my early twenties and still under a driving ban, of course.

Today, Angelina has asked me to bring in a recent article about Gaultier finally serving jailtime for offences in Toronto. I'd Googled him for the first time in years and felt fear and disgust swim up from the depth of my stomach when I'd found a news piece, accompanied by a photo of him. His eyes stared out at me through my laptop screen, the corner of his mouth curling, almost indiscernibly, into a tiny smirk.

I hand over the printout and Dr Kwan sticks it up on the wall behind her, at eye level.

'Now, stand up,' she tells me. 'Face him. The photo of him. Talk to him.'

'I . . . I dunno, Dr Kwan. Feels kind of silly,' I say.

'Maybe it is. But humour me. Give it a try. There must be things you want to say to him.'

I follow her instructions. He looks somehow smaller than I remember. His hair is thinning and he's attempted a strange combover that makes him look like a pervert.

If the cap fits, I think.

I think a lot of things. But, when I open my mouth, nothing comes out. Eventually, Dr Kwan tells me I can sit down again.

'Maybe next week,' she says.

'I don't get it,' I tell her. 'I have nightmares about him all the time, so it's not like I'm not used to seeing him. This is just a picture.'

'Do you ever speak to him? In your dreams?'

I look out of the window again. 'No. No way. I try to get as far away from him as possible.'

'So . . . what if next time you dream about him, you *don't* run? What if you face him?'

'I don't know if I can control it,' I say.

'Try,' she replies. 'I believe our dreams exist for a reason. Our psyche attempting to reveal something or help us solve a problem, like our brains trying to complete a circle that has a piece missing. Or like when you get a song you've only heard a fragment of stuck in your head. If you find you can't engage with him in your dream, write it down when you wake up. As much detail as possible. And we'll talk about it when we meet.'

Another session over, I gather my things. As I do, Dr Kwan reminds me: 'Complex PTSD is just that. Complex. It's not easy to identify and it's very complicated to treat. So don't get

362

disheartened that things aren't changing overnight. This is a marathon, not a sprint.'

On the ride over to Venice Beach, I fantasise about tearing human earworm Gaultier out of my head and crushing him underfoot. Then, I think of Lilith. How, bizarrely, I still miss her sometimes, despite all she's done. It's a familiar feeling given how I spent years bouncing between feelings of love and contempt for Gaultier. I'd be standing in the mall as someone wearing his cologne wafted by and be suddenly plunged into a memory of him. I'd find myself overwhelmed with yearning. Or I'd hear a song he loved, warped and re-versioned for elevator music, and I'd start to sweat, my hands turning clammy.

I think of the dream I had not so long ago. A dream that saw me airborne, flying over broken and arid land before sacrificing myself to Lilith, allowing her to swallow me whole. I wonder now how I could've ever thought that was freedom. I'd not been able to feel my wings or feathers, after all. I hadn't flown either.. I'd floated. Directionless and carried by the wind.

Mumtaz and Veronica have chosen a smoothie bar for us to meet Bridget at and, when I arrive, all three of them are already there.

'Sorry I'm late,' I say. 'Therapy ran over a little.'

'No worries, girl. Self-care is pivotal,' V replies, taking a long sip through her straw.

'Exactly,' Mumtaz says. 'It's great you've finally found a therapist you connect with.'

Bridget jumps off her stool to give me a hug. We haven't seen each other since shortly after the retreat and I'd forgotten how infectious her energy is. She smells like strawberry-flavoured candy. Or like the whiff of sweet scents you get as you walk past a Yankee Candle store.

'The girls were just telling me about your exhibition!' she squeals. 'I'm so, so excited for you.'

'Ah, it's a small thing really,' I say dismissively, as I sit down. It's hard not to smile, however.

'Well, we could make it a big thing, if we wanted to? I could contact my friend Bernard, who writes for the Arts and Culture section. Get him to write up a preview?'

It's a sweet offer, but I'm not sure I'm ready for anything more than a lowkey event. Putting myself out there like this, for the first time, is already scary enough.

'Can I think about it?'

'Sure,' Bridget says, brightly. 'But only if you promise to *really* think about it. It's a serious offer. It deserves serious consideration.'

'Of course. I will let you know by the end of the week. Promise.'

'V's coming to my favourite yoga class next Wednesday,' Mumtaz says, changing the subject.

'Really?' I say, surprised. No one needs to remind any of us what happened last time Veronica was invited to a class. The memory hangs between us silently.

'My teacher's brilliant. Makes every session super accessible. Both physically and financially. And you will not hear a *single* "Namaste",' Mumtaz chuckles. 'You should come too sometime.'

'Mumtaz is coming to my pole dance class this week,' V says.

'I'm terrified,' Mumtaz tells us, eyes widening in mock horror.

'You'll love it. I promise,' Veronica assures her. 'We all totally support each other there. It's a safe space, full of all types of women with all types of bodies.'

'I've kind of always wanted to try pole,' I say.

'Me too!' says Bridget, enthusiastically.

'Well, whichever one you choose . . . and I hope you try out both . . . what's most important is that you guys are reminded how good it feels to get out of your head and into your body,' Mumtaz says. 'Don't let Lilith and her creepy cronies ruin that for you.'

'But, also, none of us need a teacher or a class to move, right?' Bridget says. 'We should go out dancing!'

We clink our smoothies together, toasting to a future night of fun, and then order what the bar menu describes as 'light bites'.

Bridget tells us more about what to expect from her article, which will be published the day after my exhibition. She's managed to pull together some fairly damning interviews from former Deep Flow devotees, most notably Mackenzie Crawford.

'You got her to talk?'

'Well, her hero of a lawyer did,' Bridget replies, as Mumtaz takes a tiny, theatrical bow. 'We've had to be *really* careful in terms of what she can and can't say, because the case is ongoing. But it still feels like a fairly big coup.'

It's eighty-eight days before the trial and I've been marking red X's onto my calendar as each day passes. In truth, I can't wait. The opportunity to give evidence against Lilith feels like less and less of a betrayal the further away my time with her becomes.

'This will be good for you,' Dr Kwan said, when I told her what I'd signed up to do.

'I know,' I replied, feeling more sure of myself than I have in years. It's been well over a decade since I backed out of facing Gaultier in a Canadian courthouse. This time would be different.

'What do you think is gonna happen to Mackenzie?' I ask Mumtaz.

'Well, she's definitely going to do jail time. That's unavoidable. But the mitigating circumstances we're presenting are strong. The class action lawsuit we're putting together against Lilith and Jeremy is also looking good. We're painting a *very* clear picture of how Lilith ran Mackenzie into serious debt and then offered her a twisted way out. That she was under immense pressure to shoot up the studio, and that Lilith has set up events like this before within Deep Flow.'

She leans in. Lowers her voice.

'I've also heard from some friends in law enforcement that Jeremy's days are numbered too. Do not be surprised if you hear about him getting arrested within the next couple of weeks. We're talking multiple charges. Fraud, for sure. But the biggie is a potential sex trafficking charge. His Love Guru business – there's evidence he brought some of the girls he used from out of state under false pretences. Some of them from other branches of Deep Flow, women who were looking to pay off debts by working for Jeremy but never expected to be pushed into sex work.'

Mumtaz's words have a visceral effect on me and I can almost feel the blood draining from my face as she talks.

'And because Lilith made the introductions, like, virtually brokered the relationships between Jeremy and these women, if Jeremy goes down, she isn't far behind him.'

'That won't help Mackenzie much, though, will it?' I say. 'The damage to her life is already done.'

'You forget who you're dealing with,' Mumtaz says. 'We're talking about a middle-class white woman. A mother. From a "good family", right?'

Mumtaz does air quotes to illustrate her point. 'Juries – and judges – lap that shit right up. They might feel the time she's already served in jail while awaiting trial is long enough for her to be separated from her children. If the class action lawsuit goes well, we could get well over three million out of Lilith and Jeremy. Certainly enough to dig Mac and her family out of financial ruin. Not to mention all the other ex-Deep Flow members the Winters' crimes have impacted.'

Mumtaz is right, I realise. And I don't doubt that, if anyone is going to pull off such an intricate takedown of Lilith et al, it'll be her.

'There's something else I want you to think about, Sadie,' Bridget says.

'Oh yeah?' I say, only half listening as our food arrives and my stomach rumbles loudly.

'Look, I know you're featured in the article about Deep Flow – anonymously, of course. There is a lot of freedom in speaking your truth in that way. But . . . I wondered if you'd one day consider telling your story from the beginning.'

'What do you mean?'

'Well, you told the three of us about what happened to you,

as a teen. Then your subsequent criminal record, your driving ban, how you made a new life for yourself. And, obviously, I will take that story to my grave if that's what you want. But, if there's any part of you that feels like you still can't live your life fully because you're always wondering about people finding out, I do believe there could be power and freedom in putting the story out there yourself. You know, so you can make sure you're in control of the narrative.'

'I think it's a good idea,' Veronica says, almost immediately.

'What?' I say, astounded. To me, it sounds like the worst idea I've ever heard. My biggest nightmare brought to life.

But, then, Veronica looks at me and something in her face tells me that, somehow, she truly understands.

'You've been through so much I can't imagine, but I do know how it is to feel like you have to hide a part of who you are. It's not the same thing, but hear me out, okay?'

I nod.

'When I first transitioned, I cared *so* much about passing. Like, I was *obsessed*. Then, one day, I found this old picture of myself from when I was a kid. A school picture where I'm doing this fake smile, all gap toothed and dead behind the eyes. And I remembered just how unhappy I'd been that day. How I'd spent most of it hiding in a toilet cubicle.'

Mumtaz squeezes Veronica's leg under the table. V puts her hand on top of hers.

'It was a sad moment, thinking about that kid. About what she went through. But, you know, against all odds, she survived. So, I realised that I'm proud of her. Maybe I don't want to just pretend she never existed. And you know what else?' Veronica asks, pausing for effect. 'It made me realise that my new life isn't about passing. About flying under the radar. That's not what makes it a success. It's about living authentically. Whatever shape that takes. And that realisation is liberating.'

Head full of thoughts, I'm quieter throughout the rest of our lunch date, but no less happy. The taste of freedom is so close now I can feel it sitting on my tongue like a sweet drop of honey waiting to be swallowed.

As we stroll past vendors selling crystals and offering tarot readings and healing rituals, I confess I want to do something to herald my new beginning.

'We should do a spell!' says Veronica, causing both Mumtaz and me to dissolve into laughter.

'I meant . . . I dunno . . . maybe I'll get a card reading or something,' I say.

'*Or* we could do our own thing?' Veronica says, suggestively. 'I've done it before. Friend of mine was having a terrible start to the year a couple of years back and I did a cleansing spell to get rid of all the bad juju. It worked.'

She reacts to our sceptical looks. 'For real. He went on to get a six-figure book deal, like, three weeks later.'

'I had no idea you were so into all this,' I say, chuckling. 'Especially being a woman of God.'

'Girl, a spell is just a prayer with props. Come on, let's go get some materials and head back to my place.'

An hour later, the four of us are gathered around a hastily drawn sigil with three candles at the top and two crystals at the bottom. Veronica lights the candles and then some incense.

'So, what does all this mean?' Mumtaz asks.

'Honestly, this is just a bunch of ideas I've stolen from movies and books. But my thinking is that even if we are sort of making it up as we go along, telling the universe what we want can only be a good thing, right?'

Strangely, Veronica's refreshingly honest approach doesn't make me feel like the spell has any less chance of working. Instead, it puts me at ease.

The four of us write down things we want to get rid of onto tiny bits of paper and then burn them in a copper pot. There's a brief interlude, which mostly involves us ordering pizza, then we giggle our way through some chants and take turns in shouting out what we want the universe to deliver to us. If nothing else, it's a great bonding experience and I go home afterwards feeling full and happy.

Almost a whole week goes by before I dream of Gaultier again. This time, I'm standing in the corridor of my old dance academy. It's dark but I spot a room at the end of the hall and the light from it dapples across the shiny tiled floor and metal lockers. When I arrive at the room, however, I realise it doesn't belong to the academy at all.

It's grey and dank, as if the colour scheme is based on the inside of a snail's shell, and there are two rows of tables with two chairs at each. At one of the tables sits Gaultier, dressed in a bright orange jumpsuit. At the sight of him, it is as if I can suddenly feel the blood pumping through my veins and I want to turn and head right back the way I came.

Then, a tiny voice in my head reminds me not to.

'What if, next time you dream about him, you don't *run? What if you face him?'*

I notice, then, that one of Gaultier's ankles is shackled to the table leg and the sight of this gives me the confidence to approach him cautiously and slide into the chair opposite.

'You look like a fucking tangelo,' I say, my voice laced with vitriol.

Gaultier doesn't say a thing. Just reaches for my hand – the hand I have carelessly left on the table. His touch knocks ten bells of terror and revulsion through me. I open my mouth to scream, but, instead of sound, a thousand little bats pour out, engulfing him.

I write down everything I can remember as soon as I wake up. Then, I head to the studio and paint for four hours, stopping only when Derek comes in, insisting I eat something.

'This is pretty intense,' he says, looking at my work. 'I like it.'

'I'm thinking I might add it to my collection. For the exhibition,' I tell him.

I've named the event *Catharsis: Nightmares and Aspirations*, and this carmine-stained vision of the inside of a prison would certainly fit within the themes. The rest of the collection is made up of depictions of ballet dancers and birds. Of dark, tortured streets and clouds bursting with light. In the centre of this piece is a diminutive orange man, barely visible, trapped between dark lines and vivid, violent brushstrokes. His head is tilted down, as if to look at something in his lap and I use a pencil to draw several hairs across the top of his scalp. No more than he deserves.

How's that for channelling my vulnerability? I think.

*　　*　　*

'You look like a fucking tangelo,' I tell my therapist. It's a drizzly Tuesday afternoon and we have now repeated this phrase back and forth at least ten times. The rain taps against the window like someone begging to be let in, but, inside, the room is warm and welcoming.

'How does this phrase make you feel?'

'Hearing it or saying it?' I wonder.

'Both,' Dr Kwan answers. 'Some schools of thought say that everything and everyone in our dreams are representative of ourselves. Fragments of who we are.'

I smart at this. The idea of Gaultier being a part of me makes me sick.

'Okay, Freud,' I say, dripping in sarcasm.

Angelina smiles. 'Maybe that ideology isn't for you.'

I shake my head.

'Let's get back to the question.'

'Uh . . . hearing it makes me feel stupid. Saying it makes me feel . . . powerful.'

'Powerful. Okay. Let's expand on that.'

I shrug. Dr Kwan waves her hand in a way that means 'go on'. I tut and tell her it's not just about the phrase itself. It's about the way I say it.

'Like a latter-day Daria Morgendorffer,' I say, grinning.

'The cartoon character? With the glasses?'

'Yeah. She had this monotonous voice that always made it sound like she didn't give a shit about anything. She was cool, you know?'

'Is that what you want? To not "give a shit"? To not care?'

Vigorous nodding from me this time.

'Okay. Let's try something,' Dr Kwan says, clicking the cap onto her pen. 'If you feel ready and comfortable, I'd like to walk you back into your dream. Would that be okay?'

She moves the chairs, creating more space for me while she sits with her back against the wall. I stand in the middle of the room, eyes closed as per her instructions. She finds a playlist on her phone that starts with the sounds of a tropical rainforest. Birds call to one another. Branches creak as monkeys swing from the limbs of trees. Frogs belch and hop through the undergrowth. And all around is the buzz of cicadas. A sound that felt so permanent back when I lived in Georgia.

Dr Kwan walks me through this soundscape, asking me to imagine dirt and plantlife underfoot, a warm breeze on my skin, the smell of exotic flowers. What I assume is a harp begins to play as I head towards a large lake and then I hear the sound of its waves lapping softly against the shore. Dr Kwan tells me there is a wooden raft nearby and I push it into the water and climb aboard, lying on my back, face turned up to the sky.

'Notice how perfectly blue it is. Are there birds? Any flying insects? Notice them too.'

I listen to her talk and, in the palace of my imagination, I see it all.

Eventually, I drift towards another shore, this time arriving at a more American-looking forest. Dark-wooded pine trees stretch up into the blue and their needles crunch softly beneath my feet. There are squirrels scaling the branches above and I spot a small gray and yellow bird dart across my path.

'Selma?' I whisper. But even in my meditative trance, I know Selma is gone for ever.

Angelina guides me to a tumble-down house built of well-worn stone and I push at its wooden door, soon discovering that the inside is nothing at all like the outside.

'You have arrived in your dream,' Angelina tells me. 'This is the corridor where the dream began. If you feel ready, walk down it.'

I move slowly, and yet within seconds I arrive at the room at the end of the hall. Dr Kwan's music begins to drop away and is replaced by the song that has lived in my head for longer than I care to consider.

God only knows what I'd be without you . . .

I walk into the prison meeting room. And there he is. Small, graying and totally alone.

'You look like a fucking tangelo,' I say. He reaches for my hand, but, this time, I snatch it away.

'No, no,' I tell him. 'You don't get to touch me. You don't get to hurt me. Not any more.'

He smiles a strange smile, exposing a mouth full of yellowing teeth.

'Don't be silly, Sadie,' he says. 'You love me. You always have.'

'Oh, Gaultier. It was never love. It was trauma bonding. You manipulate and exploit because that's the only way a shit stain like you thinks they can get something that resembles the adoration you so desperately crave. None of its real.'

As I speak, I feel as if I am growing physically lighter. As if my bones are hollowing themselves out while my organs shrink within my ribcage. I look down at myself and realise a generous layer of feathers is beginning to grow all over my body.

It's time, a little voice says, and I get out of my seat and head towards the door.

'You can't just leave me here, Sadie,' Gaultier shouts.

'Yes, I can,' I say, closing the door on him before I walk back down the corridor towards the light. The faster I move, the more buoyant I feel, and so I break into a jog. I'm barely outside again before my momentum forces me to take flight.

I glide over the dark American forest, across the lake and through the tops of the trees that fill the tropical paradise I started in. Beyond that is a village and soon I am flying over a city, through rain clouds and past the windows of office blocks and skyscrapers. After that, civilization begins to peter out and I find myself approaching a barren wasteland swirling with sand, right at the end of the world.

I've seen it all before, of course. Only, this time, I don't float aimlessly. I am aware of every feather, every bone, each breath that rattles through me. Lilith waits below with arms outstretched, but I do not stop. Instead, I soar over her, wings flapping, lungs full, heading for the horizon.

ACKNOWLEDGEMENTS

There are a great many people without whom this book would never have made it into your hands. Let's start from the beginning.

Mum and Dad, thank you for teaching me to read and write, and to love books enough to read them under the covers at night when I should have been sleeping. Thank you, Mum, for taking me to the library so regularly when I was kid and for helping me carry home the maximum number of books allowed. Thank you for leaving me alone for hours and hours when I was a teenager so I could escape into fiction – my desire to write started there and those were the books that built the foundations of the writer I am today.

Thanks to my brother also, for listening to me prattle on about all of my dreams for so many years, and for your optimism, however cautious!

I am quietly devastated that, like my Dad, Ms Dr Andrews, my high school Creative Writing teacher, didn't live long enough to see this novel published. She was the first person who made me feel like my writing was really worth anything. And, no, *Ms* Dr Andrews is not a typo. Any of her other students who happen to be reading this will know exactly why we all called her that and how it encouraged so many us to never be defined by whether or not we are married.

Thank you to Gurpal, who makes everything easier. Thank you for inspiring things in me I could never have anticipated, for continually nurturing my confidence and for providing me with so much necessary time and space to create. Whilst not defined by it, I am phenomenally happy to be married to you.

My first readers – Angela Kirwin, John Beaumont and Georgia St. John-Smith: I'm so grateful to you for taking the time to read and for your thoughtful feedback. Your words of encouragement made me believe getting this book into the world could be possible. I'm also incredibly thankful to my dear friend Daniel Rusteau, my favourite person to commiserate and celebrate with when it comes to the highs and lows of writing. Thank you for always being there.

Thanks to Alex Muirhead and Lauren Witt for your crucial help during the final stages of editing. Forever grateful to you both.

My agent Ben Dunn must be some kind of superhero to have ridden the waves of this journey with such kindness and grace. Ben, thank you for believing in me, always, right from the very first three chapters of my very first novel. Thank you for your brilliant edits, hilarious voice notes and sage advice. I appreciate you so very much.

Tori Kob, thank you for your ambition, tenacity and conviction. I leave every one of our conversations feeling excited about the future and able to take on whatever comes next.

Thank you to everyone at Headline and Mountain Leopard Press for all of your incredible work on this novel. Jessie Goetzinger-Hall and Jennifer Doyle – I am so grateful for your inspired, incisive notes and the kindness with which you've always delivered them. This book is infinitely better because of you.

Finally, I'd like to thank Julia Beuno. Julia, we have never met but your book *The Brink of Being* guided my exploration of miscarriage within these pages. You taught me how to speak about the unspeakable. To all those who have experienced pregnancy loss, I hope that talking about miscarriage more openly will mean that, one day, the world will be better at holding your hand through your grief.

RAISING READERS
Books Build Bright Futures

Dear Reader,

We'd love your attention for one more page to tell you about the crisis in children's reading, and what we can all do.

Studies have shown that reading for fun is the **single biggest predictor of a child's future success** – more than family circumstance, parents' educational background or income. It improves academic results, mental health, wealth, communication skills and ambition.

The number of children reading for fun is in rapid decline. Young people have a lot of competition for their time, and a worryingly high number do not have a single book at home.

Our business works extensively with schools, libraries and literacy charities, but here are some ways we can all raise more readers:

- Reading to children for just 10 minutes a day makes a difference
- Don't give up if children aren't regular readers – there will be books for them!
- Visit bookshops and libraries to get recommendations
- Encourage them to listen to audiobooks
- Support school libraries
- Give books as gifts

Thank you for reading: there's a lot more information about how to encourage children to read on our website.

www.JoinRaisingReaders.com